First printing March 2023

Library of Congress Cataloguing-in-Publication Data

Stone, Deborah
semi-detached / by Deborah Stone

ISBN: 9798386990992

Published by Simply Affirm, LLC
contact@simplyaffirm.com
simplyaffirm.com

Interior Design by Eva Myrick

Semi-Detached

by Deborah Stone

For Charles and James

Part One

2012

Clare

Chapter 1

Clare

It took me many years to realise that the more hopeful you feel about something, the more disappointed you will inevitably be. However, back then, as a student excited to show off my new boyfriend to my doting mother, it never crossed my mind that things might not go exactly according to plan. These days, I am far more circumspect and urge myself to expect the worst.

But let's face it I could never have prepared myself for what actually occurred that day. Jack and I were driving home for the Christmas holidays after a gruelling first term of my third year at university in Bath, alternately negotiating roadworks, contraflows, tailbacks and bad drivers, the ones who only took their cars out on high days and holy days. The radio in the Fiesta that Jack had hired was malfunctioning, so I had turned it off, despite Rihanna's valiant attempts to warble about her diamonds over the static and frequent drops in signal. Both of our phones had died and the car had nowhere to recharge them, so Jack and I were forced to entertain ourselves by singing tuneless acapella karaoke and, at our most desperate point, resorting to I Spy.

'Do you think your mum will like me?'

'Of course she will. Why wouldn't she?' I sighed and shifted in my seat. 'Is it sheep?'

'No, it's not sheep. Can you spy any sheep in the middle of the M4 in the dark?'

'No, but I've run out of things beginning with 's'. Will this bloody traffic ever move? I need the loo.'

'I've got an empty Coke bottle here if you're really desperate.'

'Months of sleeping together and you still know nothing of my anatomy!' I wriggled in my seat as we inched forward.

'Getting back to your mother.'

I groaned, but Jack persisted.

'Your mum is bound to feel over-protective of you, given that you're her only child and I just don't want to get off on the wrong foot.' Jack released the brake, and we rolled forward a half inch.

'Stop stressing. You'll have loads in common with her. And my mum is so easy-going. She likes all my friends.' I leant over and planted a noisy kiss on his cheek. 'And anyway, it's not like you're intending to propose or anything, is it?' I teased, deliberately staring straight at Jack.

He paled. 'No, of course not.'

'Well, there's nothing to worry about then, is there? She'll adore you. Crisp?' I shook the dregs that remained at the bottom of a large packet of Walkers' cheese and onion. 'I think I've finished them already, sorry.'

An hour or so later, we drew up outside my mother's flat in Kentish Town. It was raining with monsoon intensity, so I bolted out of the car and ran up the steps of the block as fast as I could, pressing continuously on our buzzer until my mother let me in. I raced up the two flights of stairs to our flat, straight past my mother who stood waiting to greet me in the open doorway, and shot into the toilet.

'Sorry, Mum, I'm busting,' I called, slamming the bathroom door shut.

Re-emerging a few minutes later, I realised that Jack was still outside in the car.

'Better now?' my mother asked, smiling.

'Yes, much. We should have stopped at the last services, but we wanted to crack on. The journey took forever.' I held my arms out and Mum enveloped me in her familiar warm embrace, her scent reassuring and instantly relaxing. I was home.

My mother was on the large size – chunky, you might call her – but I had always loved her bulk. It had allowed me to sink into her lap and rest my head on her ample chest as a child, and even as a sulky teenager, when my hormones demanded it. To me, she represented pure, unadulterated comfort.

'Hang on a minute while I go to rescue Jack.' I peeled myself away and ran back out of the flat and down the front steps to the car, where he sat shivering.

'C'mon Jack, jump out,' I instructed him as I opened the car door. 'We can leave the car here until nine tomorrow, but then we'll have to move it before the wardens start patrolling. They're real bastards round here.'

Jack jumped out, blinking away the rain that flooded down his face the moment he emerged. He opened the boot, and we grabbed our bags as fast as we could. By the time we had shut the front door of the block, we were soaked.

'Just dump the bags by the front door, Jack. We can sort them out later.'

Jack did as he was told and as he straightened up, I introduced him to my mother, who was still waiting by the door. She held out two towels, handing one to each of us.

'Thanks, Mum. So, this is Jack. Jack, this is Mum.'

'It's a pleasure to meet you,' Jack said a little too loudly, shaking her hand so vigorously that water from his sleeve sprayed the front of my mother's cardigan. 'Gosh, I am sorry,' he gasped, offering the towel back to my mother for her to use.

My mother did not take it, nor did she reply. Her hand lay limp in Jack's and her mouth hung open. Jack glanced at me, and I shrugged.

'You OK, Mum?' I asked, placing my hand gently on her shoulder.

She started at my touch. 'What? Oh yes, Clare, I'm fine. It's a pleasure to meet you, Jack. Clare has told me so much about you. Come into the flat, both of you, and dry off properly by the gas fire. You're wet through.' My mother stopped momentarily and turned back to stare at Jack again. She shook her head, as if trying to clear a blockage. 'Come into the kitchen and let me make you both some tea. It will warm you up.'

Jack and I settled ourselves around the Formica table in the small kitchen, which was somewhat cracked and worn from years of meals eaten, homework pored over, and arts and crafts badly made. There were very few indicators of the festive season in the flat. A sad string of fraying red tinsel hung down from the light-fitting over the table and in the hall. There was the smallest plastic, silver tree with a couple of chipped baubles hanging from it. Underneath was a solitary present for me, to which I would add mine for my mother – when I finally got around to buying one for her.

Mum busied herself for a strangely long time with the tap and then the kettle and for even longer in her strange quest to arrange six Hobnobs intricately on a small plate. 'I haven't made dinner yet, as I couldn't be sure what time you were arriving.'

'Don't worry. We got stuck in terrible traffic and our phones were out of charge, otherwise I would have called. We ate all sorts of crap on the way, so we will live.'

'Clare! Language!'

I rolled my eyes at Jack.

Mum set down the biscuits and placed a mug of tea in front of each of us, her hands trembling. She splashed some down her front, leaving a brown stain on her long, white cardigan. She moved over to the sink and grabbed a tea towel, absently dabbing at the mark while standing next to the calendar hanging on the wall. It featured the sports in the 2012 London Olympics, which I had given her the previous Christmas.

Suddenly, my mother slammed her mug onto draining board, causing Jack and I to jump. 'Could you excuse me for just a moment?' she whispered, rushing out of the kitchen.

Jack looked at me and mouthed 'What the fuck?'

'I've no idea what's up with her. Maybe she's ill or something,' I muttered. 'Let me go and see if she's alright.'

I padded across the small flat and knocked gently on my mother's bedroom door.

'Come in,' she answered in a flat voice. I opened the door, and found her sitting on the stool by the small fold-up table, which served as her dressing table by the window. She was afforded a clear view of the drab, frenetic high street below with its shops now closed and shuttered for the night apart from the bustling twenty-four-hour store.

'What's the matter?'

She made no reply, continuing to stare out of the window, seemingly fascinated with the comings and goings in the shop opposite. 'You and Jack. Have you? Are you?'

'Seriously? What kind of question is that? You've not even spoken to Jack yet and you're already worried about whether he's deflowered me? I'm twenty-one, Mum, not fifteen - and it's not the bloody dark ages.'

'No,' she replied, almost inaudibly. 'I know all that, Clare, but I need to know. Have you had sex with Jack?'

'What the hell is wrong with you?' I leapt up off the bed, banging my back against the wooden knob on the wardrobe door. 'Since when has my sex life been any of your bloody business?'

My mother swivelled around to face me. 'It's not. I am well aware that I have no right to pry.'

'So why the hell are you behaving like this? Jack and I have been going out for ages, so what do you think we've been doing? Drinking tea?'

'You must stop seeing that boy right now.' My mother began to weep, hiding her face in her hands.

'What the hell are you on about? You haven't even made the slightest effort to get to know Jack yet.'

'You just have to trust me on this one.' A solitary streak of mascara stained her cheek.

'You are being completely ridiculous and irrational, Mum! If you won't come out of your room right now and be civil to Jack, then I'll leave with him. I love him. I've never felt this way about anyone before.'

My mother raised her head and stared at me, wild-eyed. 'Clare, sweetheart. You must listen to me. Go back in there right now and tell him he must go. Use me as an excuse if you must. I really don't care what you say to him. Just get him out of your life right now.'

'You are totally un-bloody-believable, you know that?' I screeched, tears pricking at the corners of my eyes. 'If you want Jack out of my life, that's not going to happen, but as of now, I'm going to be out of yours.'

I turned and left the bedroom, slamming the flimsy door behind me.

'Come on, Jack. We're leaving. Grab the bags.'

Part Two

1990

Amanda and Fiona

Chapter 2

Amanda

I was peeling potatoes at the kitchen sink in my coat. It was cold inside the house, but I did not dare to turn the thermostat above 18 degrees, as Bill would be home any moment and there would be hell to pay if he detected the slightest hint of warmth in the radiators. He did not believe in squandering money on the heating when you could just as easily pull on another layer, or even think yourself warm, because being cold was all in the mind, apparently. I shivered as I rinsed another naked spud under the cold tap, my hands raw and chapped.

The front door slammed, causing me to flinch. The hall tiles shook as they absorbed the shock of Bill's heavy footsteps thudding across them towards the kitchen. I had long ago given up any hope of him removing his boots before he trekked all his muck from the building sites across the floors. After all, as he reminded me often, he had been working hard all day.

'What's for dinner?' he barked, pitching himself onto one of our rickety, wooden chairs. It shuddered beneath his weight. He removed his suit jacket, lobbing it over one of the other chairs, and picked up the newspaper that I had left folded on the kitchen table for him.

'Hot pot.' I hesitated. 'But it won't be ready for an hour or so. I'm about to slice the potatoes.'

'Christ, Mandy, I'm bloody starving.' He rubbed the sole of one of his heavy Timberland boots, before raking through his thick brown hair with a heavy, dusty hand, leaving a badger-like streak through the front of it. 'Make me a mug of tea, will you. Mand? And I'll have a couple of biscuits if dinner's not going to be ready for a while.' Bill reached down and began to untie his boots, sand and mud flaking onto the floor.

I moved to fill the kettle. 'So how was your day?'

'Exhausting. This new client is hugely demanding and wants everything done like yesterday. Then I had to meet with the accountant to prepare for year end. It's just one thing after another.'

Bill threw one boot and then the second towards the back door, clods of earth spraying the kitchen floor. He ran his own small construction company and wore the same two navy suits to work on rotation– Marks & Spencer obviously, as Bill maintained that there was no point of buying anything expensive when one suit was just the same as another– but always with his heavy boots so that he could move around mucky sites whenever he needed to do so. I wished that he would just leave them in the car with his hard hat. I moved over to the back door and righted his boots, sweeping the flecks of dirt towards the mat with my slipper.

I placed a large mug of tea and a plate of chocolate digestive biscuits in front of him. Bill lifted the paper and began to skim through the news. 'Looks like Thatcher is hanging on by a thread, but I'm not sure there's any decent alternative out there. I think the Conservatives are for it if we have another election.' He bit into two biscuits at once, scattering crumbs over his belly, which was trying to fight its way out of his shirt.

'I think it's been marvellous to have a lady PM. And she was just a grocer's daughter. It's an amazing achievement really, don't you think?' I rummaged in the biscuit tin for a digestive.

'You want to watch those biscuits,' Bill commented from behind his paper.

I grimaced and moved back to the sink to begin the potatoes. 'By the way, I think they've sold the semi next to us,' I commented, staring through the rear window and into our garden. 'I saw a couple here last week and they came back again today with the estate agent. From what I overheard, it sounded like they had made an offer and it has been accepted.' I placed the potatoes on the chopping board before rifling through the utensils drawer in search of a sharp knife.

'Oh, yes? Have you been twitching the curtains again rather than cleaning the house? So, go on then. What were they like? Hopefully, they won't be too noisy if they do move in. That old couple were lovely and quiet. Inconvenient really that they had to move into an old codgers' home. We just don't know who we'll end up with.'

'I didn't get that close a look at them to be honest, but I'd say they were about our age – well, my age, not yours. He drives quite a flashy car.'

I attempted to slice through a potato, but the knife was quite blunt, and the potato shot straight back into the sink.

'What kind of car was it?'

'Oh, I don't know, do I, Bill? You know that I know nothing about cars. It was a red one. New, by the looks of it.'

'A red one! Well, that's very informative, Mand. Thank you for that.' He flicked to the end of the paper and then threw it towards the bin, missing. 'Grab me a beer, would you?'

I opened the fridge and handed him a can of Tennent's. Bill rose and sloped off into the lounge to watch the six o'clock news. 'Call me when dinner's ready,' he called over the dulcet tones of Sue Lawley.

I turned back to the sink and stared out of the window. 'My day was OK too, thanks for asking, Bill,' I muttered to my silent reflection in the window as I stabbed at another potato.

Chapter 3

Fiona

'I hope this is the very last time we are moving. I'm sick of humping boxes and of packing, unpacking, and repacking. And I've broken another one of my nails, look!' My nail was broken halfway across: too far over to be salvaged, yet not far enough for me to bite it off.

Terry dropped the heavy box he was carrying. It thudded onto the tiled floor.

'Careful. That could be fragile, that could.'

He laughed, smiling broadly. 'Well, if it was, it's too late now!' He moved towards me, wrapping his arms around my waist and planting a wet kiss on my lips. 'Let's have a look at that nail, shall we, Princess?' He took my finger to his mouth and gently nibbled off the broken nail. 'You can get that fixed tomorrow before we leave on Thursday. Chances are you'll break a few more before the day's out.' He patted my bottom and moved back to the box on the floor. 'I need to label this one. Where's the marker pen?'

'Can't you do that in a minute? Shall we have a cuppa and put our feet up for a second?'

'Well, fortunately the kettle remains unpacked. There's no milk, I'm afraid, but we can have black coffee.'

'Sounds perfect,' he replied, plonking himself down onto another unopened box. The lid sagged slightly under his weight.

'I hope you're not going to smash my good plates with your big, fat arse.'

'Are you suggesting I have a large bottom, my love? I'll have you know that women all over England and quite a few blokes lust after my behind, as you well know. My arse could win awards if there were such things.'

'Maybe we should create one and name it after you. The Terence Blackwood Arse Award.'

'Charming, I'm sure.'

I carried the mugs over to him and put them down, spilling the coffee onto the kitchen table.

Terry raised his mug and held it towards me. 'A toast. To starting over.'

'To starting over – but let this be for the very last time, please, I'm begging you. Please. Promise me,' I pleaded, clinking my mug with his and taking a sip. 'Ow, that's hot. I've burned my tongue.'

'Well, there's only one remedy for that, isn't there, Princess?' Terry stood up and placed his mug on the draining board before moving back to the table and taking mine from me. Then he lowered me onto the small space still available on the kitchen floor.

Chapter 4

Amanda

I was jolted awake by the sound of truck juddering to a halt, its air brakes releasing a gigantic sigh, as if it was relieved to have reached its destination with its precious cargo intact. I lay there, listening as the bolts on the heavy back doors were flung open and raucous voices yelled at each other across the length of the vehicle.

'Jesus H Christ, what the fuck is that?' groaned Bill, rolling towards me with one eye half open. 'It's Saturday morning, for Jesus' sake. What time is it?'

I stared at the bedside clock, trying to focus. '7.55,' I replied, rubbing my eyes.

Bill burped, filling the stale bedroom air with the odour of the several pints of lager he had consumed last night when he got home. On a Friday Bill allowed himself to have a few drinks, as it was the weekend, and he did not have to get up for work the following day. He was very disciplined like that. Sunday to Thursday, he was teetotal, Friday he drank, Saturday we scheduled sex, but it had to be over before *Match of the Day* began. He was religious about Des Lynam.

'Go down and tell them to shut it, would you? I get up before God five days a week and I don't need to do it on one of my two days of rest.' Bill turned away, pulling the duvet off me and up over his own head in the process.

I lay on the other side of the mattress, shivering, hoping the noise outside would quieten down, or that Bill would nod off and not notice it again.

'Careful, mate. Move it to the left, or you'll take the bleedin' leg off that table,' boomed a voice that sounded as if it was downstairs in our own kitchen rather than outside on the street. I took a deep breath and swung my legs out of bed, reaching for my dressing gown, which lay on the floor.

Bill grunted from beneath his underground lair of sheets.

I exited the bedroom and went to the bathroom for a wee, before splashing my face with cold water and running some of it through my fringe. I was thirty-one, but I looked as old as Bill, who had just turned forty, inevitably without fuss or fanfare. The greasy, lank strands of my dark-brown hair, spotted grey at the temples, accentuated the deep, black circles under my eyes and highlighted my eyebrows, which had long grown out of control below the permanent frown on my pudgy face. It was little wonder that Bill barely noticed me anymore. I could hardly bear to look at myself.

I pulled on my dressing gown and belted it tightly, bending down to pull on my faded pink slippers. Then I trudged down the stairs and unlocked the front door. There was a sharp frost outside – not dissimilar to that inside the house. I picked my way gingerly to the garden gate, my slippers soaking up the moisture on the path with every step.

The removal truck was gargantuan, packed from front to back and from top to bottom. I wondered how the new residents would manage to stuff it all into one small semi-detached house. It would be like attempting one of those Guinness World Records, where you cram as many people as possible into a Mini or into an old red telephone box.

There was a scruffy bloke sitting at the back of the truck rolling a cigarette. He wore a T-shirt and denim shorts, seemingly oblivious to the bitingly cold air.

'Excuse me,' I called.

He made no reply.

'Hello?' I tried a little more loudly.

'Y'alright?' He was attempting to light his cigarette, which he was sheltering in his cupped hand, fighting against the wind.

Yorkshire, by the sound of him. I glanced at the side of the truck, itself proclaiming 'Heavy Hauliers of Harrogate', which seemed to confirm my assumption. They must have left in the very early morning to reach Crouch End by this time

'Is there any chance you could keep the noise down? It's just that my husband is trying to sleep. He's been working hard all week.' I clutched my dressing gown to my chest, attempting to keep out the chill.

'Haven't we all, love,' he chuckled. 'Look, we can try, but I can't promise. We've got this massive load to take in, and then we need to be back in Yorkshire by teatime. Tell him to put a pillow over his head!'

And I could press down hard on it.

'OK, well, thanks anyway.' I turned to go back into the house, having done my best.

At that moment, the red car I had seen a few weeks before screamed up the road and came to an abrupt stop right behind the truck, causing the man on his fag break to leap like an Olympic high jumper into the back of the truck for fear of losing his legs. The driver's door flew open and the man I had glimpsed talking to the estate agent a few weeks previously emerged from the driver's seat. He was wearing ordinary blue jeans and a red, checked shirt, but somehow, he wore them in such a way that you felt that his clothes must be supremely grateful to be covering his body. His musculature seemed to possess them like Bruce Willis in *Die Hard*. His blonde hair flowed almost to his shoulders, and he flicked it out of his eyes as he strode around to the passenger door. I had not seen anyone open a door for anyone else around here since I was small – and even then, it was a rarity. He held out his hand and it conjoined with another one, which sported immaculate red talons attached to a slender, yet curvaceous body, attired similarly in jeans and a shirt and topped off with a faded brown leather flying jacket. It was like watching one of those fashion advertisements in *Cosmopolitan* magazine come alive before your very eyes.

'Princess, welcome to our new home,' crowed the man, enveloping the woman in his arms and kissing her deeply and without shame in front of the removal man. 'Let's get you inside before you freeze to death.'

They glided together up their drive, hand in hand, while I shuffled back up my own path in my sodden slippers.

Chapter 5

Fiona

'I must admit that I think it's a bit off to say the least that the neighbours haven't popped over to welcome us, but "there's nowt so queer as folk," as they used to say up North.' I opened a cupboard and closed it again. 'I can't remember where I've put anything. We need to settle for good this time, Terry, if only so I can find the jam!' Still laughing, I moved over to the sink to fill the kettle.

'I can't promise how long we'll be here if I'm absolutely honest. We'll have to see how everything goes. At some point, we may need to move on again if work demands it, which is usually the case.' He ran his fingers through his thick mane and smoothed an eyebrow down. 'Make us a coffee while you're there, will you Princess?'

I put the kettle on to boil, staring through the kitchen window as it began to rumble away. 'You don't see him next door at all, do you?' I commented, straining to get a better view of their back garden. It was fully concreted, with a cheap plastic garden table and a couple of mismatching chairs. There were no flowers or plants. In the corner was a large black wheelie bin. The only colour came from a mountain of beer cans strewn around it.

'I think he goes out very early. I've heard his car start up in the morning. What about her? Have you seen her out and about at all?'

'She's an odd one. She seems to scurry in and out of the house like a little mouse. In fact, she looks more like a hamster, with that awful hair and puffy face. Mind you, I've never seen a hamster wear a mauve coat! They have better fashion sense.' I turned back to face Terry. 'Oh, I'm such a bitch, aren't I? Anyway, I don't get the impression that she works or anything, as she seems to be around most of the day, but it's terribly quiet over there. They don't appear to have any visitors. It's all rather weird.' I poured the boiled water into our new, over-sized, stripey John Lewis mugs and spooned two generous heaps of coffee and sugar into each, before walking over to kitchen table and handing one to Terry.

I sat down. 'She certainly spotted us when we first arrived, because I saw her loitering on the path in her dressing gown. She was talking to one of the removal men at whatever that ridiculous hour of the morning it was that we arrived here. Christ knows what she was doing outside at that time, but whether it was us or something the bloke said, she made herself scarce rather sharpish.'

'Well, it seems to me that the kindest thing to do is to make the first move, be friendly, don't you agree? You're great at that kind of thing, Princess. Maybe they are both just very shy. Go round there say hello. Invite them over. It's good to get to know your neighbours in case of emergency, isn't it?' Terry blew on his coffee and took a sip. 'Jesus, that's hot. How you can drink your coffee straight from the kettle is beyond me,' he commented, as I drained the last of mine.

'Do we really have to?' I countered. 'Remember the last people two doors down that you insisted we get friendly with. They were both such hard work. I never understood why you persevered with them.' I swirled the dregs of coffee around in my mug.

'Well, you can't always guarantee that other people will reciprocate your friendship, but we can at least try. It's the decent thing to do and not everyone is the same. For all you know, these guys might be great fun to be with.'

'Seriously?' I got up to re-boil the kettle.

'You're having another coffee already?'

'You know I'm a caffeine junkie. I just can't function without it.'

'Well, whatever works for you, Princess. That's what life's all about, figuring out what works for each of us.'

Chapter 6

Amanda

'What did this cake cost?' Bill demanded, wolfing down a giant slab.

'Nothing,' I replied. 'It was a gift.' I had considered eating it all before he got home, but even I could not possibly have managed it, and I made it a rule never to throw food away.

Bill paused momentarily. 'From your toy boy, I assume?' He burst out laughing. 'Sorry, but you're going to have to come up with a better excuse than that. Just admit that you forked out for expensive cake. Go on, fess up.'

'It was a gift, just like I told you.'

'But you don't know anyone. It wasn't from your family, was it? Have you told them where we are?'

'No, of course not, Bill. It was her,' I nodded my head to the right, 'the new woman next door,' I gulped. 'Fiona. She came round earlier today and introduced herself. She brought the cake to say hello and we had a quick cup of tea. I suppose we should have made the effort to introduce ourselves already, but I know that you're not keen on getting to know people in the road, so.'

'She bought the cake, did she? How very generous. So, what was she like, this fancy Fiona?' he enquired, cutting himself another huge slice of cake and stuffing his mouth. 'She looks very thin. Did *she* eat any cake?'

I bit the inside of my mouth. 'She was lovely, actually,' I answered, remembering my horror as I had opened the door.

Fiona had stood there in her glamorous, brown leather flying jacket, proffering a massive cake box adorned with a stunning pink ribbon, while I froze in my woolly socks and puffer coat with a dishcloth in my hand, water dripping onto the floor at her feet

'Hi, I'm Fiona Blackwood, your new neighbour.' She smiled brightly, as she sailed past me into the hall. 'We moved in next door a couple of weeks ago, so I just thought I'd just pop in and say hello now that we've settled in.'

'Er, hello,' I replied, closing the front door behind me. 'I'm Amanda. Amanda Whiteread.'

'Amanda, it's so great to meet you. I hope this isn't a bad time, but I was out and about, and I thought I'd buy you a cake from that gorgeous bakery in Crouch End high street. Do you know it? The one at the top of the high street?' she asked.

'I think I know the one you mean,' I replied. The name on the box, *Louis*, was very familiar to me. I dawdled past that particular bakery often, jealous of the women seated inside, nibbling on the posh French pastries while nattering with their friends and entertaining their children.

'Oh, I'm so glad you like it there. We will have to go together soon. But for now, I have brought the shop to you.' She presented the box to me with a flourish.

'Er, thank you. That's very kind. Just a moment while I get rid of this cloth.' I walked through to the kitchen with Fiona tottering behind me in her high-heeled boots. I lobbed the dishcloth towards the sink, but missed, and it landed in a soggy heap by the cupboard. 'Would you like a cup of tea?'

'If you are making, I'd love one, thank you,' she answered. 'Now, tell me where you keep your plates and I'll do the honours with the cake.'

'I'll get them. Please sit down.'

Fiona sat where Bill normally lounged: a platinum goddess in the place of my dusty, grumpy husband.

'I'm sorry it's so very cold in the house,' I ventured. 'The heating appears to be broken at the moment and I can't seem to find a decent plumber to fix it.' I felt my face flush red and I turned away to make the tea.

'I'm sure that Terry – that's my husband – can find you one. He's very well connected. I'll ask him as soon as I get home.'

'No!' I replied, a little too loudly. 'I mean, please don't go to any trouble. I'm sure Bill is onto it. He's in the trade as it happens and he's very efficient usually.'

'OK, well, as long as you're sure, but please don't hesitate to ask if Bill can't find anyone. Good plumbers are like gold dust, aren't they?'

'Absolutely,' I replied. 'Sugar?'

'Oh no, thank you, I'm sweet enough – or that's what Terry always says, anyway. Now, would you like a slice? It's Sachertorte. I hope you like it. It's one of my favourites.'

'Oh yes, that's my favourite too,' I replied, despite the fact that I had never even heard of it. Truthfully, I liked eating any kind of cake.

Fiona slid the knife that I had passed to her through the glistening brown icing and cut me a very decent slab. I noticed that she took a much smaller piece for herself, which I thought was very polite, given that she had paid for it.

'Do you have any cake forks?' she enquired, but she must have seen the look on my face, as she immediately said, 'Oh, let's not bother. Fingers are best for cake, don't you agree?'

I could not place her accent.

'So, let me tell you a bit about us as we are going to be – well, we are in fact – your new neighbours. Terry and I have just moved down from Harrogate. We loved it there, but Terry's business requires him to be down in London now, so he said it was sensible to make the move to the Big Smoke. It's exciting, I suppose, but a little daunting at the same time. You know what it's like, a new area to get to know and making new friends.' She picked up her cake and bit into the end of it. I had almost finished mine.

'That sounds very exciting. What does Terry do?' I enquired, staring at the cake, desperate for another piece.

'Oh, he's into all sorts of things. Property mostly. I don't get too involved if I can help it. I just enjoy the fruits of his labours.' She laughed, throwing her head back to reveal two rows of perfectly straight white teeth. 'And what does your husband do?' She recrossed her slender legs and leaned forward.

'Er, well, he runs a small construction company.'

'Ooh, how sexy. I do like a man in a hard hat.'

I took a large gulp of tea and dribbled some of it down the front of my coat.

'I like that colour on you, by the way,' Fiona commented. 'It suits you.'

I looked down at my tatty, mauve puffer, now tea-stained and fraying at the edges. 'Thank you. It's very old.' I scratched at the sleeve with my nails.

Suddenly, Fiona stood up, leaving more than half of her cake uneaten. 'It's been so lovely to meet you,' she gushed, 'but I must go now, because I've got a nail appointment at four. By the way, Terry and I would be delighted if you and Bill would come over for a drink one evening. Are you free at all this weekend?'

I opened my mouth, but nothing came out.

'Look, I'm sure you must both be super busy, and that you'll need to chat to Bill, but when you've had a chance to consult your diaries, just let me know. We are really looking forward to getting to know you both.'

'OK, I'll ask Bill, but he's not a great one for going out,' I murmured.

'Well, he only has to pop next door to see us, so it's not far to go now, is it? Anyway, ask him if he feels like it. I'll make some food and we can get further acquainted over a bottle or two – or even three!'

Fiona shrugged her shoulders back into her jacket and flicked her long, glossy blonde hair over the collar. Then she toddled over to me and gave me a quick hug, kissing me on the cheek before sashaying out of the kitchen.

'Let me know,' she cooed as she shut my front door behind her, leaving me frozen, marble-like, in the middle of the kitchen. When she had gone, I finished off the end of her cake.

'Well, if they are going around buying expensive cake for people that they've never met without a second thought and are inviting us in for drinks, I think we should go, don't you? After all, it's free food and booze, so what do we have to lose? Feel free to tell Fiona that, having compared our diaries, we find ourselves free this Saturday evening.' Bill rummaged in his pocket and pulled out a wad of fifty-pound notes, from which he peeled away one. He handed it to me. 'I guess you'll need something to wear, so go and buy yourself a decent outfit. Spruce yourself up a bit, but I'll expect some change out of that, so don't go mad. And keep the receipts. That way you can return the clothes next week as you'll be unlikely to wear them again.'

Bill smiled for the first time in longer than I could remember.

Chapter 7

Fiona

'So, they're coming over on Saturday – the neighbours. I'm telling you, Terry, it's going to be fucking hard work. I struggled to get a single word out of her. And the house was like a bloody ice box and had a very unpleasant smell. I really didn't want to hang around for too long if I'm being honest. Although in a funny kind of way, I did feel a bit sorry for her. She seemed to me to be rather lonely – a bit of a recluse, in fact. I gave her a hug as I left, and the poor thing completely froze. Maybe she's one of those people who doesn't like to be touched or something? Anyway, perhaps coming over here will bring her out of herself a little. Of course, he may be the same as her, in which case we'll need a lot of booze to get through it!'

Terry smiled.

'So, this is what I'm thinking. A few hors d'oeuvres with cocktails, pate and biscuits, you know the sort of thing - and then, let's keep it simple. Maybe a steak with salad and a cheesecake? I can buy the cheesecake from Waitrose. We'll need plenty of beer and wine. Can you sort that out at Majestic?'

We were lying in bed on Friday morning having made love. Terry was stroking my back as I nestled into his chest.

'Hmm? How is it that your skin is so soft in the mornings, Princess? I've never understood it. It's barely there.'

'Must be the effect of my beauty sleep,' I spoke into his curly chest hair. 'I think you're getting hairier, you know. Your chest tickles my nose when I lie here, and it never used to.' I reached up and kissed him.

'An added bonus for you, Princess. Now, you were discussing tomorrow. Sounds like a plan. And wear something sexy, so I can spend the evening thinking about what I'm going to do to you afterwards.' Terry tickled my back and I squirmed. 'This is my favourite outfit of all, of course.' He rolled on top of my naked body and began kissing me again, but I pushed him away and rolled out of bed. 'Sorry, but once is enough for this morning. I need to get to the shops and I'm having my highlights done at lunchtime, so I need to get on. You stay right where you are and get some rest.'

Chapter 8

Amanda

'You ready to go?' Bill yelled from outside the bathroom door.

I gulped, sweat trickling down the small of my back and between my breasts, spattering damp patches randomly across my maroon dress. I should have bought something in a lighter colour, but then I would not have been able to wear thick, black tights and I could not wear sheers with my legs. They showed off all my veins. I hunched over on the toilet seat, attempting to breathe. I was not used to engaging in any real social interaction or conversation. In fact, the tea I had shared with Fiona was the first time in two or three years that I had chatted to another human being without being at a supermarket checkout – except for Bill, of course. And he did not exactly count as social.

I rose and moved back to assess myself in the bathroom mirror for the thousandth time, smoothing my dress down over my stomach as I tried to suck it in. It protruded like a shelf below my waistband, and I felt my face flush with shame.

I had bought a floral maxi dress in a sort of jersey material with long sleeves and a high neck, having loitered at the entrance of C&A in Brent Cross shopping centre searching the window for both inspiration and courage for a good half an hour, while other busy shoppers barged past me with bulging shopping bags. The racks of clothes inside the store resembled an impenetrable forest to me, and I had no idea which rail to hack my way through first. So, I just stood there like an idiot, tears forming at the corners of my eyes, knowing I had to enter yet desperate to go home.

A shop assistant who was refolding some minuscule knickers on a table near the door nodded to me unsmiling. She was tiny, doll-like and so thin that I could have snapped her in half with a handshake. Her midriff was bare and almost concave, and she wore harem pants, which somehow accentuated her slenderness even more. As I finally took the plunge and crossed the threshold, she walked towards another assistant at the back of the store, and they began to whisper. I felt as if I was about to vomit.

I turned and knocked into the rack on my left. I apologised to the inanimate object out of sheer habit. There were some dresses hanging there, so I hoicked a yellow dress off the rack and held it to my chin. Turning to regard myself in the wall mirror, it made me look jaundiced. I shoved it back on to the hanging rail and grabbed the same dress in maroon. Holding it up, it looked a little better.

'You wanna try that on?' called the assistant from the back wall of the shop over the overly loud sound of INXS' 'Suicide Blonde'.

'Oh no, thank you,' I blustered. The thought of taking my clothes off in a public place was horrifying to me. She may as well have asked me if I would like to run naked through Marks & Spencer. 'I'm sure it will be fine, and I can return it if not, can't I?' I spluttered, knowing full well that I would in any case. 'Do you have this in a size fourteen? Or actually a sixteen might be better.'

The girl glowered at me from under her heavily kohled lids, rifling through the dresses. She passed the dress to me.

'Thank you.'

I followed her meekly to the till, where she stuffed the dress into a plastic bag, and I fled.

'Amanda, get out of the fucking bathroom, will you?' Bill shouted through the door. 'We're late.'

I grabbed a piece of toilet paper off the roll and dabbed at my eyes, before taking a huge breath and opening the door.

'How do I look?'

'Fine. Now let's go.'

I followed him down the stairs, feeling light-headed. 'Do you think we should take anything round?' I asked, suddenly thinking that it might be the polite thing to do.

'They invited us, didn't they? I don't see why we need take anything. And anyway, what did you have in mind exactly? We've only got a six pack of Tennent's Extra in the fridge and an opened packet of digestives. Let's just go and get this over with. I'm sorry now that I ever said yes. We'll stay for one drink. If they ask us to stay for food, I'll make an excuse.'

Bill jerked our front door open, and I traipsed down our drive and back up to the neighbours' one to their side of the semi like a cowed little dog who did not want to go for a walk. When Bill pressed their bell, it pealed to the chimes of Big Ben.

'Jesus Christ, listen to that,' said Bill as we waited on the step. 'How corny.'

The door flew open. 'Bong,' laughed Terry. 'It's funny, isn't it? Makes me laugh every time. Well, don't just stand there. Come in, come in and take a load off!'

Terry held out his hand and shook Bill's firmly, before reaching over and planting a strong kiss on my cheek. 'Terry Blackwood. It's so great to meet you both finally. I've heard such good things about you from Fiona.'

Terry ushered us through the hallway, which was the total antithesis of ours - not structurally, but in every other way. The walls were painted a pale cornflower blue, with framed abstract prints of landscapes punctuating the space at perfect intervals. When we entered the lounge, the damson sofas were illuminated by the flames from the gilt and black gas fire in the centre of the fireplace. Ours was sealed off and used as a receptacle for old shoes and magazines. Their glass coffee table sparked with its twisting chrome legs and was laden with crisps, nuts and other treats. Sinead O'Connor warbled through two immense speakers that stood sentinel at each side of the room.

But it was Terry who shone the most. He wore a cream silk shirt, which clung to his muscular chest as if it had been painted on to him. More of his buttons remained undone than fastened, exhibiting his luxurious mane of chest hair.

'Sit, sit down, please.' Terry beckoned towards the enormous three-piece settee. 'Now, what's your poison? I've got beer, wine, gin, vodka, brandy, whisky?' His teeth were immaculate. 'Amanda?'

'I, well, I don't know. It's such a choice.'

'She will have a small glass of white wine, thanks Terry, and I'll have a beer,' Bill interjected, heaving himself down onto the low sofa.

'No problem at all,' replied Terry, moving over to a large globe in the corner of the room. He pulled open the top to reveal a full bar. 'Cool, isn't it? I saw it in a vintner in Piccadilly the other day and I just couldn't resist buying it.' He proceeded to open a bottle of wine with one of those fancy bottle openers with legs, pouring out a very large glass before handing it to me. 'There you go, Amanda. It's a nice little Sauvignon which we brought back from our last trip to France. We like to drive over to Calais and hit the hypermarket a couple of times a year.'

I nodded and took a small sip. It tasted sweet. 'It's very nice, thank you.'

'Help yourself to nibbles, please,' Terry offered, pointing to a plate loaded with cubes of cheese on sticks. 'Fi will be down in a minute. She takes bloody ages to get ready. Women, eh?' he commented, rolling his eyes at Bill.

'You don't need to tell me about it,' Bill responded. 'I can never get her out of the bloody bathroom.'

'Well, it's worth it because you are a vision tonight, Amanda. That colour really shows off your beautiful eyes,' Terry commented, passing a pint glass to Bill, who nearly spilt it.

I felt my face flush with heat. I glanced up at Terry and he was smiling down at me. I looked back quickly into my wine glass on my lap and took a larger swig.

At that moment, Fiona shimmied in, resplendent in a tight black dress that clung to her curves and vertiginous heels. I wondered why on earth she was wearing such dressy shoes in the house, especially if she was cooking. Bill made to get up, but she stopped him. 'No, don't stand up for me, please. It's so lovely to meet you, Bill.' She bent down and kissed him on the cheek, her ample cleavage almost touching his face. 'And you, Amanda, how are you? Oh, I really love your dress. Where did you get it?'

Before I could reply, Terry was asking Fiona what she would like to drink, and she was insisting that I took several cheese sticks at once. 'And help yourself to crisps, please, otherwise I'll eat them all. I'm such a pig.'

Fiona perched her slender frame on the arm of the sofa next to me and Terry sank into the armchair next to Bill. 'So, Bill, I hear you're in construction. How's business these days?'

'It's busy,' Bill replied, puffing out his chest in a gesture I liked to think of as his Buxted turkey. 'We're building a new estate out in Woodford. It's a massive project, so it will keep me out of mischief for a year or so.'

'I'm working on a few property-related deals myself at the moment, as it happens,' replied Terry. 'I'm trying to raise funds for a couple of projects that I believe will turn a tidy profit. At least, I hope so. I need to keep the missus in the manner in which she has been accustomed. Right, Princess?'

'Right, babe,' Fiona replied, draining her wine. 'Top us up, will you, Terry?'

As Terry moved back to his three-dimensional map of the world, Fiona asked, 'So what about you guys? Where are you from and how did you meet? I love hearing stories about how people first got together. Terry and I met in a nightclub in Manchester.'

'I was throwing shapes on the dance floor, and she simply couldn't resist my moves,' Terry interjected.

'He thought he was bloody John Travolta. And you two?'

'Well,' I began.

'We met through mutual friends,' Bill interrupted.

'In London?' Fiona enquired.

'Yes. But in South London, not round here.'

'And do your families still live in London?'

Bill shot me a look. 'My dad left when I was young,' he said. 'My mum never remarried and now she's dead.'

'Oh, poor you, Bill. That's so sad. And you?' Fiona asked, turning to me.

'Mandy doesn't see her parents. They live a long way away and she's not close to them,' Bill interrupted, with a finality which made it clear that Fiona should desist from that particular line of questioning.

Fiona drained her second glass and rose from the arm of the sofa. 'So, are you both hungry? Shall we eat? I've got some gorgeous rump steak from the butcher, not Dewhurst's but the family one next to the shoe shop, and some lovely fresh asparagus. When we pee later, we'll all smell of petrol, won't we? It's so weird.'

I glanced at Bill, unable to answer the question.

'Why not? I'm very partial to a decent steak if I say so myself,' Bill replied.

Terry settled himself on the sofa between Bill and myself, while Fiona busied herself in the kitchen. Terry chatted away to Bill, and I was mostly ignored.

Chapter 9

Fiona

I loaded the dishwasher while Terry carried the remaining glasses through from the dining room.

'We'll have to wash these by hand, as they don't fit in the dishwasher and anyway, they might break.' He lowered a tray of glasses carefully onto the work surface.

It did not seem to matter how much Terry drank. He never appeared to be any worse for wear and was always in control, whereas I felt somewhat shaky on my feet, grateful that he was handling the glassware and not me. 'Shall we do those in the morning and just have a nightcap now? I'm totally knackered.'

'Sure, Princess. What would you like?' he asked, reaching up for two more glasses in the top cupboard.

'I'll have a brandy please. Just a smidgeon, though. I don't want to wake up in the night to a spinning room.'

He disappeared into the lounge to consult his booze globe and I wobbled behind him, removing my shoes once I reached the lounge. My feet throbbed.

'I swear to God that removing my stilettos after a long evening is better than sex,' I commented, abandoning my shoes on the rug, and throwing myself onto the sofa.

'I take that as an enormous insult,' Terry protested, handing me a brandy balloon that was half full.

'Is that your idea of a small one?'

'Are we still talking about the glass?'

I lay back and rested my feet on his lap. Terry massaged them gently.

'Well, what did you think of them then?' I asked. 'It wasn't the easiest of evenings, was it? She hardly speaks. Oh, that's good. Just a bit more pressure on my instep, please.'

'Yes, she's rather timid, isn't she and she's rather let herself go given she's probably only the same age as us, but she's so staid. He's clearly older, so maybe that's why.' Terry sipped his whisky and closed his eyes, resting his head on the back of the sofa. 'I think she could actually scrub up to be quite attractive if she lost some weight and dressed better. She's not got a bad face.' He opened his eyes and stared at me. 'She'd be a great project for you, Princess. You're so talented at makeovers.'

'I can't just waltz in there and suggest she sorts herself out, Terry. She'd be really offended.'

'No, but I think the poor thing lacks confidence. It doesn't sound as though she's got any friends, or even family to talk to. I felt quite sorry for her.'

'That's what I love about you,' I half-slurred, draining my brandy. 'You're always thinking about other people rather than yourself. You're a much better person than I am in that respect.' I turned around so that my head rested on his shoulder.

He put his arm around me. 'Don't be ridiculous, Princess. You're the kindest person I know.' He leant down and kissed me.

'And what about Bill? What did you make of him?' I asked.

'He seems like a bit of a disappointed man to me. Maybe work is unsatisfying, or maybe he's just got a small cock.'

I could not help but giggle. 'You are so mean!' I slapped Terry's thigh lightly.

'He did seem to loosen up a little after a few beers, so maybe he will get more interesting as we get to know him. First meetings are always tough, because everyone puts up a façade when they meet other people initially, don't they?'

'Not everyone. I felt like I knew you inside out from the first day I met you.' I lifted my head and kissed him again.

Chapter 10

Amanda

A fortnight later, Terry had invited Bill to join him at a race meeting at Kempton Park. What was more shocking than the invitation – because I just could not understand why Terry would want to become all pally with someone like Bill, who did not seem to be his type at all – was that Bill accepted. Yes, of course, Bill had always liked a small flutter on the horses, but he was far too risk-averse to bet more than a couple of quid. Yet here he was, all trussed up in his special occasion suit and sporting a proper pair of leather loafers, just because Terry had a box. He came down to breakfast whistling. Whistling!

'I don't know when I'll be back, because I think it takes a good hour or so to get to Kempton, so just make me a sandwich for when I get home, will you? I think there will be proper catering at the races, so I hope to get well fed and watered.' He patted his ample beer gut, which rumbled in anticipation of its future feeding frenzy.

'Sure,' I muttered, as Bill unrolled a wad of fifty-pound notes and began to count them out on the table. When he had finished, he rolled them back up and secured them with an elastic band, before kissing the bundle and returning them to his trouser pocket. 'Grow and multiply,' he whispered to the protrusion.

'Make sure you take that dress back. You will probably never wear it again, and I don't want to pay for stuff just to let it rot away in your wardrobe.'

I made no reply.

'Right, well I'm off. Terry's driving us down in his Audi, so we should fly there. See you later.' He rose from the table, his jacket slung over his shoulder and his tie in his hand. I heard the front door slam with gratitude.

I sank into one of the rickety kitchen chairs and rested my head in my hands. I have no idea how long I stayed there like that. Another whole day of emptiness stretched ahead of me, so there was no hurry.

Suddenly the telephone rang, shattering the chilly air and I froze. No one ever called because no one had our number. Even I did not know what it was, because Bill had set up the account. He said he had done this for my own protection, to save me from the temptation to call my family.

When I first met Bill almost ten years ago in the chip shop where I worked in Clapham, he was so sweet and rather shy. He was unlike the other boys, who simply wanted a snog round the back and more than that if they could get it. But my parents and my brother never took to Bill, thinking he was far too old and more than a little odd. They made me choose and I chose Bill. We moved north of the river, cut off all communication with my family, and I was free to concentrate on Bill to the exclusion of all else. This was married bliss.

The telephone persisted, so I rose to answer it. 'Hello?'

'Hi, can I speak to Dawn please?' asked a woman's voice.

'I think you've dialled the wrong number,' I apologised.

'Is that 427 6548?' she demanded.

'I'm afraid I really don't know.'

'Excuse me? Are you simple or what?'

'Yes,'

The voice was right. I was clearly a bit of a simpleton. I replaced the receiver and went to fill the kettle to make myself another cup of tea. I drank it slowly, munching my way through a whole packet of Rich Tea biscuits without even realising, mesmerised by the barren view of my paved garden, where nothing green ever grew and no birds came to sing.

Chapter 11

Fiona

I had to hand it to Terry. Every time we moved house, he launched himself into the new community and made the most of it. His work was portable, as he described it, so regardless of where we lived, he was always extremely busy and successful. He invested in various projects ('I'm good with property and people' he explained to anyone we met). I did not pretend to understand the ins and outs of it all; and whenever I did ask, he just told me how boring I would find it if he attempted to explain and changed the subject. That was fine by me. Terry was extremely generous, providing me with a healthy, weekly housekeeping allowance and never questioning my credit card bills, which could be hefty. I must admit that I did enjoy buying clothes and often popped up to Knightsbridge or the West End to mooch in Harvey Nichols or Selfridges. It was my weak spot, but I liked to look good for Terry and he never seemed to complain. He said he loved having such a glamorous woman on his arm, and the fact that I made him feel good made me feel great too. I felt truly blessed to have found such an adoring and affectionate husband. Sometimes, I got a little bored, especially when we were settling into a new place, and occasionally I made noises about going back to work – I had worked as a hairdresser up in Harrogate before we got married – but Terry would not hear of it. He was pretty old-fashioned in that respect.

Over the last couple of months, Terry had made a particular effort to befriend Bill next door, which I found admirable, because I found Bill excruciatingly dull. On the one hand, I did not approve of the way he treated Amanda as a domestic servant, expecting her to wait on him hand, foot, and finger. On the other, she was so docile to the point of being mute, so maybe he was simply bored and frustrated because she had nothing to say. It was hard to understand how they put up with each other, given that there appeared to be such a lack of affection between them.

Despite my misgivings, I thought that I had better try with Amanda, if only because Terry had already set such a good example. I knocked on her door around lunchtime on the day that Terry had taken Bill to Kempton and was somewhat surprised to see her still lounging about in her pyjamas and dressing gown, both of which had seen better days and were desperately in need of a good wash.

'Hi, Amanda, how are you? I was going to pop up to Harrods later on to do some shopping and wondered if you'd like to join me?'

Amanda froze. 'Oh, hi, Fiona. I was just about to get dressed.' She hesitated again. 'I've been absolutely rushed off my feet with the housework this morning and I'm afraid that I haven't made it as far as the shower yet.'

She tried to smile, but it was far more of a grimace. She moved to close the door on me, but I persevered. 'I can wait if you like – or come back when you're ready?'

'Well. I've got to return something to Brent Cross, so I don't think I can come into London today.'

I spotted a crumpled C&A bag lying behind her on the hall floor. 'Well, I'm happy to go to Brent Cross instead if you like. I'm in the mood for mooching around the shops, and that's as good a place as any. Shall I come back in an hour? We can go in my car if you like.' I had a minuscule, second-hand, ruby red Mini Cooper, which I loved. I could park it literally anywhere, and often did, as my many parking tickets testified.

'Oh, there's no need, really,' Amanda stuttered, backing into the shadows of the hall.

'It's no trouble, honestly. I'll meet you outside the house at two. The boys won't be back for hours, so we'll have plenty of time to shop and have a coffee and a natter.'

She nodded slowly. 'Alright then. I'll see you at two,' she replied, without enthusiasm.

I retraced my steps back home, where I draped myself on the sofa to watch a repeat of *Kilroy* for an hour. I was ready and waiting in the Mini at two sharp as promised, beeping my horn to let Amanda know I was outside. She emerged a few minutes later, and then immediately went back inside again, evidently having forgotten her C&A return. I watched as she reappeared, locking the front door and trudging heavily across to the car.

'Stick the bag in the boot. It's open,' I called through the driver's window.

Amanda did as she was told, and then crammed herself into the passenger seat. There was quite a lot of her - amplified by the ageing puffer coat which seemed to be a permanent fixture. 'It's so kind of you,' she said, struggling to fix the seatbelt, 'to give me a lift to Brent Cross. Normally, I have to take the bus and it takes forever.'

'I guess you could have used Bill's car today, couldn't you, given he's at the races with Terry?' I asked, shoving the gearbox into reverse and pulling off the drive.

'Oh no, I'm not insured on Bill's car,' she answered, fiddling with the fraying edges on the sleeves of her coat. 'In actual fact, I haven't driven since Bill and I got married almost a decade ago. He never liked the way I drove anyway, and I'm not sure I'd have the confidence anymore. Bill says I was a complete menace on the road.'

'Do you believe everything Bill tells you? Because I ignore most of what Terry says to me!'

Amanda made no reply, instead staring out of the window, seemingly fascinated by the stream of traffic on the A41.

Fortunately, it was moving, and within fifteen minutes we had reached the shopping centre at Brent Cross. I hummed along to Rick Astley's 'Never Gonna Give You Up,' because I could never remember the exact lyrics, while Amanda remained mute and motionless beside me for most of the journey.

We parked up eventually after circling the car park for a while looking for a space. 'Shall we make your return first and then we will be free to shop?' I suggested.

'Oh, there's no need for you to come with me for that. It'll only take me five minutes,' Amanda replied, clutching her plastic bag to her ample chest. I recognised the material poking out of the top of it.

'Is that the dress you wore when you came over for dinner?'

She blushed. 'Oh no. It's a blouse that I bought in the same material. I decided not to keep it as it's the same as the dress. I wouldn't return something I'd already worn obviously, unless it was faulty.'

'Of course,' I replied, but I wondered if she was lying to me. 'Are you going to exchange it for something else? I love doing that, because the thing I buy instead is always that little bit more expensive, but somehow it feels like it's less, because I've already paid for most of it, if you see what I mean.'

Amanda shifted the bag into her other hand and made no reply.

'OK, well, I'll meet you in John Lewis for coffee in half an hour then,' I suggested. 'I've got a few things I need to buy there in the meantime.'

She nodded and wandered off, while I headed towards the fashion section of John Lewis.

We met at the allotted time. 'I got you a cappuccino. Is that OK?' I asked, as Amanda approached. 'And a brownie to share.'

She sagged down opposite me. 'Thanks.'

'Success at the shop?'

'Yes, thank you.' Amanda stared into her coffee, seemingly fascinated by the froth.

She had no shopping bags with her, so I assumed she had not bought anything else. I, on the other hand, had managed to purchase a Mulberry handbag and a cashmere sweater. I had seen some similar items in Selfridges the week before, but had resisted the temptation to buy them. When I spotted them in John Lewis as well, I felt like it must have been fated.

I cut the brownie roughly in half and pushed the larger portion towards Amanda.

'Thank you.' She took a large bite and looked up from her plate. 'How do you stay so slim and still eat cake? If I eat anything at all, it immediately adds another pound of flesh straight onto my bones.'

'I've always been naturally skinny, which is lucky, but I also do my Jane Fonda video workouts religiously, which really do help – and Terry and I do have quite a bit of sex. It's a great calorie burner!' I nibbled at my brownie.

Amanda stared straight at me. 'Bill and I have sex once a week on a Saturday. We want to have children, but I keep losing them.' She made this statement without emotion, as if she was telling me that she had butter on her toast in the mornings.

I choked on my coffee and spat some of it onto the table. 'I'm so sorry. That must be so upsetting.'

'Yes.' Amanda finished off her brownie and I slid my half towards her. She finished it in two bites. 'Look at me. I'm thirty-one, but look at least a decade older, and I weigh over four stone more than I did when I met Bill. I don't know much about anything, and I can't even give him children.' Her lip wobbled involuntarily. 'We keep trying, once a week, regular as clockwork, but I just kept miscarrying. The doctors don't seem to know why exactly. It seems that we simply aren't compatible.'

A tear made its way slowly down her cheek. I reached across the table and held her hand. 'Poor you. I'm so sorry. If it's any consolation, Terry and I have been trying for ages and nothing's happened for us either, as yet. Have you been to see a doctor? I'm thinking about it.' This wasn't actually true, but I was trying to make her feel a little better.

'Bill won't hear of it. He says he's not wanking off to some porn magazine in a doctor's waiting room – his words, you understand. I wanted to consider adoption, but Bill says he's not bringing up someone else's child. He only wants his own. I really feel like I've failed him as a wife.

'Don't be ridiculous. What does your mum say about it?' I paused, realising my mistake. 'Oh, I'm sorry, I forgot Bill said you don't speak.'

Amanda hung her head and stared into her empty cappuccino. 'I've already said far too much. Bill would be furious if he found out that I had told you all of this.'

'I won't tell him,' I promised, waving to the waitress and ordering two more coffees, although in reality we really needed something much stronger. 'You can always talk to me. It sounds like you need a friend.'

Amanda gave a short smile. 'Thank you. I really appreciate it.' She hesitated and then continued. 'I often want to call my mum, you know, but our phone does not allow for outgoing calls. I have made it as far as a phone box on occasion, but I only ever dial and then hang up when someone answers. I can't go crawling back to them having not spoken for so long, and anyway, home was no picnic, so I wouldn't want to if I'm completely honest. One day, Bill and I might get lucky.'

She was weeping now, quietly, shedding long-bottled tears all over the table. 'The truth is, I hate myself. I've made all the wrong choices, I look like shit. I'm infertile, stupid, boring – I'm effectively useless.'

I rummaged in my handbag and handed her a packet of Handy Andies. 'Amanda, listen to me. You're none of those things. You've just been battered down by circumstances, and we need to build you back up. I tell you what. I can help you. You're a good-looking girl, who has just let herself get a little out of shape and certainly very much out of self-confidence. I could cut your hair properly for you for a start, and you can join me in my keep fit routines. How about it? They've done some research that says that diet and exercise can really help with fertility too.' I watched myself saying this, appalled that I was offering all of this to a woman I hardly knew and was not even sure I liked.

'That sounds great, Fiona, but I'm not sure it's possible. You look incredible, but me.'

'You have a great face and a kind heart – the only two things which matter.'

Amanda drained her second coffee and blew her nose so loudly that people in Perfumery on the ground floor probably thought that there was an elephant up on the third.

'Don't you worry about that. As of today, we will re-build you.'

'Like The Six Million Dollar Man?'

'Or rather woman,' I corrected.

'It's a lovely thought,' she sniffed, wiping her eyes, 'but rather like the TV show, it's not real life, is it?'

'Life is what you make it. Or that's what Terry always says anyway. Right. Chin up, Amanda. Things can only get better.

Chapter 12

Amanda

I closed my front door with a thud, leaning on it hard to ensure that I had sealed myself back in from the outside world. I was sweating, despite the cold inside and out, and struggling to catch my breath. What had I said and why had I said it? I had not opened up to another person like that in years, so why now and why Fiona? I barely knew her, we had absolutely nothing in common and - even though she was clearly a good person and wanted to help, for which I suppose I should have been grateful - I had exposed myself and Bill. What made it worse was that they lived right next door to us, our walls conjoined, and Bill and Terry were becoming friendly. What if Fiona told Terry what I'd said, and then Terry told Bill that I had revealed details about my past and our sex life and my inability to have children? It did not bear thinking about. Bill held me in contempt as it was, but at least I had kept quiet about our private lives – up until this point. Now I had blabbed, and soon the whole neighbourhood would know all about it. I was suddenly gripped by a violent wave of nausea and raced to the toilet, where I threw up all my afternoon tea. I was disgusted with myself, and I knew that I deserved everything I got.

Dusk had descended even though it was barely four o'clock in the afternoon. It was February, a month that I had always found even more depressing than January. It appeared to be a mere elongation of that first dreadful part of the year when everything remained dead and buried in the icy ground with seemingly no chance of renewal. I drew the curtains closed in the lounge and sagged onto the sofa, staring at the turned-off television. It was the focal point of the room, which was otherwise essentially bare of detail. The brown fabric sofa and mismatched armchair were faded and worn around the armrests. The coffee table – also faeces brown – was multifariously stained from the bases of Bill's beer cans. The carpet – once beige – was now grey, dirty, and spotted. We had hung no pictures on the walls and placed no photographs on the tables. The curtains hung limply at the centre where the hooks had fallen out long ago, never to be replaced. It was a shabby, desolate room that could have belonged to anyone, but somehow, it uniquely belonged to us. Bill and I had made no personal mark upon it, much as we made no impact on the world. The room merely existed. As I rested there on the sofa in my moth-eaten, old coat, I was indistinguishable from the furniture – cheap, slightly damaged and of no use to anyone.

I must have fallen asleep, because I was jolted by the sound of a key struggling to open the front door. I shook myself and stood up too quickly, so that I felt momentarily dizzy and had to stand still to wait for the room to stop spinning. The fumbling on the other side of the door continued, so I took the opportunity to switch off the light in the lounge and dart into the kitchen. I opened the fridge and hauled out a few random ingredients, throwing them onto the side of the sink just as Bill lurched through the door. He swayed slightly as he staggered towards the table, before lowering himself into a chair with the care of someone who was more than a little drunk.

'Did you have a good time?' I enquired, facing the draining board away from him while I attempted to slice through an old lump of hard cheddar.

'It was bloody fantastic,' Bill slurred. 'We had an amazing day. Great racing, loads of booze, good food and company.' He attempted to remove one sleeve of his jacket, but it got stuck around his elbow and he gave up.

'That's great. I was just making you a cheese and pickle sandwich.' I moved over to the bread bin and pulled out the end of a sliced white loaf, which had grown slightly mouldy at the edges.

'Bit of a disappointment after the catering we had today, but go on then,' Bill replied, having another go at jacket removal, which defeated him once again.

'Successful day?' I enquired, grabbing the pickle jar from the cupboard.

'I suppose I made a bob or two. I followed Terry's lead. He seems to know everything there is to know about horses.'

I concentrated on slathering a thick layer of butter onto the bread.

'Here you go.' The plate wobbled on the tabletop before him.

I turned back to the sink and began to run the hot water to start the washing up when I was suddenly caught by a familiar stabbing pain in my lower abdomen. I held on tightly to the sink until the contraction passed.

'I don't feel too well, Bill,' I gasped, struggling to stand up straight. But when I glanced behind me, Bill was snoring in his chair. I hobbled out of the kitchen, turning the light off on my way out.

Chapter 13

Fiona

Terry waltzed into the house with a massive grin plastered across his face. He threw himself onto the sofa next to me and planted a sloppy kiss on my lips. He reeked of whisky.

I pulled away from him slightly. 'Do you think you should have driven home?'

He ran his hand through his thick mane and laughed. 'I've only had a few, Princess. You know I never overdo it.'

I pulled a face.

'Ah, don't be like that. Come here,' he demanded, dragging me onto his lap. 'Feel that? I've had a very good day.'

'Is that a wad in your pocket, or are you just pleased to see me?'

'Let's find out,' he teased, unzipping his trousers. 'Well, Princess, what do you think?' Terry was quite clearly aroused, but instead of inviting me to do something about it, he produced a gigantic roll of notes from his trousers' secret pocket, one of which he had sewn into every pair he owned. 'Take a look at this!' He unravelled a roll of fifties, peeling off a few notes and stuffed them down the front of my shirt. 'You can treat yourself to something nice tomorrow. The last nag came in at 100-1.'

'Ooh, you *have* had a good day. And what about Bill?'

'He made a very tidy profit as well. I advised him to follow my tips, and he walked away with a couple of grand. I don't think he'd ever won so big in his life. Mind you, he was pretty out of it by the end. I had to collect his winnings for him. It's a good job I'm an honest chap. Mind you, I was rather worried he was going to throw up in the motor on the way home and wreck the upholstery. I not sure how he even made it up his own drive!'

'Lucky old Bill.' I wondered how kind he would be with Amanda once he got home in that condition. With any luck, he would just pass out until the morning.

'What are you thinking about, Fi? You look a little sad.'

'Oh, nothing in particular. I just missed you today, that's all.'

'I missed you too, Princess. But now I really need to get some sleep. It's been a long old day entertaining our neighbour.'

Chapter 14

Amanda

Weeks passed and Bill made no mention of my indiscretion with Fiona. So, she had clearly said nothing to Terry (or if she had, Terry had kept his mouth shut). After their day at the races, Bill seemed to be out with Terry almost every free moment he had. With his newly found enthusiasm, he was like a small boy: constantly knocking on the next-door neighbour's door to ask if he wanted to come out to play. More often than not, the two men disappeared to the *Queens* for a few drinks in the evening, or of late, to one of the new trendy wine bars in Muswell Hill. If anyone had mentioned a wine bar to Bill in the past, he would have entered into a long tirade about how they were all frequented by pretentious prats with more money than sense. But now that Terry took him there, he could not get enough of them. Sometimes, he even drank wine instead of beer and nibbled on mixed nuts rather than on his favourite cheese and onion crisps.

'Terry attracts a great deal of attention when we go out, you know,' Bill commented one evening, while I was setting up the ironing board with a loud scrapping noise. I plugged the iron in and water to it. It hissed and spat.

'Does Terry take any notice of them?' I enquired, starting in on one of Bill's collars.

'He flirts with them, but that's about all. But he's a good-looking bloke, isn't he? Even you must have noticed that.'

I made no comment.

'I don't think he plays around, though. Mind you, even if he did, I wouldn't rat on him to you, would I? What goes on tour, stays on tour, as Terry often says.' Bill chuckled to himself.

I smirked, wondering what particular tour Bill had ever been on in his entire life. Frankly, I did not care that he was out with Terry all the time. I was lonely whether Bill was out or if he was at home. And these days, on the nights that Bill did stay in, because Terry was spending time with Fiona, he sulked like a small child.

'Not seeing your best mate tonight then?'

'Nah, he's taking Fiona to see some poncey French film with subtitles. I can't see the point of paying for the cinema personally, when you can just watch something on TV, but I suppose he needs to keep a woman like her entertained to some degree, or she might bugger off with someone else. At least you're not vaguely bothered about going out.' He rubbed his protruding belly button absently through the gaping hole between the shirt buttons.

I ignored him, busily hanging an ironed shirt on a wire hanger and reaching down into the basket to retrieve another one. 'And how's work?' I enquired.

'Oh, you know, the same old stuff. Problems with this and that, but in general it's going to plan. The problem is, it's just steady. Terry tells me that he has a few interesting investment opportunities lined up that he might discuss with me. Get me in on the ground floor, as it were.' He cracked open another beer and took a long swig. 'Terry thinks that I will never manage to grow the firm more than I already have and it's basically a waste of my abilities. I hadn't even thought about it like that before.'

'What kind of business opportunities?' I queried.

'None of your fucking business opportunities - that kind,' he barked, before continuing, 'Look, I'm only thinking about options at the moment. I've always taken the view that cash is king, but Terry says there's money to be had longer term if you are prepared to take a bit of a punt on property. He says that's how he's made all his dosh. And he clearly knows what he's doing. He's made an awful lot of money after all, and he definitely has an inside track on things. He's opened my eyes a bit.' Bill finished his can, crushing it in his left hand, before lobbing it at the bin, missing as always.

'I think it might be helpful if you seemed more interested in the world outside of these four walls,' he continued. 'It would be helpful for me if Terry and I do agree to do some serious business together. Terry often tells me what a business asset Fiona can be at times.' He looked me up and down as if I were a prize heifer that he was considering buying at auction.

I tasted blood in my mouth. It seemed that I had been biting my lip without realising, but I could no longer stay silent. I watched myself explode from somewhere else, from somewhere outside myself. 'Why would I have ever needed to make an effort, Bill? I've never gone anywhere, *we* have never been anywhere – or at least we never have so far in our decade together. You've always moaned if I spent money on clothes or got a decent haircut. We've never even been on holiday because you're so Scrooge-like with money. You've never wanted me to work so that I could earn my own money, because you have always wanted me to be right here at home getting your tea ready and doing your laundry. I can't see my family – even if I wanted to. We make love like dead people, which is probably why we cannot create any kind of new life. No one would notice if I dropped dead tomorrow – except perhaps you, because you'd get no dinner. And now, out of the blue, you want me to be Fiona!'

I stopped, suddenly drained of all energy, and collapsed onto the floor by the sink, burying my head in my hands. I no longer cared what Bill did or said in response.

'For Christ sakes, stop feeling so bloody sorry for yourself,' Bill growled. 'I have always worked every hour God sends so that you can have a decent roof over your head. I put plenty of food on the table. Let's face it, you're not exactly wasting away, are you? I'm just asking you to sort yourself out.'

I remained motionless as he thumped his way out of the kitchen and down the hall, slamming the front door on his way out.

The house was completely silent, as if it also had no further comment to make - its walls sick and tired of listening to our constant bickering, its floors bowing under the weight of the boredom and contempt that walked on them every day. I stood up slowly and shuffled my way to the stairs, suddenly exhausted. The pain in my abdomen had returned, stabbing me as I moved up to the bathroom. I pulled up my dress and lowered my tights to urinate. As I did so, the pan was pink. I had not told Bill this time that I was pregnant. I saw little point in both of us suffering loss yet again.

I opened the wall cabinet and pulled out a box of sanitary towels stuffed towards the back. I rummaged to the bottom of the box and recovered a tub of aspirin and six miniatures of whisky, which I kept hidden there. It was the one place that I knew Bill would never look. I kept it hidden away and had so often thought about using this way out of my sad, sorry life, but in the past something had always held me back. But now, I was so utterly exhausted, and I knew that I could not keep repeating the endless cycle of momentary hope that life would change followed by crushing disappointment.

I grappled with the childproof top on the aspirin, cursing the ineptitude of my fat fingers. Eventually, I wrenched it open and emptied the contents into my hands. I filled the tooth mug with water and swallowed all the tablets down, chased by the six miniatures. The harsh liquid made me squirm as it scorched my throat. Then I turned to head back downstairs, switching on the television to watch Coronation Street. I hoped to fall asleep before the episode ended and not wake up to see the next one tomorrow.

Chapter 15

Fiona

'How's the chocolate mousse?' mouthed Terry, his own lips glued together as he worked on an enormous slice of cheesecake.

Terry had treated to me to a night out at Le Caprice in St James off Piccadilly, one of London's swankiest restaurants and great for people watching. Sadly, we had spotted no celebrities this evening, although the maitre d informed us that Tom Cruise had dined there the night before. 'He's much shorter than you think,' he had confided to us with some satisfaction.

'Mmm, it's delicious,' I cooed, licking the rich chocolate off the spoon as slowly as I could. I liked to savour my food, whereas Terry ate so quickly that I doubted that he ever tasted any meal at all. 'This was a much better idea than going to see that foreign film – if rather less intellectual.' My face flushed. The effect of the second bottle of wine was starting to kick in and I was feeling pleasantly disorientated. 'How did your new best friend take it when you told him you couldn't see him tonight?'

Terry raised an eyebrow. 'He's not my best friend. We might do some business together, and there's things to discuss, that's all.'

I spluttered, sending a small piece of mousse onto my lip. 'Business with Bill! That doesn't make any sense.'

'Fiona, you understand nothing of the world of work, and nor should you, but I have a couple of investment opportunities and Bill has cash – more than you might think, in actual fact. He's running a business which appears to be extremely hard given its very small turnover and profit margin. Look, he's not my normal kind of investor, you're right, but I'm just trying to help the guy out, you know. It might improve his lot, and maybe even help his wife out as a result. You know how much I like to help people.' Terry polished off the last of his cheesecake, scraping his plate with his spoon. 'That was very good,' he commented, patting his six-pack. He could eat anything he wanted and never gain any weight. He was bloody irritating that way.

'Right, Princess, it's about time I took you home.' Terry raised his hands to signal to the waiter for the bill.

He paid, and we threaded our way through the small, tightly packed bistro, me clinging to his arm to prevent myself from swaying too much. Fortunately, the car was parked just up the street.

'Are you sure you're OK to drive?' I questioned.

'Of course I am. It's not me who's so tipsy that I can't quite stand up straight, is it? Anyway, as I've told you many times, alcohol has absolutely no effect on my cognitive abilities. Just strap in and enjoy the ride!' He revved the Audi like a teenage boy racer, and we sped off up the street.

It was past midnight when we turned into our road and saw blue flashing lights illuminating the buildings. 'What the hell is going on?' muttered Terry, dropping his speed as we approached the house, just in case it was the police. As we parked up, we spotted a stretcher being loaded into the ambulance.

'Christ, Terry, what the hell is going on?' I shouted louder than I had intended as I opened the car door. I stood up and wobbled, the alcohol and the evening air colliding.

The ambulance crew slammed the doors at the back shut with a loud clang, and the driver started the engine. I glanced over and saw Bill framed in the doorway, the light behind him illuminating his bulky frame.

'What's happened, Bill?' I called. 'Are you alright? Has something happened to Amanda?' I began to wend my way up their drive, but before I got halfway up it, Bill had turned around and slammed the door.

'Do you think you should go and see if he's OK, Terry? Maybe he would rather talk to you?'

'I'll knock on the door. Don't you worry. You go in and I'll be back in a minute.'

Terry strode down Bill's path and rang the doorbell. Bill answered immediately, and Terry disappeared into the hallway, closing the door behind him.

Later – although I have no idea how much time had elapsed – Terry shook me awake on the sofa, where I had nodded off waiting for him.

'Come on, Princess, let's get you to bed.'

'Is everything alright?' I slurred, rubbing my eyes.

'Yes, it's fine. Amanda has suffered a bad attack of food poisoning, that's all, and she couldn't stop throwing up. They've taken her in for observation as a precaution overnight, but she'll be OK.'

'Oh, thank goodness. But what could she have eaten that made her so ill that she had to go to hospital?'

'Let's face it, it could be anything in that house. It's filthy. I don't think that woman ever cleans.' Terry reached out a hand to pull me up off the sofa, but I could not move.

'Are they sure it's food poisoning?' I queried, rousing myself a little.

'Well, that's what Bill said, and I can't see why he'd lie about it – unless he tried to poison her!'

'Do you think he might have done?' I gripped Terry's arm.

'Don't be ridiculous! You watch too much of that true crime crap on the telly. Bill may be unpleasant to her sometimes, but he's not a murderer, I can assure you of that.'

'But what if he did hurt her?'

'Old Bill couldn't hurt a fly. He's all talk and no trousers. Come on up to bed. You can go to see her when she gets home tomorrow.'

Chapter 16

Amanda

I was surrounded by a fierce brightness searing my eyelids. I had never believed in all that rubbish people spoke of when they described their near-death experiences of moving towards the light, the light at the end of the tunnel, the whiteness of heaven, although why I would end up in heaven was a matter of sheer conjecture, given that I had never been inside a religious establishment in my life. Even my elopement with Bill had culminated in our marriage in a prefab Nissen hut, which posed as a temporary registry office on the dreary Edgware Road.

My eyelids fought to open but failed. I was blind, unable to appreciate my newfound utopia. The light began to hurt the inside of my eyes. Panic seized me and I began to thrash around, my arms and legs flailing, as if such frantic exercise might miraculously force my eyes to peel awake. Yet they remained steadfastly stuck.

A voice called to me from very far away. 'Amanda, can you hear me?' I attempted to reply, but I could not speak. I seemed to have escaped one life, where I had been totally paralysed, merely to dive into another where I had been struck both mute and blind. Yet not deaf. In both, I could hear the demands of others, but I still failed to make myself heard. The light thrumming against my eyes faded, and my mind grew dark, returning momentarily to peace.

This exact sequence kept recurring. I have no concept of how long or how often it continued, but I moved from darkness to light and back again with monotonous regularity, interspersed with short, fraught attempts to reconnect, to resurface. I heard men, women calling my name, pulling me up, yet each time I sank straight back down again.

And it was only then I realised that I had merely achieved limbo, a different kind of limbo from the one where I had previously resided. I had wished to free myself from my life, but where was I now?

Chapter 17

Fiona

'Look, I'm no doctor, but don't you think it's a bit odd that Amanda has been in a coma for the last two weeks due to food poisoning? I mean, I'm not the suspicious type, but you don't think that Bill had anything to do with it, do you? I know I've said it before, but I really do wonder.' I was perched on a stool at my dressing table, painting my nails a fluorescent pink, an even brighter hue than shocking.

Terry was lying on the bed in his pyjama bottoms. 'I think you're letting your imagination run away with you, Poirot,' he chortled. 'Bill may not be the kindest of husbands – unlike yours truly – but, as I've already told you, he does not seem to me to be the murdering type. I'm really not sure he's got the imagination.' He scratched his balls and continued. 'And he's been totally distraught ever since she's been in hospital.'

'Probably because he's having to fend for himself. Shit, I've smudged my thumb,' I moaned, reaching for the acetone.

'That's rather uncharitable of you, Princess. If the same thing happened to you, I'd be destroyed.' He moved off the bed and came up behind me, kissing my head.

'Go away, Terry. My nails are wet,' I scolded.

He moved off to the chest of drawers, pulling out a pair of boxer shorts, which he swopped for his pyjamas.

'I think I'll go to visit her,' I mused. 'I think I should. They say that if you talk to people in comas they can still hear you and that often it can bring them round.'

'I'm not sure they'll let you in, Fi. Bill says he's the only one allowed to visit.'

'Yes, but let's be honest, Terry. Bill prefers it if no one else ever talks to Amanda except him. He controls her.' I raised my finished left hand, pleased with the results. My right hand had once again tragically suffered a badly broken nail, so did not look so good. 'And as far as I'm aware, he's not been to see her at all. It's pretty shocking.'

'I don't think you know them well enough to know what goes on over there, do you?'

'I know more than you think I know. He's not kind to her, and she's been very unhappy. Ooh, you don't think she tried to top herself, do you?'

'For Christ sakes, please stop being so over-dramatic. The woman ate a dodgy piece of chicken and now you've decided that he laced it with arsenic or something. Calm down, Princess. Really.'

I blew on my nails and then switched on the hairdryer to see if I could get them to set any faster. 'You're probably right, Terry. You usually are. But I can't help feeling that there's something else going on.'

But Terry was pulling on his jacket and rattling his keys. 'Don't worry that gorgeous little head of yours. Now, I've got to get on.' He took out his wallet and left a new credit card with my name on it on the dressing table. 'Go out and treat yourself.' He kissed my cheek and ran downstairs. I watched out of the bedroom window as his red Audi sprang into life and shot off down the road.

Chapter 18

Amanda

The voices grew louder yet they were still very much indistinct. I was aware of some prodding and poking, of damp flannels being applied to areas which no one else had been privy to for some time, but it no longer mattered to me. My shame had evaporated in my current state.

I was a mere onlooker, viewing proceedings from somewhere far off. I felt disconnected, yet at the same time oddly connected, as if the thinnest strand held me in place preventing me from floating away entirely. Sometimes I swam closer to the surface of the action, only to be dragged back down into the murky depths again. It was as though I could not decide whether to return, or to leave permanently. In an odd way, I was enjoying the freedom to choose, the deliciousness of not being beholden to anyone or anything. In another, I felt as frustrated as I had in the past. I was unable to make any kind of firm commitment, stuck in a position from which I could see no easy way out, if indeed I could leave it at all.

Occasionally I floated alongside my babies - those tiny, lost foetuses, who had been unable to form fully and who had slipped away long before I could touch them, hold them, nurture them. Yet here, in this strange place, I met with them, fleetingly. And each time they left me again it was as though tiny fragments of myself fell away, rendering me less whole, depleting me, just as they had when I lost them the very first time.

Chapter 19

Fiona

I stopped off at the hospital shop to buy a *Get Well Soon* balloon and a small teddy bear bearing the same message. I realised the folly of these purchases the moment that I reached Amanda's bed, which was pushed into a small anteroom off the main ward. She was hooked up to various machines, which beeped and whirred with irritating regularity, and she had a tube protruding from her throat, through which she produced small, rasping noises. Her skin had the pallor and texture of cold porridge. I gasped out loud when I first saw her. I did not know quite what I had been expecting, but it was not this. Perhaps I thought she might resemble Snow White before the prince brings her back to life with a kiss. But this was no fairy tale.

I froze in the doorway, wondering what had possessed me to come in the first place and why I had presumed that I might be able to make a difference where skilled medical staff had failed. But I was here now, and the nurses had seen me arrive. I could not very well simply turn around and leave straightaway. That would be too cowardly and callous. So, I took a deep breath, inhaling disinfectant and disease. I moved closer to the bed where Amanda continued to whirr and rasp. Her catheter bag hung from the sheets, almost full of dark, yellow urine.

'Hi, Amanda. It's me, Fiona, from next door.'

Amanda lay on her back, both eyes closed.

'I brought you a balloon, which I realise now was a pretty stupid thing to buy for you as you are asleep, but I also brought you a lovely, cuddly teddy bear. I thought you might like something to hold while you're in here.' I moved slightly closer, holding out the balloon and the bear in my outstretched hand, unsure what to do next.

The monitor connected to Amanda showed a steady pattern. It never wavered. I turned and pulled a plastic chair closer to the bed, so that I could sit down and talk to her. Standing over Amanda felt uncomfortable for both of us. I seated myself and tied the balloon around the arm of the chair. I held onto the bear, hugging it to my chest for company and courage.

'I'm sorry you've been so ill, Amanda. I can't believe that you can fall into a coma from food poisoning. I've been super careful ever since it happened. I'm sniffing everything before I cook it like a sodding bloodhound.' My half-hearted laugh echoed around the stark room.

Amanda beeped.

'Bill is completely lost without you. He seems so miserable. I've invited him over several times, but he doesn't ever seem to want to take me up on it. He prefers to go for a drink with Terry instead. I suppose it's easier for them to chat man-to-man without me there. Terry is being extremely supportive to Bill, but he's like that. He's such a decent guy - always thinking of other people before himself. He puts me to shame, he really does.'

Not a flicker.

'So, other than that, there's not much to report. Terry is very busy with work and is out a great deal of the time, so I spend most of my evenings washing my hair or watching Beverley Hill 90210. It's a pain really, because I've often gone to bed by the time Terry gets back, and then he always wakes me up with his noise.'

Amanda made no comment.

'I've been shopping, which won't surprise you. I bought a fabulous pale blue cashmere coat from Harvey Nichols last week. It was so expensive that I haven't dared to show it to Terry yet. And I found the most wonderful pair of black leather boots in a small shop on Knightsbridge. I'll show them to you when you're feeling better. They are thigh length, so a little bit naughty. We'll have to move again soon just so that I can get a bigger wardrobe. But Terry doesn't seem to mind. He keeps giving me new credit cards and telling me to go for it, so who am I to complain?'

I looked over at Amanda, realising that I had been looking anywhere except at her. 'Oh, I'm sorry. Listen to me, rattling on about trivia when you're in this place.' I leaned in closer and bravely took Amanda's hand. Her machine gave a little bleep and the line wavered just a little. I squeezed her hand and it happened again.

'I hope you can hear me, Amanda. They do say that people in comas can hear people talking to them. Bugger! Do you even know you're in a coma? Sorry if you didn't. I always say the wrong thing.' I felt very warm suddenly and shifted on the plastic chair where my legs had stuck to it. I should have worn trousers.

I released Amanda's hand and placed the small bear in the crook of her arm. 'I'll leave the bear on your bed with you. When I come back next time, we can decide on a name for him.' What was I saying? I was already committing to coming again. But if I could try to make a difference, I would. Terry had told me that Bill had not visited because apparently, he had a phobia of hospitals.

'But it's his wife,' I remonstrated with my husband.

'Bill's not a strong character, Princess. That's why he needs us to support him,' Terry had said. 'He's extremely vulnerable right now.'

I had raised my eyebrow but said nothing. Terry was usually right about these things.

I squeezed Amanda's arm and turned to leave, glancing back at the poor girl with her mind trapped inside her immobile frame. 'I'll come again soon,' I promised and left the room, tears stinging the corners of my eyes.

Chapter 20

Amanda

There was a voice that became familiar to me. A woman who sat beside me on a regular basis. She rambled on to me about nothing in particular, but the frequency of her visits and the cadence of her voice reassured me. My random manoeuvres between dark and light grew more controlled. When the woman came, I was increasingly able to drag myself upwards, to listen attentively, even if I did not catch every word she said. I felt that I knew her somehow, and yet I did not know her at all. But what she did make me feel was that she was someone who cared about me. She was somebody who thought enough of me to continue returning. Perhaps I should consider doing the same.

Chapter 21

Fiona

'Oh my God! Oh my God! I think her eyes flickered,' I had jumped up from the plastic chair and screamed far louder than I realised, as a nurse came running in, red cheeked and flustered.

'Is everything OK?' she asked, rushing over to Amanda's bedside and checking the monitor. 'What happened?'

'I'm not sure,' I replied in a whisper. I have no idea why I was whispering, but maybe it was because now I had made a fuss and it might be nothing. 'I thought I saw her eyelids try to open.' I stared at Amanda, who lay there as motionless as she had for the last six weeks. 'At least, I think I did.' I slumped back into the chair.

'It might have just been a reflex reaction,' the nurse responded. 'Let me take a look.'

I obliged by standing up once again and moving towards the wall at the back of the room. The nurse considered the monitor. 'Her pulse does appear to be slightly faster, but her blood pressure is the same. I think it's probably just a blip, I'm afraid.' She scribbled something on the chart, before hooking it back onto the bedpost and heading for the door. 'I'm sorry. It's very easy to imagine these things when you sit here for a while. But I'm sure she'd really appreciate the fact that you come so often. Do you go back a long way?'

'No, not at all. She lives in the semi next door to me, that's all. I've got to know her a little and her family don't live close by.'

The nurse looked me up and down. 'Well, I'm sure she appreciates it all the same. She doesn't get any other visitors. It's sad really, for such a young woman.'

She bustled out of the door, and I returned to Amanda's bedside. She had lost quite a bit of weight, which was probably unsurprising, given how that she had lain immobile for so long.

'You're looking great, by the way, Amanda. You've lost so much weight. I think you've dropped at least two dress sizes. I know it's not the best way to diet, but just think! When you wake up and you feel a bit better, we can go shopping for a whole new wardrobe.' I stopped, pondering whether I had been a little tactless, given Bill's meanness with money. 'My treat. What do you say? Terry doesn't seem to care if I max out my credit cards every month, and he won't need to know that I'm not spending on myself. As long as I look good and have sex with him on demand, he's happy.'

I reached out and squeezed Amanda's hand. I know I must have been imagining it, but I'm sure, or almost sure anyway, that I felt the tiniest bit of pressure on mine.

Chapter 22

Amanda

It was Fiona who collected me from the hospital. Bill was busy with work, and she said she didn't mind at all. Secretly, I was relieved to be able to go home for the first time in almost two months without having to face Bill with his inevitable recriminations straight away.

The day before I left, I had been visited by a psychiatric doctor, who was required to assess me prior to releasing me back into the wild. He was quite young – I'm guessing he was newly qualified and only a few years younger than myself. He was tall and gangly, with almost translucent skin, lacking in any colour apart from the two scarlet blotches that flamed on his sunken cheeks.

'Hi, Amanda. I'm Doctor Gerrard, but please do call me Mike.'

'Hi, Mike,' I murmured, as I slumped in the small, uncomfortable chair in my ratty dressing gown, which Fiona had brought for me from home. Doctor Gerrard – Mike – perched on the edge of my unmade bed with his clipboard and ballpoint pen, the end of which he kept pressing in and out with irritating regularity.

'So, Amanda, before you leave, I need to have a chat with you, just to make sure that you're ready – and of course safe – to go home. I'll start with the basics if that's OK?' *Click, click, click.*

'Sure,' I whispered. My throat was tight and dry from lack of use.

He rattled through the basics – where I lived (Crouch End), whether I was married (yes), had I had children (almost), where I went to school (Clapham), where my parents lived (Clapham), what siblings I had (one brother), whether we were close as a family (maybe once, not now), why was that (we drifted apart after I married Bill). He did not enquire further as to the reasons behind to this last response, which made me wonder whether this was nothing more than a box-ticking exercise. I did not intend to elaborate further if he could not be bothered to ask.

Did I take drugs (no), why had I taken so many paracetamols on this occasion (I was drunk, and it had been a mistake), did I often get so drunk that I did not know what I was doing (no, never). He did not delve any more into why I had overdosed on this particular occasion, and I felt far too weary to fill him in.

How did I get on with my husband (fine), had he ever abused me physically (no), was I looking forward to going home (I supposed so), did I exercise (no), did I drink regularly (no), did I feel ready to go home? I made no reply, but I knew that they were desperate to refill my bed with another warmish body, so the question was effectively redundant.

The doctor filled in his boxes and signed the bottom of the form. 'I think it's fine to discharge you. I will recommend that you see your GP for ongoing consultation. If this was genuinely a one-off incident, I think you should be perfectly OK from now on, Amanda. Just take it easy when you drink. Moderation in all things as they say.' He trailed off in mid-sentence, clicking his pen for the thousandth time, while smiling in a manner which suggested sympathy without empathy. He leant over, patted me on the knee and left the room. I heard his *click, click, click* ringing in my ears as he meandered along the corridor.

I cannot remember how long I sat there, staring at the blank, yellowing walls. '*You should be perfectly OK from now on*' whirled around my brain, making me feel quite dizzy.

Fiona busted through the door, startling me out of my reverie.

"Hi, ready to go home?' she called with far too much enthusiasm.

I shrugged. 'I guess so. I've been told that I am, anyway.'

Fiona lowered her gaze and soldiered on regardless. 'Here, I got you a present. Open it,' she urged, handing me a large Selfridges bag.

I put my hand inside and drew out a red-patterned, peasant top, followed by a pair of denim jeans. I frowned at Fiona. 'These aren't my clothes.'

'They are now. I bought them for you this morning. I hope you like them, as I've already cut all the labels off. I hate labels. They are so scratchy. I'm guessing you're a size 12-ish now, so go on, try them on. There's some new underwear at the bottom as well, and some seriously cute sandals. I bought them for you at Russell and Bromley.' She hopped from foot to foot in her excitement.

I stared from the bag to Fiona and back again. 'Oh, Fiona, I really can't accept these. I don't have the money to pay for them and they look very expensive. They're probably won't even fit me.' I had not been a size twelve for many years. 'It's extremely sweet of you, but you'll have to return them.' I shoved the clothes back into the bag and held it out towards her.

Fiona shook her head. 'It's a welcome home present, and I can't return them, so you're stuck with them. Stop messing about and put them on. I've got the car in the hospital car park and it's costing me a bomb.'

I remained motionless in my chair. Fiona rolled her eyes at the all-seeing wall. 'Look, I'm going to pop outside this door for five minutes. If you've not dressed by the time I come back in, you'll have to walk through the entire hospital and get into my car in that horrible old dressing gown of yours.' I wondered when she had become so familiar with me that she could say such rude things like this. 'Now come on, Amanda. Let's crack on!'

She winked at me and tottered out of the room, her high heels clattering on the linoleum. I did not move, sitting there clutching my bag full of designer goodies. A minute later, Fiona rapped on the small window in the door and made a show of tapping the face of her watch. I sighed. With difficulty, I shuffled out of my chair, stood up and emptied the contents of the bag onto the ruffled, unmade bed, which had been my home for the past six weeks. My legs felt rather weak and unsteady, as if they could not deal with my torso being vertical.

Fiona, clearly lacking any patience, flounced back in through the door, her ample cleavage jiggling under her shirt. Not for the first time, I wondered if she had had a boob job, although I would never dare to ask her. 'OK, time's up, my friend. Let me help you.'

I stared at Fiona, but I allowed her to dress me, as my mother had done when I was a small child a million years ago. I stood up, I sat down, I lifted various limbs to order as if I was sleepwalking. I even allowed Fiona to slap some moisturiser onto my face.

'Now for a little foundation. Put your head up,' Fiona instructed, stroking the product all over. 'Wow, that's a great colour on you. You don't look quite so washed out now.' She rubbed some blusher to my cheeks. 'Now, pout,' she ordered, and I pouted. I was not aware of ever having pouted in my life before. 'A slick of lipstick and voila! Now stand up again, Amanda.'

I stood on command, wobbling slightly. Fiona looked me up and down and then walked around me. 'Amanda, you do scrub up very nicely if I may say so. In fact, you look absolutely beautiful,' she cooed. 'Now, let's get you out of here before all the doctors start to fight over you.' She hooked her arm through mine, and we hobbled along the corridor towards the exit, the smell of bleach following us.

I had felt dead inside for an eternity. As I hit the fresh air, supported by my new friend and wearing my new outfit, I realised that I wanted to start to live again. Somehow, despite the hallucinations I had suffered in hospital - those strange visions of lives lost, and opportunities squandered - I had managed to return and, if I was going to go back home, as everyone assured me that I was, things were going to have to be different this time. I was going to begin to fight back. I squeezed Fiona's hand as we reached the car. 'Thank you,' I whispered, 'for being such a good friend to me.'

Chapter 23

Fiona

I had offered to get some food in the fridge for Amanda's return, but Bill had told me in no uncertain terms that he would make everything ready. But I knew as soon as Amanda turned the key in the lock that he had not done so. The hall was dark and cold, despite the warmth of the spring day. Small shafts of light, forcing their way through the minute pane of glass in the front door, revealed myriad layers of dust floating in the air. It was like walking into an old, decaying house which had lain uninhabited for years.

I followed Amanda through to the kitchen, but the stench reached me before I got halfway down the hall, and I retched. There were piles of pizza boxes and balls of old newspaper concealing the remnants of fish and chips. Dozens of empty beer cans littered the table and the floor. Rotting food lay in the sink, layered in feasting flies.

Amanda threw open the kitchen window over the sink and was then promptly sick into it. She grabbed the side of the counter to steady herself. I moved over to her and led her away without speaking into the living room. 'Sit down and I'll make you a nice cup of tea. Then I'm going to clean.' Fortunately, the living room was in a marginally better state with only beer cans scattered about, but no food.

Amanda opened her mouth to reply, but nothing came out. 'Don't worry. Everything will be OK,' I reassured her, even though the thought of cleaning up her house made me nauseous.

I made Amanda a large mug of tea and then dashed next door to throw on some old sweats and to grab my rubber gloves and cleaning equipment. When I returned, Amanda had already fallen asleep on the sofa, snoring. I pulled the door to and set to work.

I was ruthless. Even though this was not my own home, I made cut-throat decisions about what to throw out – virtually everything – and what to keep – essentially nothing. I filled so many bin bags that I had to go back home to fetch another roll. When I had cleared the surfaces and the floor, I scrubbed the kitchen with a passion that I did not know I possessed. I hated cleaning, but then again, I had never lived in a cesspool like this. There were several things that were beyond help, such as the kitchen table, which was so cracked that it was hard to clean in places, but a couple of hours later the kitchen no longer resembled a rubbish tip, and you could at least breathe in there again. I sat back on my knees as I finished scrubbing the floor. I was sweaty and tired, but I had succeeded.

I checked on Amanda again. She was snoring louder now, her nostrils flaring, like Terry's tended to do after too much whisky. I closed the door again and headed upstairs. I entered her bedroom, which reeked of male body odour and stale cigarettes. I opened the window and started on the bed, stripping it of its covers and stuffing the dirty linen into a plastic bag, hoping that I could find a clean set somewhere in the cupboards to replace it. An hour later, the room was habitable at least. Then I moved onto the bathroom. I'm not going to describe what I found in there, but I held my nose and ploughed on.

I finished around five in the afternoon. I had filled fifteen bin bags, used up all my cleaning products and suffered three broken nails. I ached in parts of my body that I had not previously known existed.

Amanda had woken up by the time I went back downstairs and was wandering, dazed, around the kitchen. As I entered, she turned to me, her face alive with wonderment as if she was a small child who had just met Father Christmas as he came down the chimney. 'Fiona, I don't know what to say,' she spluttered, tears dripping from her eyelashes.

I walked over to her and took her in my arms, while she sobbed until she had no more tears to shed.

Chapter 24

Amanda

It was dark when Bill got home, but I had absolutely no idea what time it was. Since Fiona had left, I had lay prone on my bed, staring at the misshapen, brown mark on the ceiling, which had been caused by a flood we had suffered the previous year. Bill had promised to fix it, but inevitably he had never got round to it. When I heard his key turn in the front door, I did not move. He could come to me.

He banged around downstairs for about ten minutes, perhaps attempting to undo some of the miraculous work that Fiona had performed earlier. Eventually, his heavy tread sounded on the stairs. I could tell that he was still wearing his boots. He shoved the bedroom door open and flicked the light switch. The sudden illumination stabbed at my eyes.

'So, you're back then,' he stated, slamming his broad backside onto the bed and beginning to untie his boots.

I concentrated hard on the mark on the ceiling.

'What's for dinner?'

I made no reply, rolling over onto my side to face him. 'I have just got home, and as far as I am aware, there is nothing for dinner, so you'll have to order another one of your take-outs. You seem to have been thriving on them while I've been in hospital.'

I rolled away from him and swung my feet onto the floor on my side of the bed. My vision wavered as I righted myself. I waited a moment for the dizziness to subside before standing up, smoothing my blouse and tucking it back into my jeans. When I turned towards Bill, he was staring at me.

'Blimey, you've lost a lot of weight. Was the food that bad in hospital?'

'I didn't eat much, Bill, because I was unconscious most of the time.' I moved towards the dressing table and considered my reflection in the mirror. My lipstick was long gone, but I was still wearing most of the foundation Fiona had applied, and my face had retained a faint tint of colour.

'So where did you get those clothes?' Bill demanded.

'They were a gift from Fiona. She realised that none of my own clothes would fit me now. It was extremely thoughtful of her'

'Well, I'm not reimbursing her, if that what she thinks is going to happen.' He took a step towards me, but I did not move.

'She doesn't expect anything from you, Bill - and neither do I.'

He stepped closer, so that there was no space separating us. I concentrated on my breathing, in and out, in and out. Tears prickled at the back of my eyes. 'You have no idea of how embarrassed I was by what you did, and how difficult it's been for me. What have you got to say for yourself?'

'Nothing. But if you want me to leave, then I'll go. If I'm that much of an embarrassment to you, I'll get out of your way with pleasure,' I gulped.

'You're going nowhere. Just apologise for what you've done, or at the very least, explain why you did it, and then we'll carry on as before, OK? You can start by making me some sodding food.'

I inhaled and grabbed both his arms, pinching the skin as hard as I could with my razor-sharp nails, grown long from weeks of lack of use. 'Make your own dinner, Bill. I'm going to bed.'

I released his arms, noticing with satisfaction the raised, reddening welts I had left on his skin, marching out of the bedroom and walking with purpose towards the bathroom. I slammed the door behind me and locked it, waiting for Bill to begin pummelling on it. But there was complete silence. I cowered on the toilet seat, waiting, the sound of my heart beating filling the small room, until eventually I heard Bill tramp back down the stairs and back out of the front door. I let out the breath I had been holding. This was a tiny beginning. I was no longer going to allow him to decide how I could live my life. I had no idea how or in what way it was going to happen, but things were definitely going to change. I had changed my life once before when I set my eye on Bill, knowing I could get him to marry me and remove me from my first hell. I could do it again.

Chapter 25

Fiona

I struggled through the front door lugging a couple of buckets containing a variety of cleaning products, and wearing a pair of torn, yellow rubber gloves. I shoved the door closed with my grubby bottom, before dropping the buckets onto the hall floor. I felt exhausted. My perm had drooped, so that it hung limp around my face, and when I glanced in the hall mirror, splodges of mascara blackened my eye sockets.

'You're looking more than a little worse for wear, Princess. Have you taken a job as a charwoman?' Terry enquired, gliding out from the lounge with a whisky in his hand.

Normally, I would have laughed, but now I merely shoved my shoes off my aching feet, leaving them where they fell. I sloped past Terry and into the lounge, where I collapsed onto the sofa.

'Pour me a gin and tonic, would you? I'm completely buggered.'

'Who by?' Terry quipped, but once again, I failed to laugh at his off-colour joke.

'Wouldn't you rather shower first, Princess?'

I was aware that I stank of sweat, and that my clothes were smeared in dust and grime. We had only just bought this sofa and I did not want to mess up the velour any more than Terry did, but now that I had sat down, I could not rouse myself again.

'I need a drink first, OK? Just get me one, please. It's been a very, very, very long day.'

Terry ambled over to his globe and flicked open the lid. He never seemed to tire of his favourite toy. 'Let me grab some ice.'

I closed my eyes and listened as Terry moved through to the kitchen and cracked a few cubes into a bowl. He returned to where I lay motionless on the sofa. 'So, what have you been up to then? You look like you've been down the mines,' he laughed, pouring a copious amount of gin into a glass, and topping it up with tonic.

"I went to collect Amanda from the hospital, and then I cleaned her house. I had to. Jesus, you wouldn't believe the state of it. Bill left it like a total pigsty.' She accepted the drink and downed it in one.

'Another?'

'Hit me,' I replied, feeling some colour slowly returning to my cheeks. 'The house wasn't anything like as bad as that before Amanda was ill, but he's clearly never cleaned anything up. He hadn't even washed up. He's lived on take-outs. There were empty cartons and rotting food everywhere. And the beer cans! I'm not surprised he's got a massive great belly.'

Terry patted his own six-pack and sat down at the end of the sofa, removing my socks. He began to massage my feet. 'So, how is the old girl anyway? Better?'

'Well, she's awake and out, so I suppose so. She was quite quiet, but I expect she is still very tired. Mind you, she's lost a shedload of weight.' I took another sip. 'It suits her, actually. I bought her some clothes because she had nothing that fitted her and, well, you know, her stuff is dreadful anyway. Let's just hope she doesn't eat anything dodgy again. What happened to her was awful.'

Terry hesitated. 'You know, I don't think that it was food poisoning. I know that's what Bill told us originally, but I think she's got a little bit of a problem. He told me in confidence that she drinks and takes too many pills. That's why he doesn't give her any money.'

I sat bolt upright, narrowly missing my gin and tonic on the side table. 'You think she's an alcoholic and a junkie? Are you telling me that she overdosed? Do you really believe *Bill*?'

'I don't know. I'm just going by what he said to me. I don't see why he'd make it up and anyway, think about it. You don't normally fall into a coma with food poisoning, do you?'

I suddenly felt tearful. 'Oh, poor Amanda. I suppose it sort of makes sense. She was very emotional, but I just assumed she was over-tired and anxious about going home. To Bill, I mean. But if she does drink and take pills – and I must admit that I've never noticed it in all the times I've seen her – she must do it because of Bill. He's not very caring.'

'Well, soon she'll be all over him, Princess. He's going to be pretty well off when I'm done with this deal he's buying into.'

'Well, let's hope that more money makes him a better man. Amanda may be a little dull, but she's a nice person, and I think she deserves to be happy.'

'And so do you, Princess. Speaking of which, why don't I run you a hot bath and I can get in with you to help you scrub off all that muck and grime.'

'Terry, I'm not sure that I've got the energy. I'd love a bath, but on my own, and after that I think I'd just like to eat something and go to bed.' I stretched, my breasts straining against my filthy T-shirt.

I saw Terry's jaw clench. 'I tell you what. I'll get that bath going and then we'll see if I can persuade you. Alright?'

'No, Terry. I mean it. Not tonight. I'm absolutely knackered.'

He turned away and stomped upstairs to the bathroom, where I could hear him beginning to run the water. I hoped that he had remembered to pour a generous amount of Molton Brown bubble bath under the tap. I heard him running back downstairs. He had stripped off my shirt and stood in front of me for a moment, stroking his chest, before removing his jeans. His erection twitched beneath his underpants.

'Come on, Princess. Your bath awaits.' He held out his hand and I took it so that he could haul me off the sofa and help me to relax in the bath.

Chapter 26

Amanda

Bill seemed oddly relieved now that I was home. Although I think it was mainly to do with the fact that the house had been a shambles without me. Bill had never regarded housework as part of his remit, given that he worked flat-out all day long as it was. He was always ready to remind me that his mother - God rest her soul - had always instilled in him the belief that a man's home was his castle, and a woman's job was to clean it. She had never asked nor expected him to so much as pick up a plate at their house. Dirty clothes dropped wherever he left them, re-appearing the next day, clean and pressed in his wardrobe.

'You know what she used to say to me, Mandy?'

Of course, I did. I had heard it a thousand times.

'She used to say to me, "William, you need to be looked after properly. And I'll always be here to do that for you, so you never need to worry." Then she would kiss me on the top of my head, scurry off, and return with a mountain of biscuits on a plate covered with a paper doily and a steaming mug of tea.'

It had been just the two of them at home. Bill's father was a merchant seaman and was therefore hardly ever around. When Bill was ten, his dad left for yet another voyage and never returned. A year or so later, his mother received a telegram from him informing her that he had visited Australia on his travels, liked the people there and decided to stay. He wished both of us all the best for the future, and they never heard from him again.

'My mother simply smiled,' Bill told me. "Goodbye and good riddance to bad rubbish," she declared, screwing up the telegram and throwing it onto the fire, where it briefly flamed orange before incinerating to dust. "You and I need your father like a hole in the head. He was a useless bastard at the best of times. It's just you and me now, William – as it should be."

And it was just as it should have been, at least until Bill was twenty-six, when one summer evening, his mother retired to bed complaining of a terrible headache, and she never woke up again. She was fifty-four.

His mother, Florence, had taken in alterations and washing to earn their keep, so she left nothing of any value behind besides an old Singer sewing machine. Apparently, no one came to her funeral, because Florence had always maintained that she and Bill had no need of other people in order to be happy. But then, when she was gone, so suddenly, I think the cruelty of it lacerated Bill, effectively orphaned at twenty-six. I think he felt as bereft as if it had happened when he was just a toddler.

When I first met Bill, he worked as a jobbing labourer on a variety of building sites, having never been much good at school. His lack of academic prowess never bothered Florence, however, who believed that you did not need brains to get on in this world, just sheer grit and determination. So, Bill gritted his teeth as he shouldered hods of bricks and slathered them miserably in mortar day after day, before trudging home each evening via the fish and chip shop. He always paid his bill there promptly at the end of every week, as soon as he got paid, having been brought to believe that any kind of debt was a sin. As far as I was aware, he spent money on nothing else, as he had nothing else to spend it on.

I did not get the impression that Bill tended to make friends easily and he rarely talked about any of the others on site. He told me once that his colleagues had nicknamed him *Mummy's Boy*, but that he did not care. "'Sticks and stones may break your bones, but words will never hurt you, as my mother used to say." It was her mantra, you know.'

I often wondered how many mantras one woman could have.

Between the time of his mother's death and meeting me, I understood from what Bill told me later that he limped on like this for a couple of years, entrenched in his solitary weekly routine of work, deep-fried food and stuffing any additional banknotes he had left into a shoebox under his bed. I had seen Bill around and was aware that the people whispered behind his back, calling him a sad soul and a bit of a weirdo. I did not know if Bill noticed or even cared, or perhaps he did not know how to care, having been schooled to be dismissive of social contacts.

So, I was quite surprised, wary even, when I first met him at the chippy. He popped in on his way home one Friday, as I learnt later was his custom. It was my first day working there.

'Evening,' I chirruped as he entered the shop. He glanced behind him to see who I was addressing, but he was the only person there.

'Evening,' he whispered, his voice hoarse from underuse.

'It's nippy out tonight, isn't it? Have you been working outside all day?'

I deduced this from the fact that he was caked in dust from the site.

'Yes,' he replied, head down looking at his filthy boots.

'Well, I suppose if you're on the move all day, it must keep you a little bit warmer. And it's certainly hotter than hell in here, with all this chip fat boiling away all day long. I've only been here a day and I don't think I'll ever get rid of the smell of fish off my hands.' I laughed, revealing my set of tiny, white, crooked teeth, which I loathed. 'What can I get you?'

'A cod and two chips, please.'

'Right you are. Mushy peas?'

'OK,' he replied, but he looked uncertain. Much later on in our friendship, he told me that he hated mushy peas, or in fact vegetables of any kind. He just did not want to say no to me as I was being so nice.

'Can I settle up for the week please?' he whispered as I handed him his meal rolled up neatly in newspaper. He passed over a couple of notes, which I duly placed inside the till.

'Look forward to seeing you next time,' I called as he turned to leave the shop.

Bill made no reply.

I saw him in the chippy most nights from then on, whenever I was on shift. I always gave him a warm greeting and a broad smile as he walked through the door, the bell tinkling over my head. He attempted to smile in return, but somehow his face refused to cooperate, and he could only ever manage a gruff nod towards the cracked lino on the floor. We went on in this manner for weeks, which necessitated him buying a portion of mushy peas each time, which he apparently chucked into the bin almost as soon as he got home.

One Friday evening, I decided to introduce myself formally.

'I'm Amanda, by the way,' I told him, shovelling an extraordinary amount of extra chips into the newspaper. 'I thought I had better introduce myself finally as I see you pretty much every day.'

He made no reply, merely fiddling with the notes he had drawn from his pocket to pay the bill.

'And you are?' I pressed, leaning across the counter to accentuate my cleavage.

He backed away slightly. 'William,' he stammered, 'or Bill for short, but my mother never liked Bill. She said if she had wanted to call me Bill, then she would have done so, but she didn't.'

'Do you like being called Bill?' I asked, wiping the counter with a damp J-Cloth.

'I do, I suppose.'

'Well then, Bill it is. So, Bill, I finish early tonight, so would you like to buy me a drink down the Avalon?'

He blushed scarlet, and then began to sweat as if he had just run for the bus or something.

'Cat got your tongue, has it? Look, it's only a drink. I'll be in there at eight o'clock, so please yourself if you come or not.' I turned away to jiggle the chips in the deep fat fryer.

The bell tinkled and a couple of local lads came in. 'Hello, darling, you're looking lovely today. How's tricks?' one of them enquired, leering at me across the steam.

It was my turn to blush. I looked down and by the time I regained my composure, Bill had left. I had no idea whether or not he would come along to meet me later, but I resolved to go along anyway. You never knew, did you?

When I arrived at The Avalon, the pub was rammed with people and the noise was deafening. The air was thickly fogged with tobacco smoke, making me cough as it caught the back of my throat. I glanced around, but there was no sign of Bill. I should have realised that he had no intention of showing up. I turned to go, but just as I did so, I spotted him: a hunched figure alone at a table right at the back. He caught my eye and gave me a tiny, shy wave. I nodded and took another deep breath, before threading my way across the room towards him.

'Hello, Bill. You came. I'm so glad.'

'Yes, hello,' he stuttered, standing, and knocking the table so that his pint spilt down the front of his trousers. I laughed.

'Shall I get you another drink?'

'I guess so,' he replied without moving. I looked at his glass, which was almost empty. 'Would you like another of the same? Draught, is it?'

'Yes, please,' he replied, dabbing hopelessly at his trouser leg with his handkerchief.

'Alright.' I turned to thread my way back towards the bar. I was not of a size which meant that I could fight my way through easily, but I got there in the end. I ordered the wine and a pint of bitter. I did not drink that much generally, but I felt that in these particular circumstances, I might need a couple.

I made it back to the table without too much spillage and sat down.

'Thanks very much.' Bill took the pint glass from me. 'Cheers.'

'Cheers.' I took a long slug of wine and it felt good as it went down. I was thirstier than I had realised, as my glass disappeared in minutes. Bill returned to the bar for another round, having hardly spoken to me at all yet. I did all the talking, my own words washing over him like small waves lapping on the shoreline.

'So, after that I left school at sixteen, but I had no idea what to do and my mum and dad did not want me working in a bar or anything, because they thought men would just try to chat me up all night. Fortunately, the local newsagent needed an assistant, so I did that for a couple of years, but then he had to go back to Pakistan and someone else took over, who did not need me anymore, so that's why I've ended up at the chippy. My dream is to train as a beauty therapist, but it costs a bomb and Mum and Dad aren't too flush at the moment, so I need to save up myself. Anyway, enough about me. What about you?' I paused for breath, finally, and sipped at my wine. I did not want him to think that I was one of those girls who drank too much.

'Not that much to tell really,' Bill muttered into his pint. 'I work on building sites as you know.'

'What about your family?'

'Well, my father left us years ago and lives in Australia, but I haven't heard from him in over fifteen, no sixteen years. My mother died two years ago, and now I live alone. That's it.'

'Oh, you poor thing,' I replied, tears pricking at my eyes. I reached over and touched his hand. An electric shock passed between us, I assume from the cheap nylon covering on the chairs. 'I live with my mum, my dad and my older brother, Dave, who works with my dad as a painter and decorator. Mum works in Debenhams on Oxford Street. Do you wish you'd had brothers and sisters?'

He shook his head. 'Mother and I were perfectly happy as we were, just the two of us, but it's difficult now of course, without her. I guess that's why I live on a diet of fish and chips. I never learnt to cook and frankly, I don't want to. I don't think men should, do you?'

'But some of the best chefs are men, aren't they? There's a few of them on the telly now.'

'Mother always said Fanny Craddock was the best, although she didn't like that fact that she was assisted by her husband, Johnny. She thought it was unmanly of him.'

'I don't know who that is,' I replied, finishing her drink. 'Look, would you like to come over for tea at my house sometime. I know my Mum wouldn't mind. She likes a houseful.'

'Oh, I don't know, Amanda,' he responded. 'I'm not that good with people.'

'Oh, don't be so silly, Bill. They'll like you. They are always telling me to grow up, so they'll be impressed when I bring home an older man. And anyway, it'll mean that you can enjoy something which isn't fish and chips for one night at least. Surely that's got to be worth it, eh? I'll find out what night suits Mum best depending on her shifts, and I'll let you know when you next pop into the chippy, OK?'

And that's how it started.

Bill finally accepted a dinner invitation to my house a few weeks later, having run out of random excuses as to why he could not go when I kept badgering him in the chippy. My family lived in a terraced house, not unlike Bill's in fact, except that my dad owned ours, while Bill still rented. He told me once that he had saved enough to get a mortgage, but just could not see the point at the moment. Cash seemed safer to him, and he was not keen on getting into debt. It was the one of the many things Florence had drilled into him – to live according to his means and no more.

The doorbell rang out without stopping.

'Jesus, some twat's jammed the bell in again,' I heard from the living room, as I saw the short, squat shadow of my brother, Dave, stomp towards the door. He yanked it open with force. 'Yes?' he bellowed, sticking out his chin with its poor attempt at a beard on the end of it. 'Can I help you?' he asked,

Deborah Stone

jabbing at the doorbell with a screwdriver. 'Bloody thing is a constant fucking disaster,' he moaned, as the ringing finally ended.

'Hi, I'm Bill.'

'Bill?'

'Yes. Amanda invited me for dinner.'

'Oh, she did, did she? The sly minx. Well, you'd better come in then. Amanda, it's your fancy man,' he yelled.

I wished the floor would open and swallow me up.

I emerged from the kitchen at the back of the house. 'Hello, Bill. I'm so glad you came. This is my brother, Dave. Dave, this is my friend, Bill.' I felt quite pink in the face, I guessed from cooking.

'Yeah, we just met,' Dave frowned, slamming the front door closed. 'He knackered the bell again.' He stalked past the two of us and ran upstairs, taking the steps three at a time.

'Don't mind Dave,' I reassured Bill. 'He's a total prat. Anyway, come on. Come in and meet Mum and Dad.'

I led him by the hand into the lounge. Mum and Dad were sitting side by side on the sofa, but they stood up as we entered.

'Hello, Bill, it's lovely to meet you,' said my mother. 'My name is Dawn, and this is my husband, Roger.'

'How d'you do,' muttered Roger, before settling himself back into the faux-leather off-white sofa. They told me later during dinner that they had bought it last year in a particularly good sale at DFS. My father was a slight man in his late fifties, wearing brown slacks and a checked shirt. His shoes shone with newly applied polish, which made me instantly self-conscious about the state of Bill's boots. Did he not own another pair apart from his work boots? They looked terrible.

I looked just like my mother, only Mum was much larger, a portrait of what I would become. She was bubbly just like me, unlike the men of our house, who seemed to regard any intrusion into their personal lives as a minor irritant.

'So, Bill, tell us all about yourself,' Dawn instructed.

102 | Page

Bill provided his potted history: working on a building site, dead mother, absent father, lived alone. It took all of one minute. There was a prolonged silence.

'So, Mum, shall we have dinner now?' I suggested when no one else tried to spark further conversation.

'Yes, of course. I've made shepherd's pie. Is that OK with you, Bill?'

'Yes.'

'OK, great, let's eat then.'

We moved through to the kitchen and sat down at a square, wooden table, which I had laid neatly with cutlery and paper towels. The kitchen was immaculate, with no sign that cooking had recently occurred. On the table was a steaming bowl of peas.

'Would you like a beer, Bill?' Roger enquired.

'Er, yes please,' he replied.

Dad opened a can of Sam Smiths and poured it into a chipped pint glass, handing it to Bill, before doing the same for himself and Dave, who had now appeared in the kitchen ready to eat. Mum and I watered our beer down and made a shandy.

Mum served the shepherd's pie, while I proceeded to prattle on about my day at the chippy. When we began to eat, Mum moaned about some difficult customers in Debenhams earlier that day. 'Ooh, she was a right stuck- up old cow, I can tell you.'

'And how was your day, Bill?' she enquired, offering him some peas. He shook his head at them.

'Same as usual. There's rarely anything to report.'

There was a brief pause and then everyone began talking across each other. Bill concentrated on his shepherd's pie, which was tasty enough if you added a decent amount of ketchup to it. There were tinned peaches and cream for pudding, which was a treat.

When we finished, Bill thanked my parents and rose to leave.

'Are you going already?' I asked, somewhat crestfallen.

'Yes. I've got work tomorrow.'

'Oh, OK. I tell you what, I'll walk halfway home with you as it's still early. Would you like that?'

'I suppose so.'

Bill said his goodbyes to my parents and Dave, who barely responded, and we walked slowly along the road. Once the house was out of sight, I threaded my arm through his, making him jump slightly.

'Thanks for coming over. I think they really liked you.' I paused. 'You were quite quiet, though. Was everything OK?'

'Yes. The food was nice. Your parents were fine. Thank you.'

I stared at him, puzzled and we walked on in silence for a while.

'I think this is about halfway back,' Bill commented when we reached the bridge that straddled the two halves of the town.

'Right, OK. Goodnight then.' I reached up to plant a kiss on his cheek.

Bill shook my hand in reply. 'Night Amanda. See you tomorrow as usual at the chip shop.'

After that, Bill began to linger a little longer each night at the chippy, even eating there sometimes when I had a break. He had not returned to my house since we had had dinner with my family, but that suited me fine. They were rather loud and intrusive and not to everyone's taste. And my dad did not like the idea of me having a boyfriend, especially not one as old and odd as Bill. I chatted to Bill when he came into the chippy, or sometimes not, depending on how he felt, because sometimes he just did not want to talk. After a few more weeks, I began to go over to his house and Bill said I was a great help to him. I tidied up, did a little cooking, and even did some washing, which Bill was pleased about, because it saved him paying the laundry woman. Sometimes, however, it seemed that I went a little too far.

'What are those?' Bill demanded one day, when he came into the kitchen for tea.

'Daffodils. I picked some in the park. I thought it would brighten the place up a bit. It's terribly dreary in here.'

'I've managed perfectly well here without flowers up until now – and you shouldn't steal them from the park. It's theft.'

I felt as though I was about to burst into tears. I slumped onto the kitchen chair and put my head in my hands.

'Look, I know you're just trying to be nice to me, and your help around the house is really very much appreciated.' He walked over and patted my shoulder. I reached up and held his hand and it felt warm and comforting. We had had no physical intimacy of any kind yet. I might reach up to give Bill a peck on the cheek and try to hold his hand occasionally. Yet he seemed nervous to make any sudden moves, maybe because I was so much younger than him and at some level – one that I did not want to explore too deeply – he perhaps could not understand why I wanted to spend time with someone as dull as him.

Bill clearly had had no experience of sex, apart from perhaps by himself, but I think he even felt guilty about that. Probably his bloody mother again telling him that it was a sin to handle himself down there. Bill told me he did not believe in sex before marriage, as the only reason we were put on this Earth was to have children and that had to be within wedlock. Sex outside of that was apparently an unforgivable sin. I could guess where he got that idea from.

Bill wandered into the chippy at his usual time the following day. I was serving two spotty youths, who were bantering with me, and I was laughing with them. Bill looked uncomfortable as he waited for them to grab their chips and leave, which they did eventually, one of them jostling Bill accidentally on purpose as they went out of the door.

'Hi,' I called, wiping the sweat off my forehead with the tea towel that I kept slung over my left shoulder as I worked. 'Do you want your meal now, or shall I come over later with portions for the two of us?'

Bill hopped from foot to foot, before replying, 'I think I'll take it now if that's OK, as I'm going to pop to the shops shortly to look for some shoes.'

I opened my mouth wide, and then closed it again.

'But I did want to ask you if you'd like to go out for dinner tomorrow evening. My treat,' he offered, the words struggling to leave his throat. 'I thought maybe we could try that new Italian place down the road. I forget the name of it.'

I was so thrilled that I lifted up the flap in the counter and raced over to him. I reached up and hugged him around his thick neck. 'Oh, Bill, that would be fab. Thank you.'

He froze, waiting for me to let go.

At this moment, my manager appeared from a door at the back of the shop and bellowed, 'What are you up to, young lady? Stop fraternising with the customers and get back behind the counter.'

'Yes, Mr Marshall,' I replied, bursting into fits of giggles the moment he disappeared.

'You'd best get on,' Bill said, clearly not approving any more than my boss did of me slacking on the job, and he promptly left to pop into Millets to look at boots. When I saw him later, he was sporting a new pair, which were a strange muddy grey colour with a mark on the front of the left shoe, but they had been much reduced in the sale, so Bill had decided to splash out.

The Italian restaurant was acceptable – red checked tablecloths, small, uncomfortable wooden chairs and candles rammed into empty wine bottles, with a variety of different coloured wax stuck to their edges. The waiter was unnecessarily effusive, insisting that he was giving us the best table – there were only eight in the place, and I guessed by best he meant the one that was not next to the toilet. The plastic menus were enormous, so much so that I disappeared behind mine completely when I was holding it to read. The choice on the menu was overwhelming and essentially all a mystery to both of us. I had not eaten pasta or pizza before, and I had no idea what the difference was between a margherita and a quattro stagioni.

There was a fish option and also a steak, but they were both very expensive. I did not want to appear to take advantage of Bill and go all out with my choices.

'What are you going to have?' Bill enquired, looking rather warm despite the fan whirring over our heads.

'Oh, I don't know. This menu is mental, isn't it? Do you want to share a pizza? They look ginormous,' I commented, looking over at one being delivered to another table.

Bill breathed out loudly. 'Sounds good to me. What would you like to drink?'

'I'm happy with a beer.'

'Oh, I think we can do better than that as we are out for a special meal, don't you?' he suggested, beckoning to the waiter.

'Yes, sir. What would you like?'

'One pizza. Something relatively plain please.'

The waiter sniffed. 'A margherita is our basic, sir. It's tomato and cheese.'

Bill considered a moment, glancing over at me. I nodded encouragingly.

'That sounds good, thank you. And we'll have a half carafe of your house wine, please.' Bill handed the menu back to the waiter, feeling more in control.

'Red or white, sir?'

'Excuse me?'

'The wine, sir.'

'Ah, yes.' Bill paused, thinking that there must be a right answer if you were going to be eating pizza. The waiter and I gazed at him. 'Er, white, I think.' I thought I noticed a raised eyebrow from the waiter, but I could not be sure. Bill hesitated. 'No, make that red. Yes, red would be better, thank you.'

'Perfecto,' shouted the waiter, before sliding away across the restaurant towards the kitchen.

The pizza arrived extremely quickly, cut neatly into six slices. I tore one off and Bill followed my lead. It was quite tasty, and the wine complemented it very well.

'So, how long do you think it will take you to save up for beauty school?' he asked me.

'Oh, I don't know exactly, but far too long. I'm desperate to get started so that I can move out from home.'

Bill choked on his pizza and coughed. 'But why? Isn't it nice living with your mum and dad? They must look after you well.' He did not include Dave, as I knew he clearly assumed that living with him must be something of a trial.

'It's, well it's difficult sometimes, that's all.' I picked up my wine glass and drained it.

The waiter returned and, noticing the carafe was empty, asked if we would like a refill. Loosened by the pizza and more particularly by the wine, Bill threw caution to the wind. 'Why not! After all, it's special occasion.'

'What's the occasion?' I asked, swallowing the last of my pizza crust.

'Well, you know, Amanda. You and me being out together somewhere posh, telling each other intimate details about our lives. It just seems special to me, that's all.'

I reached across the table and took his hand. 'Oh, Bill, you're so sweet. You're not like all those other boys, the other men, always wanting something else, if you know what I mean.'

Bill seemed unsure, but nodded.

'Bill, are you OK? You seem miles away,' I asked, touching his sleeve, snapping him back to the present.

'Yes, I'm fine. Never better.'

He grabbed my other hand. 'Amanda, we've known each other a while now and I think we get on well, don't we?'

I nodded.

'And if you want to leave home and move on and I'm on my own, I was wondering if, that is, I thought we may as well.' He paused, his palms sweaty in mine.

'Yes, Bill, you thought we may as well what? That maybe we should get married?'

'Well, um, not exactly.' His face grew puce. 'I was going to suggest going steady for a while, so we could get to know each other better.'

'But we already know each other really well, don't we? I virtually live at your house as it is – except at night-time. So, surely the next step is to tie the knot? You're without your mum, I want to leave home. Given the circumstances, getting married suits both of us.'

Bill's eyes grew wide, and I gulped, tightening my grip on his hands.

'I'm sorry, Amanda. I'm not sure. We hardly know each other, after all, and.'

'Bill this is just you, too afraid to take the leap, but why not? What's stopping you?'

He looked down at his empty plate.

'Bill. I'd love to marry you. Let's go for it. What have we got to lose?'

Bill looked up at me and nodded. It was agreed.

Well, all hell broke loose after that. I went home and told my parents, who told me in no uncertain terms that marriage to Bill was never, ever happening. Dad asked if I was pregnant, and I said no, obviously.

'Well, I suppose it's a natural conclusion to jump to,' Bill commented when I told him what happened.

I stared at him wild-eyed, my eyes red and swollen. 'I think we should get married as soon as possible. Maybe they'll come round to the idea once they get to know you.'

I left my home in a huff to start my evening shift at the chippy. When I returned home, there had been ructions. Bill was at his house settling down to watch *Coronation Street* when there was a loud knock on his front door. Bill had peered through the front window to see Dave: his short, squat form barely visible in the dark in his black jacket and Doc Martens. Dave had banged loudly again.

'I know you're in there, freak. Open the fucking door!'

Bill said he had been minded not to open the door, but Dave was shortly to be family, so he thought that he had better be polite, and also that if he did not open it soon, Dave was more than likely to break it down.

He opened the door and Dave lunged at Bill, shoving him backwards into the banister rail.

'What the fuck are you doing with my sister, you paedo? You'd better leave her alone, or we will come for you, do you understand? What is this place, anyway. It looks like something out of the last century – and it smells.'

Bill said to me later that he had thought that this last comment was particularly unkind given that I had only cleaned the house the day before, but he let it go.

'Well?' Dave demanded. 'Are you going to fuck off and leave her alone, you weirdo? Have you ever even had another woman apart from my sister? Rumour has it that you did have one once – your own fucking mother!'

I think that Dave could have said almost anything else but that. Bill swung his fist towards Dave's face and hit him full on. Bill was much larger than Dave in both height and girth and to his own surprise, packed a powerful punch. He had heard the snap of cartilage in Dave's nose and cut his fist on the two teeth he broke.

Dave had staggered backwards towards the open front door, clearly in pain, blood pouring from his face and onto his leather jacket. 'I'll be back, you bastard- and next time, I won't come alone,' he had gabbled, backing out of the front door before turning and running.

I had been regaled with the full story by Dave on my return from work, who lay stretched out on the sofa as if he had been shot.

Bill had apparently closed the door and went into the kitchen to run his hand under the cold tap. Then he had bolted the door and headed up to bed.

He had just cleaned his teeth and changed into his pyjamas when he heard another knock on the door. He moved into the bedroom, which was at the front of the house, and pulled back the curtain just a crack. It was me, standing on the doorstep. He unlocked the sash and pulled it up.

'What are you doing here at this time?' he called down.

'Come down and let me in. Please.'

'Are you alone?' Bill asked, fearing that Dave might be hiding around the corner with some lunatic posse.

'Yes, of course I'm alone.'

Bill came down and opened the door, tying up his dressing gown. I rushed in, slamming it shut behind me.

'Jesus, Bill, what did the hell you did to Dave? You've caved his face in,' I wept.

'He attacked me first - and he was extremely offensive about my mother.'

'Did you really have to hit him so hard? Dad went totally berserk. He threatened to call the police to ask them to charge you with assault and to send me away to my aunt's house in Brighton. I had to do whatever I could to stop him. But now we've got to leave here Bill. We've got to go tonight.'

'Calm down, Amanda. It'll all be OK. I'm sure when everyone settles down, we can sort things out. What does your mum have to say about it all?'

I snorted. 'Mum? You really think she'll come to my rescue? She's turned a blind eye to everything that goes on in our house since I was a little girl.'

I was clearly not making much sense to Bill, but he could see that I was scared.

'Look, Amanda, let's talk about this in the morning. It's late now and we can try to get a better perspective on everything tomorrow. Go home and we'll talk again then.'

I grabbed his dressing gown and pulled him towards me, my face contorted, thick snot pouring from my nose. 'I can't go home, Bill. I can't go back there now. Don't make me go back.'

It was only then that he spotted the small suitcase by my feet.

I was jumped awake from a deep sleep by a sharp ring on the doorbell. I struggled to prise my eyelids open and to locate my watch. It read six-thirty in the morning. I felt my chest tighten as the bell went again. I slung my legs off the sofa, where Bill had reluctantly allowed me to sleep last night, and I opened the front door. My mother stood huddled in the doorway, shivering in the early morning air.

'I thought you'd be here,' she howled loudly enough to wake the rest of the street. 'Your father is, well I don't know how to say it,' she sobbed. 'Mandy, he's dead. I don't know what happened, but a few hours or so after you left, he started to vomit and then he had a terrible fit. They took him to hospital by ambulance, but by the time they arrived, he had passed away.' she cried. 'I just can't believe this is happening. Please come with me. I really need you to come home.' She stepped across the threshold, and I closed the door behind her. Her face was horribly red and swollen from crying.

I shrugged. 'Bill's asleep, Mum. You'll wake him.'

'I suspect you've kept him awake all night as it is. It's not right, Mandy. You're throwing your life away. I mean, do you seriously think that you are going to marry this guy? He's a right weirdo, Mandy.'

'At least Bill's a decent man and has proper values.' I ran my fingers through my hair, but they seemed to get stuck.

'I'm not sure what that's supposed to mean, Amanda.' My mother pulled her coat tighter around her body, her sobs subsiding.

'You know exactly what it means, Mum. The fact that you've chosen to turn a blind eye to what Dad has been up to at home for all these years doesn't mean it doesn't happen.'

Her face twitched.

'At first, I didn't understand what was going on, and then, when I was old enough to get it, there was nothing I could do about it. But you knew. You've always known, and you've done absolutely nothing to help me.' A small sob escaped from my mouth, like a hiccup. 'But I'm eighteen now, Mum, and I don't have to put up with Dad creeping across the landing anymore. You go back and bury that sicko by yourself. He had it coming.'

'Amanda, I'm sorry. I...'

'It's too late for sorry, Mum. Sorry doesn't begin to hack it. It's just how it is.' I stared at her impassively.

'Please come, Mandy. I need you.'

'But I don't need you, Mum.'

'Mandy, love,' my mother pleaded, reaching out to touch my sleeve. I pulled away and then moved past her, flinging the front door open.

'Bye, Mum. You'll be better off without him too. You'll see.'

My mother turned away, her shoulders slumped. She exited through the front door, without looking back and I closed it behind her, giving it an extra shove with both hands to ensure it was shut. Then I shuffled back into the lounge, where I flumped back onto the sofa, hoping that Bill had not woken up nor overheard the conversation.

An hour or so later, I got up and put the kettle on. I filled a mug and knocked on Bill's bedroom. He jumped as I opened it and hauled the blankets right up over his chest.

'Morning,' I sang brightly.

'Morning,' he replied. 'I can come down for my tea, thank you.'

'Nonsense, Bill. We'll be married soon, and then I can spoil you like this every day.' I placed the mug on the side table by his bed and sat on the edge of the blanket, causing him to flinch. 'Did you think about what I said last night, you know, about making a whole new start, moving away from here and beginning again?'

'Well, I don't know about that, Amanda.'

'Call me Mandy, or Mand.'

'OK, Mandy,' he stuttered. 'I've always lived here with Mother, and I'm not sure I could leave her.'

'But your Mum's dead, Bill.'

He blinked hard.

'She's gone,' I continued, 'and it's time to start again. It's fate, isn't it, Bill? Us meeting like this gives both of us the chance to begin new lives, and to do it together.' I leant forward and kissed him on the cheek. 'You are going nowhere here, and neither am I. This house just reminds you of your mother and everything you've lost. And I know that if you leave here and start again somewhere fresh, you could really make something of yourself. I know other people think you're a bit odd, but I just think you're shy and that they haven't made any effort to get to know you. I am certain that you can be better away from here Bill, and if you think about it, so do you. And I certainly want to make a new start. So, let's both of us be brave and see if we can make a good life together away from our families.' I sat on the edge of the bed and patted his knee.

Bill picked up his mug from the side table and sipped his tea. For a long while, there was silence, before Bill asked, 'What have you done, Amanda?'

'I don't know what you mean,' my voice responded in an abnormally high pitch.

'I think you do. I know you think I'm stupid and desperate, and in a way, I might be the latter, but I am definitely not the former. You misunderstand me completely.' He took another long draught of tea. 'In case you're wondering, I did overhear the conversation you had with your mother this morning. She told you that your father had died, and you didn't bat an eyelid. Now, I'm guessing that you and he did not necessarily have the best relationship, which is why, I assume, you've been so keen to marry me, but you seem to have reacted particularly badly on this occasion, and that's why you need to run away so quickly.'

'I don't know what you mean.' I stood up and walked to the window, peering out through the gap in the curtain at the street beginning to come to life in the early morning.

'I think you know exactly what I mean, Amanda.' He paused and looked at me directly. 'So, I think you are left with two choices here. Number one: I report you to the police, telling them that I suspect that you might have something to do with the sudden death of your father, or number two: I take you away from here and marry you as requested, but the relationship from here on in will be on my terms.'

I turned away from the window. 'What are your terms?' I whispered.

'They are straightforward really. You look after the house and after me, just as my mother did. We will have marital sex only when I schedule it and you will raise any resulting children according to my rules. Otherwise, you will see no one without my consent, especially not your mother and brother. I will control the money and give you what you need for running the house and family. Those are my terms.'

Bill gave notice to his landlord, and we moved into a tiny flat in Crouch End. Three weeks later, we married in the Haringey registry office in Wood Green. Before Bill left his old house, he ventured into his mother's room and checked that all the drawers and wardrobes were empty. I think he already knew that they were, as he had given her clothes to charity after she died, and other than that, she left nothing except that rusty sewing machine. She had not even kept her wedding ring. I heard Bill talking to himself in there.

'Well, Mother, I'm moving on,' he informed the echoing, dank room. 'I've made a decision, rightly or wrongly, but it's time to move on.'

The room made no reply, but I had no doubt that that his mother would follow us wherever I went. As he closed the bedroom door behind him, I felt a damp breeze around my ankles on the landing. She was there.

When we got married, Bill had no idea what to expect when it came to sex. Sex was, after all, merely a means to procreation for him, which was a gift from God, but was not something that was meant to be enjoyed apparently – whatever the lads at work suggested. We spent our honeymoon night in our new flat, which was above a Coral's betting shop on the main road. The windows did not close properly and the noise from the traffic was constant. Bill allowed me to use the bathroom before him and I was already lying under the sheets in my fleecy nightdress when he came back into the room. He lay down beside me on top of the covers and we remained stock-still for quite some time, like we were playing a game of sleeping lions.

'We should have sex,' he stated.

I made no reply, but merely pulled back the covers, raising my nightdress to my waist and opened my legs. Bill stared at my body, fascinated by the thatch of thick, dark hair that crowned my pubis. I closed my eyes, and he rolled on top of me, untying his pyjama bottoms. He fumbled about, struggling to enter me, uncertain of where he should be aiming. During the whole procedure, I did not move a muscle or say a word. When Bill had finished, I merely pulled my nightgown back down and rolled away. It was what I had been used to, just with someone else.

From then on, that was the pattern of our lovemaking. We never kissed. We just performed the act. And when I fell pregnant six months later, we stopped, because we had achieved our goal. But then I lost the baby and we had to start all over again. Then I lost another one. This soul-destroying pattern continued every couple of years. Our marriage was a failure.

So, there we were, Bill almost forty and me nearly thirty, marooned together in a poisonous relationship. But marriage was marriage, and Bill certainly had no intention of running away from his responsibilities like his own father had. And I had nowhere to run to.

At least Bill had prospered at work, eventually building up his own modest construction firm and buying our semi-detached around the corner from the original flat. We rubbed along together somehow, with Bill going out to work and me looking after the house as his mother had done. Some days I wondered if it might have been easier to have gone to jail.

Chapter 27

Fiona

I had popped over to check on Amanda. We sat at her uncomfortable kitchen table over several mugs of tea, as she suddenly opened up and began to tell me all about how she first met Bill.

'Wow, it sounds quite romantic in its way,' I exclaimed, nursing my now cold mug.

'Would you like some more tea?'

'I don't think I could. Thanks anyway.'

'So, tell me, how did you meet Terry?'

'We met three years ago in a club in Harrogate. Terry was drinking whisky at one of the private tables on the balcony. I spotted him while I was strutting my stuff with a couple of girlfriends to that irritating song *Venus* by Bananarama. I had really dressed up that night, hoping to meet someone I suppose. I wore a skimpy, silver Lurex halter neck top, which kept slipping slightly to the side, which annoyed me all night. Anyway, I could feel his eyes boring into me like lasers and when I left the dancefloor and returned to my table downstairs, he sent over a bottle of champagne with a note. I read it, looked up to the balcony and he nodded to me. I drank the champagne with my mates, and when they wanted to leave, I made an excuse about spotting an old friend and stayed behind. I climbed the spiral stairs up to Terry, who met me with his smile, you know the one he has. It's irresistible.'

'Hi, I just came up to thank you for the champagne,' I shouted over the din of the disco. I sat down and sidled around the table to where he was sitting.

'It was my pleasure, Princess.'

I giggled. 'It's Fiona, actually.'

'What a beautiful name. And I'm Terry.'

'Pleased to meet you.'

'Not as pleased as I am to meet you,' he whispered into my ear. I felt myself shudder involuntarily.

He ordered another bottle of bubbly, while I told him all about myself. I worked as a hairdresser, lived alone, had one sister, who was married with two kids but who I not really get along with, and that my mum and dad had recently retired to Wales. I said that liked Harrogate. It was a wealthy town, and I had good clientele who tipped well.

'And what do you do, Terry?' I slurred, laying my head on his shoulder about thirty minutes into the bottle.

'I'm in finance. Property mostly.'

'Ooh, that sounds super interesting,' I downed the last glass of champagne.

'Fancy a nightcap back at mine?'

I nodded and he supported me down the stairs. The doorman hailed us a cab.

Terry's apartment was a penthouse in the centre of town.

'Wow, what a great pad.' I wobbled from chair to chair stroking the velvet upholstery.

Terry made no comment, apart from taking me by the hand and helping me into the bedroom, pushing me gently down onto the circular bed. Within moments, he had undone that flimsy halter neck and explored further from there. We had sex on and off all night, until I literally had to beg him to stop.

I saw Terry several more times over the next few weeks and we really enjoyed each other's company. He was always kind and happy to see me. He took me along to a couple of business dinners to impress his clients, which he said I was good at, because I could disable any man with my stunning body encased in my skin-tight dresses (his words, you understand. I don't mean to boast!) while I was able to befriend the women as if I was the girl next door. Terry believed I was quite the asset.

But then one evening when we lay in bed together, Terry told me that his dealings were coming to a close in Harrogate and it was time for him to leave. His next project was in Manchester. I felt quite distraught, until he asked me if I fancied coming with him.

'But what about my job, Terry? I can't leave here without a job to go to.'

'Don't you worry about that, Princess. How about you come with me, and I'll pay you a wage.'

'For doing what?'

'To support me in my work, you know. Come out for a few dinners, do the shopping, and shag me senseless.'

'I'm not a hooker, Terry.'

'How many hookers do you know who do the shopping? Just think about it. The offer is there for you if you want to take it.'

And I did. But unfortunately, we did not stay in Manchester for very long.

'Fiona, the deal is wrapping up early,' Terry told me one night in our flat in Didsbury, six months into our stay there. 'I've got a new prospect in Newcastle, so I'm going up there for a few months.'

I stared at him, big-eyed and sleepy as I always was after Terry had made love to me for hours. 'But what about me, Terry?' My lips trembled.

'What about you, Princess? You're coming with me, of course.'

I rolled on top of him and kissed him. 'Oh, Terry, I love you.'

We moved over the next few days. I was sorry to leave Manchester. It was a happening place, and I enjoyed the vibe in the clubs including the fabulous Hacienda, which was a venue that Terry frequented, and I joined him there occasionally.

'We do seem to be rushing this a little, Terry. Couldn't we stay a few more weeks? I like it here.' I was packing my suitcase extremely badly, so that there was no way it was going to close.

'Sorry, Princess. I'll miss this deal if I'm not up in Newcastle by Friday.'

But I must admit, whilst I had my reservations, Newcastle was terrific, and we were loving life up there. But then something unexpected happened.

We were enjoying a meal in Fisherman's Wharf, the best restaurant in Newcastle, where Terry had ordered a particularly expensive bottle of wine to celebrate closing his latest deal. But when the waiter offered some to me, I had to decline.

'Don't you fancy red tonight, Princess? Did you want something else? Champagne maybe?'

'No, I'll stick to water thanks.'

'Are you ill?'

'No, Terry. I'm not ill. I'm pregnant.'

He dropped his fork, and thousand island sauce from his prawn cocktail spattered the front of his new silk shirt. 'Shit, this shirt is new and now it's fucking toast.' He plunged his serviette into my water glass and dabbed furiously at the stain, which merely spread.

'Terry, did you hear what I said?' My eyes were moist with heavy tears, which threatened to spill down my cheeks.

'Yes, of course I heard you. Sorry, I'm just pissed off. This shirt is screwed.'

I was crying now, and other diners were looking over. He reached out and held my hand to quieten me down.

'So, do you want to keep it?'

I flinched. 'Well, of course I do, Terry. I'm a Catholic.'

'Really? That's the first I've heard of it.' He downed his glass of wine and filled it again to the brim. 'I thought you were on the pill?'

'I was, but I forgot to take it when I had that terrible hangover the other week, didn't I, so I think it hasn't worked so well.'

'Right. Fuck. This is a conundrum.' He took another slug of wine.

I stared at him, my face wet, mascara running everywhere. 'I thought you might be pleased. I thought we had a good thing going here, Terry.'

'We have, Princess, we have. It's just a bit of a shock, that's all. I need to process it.' He managed a tight smile and finished off the bottle.

That night, neither of us slept very much at all. In the morning, I woke up all puffy-eyed and blotchy.

Terry rolled towards me. 'Well, Princess, I guess I'd better make an honest woman out of you.'

I hugged him and then sobbed into his chest hair. It was not our most romantic moment.

Two weeks later – I did not want to be wearing a bump in the photos, so we moved sharpish - we married at the registry office in the Civic Centre in a bare-walled room with splintered wooden chairs. I wore a white shift dress and carried a small bouquet of white lilies. I cannot even remember what Terry wore, but I do not think he bought anything special for the occasion. We held a short champagne reception for fifty distant acquaintances, which lasted less than an hour. A month later, I lost the baby and three months after that, we moved back to Harrogate, as Terry's work in Newcastle had finished.

'So, you lost a baby too?' Amanda whispered.

I nodded, a solitary tear falling into my empty mug.

Frankly, even though I was distraught about my miscarriage, I had nothing to complain about. Terry was extremely generous to me, allowing me to buy expensive clothes and taking me out to fancy restaurants, as well as banging me senseless on a regular basis.

We were happily settled in Harrogate for almost year. It was a great town and both Terry and I were doing well. But then, all of a sudden, he said we had to move again. I was not at all keen. I had re-secured my job at one of the leading hair salons and enjoyed working there. The two of us had quite a few arguments about moving to London.

'Terry, I really love my job here. I know it's only hairdressing and not high-powered like your stuff – whatever it is that you actually do. I know you've sort of explained it, but it all sounds so ridiculously complicated. Anyway, couldn't we stay on here for a little while longer? I'm sure things will improve for you, love.' I snuggled up to him on the sofa, my breasts begging him to concede defeat, but he held firm.

'Fiona, the world of finance revolves around London, and so that's where I need to be. It's time to move onwards and upwards. And we need to shift ourselves sharpish, as I've got something going down which I can't afford to miss.' He put his arm around me and pulled me close. 'We'll be fine, Princess. And you can stop working for a while. Have a break.'

'And maybe we can try for another baby, Terry? I know I went to pieces when we lost the last one, but I do feel ready to try again. Shall I come off the pill?'

He coughed. 'Let's get settled first, Princess, and then we can talk about it. After all, there's no rush, is there? We've got our whole lives ahead of us.'

My bottom lip wobbled.

'Hang on, Princess. I've got a little something for you to take to London.' Terry produced a brand-new Chanel bag which he had hidden behind the sofa, and I momentarily forgot how upset I was with him.'

'So, that is how we ended up living next to you guys,' I smiled.

'I'm glad you did,' Amanda replied, reaching out and squeezing my hand.

'Me too.'

Chapter 28

Amanda

Around lunchtime one Wednesday, the doorbell buzzed, and I roused myself out of my daydream to answer it, thinking that it would most probably be Fiona.

She popped over most days now, and I was more than grateful for her friendship. Slowly, we were talking things through, and it was very helpful to me. Until I had spoken to her, I had not opened up to anyone about the trauma of all my losses.

'Bill clearly blames me for failing to have children,' I moaned to Fiona over coffee in my kitchen. 'He's got some weird belief that the only point of marriage is to produce offspring, and without it, it's all a complete waste of time. It's as if I've betrayed him somehow.' I paused, my throat stopped with emotion, 'And yet he has no understanding of how devastated I was each time it happened, how devastated I still am. I've offered to leave him, but he won't have that either. He says he doesn't want to be a bolter like his father.'

'At least Bill wants kids,' Fiona had mused, staring deep into her coffee mug, her long legs wound up underneath her. 'I'm not sure Terry does. He keeps telling me that it's still the wrong time to try again. I don't know why. He's doing ever so well with work and everything.'

'Are you on the pill?' I ventured.

'Yes.'

'So why not come off it and see what happens?' I was shocked by my own audacity, but something had changed when

I was in hospital. My confidence, buried for such a long time, was resurfacing.

'It wouldn't make any difference. Since the last accident, Terry always wears a condom. I think he'd wear two given half a chance!' She paused and looked up at me.

'What about you?'

'Me? Sex has never been a thing for me.'

'And Bill?'

'It is more of an obligation for him more than anything else. Neither of us enjoy it.'

'Wow! That's so totally weird.' Fiona checked herself. 'Sorry, I mean, Terry is completely the opposite. He's always up for it, whether I want to do it or not. He can be a bit of a pain like that.'

I stared at Fiona and could completely understand why any man would have the permanent hots for her. She was beautiful, whereas I was middling at best. And more than that, I was damaged goods.

The bell trilled again, reminding me that someone was still waiting outside, and I hurried to the door. When I opened it, I was somewhat surprised to see Terry standing there, his hand resting on the doorframe.

'Terry, hello. I'm so sorry, but Bill's at work. He'll be back around seven, as he said he had a late meeting tonight,' I blustered.

'I came to see you actually.' He stepped over the threshold without waiting to be asked and closed the door behind him. 'I was supposed to be entertaining a client at lunchtime, but she never showed up. Unusually, I found myself with an hour spare and as I haven't had a chance to catch up with you since your illness, I thought I'd pop in to see how you were doing.'

I felt my face flush. 'That's very kind of you. I'm fine, thank you.'

'Brilliant. That's great to hear,' he exclaimed, moving past me towards the lounge and springing onto the sofa like Tigger. The broken springs groaned. 'Any chance of drink? I'm gasping.'

'Yes, of course,' I mumbled and scurried off to the kitchen. While I boiled the kettle, I attempted to compose myself. Terry unsettled me, disturbed me, in a way I could not quite explain. He was remarkably handsome, and when he spoke to me, I felt an odd, dizzying sensation, which frightened me.

I made two mugs of tea. 'Terry, do you want milk and sugar?' I croaked through from the kitchen.

'Don't bother with tea, Princess. Have you got something stronger?'

'Well, I've got some beer and I think there might be a half bottle of whisky somewhere. I think Bill brought it back from one of your evenings out together.' I glanced at the clock as I re-entered the lounge.

'Live a little.' Terry patted the faded brown sofa cushion next to him, indented by Bill's bottom. 'May I call you Mandy?'

'Sure,' I faltered, placing the mugs onto the table. 'Let me see if I can find the whisky.'

I bolted back into the kitchen, fumbling around in the cupboard. When I found the bottle, I returned with it to Terry carrying two mismatched tumblers.

'So, Mandy, you're looking terrific if I may say so. I hadn't realised what a stunning figure you've got.' Terry relieved me of the whisky and poured two generous glasses, handing one to me.

I blushed even harder and sipped. The harsh taste made me squirm.

'Sit, sit,' Terry urged me.

I perched at the far end of the sofa.

At least I was bothering to get dressed these days, and I was pleased that I was wearing the jeans and peasant top Fiona had bought me, because she had good taste even if I lacked it.

'Bill's a very lucky man, you know,' he continued. 'I hope he knows it.'

I shrugged, not knowing what to say in reply.

Terry shifted closer towards me and ran his hand along the back of the sofa. The hairs on the back of my neck stood to attention.

He downed his whisky and poured himself another, even larger one. 'I don't think you've had much love in your life, have you, Mandy?' He stared straight at me.

'Well, I, erm, I.'

'That's a shame because women are special you know. I've observed you, and my assessment is that life hasn't treated you all that well so far. I think a beautiful woman like you deserves some proper TLC.'

He slid his hand from the back of the sofa onto my shoulder and squeezed it lightly. I felt a strange tingle in my groin.

'I think it's so important to be loved, don't you? And part of love is being able to talk and share. Don't you agree?' I thought for the briefest moment that I might pass out. No one had paid me this sort of attention since my days at the chip shop – and no one there had looked remotely like Terry. I blinked hard, unable to respond.

Suddenly, he removed his arm, finished his whisky in one gulp and stood up. 'Anytime you want to chat, Mandy, remember I'm just next door. Don't be a stranger.' He bent down and planted the softest kiss on my cheek, before striding out of the door without looking back.

I remained on the sofa, petrified.

Chapter 29

Fiona

I lay on my back, drenched in sweat. Terry and I had just made love in several athletic poses, and I was exhausted. I glanced over him, grinning back at me, then looked away again quickly, not wanting to encourage him to think about going again. I closed my eyes. 'You know, Amanda told me that Bill blames her for all her miscarriages and thinks she's a waste of space because she can't give him kids. That's so sad, don't you think?'

'It's dreadful,' Terry mused. 'I bet the poor cow has never even had an orgasm. And she's not so bad looking since she lost the weight and you spruced her up a bit, Princess. Good job.'

'Yes, but it doesn't help her, does it, Terry? Bill seems to resent her and has kept her almost prisoner in that awful house. I think she'd prefer it if he just left her, but apparently, he won't do that either.' I rolled on my side towards him. 'How do you find him when you're with him?'

'Well, he's certainly an odd character, I'll give you that. And he wouldn't be the kind of bloke that I'd ordinarily choose to take down the pub. But he's not stupid and he can recognise a decent opportunity when he sees one – or when he's encouraged to see one. I think he's pretty close to investing in one of my property schemes, but he's rather risk averse. If he would just decide to take the plunge, he'd be so much better off. Not just financially, but it would also allow him to reach his full potential. He just needs one final shove.'

'Maybe if he did, he might be a bit kinder to Amanda and they could work things out. It's a shame, because they obviously don't talk to each other and share everything like we do.' I budged closer to Terry and lay on his chest.

'Well, you know I love to share, Princess. That's what makes this world a better place.'

Chapter 30

Amanda

I was waiting for Bill to get home, pacing up and down the kitchen, wearing out the already tired linoleum. The last vestiges of the spring sunshine did nothing but highlight the dreadful state of the shabby worktops and cracked cupboard doors. It was as if the whole house was a manifestation of our own depression.

I heard the door open and then bang shut again, Bill's heavy boots thudding towards me.

'Hello,' I ventured, as he arrived sweating through the doorway, encrusted in dust and grime. He threw himself onto a kitchen chair and began to untie his boots.

'What's for tea?'

'I don't know. I haven't thought about it yet.' I gulped. 'I, I've been out actually. I've got myself a job.' My heart was banging so hard in my chest that I thought it might break through my ribs and jump onto the floor.

'You've fucking done what?'

'I've got a job. It's not very exciting, but it will give me a bit of my own money to buy things I need and more importantly get me out of the house. I'm dying here, Bill. I need to do something with my life. I feel like a prisoner here.'

Bill's face was puce. 'Your job is here at home looking after the house and making my dinner. I give you enough money for that. Are you telling me that I don't provide sufficiently for you? That I'm a bad husband?'

I wanted to scream that yes, he was a terrible husband, who did not give me freedom, nor affection, let alone a life, but I was too exhausted to start a serious argument. 'I'm not saying any of those things. But we don't have children for me to look after and.'

'Well, you can't blame me for that.'

I blinked back the tears and soldiered on.

'I've got a job in Sainsburys. It's just on the tills, but it will be interesting enough, and we get to buy food at very reduced prices at the end of the day. I don't start until you've gone to work, and I'll be back before you, so you won't even know I've gone. And it's only three days a week.'

'I don't need any wife of mine out working. I provide for this household, and I bring in enough. That was the deal.'

'But I want to be able to buy some clothes and get my hair done properly. This way I won't have to ask you for the money.'

Bill stood up, his chair flying backwards. He came towards me, so that I could feel his hot, stale breath on my face. 'I've got plenty of money, Mandy, but I'm careful with it. And I don't trust you with it. If I give you any more of it, you'll be frittering it away like that floozy friend of yours next door. It beggars belief that Terry - who is a seriously shrewd operator, I can tell you - allows her to buy so much stuff. I don't think I've ever seen her in the same outfit twice.'

'This isn't about Fiona, Bill. It's about me. When I was in hospital, when I did what I did, I realised that I must do something else with my life. I know I've made mistakes in the past, but haven't I done my time? Working in a supermarket might not be earth-shattering, but it's a start and I'm sure we will both be grateful for the extra money, won't we?' I reached out my hand to touch his shoulder, but he batted me away.

'We don't need extra money, Mandy. I am thinking about investing in Terry's new property and if that goes the way he says it will – and I have no reason not to believe him given his track record – we will be rolling in it. I may even be able to quit the construction business finally.' He stared past me into the concrete garden. 'I'm so bored with it, and I've taken it as far as

I can. Terry says that this will allow me to make the most of my talents, to get to the next level.'

'You've been talking to him for a long time. Are you worried about going for it?'

Bill glared at me. 'No, I'm not worried. It's just that it's a leap on from what I've done before, and I need to raise more cash. I've got my savings, but I'd have to re-mortgage this place as well as selling the firm. I'm onto it. I just don't have much time, as Terry says the offer's not on the table for much longer.' He moved away from me, righting his chair, and slumping back down. I realised it was the most in-depth conversation we had had in a long while.

'Isn't it a bit too risky, putting everything you have into one deal? Not that I know much about it,' I ventured.

'No, you don't and frankly, it's none of your business, because you've never needed to contribute to our living costs anyway.'

'But only because you've never allowed me to,' I retorted.

'Because I wanted you to concentrate on being a wife and a mother'

'I'm a total failure in the baby stakes, but that doesn't mean we can't still have a life together. You liked me once, didn't you? When we first met?' I could feel tears rising, stinging my throat.

'I don't know, Mandy. Did I? You made a beeline for me, remember, and no other woman had ever shown any interest in me before you, so maybe you just turned my head. Maybe if Mother had still been alive, she would have given me better advice and I wouldn't have jumped so fast. And let's face it, you kind of moved in on me, didn't you? You were running away from, well from what you did, and I was a convenient mule to carry you off. So, I don't know, Mandy. I couldn't tell you if I liked you, or if I felt anything very much at all. You were just there, and you seemed to like me when no one else did.'

Bill looked so forlorn sitting there, like a small lost boy, and even though his words wounded me, I knew he was right.

He had been in the right place at the right time, and I manipulated him to escape from home.

'I'm sorry, Bill. But it's not too late. We both deserve to be happy. You don't have to feel constantly guilty, or even responsible for the choices you've made. We can both try to do better.' I moved over to him and raised his head with my hand. I bent down to kiss him, but he pulled away. He stood up and stalked out of the room, disgusted with me, and disgusted with himself.

Chapter 31

Amanda

Fiona had driven off to see her parents for a couple of days in Wales, and I was missing my coffee break with her. I fiddled around taking too much time getting dressed and trying to ignore the housework. Suddenly the doorbell rang, followed by three sharp raps. No one ever visited me apart from Fiona, so I was wary as I approached the front door.

'Hey, Princess, how are you today? You're looking as lovely as ever.' Terry leant on the doorpost, glowing in the mid-morning sunshine.

I blushed so furiously that I knew that my usual unpleasant, irregular blotches had bloomed across my cheeks. 'Hi, Terry, yes, I'm fine, thanks. How are you?'

'Yes, I'm great, thank you. Listen, Fiona's away for a couple of days, and I could really do with a woman's advice on something. Do you think you could help me out?'

'Erm, OK, if you really think it's something I could help you with. But to be honest, I'm probably not the best person to give advice.' I hopped from foot to foot, half closing the door.

Terry stuck his shoe in the doorway to stop it from closing. 'Oh, you'll be perfect, I'm certain of it. Can you pop over to my place with me for a minute? I can show it to you there?'

'Um, well, OK then. Let me just find my shoes and my keys. Can you give me a minute?'

'Sure thing.' I left him standing on the doorstep, whistling, while I wandered back into the house to locate my stuff. Eventually, I reappeared, stepping outside and negotiating the numerous locks on our front door, which Bill insisted on in case marauding herds of armed tribesman descended on our semi while we were out. Then I followed Terry down my path and back up his own. He unlocked the front door and ushered me inside.

'Would you like a drink, Mandy? I've just bought a case of deliciously fruity Chablis, and I can't wait to try it. I've got a bottle chilling now.' He beckoned me towards the kitchen, and I followed behind like a meek, little lamb.

'It's a bit early in the day for alcohol, don't you think? In actual fact, I don't normally drink at all.' I fidgeted in the kitchen doorway.

'Well then, that's even more reason to try some. I think it's a good thing to try different things from time to time, otherwise we all fall into terrible ruts, don't you agree?' He raised the bottle from the ice bucket, cutting the foil of the top with perfect precision, and inserting the corkscrew, centring it just right so that it would come out cleanly. It emerged with a satisfying pop. He picked up one of the wine glasses by the bucket and poured out a generous serving.

'Here you go, Mandy. Get that down your neck.'

I stood there motionless, glass in hand. Terry poured himself a glass and moved towards me. My face burst into flame once again.

'Cheers,' he laughed, clinking his glass with mine.

'Cheers,' I responded and took a small sip. 'Ooh, that's gorgeous. I've never drunk anything quite so delicious.'

'Excellent. I thought you'd like it. Now, come through to the lounge and we can sit in the comfy chairs.'

Terry sat on the sofa and set the wine bottle down on the coffee table. He held out his hand to me and I took it, while I lowered myself into the seat next to him on the sofa. My hands were shaking, and I attempted to steady my glass to stop the wine from spilling. We remained sipping our drinks for a few moments without speaking.

It was me who eventually broke the excruciating silence. 'So, what did you want to show me then, Terry?'

'What? Oh, that, yes. Well, I've bought a couple of options for Fiona's birthday, and I can't decide which one I like best. I need another woman's opinion, as I mentioned. Someone with a good eye for things, like yourself. But look, there's no rush. Sit back and enjoy the wine. It's from Provence. Have you ever been there?'

I shook my head.

'Oh, that's a such a shame. You must go one day. It's such a glamorous part of the world. White sandy beaches, luxurious hotels and such beautiful people walking around wearing so very little. It's intoxicating and super sexy.'

'It sounds incredible. Sadly, I don't think I'll ever get to go there. It doesn't really sound like Bill's cup of tea. I really can't imagine him on the beach, can you? Mind you, I'm not sure how comfortable I would be either. I'd be no match for the beautiful people.' I sighed as I emptied my glass.

'Utter nonsense! You've got to stop doing yourself down. You're a very attractive woman. Your problem is that no one has ever taken the time to tell you that. That's such a great shame.' He refilled my glass and sidled closer. My chest tightened.

'I find you very alluring, Amanda. You got a certain something about you. I've always thought so, but it's never been possible for me to tell you before. We've not had a proper chance to be alone.'

I opened my jaw and left it hanging there, like a hungry chick waiting to be fed.

'I know it's wrong to be attracted to you when we are both married and you and Fiona are friends, but I simply can't help myself. I just feel this strong, urgent pull between us, and I've been struggling to ignore it. Do you?'

I drained my second glass far too quickly and leapt up from the sofa, and in so doing knocked the coffee table with my knee, toppling the ice bucket. 'Oh, my goodness, I'm so sorry, Terry. Let me clean that up.' I ran through to the kitchen and returned with the kitchen roll. I bent down and began mopping at the spreading wine with ferocity.

He moved behind me and wrapped his arms around my waist, drawing me upright again. He ran his hands up over my breasts, and I felt my nipples harden as he touched them with his fingers. I let out an involuntary moan, and Terry span me around to face him. He kissed me hard, unbuttoning my blouse one-handed with practised fingers, before helping me to step out of my jeans. My underwear was horrific – grey, saggy, and elephantine – but I was too far gone to care. I simply dissolved into him and moments later, as he travelled downwards, I was howling so loudly that I was relieved that their house was double-glazed, unlike my own.

Afterwards, we lay there facing each other.

'You can't tell anyone about this, Amanda. I love my wife and she can never find out. This will be our little secret.'

'Don't worry,' I murmured. 'I've been keeping secrets since I was a small child. I'm very good at it.'

He stroked my leg. 'That's good to hear, Amanda, because I'd like to see you again, to do this again. But if we are going to be able to keep this going, I need you to persuade Bill to sign this deal. He's still undecided and I want him to move straight away before the opportunity disappears, which it will if he doesn't invest.'

I nodded, all doe eyed.

'The best part of getting into business with Bill would be that I would have to be around a lot of the time, and I can send Bill off to meetings and on trips, giving us more time to, well, you know.'

'I'd like that,' I murmured.

'Good. Well, you work your magic on him, Amanda and we can go from there. But remember, not a word to Bill, because it will blow us all to bits.'

'My lips are sealed,' I whispered.

Terry gave me a small pat on the top of my head, before pulling his clothes back on. 'I think you'd better go home straight away just in case Bill gets back early. Anyway, I've got other things to be getting on with.'

I nodded and reached down to the floor for my clothes to put them back on. Oddly, I did not want him to see what he had already seen, as I thought I looked less appealing in the cold light of post-passion. He left the room to make it easier and faster for me. A few minutes later, I hurried out into the hall. He was waiting with the front door open.

'Remember to talk to Bill,' he reminded her as he closed the door behind me.

When I got home, I felt like I should shower straight away and rub the sin of Terry off my skin, but I did not want to, so I got into bed and luxuriated in his scent for a while longer before washing. I felt like I had been reborn.

Chapter 32

Fiona

'I made a decision while I was in Wales,' I announced, nibbling on a piece of carrot cake. I was perched at a small table at the back of my favourite cafe in Crouch End with Amanda. As soon as I had got back, I had rushed over to see her.

'Oh, I'm so glad I caught you,' I had called to her as I saw her coming back up her drive carrying her food shopping. 'I couldn't remember if you'd started your new job yet, and if you had which days you were supposed to be working. Look, I've got something to tell you and it calls for cake. Get in the car.'

Amanda had muttered something about having too much to do, but I was not taking no for an answer, and after half an hour of her faffing about unpacking her groceries, we made it to the cafe.

'So, don't you want to know what it was?' I asked her.

'What what was?' asked Amanda, who appeared weirdly distracted. She did not look so well, if I was being honest. She appeared rather pale and drawn, and I hoped she was not coming down with something. Or maybe Bill was being a bastard to her as usual.

'My decision. In Wales. Have you been listening to a word I've been saying?' I took another tiny bite of cake.

'Sorry. Yes. What was it?' She fiddled with the paper doily on her plate.

'So, I thought about what you said before I went away, and I think you're right. I'm fed up with waiting for Terry to decide when the right time is for us to have a baby. I want one now and

I can't spend the rest of my life shopping and doing fuck all else all day. So, I've come off the pill.'

Amanda choked on her tea. 'Is that such a good idea?'

'It was *your* idea,' I laughed.

'Well, we talked about it as a possibility, yes, but I thought it was just part of a general discussion. I didn't mean that you should necessarily do it.' She worried at a hangnail on her right thumb. 'And anyway, didn't you say he always uses a condom as well?'

'Yes, I did, but I've thought about that, and I can either hide them or prick holes in his supply. And he doesn't always use one if he's feeling super randy. If he's in one of his nothing's gonna stop me now moods, literally nothing will hold him back.'

A strange sound emerged from Amanda, somewhere between a hiccup and a burp.

'Are you OK? You look a little peaky?' I asked, leaning across and taking her hand.

'I'm fine,' she replied, withdrawing it. 'I just swallowed my tea the wrong way, that's all.'

'OK, as long as you're alright.' I paused. 'Anyway, I think it's a plan. It's easy to get Terry regularly riled up in the bedroom, so hopefully it won't take too long to get pregnant, and then I just have to hope that this time is sticks. Wish me luck.' I crossed my fingers and waggled them at her.

'Good luck,' Amanda muttered, staring into her teacup.

'I get the impression you disapprove for some reason?'

'It's not for me to say, Fiona. It's your marriage and I'm no expert on such matters, as you well know. Anyway, let's change the subject. What are you doing for your birthday?'

'My birthday? It was four months ago. Why did you think it was my birthday?'

Amanda's neck flared and blotched, and her face flushed. 'Oh, I must have got muddled up somehow. For some reason, I thought it was coming up soon. I must have confused you with somebody else.'

'No, it's not for ages, more's the pity, as Terry normally spoils me rotten on my birthday - although I always end up having to pay him back in kind, if you know what I mean. Actually, it's a shame it's not, as I'd have an even better chance of getting a bun in the oven!'

'I'm feeling quite tired, Fiona. Do you think we could go home now?' She did look quite pale.

'Of course, babe. You should have said. Let me pay the bill. Here are my keys. Why don't you go and wait in the car?'

Amanda nodded and grabbed her coat, shooting out of the front door. She leant against the window of the cafe outside. She must have been feeling dreadful because she looked as though she was about to faint.

Chapter 33

Amanda

Bill had failed to come home the previous night. He was often back late these days, out with Terry discussing their joint venture. But this was the first time he had not returned before morning. I was partly relieved not to have to deal with him, still trying to reconcile having slept with Terry the week before, yet at the same time, I was a little worried about his whereabouts, because it was so out of character. Mind you, his character has been a little out for a while now – ever since he got close to Terry, in fact. Bill went out after work, he dressed in expensive clothes, he went to restaurants. It was all quite bizarre.

Since I had informed Bill about my intention to return to work, he had largely ignored me. I should have been happy that he was spending so much less time at home and being less controlling. Yet since my unforgettable and unforgivable afternoon with Terry, I was awash with a whole host of emotions, none of which I could reconcile. Firstly, I was fearful that Terry might tell Bill about our encounter and then the whole business deal would fall through. Bill would blame me and then become worse with me than he was before, that is if he stayed with me at all. Secondly, I felt hugely embarrassed that I had fallen for Terry's easy lies like some stupid, gullible, little girl. And I felt dirty for allowing myself to be used by yet another man. Thirdly, I felt immensely guilty about betraying Fiona, my only friend, who had been kinder to me than anyone had ever been in my entire life. I could not really explain why I had done it. Terry had simply overwhelmed me. Whenever I thought about it, my brain scrambled once again.

Yet, above all these conflicting thoughts, I felt an unstoppable desire to see Terry again and to make love with him repeatedly. No one, however briefly, had ever awoken me as he had, and I wanted more. Yet I had not heard from Terry since and I was in pieces, unable to control my emotions, alternately crying, then angry.

Bill finally made it home around eleven in the morning. I was sitting at the bottom of the stairs, my head in my hands, moping, and I did not hear him approach until he turned the key in the lock. Ordinarily, this would have simply irritated him, me loafing about in the middle of the morning, but instead, he asked me if I was alright. Maybe he thought I was weeping over the fact he had failed to come home and was feeling guilty. He had no idea that the real reason was that I hated him because he had been out with Terry, which was the one thing I really longed to do.

I made no reply, staring blankly. Bill moved over and perched on the step beside me.

'What's the matter?' he repeated.

'Since when do you care?' I sniffed. 'You never even came to see me when I was in hospital and now, when you've been God knows where all night, you decide to act all concerned. Got something to hide, have you?'

He blushed and scratched at his day-old stubble. 'Look, Amanda. We may not have had the best life so far, but things are about to change radically.'

'So, you keep telling me, Bill, but I get the impression that they will change for you, but not necessarily for me. Well, I might decide to make some changes of my own.'

He ignored my jibe and placed his hand on my knee. I flinched. 'Look, it's going to be a new start, and we can make it for both of us if we try. I've spent all my life insulated and afraid, but I'm slowly coming to realise that that's all been such a waste of time and that we need to learn to live before it's too late.

Maybe we could try to begin again together? Try to forget the past.'

'Are you drunk, Bill?' I shuffled away from him slightly.

'No, at least I don't think so, no. I've just been thinking about things a great deal, and I've decided that I'd like us to try to be nicer to each other.'

'I've tried to be nice to you for years, Bill, and all I've ever got in return is meanness,' I snorted. 'So, if this is some kind of sick joke, where you get me to say something nice to you and then you just put me down all over again, then I'm simply not interested. It may surprise you to learn this, but I also want a better life. I feel as if I've been dead inside for so long, and I want to start living again. But I can't do it with you.'

He wrapped his arms around my shoulders. I tried to pull away, but he held me fast.

'But that's just it. I don't want it to be like it was before. I'm about to make a great deal of money, and it will enable us to move on and go anywhere we want, do anything we want. No more hiding. Think about it.'

I laughed, but Bill stopped me short, taking my face in his hands and kissing me as if it was for the very first time with genuine feeling and passion. When he stopped, I stared at him in shock. Without speaking, he picked me up and carried me up to the bedroom, where he made love to me, slowly and carefully.

Afterwards we lay together and he told me about the property deal he was about to sign with Terry and how it would mean that the two of them would be partners in a venture to rebuild parts of Camden. Bill had raised the funds by re-mortgaging the house, found a buyer for the business and had committed all his savings to it. It meant that Terry would be an integral part of our lives for years to come.

'I wasn't sure about Terry at first. I thought he was a bit of a chancer, but now I do think that his heart is in the right place, and he's got a great business brain. He's an honest bloke. I have never believed in fate, but now I really think that it really might exist. What do you think?'

'I feel that he's a good omen,' I agreed. 'Before Terry came on the scene, we had been stagnating, merely existing. He's opened our, I mean, your eyes to all kinds of different possibilities, options, choices. I think you should do it.'

He stroked my hair. 'And I think we can begin to love each other properly, don't you?' he muttered in my ear.

Suddenly, I rolled away from him and leapt out of bed, running into the bathroom and locking the door. I lay on the cold bathroom tiles, sobbing unrelentingly. I thought I might never stop.

I only wanted Terry. If I ever saw him leaving the house or coming home, I would rush to the front door or the bedroom window to try to attract his attention, but he looked straight through me as if I was part of the glass. The rest of the time, he was with Fiona, and I avoided talking to them together. It was far too painful. Yet the less I spoke to him, the more I wanted him. It was as if he had awoken a demon in me who had taken complete control of my rational being.

I was tangled up in all these thoughts when the doorbell rang. I hastily splashed water on my face and threw on my dressing gown, Bill having already gone out again. It was Fiona. I answered the door, and she grabbed me hard by both shoulders, leaping up and down.

'Oh my God, Amanda, you're never going to believe what's happened.'

'What? Tell me!' I replied, attempting to mimic her enthusiasm.

'I'm already pregnant! Can you believe it?'

I felt an overwhelming rush of nausea. 'Oh. Fiona, that's amazing. Congratulations.' I hesitated. 'Have you told Terry yet?'

'No, not yet. I'm waiting for the right moment. Look, I must go, because we are going out for brunch with some of his associates, so I need to get dolled up, but I'll keep you posted, alright?'

Fiona kissed me on the cheek, and in that moment, I hated her more than I had ever hated anyone before. She flounced out of the door, and I collapsed onto the bottom step of the staircase.

Following my conversation with Fiona in the cafe about Terry's extreme obsession with contraception, I had remembered that Terry had forgotten to use a condom when we did it and I was not on the pill. It occurred to me that if I was carrying his child, Terry would have to see me, speak to me, continue a relationship with me. I would not care as long as I could sleep with him occasionally and to receive a little of his attention. I was good at not telling. He could count on that.

Chapter 34

Fiona.

I had been frantic all day, cooking, cleaning and setting up the dining room for our special romantic dinner. Well, when I say cleaning, I had asked my cleaner to come in early and to put in a couple of extra hours. And when I say cooking, which was not really my forte, I had driven up to the fancy fishmonger's in Muswell Hill and bought scallops pre-prepared in their shell with creamy, Thermidor sauce and then on to the butchers to purchase a ready-seasoned rack of lamb. Marks and Spencer offered bags of pre-peeled vegetables and my favourite cafe in Crouch End provided a dessert of chocolate mousse cake laced with rum and topped with raspberries. I was exhausted by the time I had unpacked it all, placed it on foil ready for baking and set the table with some fabulously scented candles.

Obviously, I had to dress myself up for the occasion as well, and I had plumped for a short, black lace number, which pushed up my boobs to a show-stopping height and barely covered my knicker line. Subtlety was never worthwhile with Terry. I needed to knock him dead as he came through the door. I spent quite a while on my face, perfecting my eyes with extra layers of spidery black mascara. I slipped on my five-inch black velvet stilettos and pirouetted in front of my full-length mirror. I smiled to myself, pleased with the results, whilst reflecting that I would not look this good for some time after this once I started to get bigger with the pregnancy.

I had given Terry strict instructions to be home by seven, and to come home alone - not with Bill in tow, nor any other of his acolytes. Not tonight. At six-thirty, I put the champagne on ice and placed two glasses next to it, which my cleaner had polished to a high sparkle earlier in the day. The scene was set.

The clock ticked past seven-thirty, but there was still no sign of Terry. I started to pace the lounge like a caged panther, and occasionally to peer through the frosted glass in the front door to see if he was arriving, although I knew he had not. You could hear his souped-up Audi three streets away. It got to eight p.m. and there was still no sign of him. I could feel irritation strangling the breath in my chest. I needed a drink to calm myself, even though I knew I had to be careful these days to not overdo it. I did not want to pop the champagne before Terry got back, so I poured myself a small gin and tonic, switching on the television to see if there was anything distracting on, but there was not.

At nine o'clock, I gobbled down one of the desserts. Terry had still not arrived, let alone called. I kicked off my shoes and threw them across the room, narrowly avoiding hitting the glass coffee table. When it got to ten, I took the food I had so painstakingly arranged off the baking trays and tipped all of it into the bin – except for the second dessert, which I now devoured. Then I weaved my way upstairs, unzipping my dress, which I lobbed in the corner of the room, where it lay crumpled and forlorn, before wiping off all my carefully applied make up and throwing on my nightdress. I lay on top of our bed, tears stinging my cheeks, as I waited for Terry to return.

I must have nodded off, because the next thing I knew I was woken by Terry crashing through the bedroom door.

'What are you doing sleeping with all the lights on?' he drawled, staggering over to bed. He threw his keys onto the bedside table and pulled his shoes off, almost toppling over in the process.

I opened my eyes, groggy with crying, sleep and alcohol. 'I was waiting for you. I had made dinner, remember? You promised to be here.'

'Oh, Princess, I'm really sorry. I had a meeting which ran late, and then the client wanted to grab dinner and I could not say no. It was important.'

'And this was important to me, Terry. I told you I had something special planned.'

'We can do something special any night, Princess. This was business.' He sat on the edge of the bed and removed his trousers, loose change tumbling out of his pockets and onto the floor. 'Don't be a pain. I've been out all day busting my balls for the two of us and all you can do is fucking nag.' He lay back on the bed wearing his shirt, underpants, and socks.

'Couldn't you have at least picked up the phone and called?'

'What are you, my bloody mother? Jesus, Fi. Give it a rest. So, what if I was late? I'll make it up to you tomorrow. We can go shopping.' He closed his eyes.

'Well, we will need to go shopping for quite a bit of stuff shortly,' I barked back at him.

'We always seem to need stuff,' Terry muttered, his eyes remaining closed.

'This is different, Terry. The reason I wanted to make this evening special was that I've got something to tell you.' I rolled towards him and placed my arm across his chest.

'Can't it wait until tomorrow? You know normally I'd roger you senseless at any time of day or night, but I'm seriously buggered tonight.'

'No, it can't wait. I've been waiting to tell you all evening and I can't keep it a secret any longer.' I rolled on top of him, and he opened his eyes.

'I'm pregnant, Terry.'

Terry shoved me off him with such force that I almost fell off the bed.

'What the fuck, Fiona? How is that even possible? I thought we had an agreement that this was the wrong time.' He sat up, facing away from me.

'No, you decided that it was the wrong time, not me. And what I believe is that you will never think it was the right time, because you're far too rational about these things. So, I came off the pill without telling you, just to see what happened.'

'And what exactly did you think would happen, you silly cow?' He threw off his socks and his underpants. 'Look, if I want to play Russian roulette with my sperm, that's my business, not yours. You can't trick me into it. It's dishonest, Fiona, and frankly, it's very distressing and disappointing. I've always been completely upfront and honest with you during our marriage, and this is how you repay me? Fuck!'

He threw back the duvet and climbed underneath it, his back facing away from me. I sidled up behind him and stroked his shoulder. "I'm sorry. I thought you'd be pleased. I really want to bring another little Terry into the world.'

He rolled over and faced me. 'This is really not a good time. I'm in the middle of such a massive deal at the moment, and I'm working so hard to try to set us both up for the future. This totally fucks everything up.'

'But it might not, Terry. It might be just what we need.'

'In what way, exactly?'

'I don't know. Think of all of the good things there are about having a baby. Think about all the joy they bring.'

'Joy! They get in the way, they cost money, they stop you sleeping, they wreck your body – yours, that is, not mine. It doesn't sound all that joyous to me.'

I stared at Terry, no longer able to hold back the tears that had been straining hard against the wall of my chest. 'But, Terry, you'll make a great dad.'

'No, I won't, Fiona. At least not right now. Now stop snivelling and go to sleep. We'll talk in the morning about what we do from here.'

'What do you mean?' I wailed.

'I don't like being double-crossed, Fiona.' He rolled away from me and hoicked the duvet up around his neck.

I fled from the bed and collapsed onto the one in the spare room, where I lay awake all night, willing this baby to stick fast, because there was no way I was ever going to let it go now.

Chapter 35

Amanda

I had done my level best to avoid Bill since that strange morning when he had taken me to bed. I organised evening shifts at Sainsburys whenever possible so that I left the house before he arrived home and I could sleep in until he left the next day. I could not begin to understand what had caused such a shift in Bill's behaviour; but whatever had been the catalyst, it seemed to me to be too late for us. Bill had treated me with contempt for so long that I could no longer reconcile myself to this new, alternative version of him. And more pertinently, I had now tasted a different kind of man, someone who had finally granted me permission to feel. In Terry's shadow, Bill was invisible.

But the situation appeared to me to be impossible, and it was making me ill. I could see no way of separating Fiona and Terry now that Fiona was pregnant. I felt permanently lovesick and miserable, still unable to attract Terry's attention for even for a second. I began to lose weight and felt nauseous all the time.

One evening, I was stationed at my till when an unstoppable wave of sickness overtook me, and I was sick in the bin where I sat. Fortunately, there were no customers waiting in line at the time, and even if there had been, they were often so inebriated themselves at that time of night that they might not even have noticed. However, Tracey at the next till did see me.

'You OK, love?' she called over. 'Here, have some of this?' she offered, throwing a bottle of water across to me. I nodded my thanks, unable to speak at that particular moment.

'Are you going to take a test then?'

I choked on the water. 'Excuse me?'

'A pregnancy test. Look, Mandy, I've got four kids and I was as sick as a dog with all of them. I recognise the signs.'

I grabbed the bin and threw up again.

At the end of my shift, I made my way to the pharmacy counter and bought a test. I shuffled off to the staff toilets and peed on the stick, before waiting anxiously for the result. I hid it in my handbag and timed three minutes by the second hand on my watch. When it was up, I retrieved the stick and stared at it for a very long time.

When I arrived home, Bill had mercifully left for the day. Instead of going to bed, I showered quickly and then camped by the front window in the lounge, peeping out of our greying net curtain. As soon as I spotted Terry heading towards his car, I sprinted out of the house and down the drive.

'Terry, hi,' I called, waving frantically.

He kept his head down and did not make eye contact with me. 'Amanda, hi. Look, I'm late for a meeting. Can I catch you later?' He did not wait for me to reply, but jumped into the driver's seat and slammed the door. I grabbed the handle of the passenger door and wrenched it open. 'This will only take a moment, Terry,' I muttered, hopping in before he could stop me.

'We can't talk here, Amanda. Fiona might see us,' he hissed.

'Well, drive round the corner. We need to talk,' I urged him, shocked by my own audacity.

He paled beneath his orange tan. 'OK, but you'd better make it quick. I'm a busy man.' He started the car with a roar and shot off down the next street, parking haphazardly, so that the tail end of the car stuck out into the street.

'What is it?' Terry demanded.

'I'm pregnant.'

'Jesus H Christ. Two of you? This is fucking unbelievable.' He ran his face through his hands.

'Is it?' I commented. 'You didn't wear a condom.'

'I didn't think I needed to, given that I thought you were infertile, or barren, or something.'

I shivered suddenly. 'Excuse me?'

'Well, I thought you couldn't have kids. Fi told me you'd lost a few babies, and now couldn't have any, or something to that effect. I forget exactly what she said.' He gripped the steering wheel with his driving gloves and stared straight ahead out of the windscreen. 'So, what exactly do you want me to do about it?'

'Well, you're the father, so I thought we had better talk about next steps. Obviously, we will have to tell Bill and Fiona. I did what you wanted and persuaded Bill to go ahead with the deal. So now, we need to work something out about how we manage the future.'

I could feel a rising sense of panic gripping my chest. This conversation was not proceeding in the way that I had envisaged.

Terry snorted loudly and looked straight at me with cold, steely eyes. 'We will do nothing of the sort, Amanda. We have no future together. And anyway, it's probably not even mine.'

'Well, I'm convinced it is.'

'And what about your best friend, my wife? Are you prepared to ruin her life as well? No-one has been kinder to you than she has. She's the only person who visited you when you were sick. She's helped you come out the other side and to be a better, more confident person. So much so that you managed to seduce me. I don't begin to understand how you could have encouraged me to sleep with you, as Fiona's husband, never mind betraying your own. Are you really going to destroy both of them and ruin everything?' He removed one of his driving gloves and rubbed his left eye.

'I didn't seduce you. It was the other way around. I thought you liked me. You told me how attractive you found me. I think I love you, Terry.'

'Don't be ridiculous woman. You and I had a fling for half an hour when you came on to me and I was vulnerable. That's not love, it's lust. You slept with me, and I've felt desperately guilty about betraying Fiona ever since. I love Fiona. And that's what I'll tell both of them if you breathe a word of this to either of them. They'll never believe that I came on to a little mouse like you. I strongly suggest that you go back home and re-connect with your own husband and leave me well alone.' He pulled his glove back on and re-started the ignition. 'And I'm warning you that, if you breathe a word of this to anyone, I'll make sure you and that child lose everything.'

It was as though he had slapped me hard across the face, jolting me out of the fantasies that I had been harbouring for the past few weeks. My wonderful daydreams where Terry leaves Fiona and he and I live happily together, making love madly every day and raising a brood of children. Or of Terry setting me up as his mistress. But not this. Never this. Tears stopped my mouth, and I knew if I opened it that I would begin to sob without being able to stop.

'Now get out of my car and go home like a good girl. I suggest that we pretend that none of this ever happened. And don't forget, any mention of this to Fiona or your husband will wreck our deal as well as both our marriages. So, what's your upside? You and Bill would kiss goodbye to any hope of making any money through me. I'm seeing him later on to get everything sorted out. Don't step on my toes, because if you do, I'll blow up your lives.'

Terry leant over and I thought for a brief moment that he was going to kiss me, but he merely grabbed the handle and shoved my door open. I got out, my legs weak and unsteady. He pulled my door shut with a bang and sped away down the street.

Chapter 36

Amanda

I had made an appointment that afternoon at Marie Stopes off Soho Square. I perched on an uncomfortable plastic chair in the waiting room, surrounded by women reading a variety of leaflets on venereal disease, contraception, and abortion. I had been handed one of these leaflets in preparation for my consultation, but I was struggling to read it. The words swam around in front of my eyes, and I was unable to focus on any of the information it contained. Instead, I folded the leaflet into smaller and smaller pieces, scoring them along the edges with my nails before tearing it into squares. Before I realised it, I had reduced the vital facts to a pile of dust.

Someone far off called my name and I jumped. They called again and I rose, following the doctor into her surgery.

'So, Amanda, how can I help you?' the doctor asked me with a gentle smile. She was in her late forties, with a kindly face, etched in wrinkles from too many hours at work.

'I think I'd like to get an abortion, please.' I dug my nails into my hands.

'You think you would?'

'Yes,' I nodded.

'OK. And why do you feel you want this?' she asked, scribbling on her pad.

'I have had miscarriages in the past and I don't want to experience it again.'

'Have you talked this through with your partner and if so, is he supportive of the decision?'

'No, and I don't know.' I stared into my lap.

'OK. Whilst this is your body and your decision, do you feel you should discuss it with him?' The doctor looked directly at me, and I looked at the wall.

I wanted to say to her that I had told him, but he didn't want me, or the baby. I wanted to scream at her that he was not my partner, but that I desperately wanted him to be. And to explain to her that I could not tell my actual husband, because I did not want to be with him. And even if I did stay with Bill, I did not want to raise another man's child as his. I wanted the doctor to understand all of this, but instead I just sat there and sobbed.

'Look, there's no hurry to decide at the moment,' soothed the doctor, passing me a box of tissues. I blew my nose loudly. 'Take this leaflet.' She handed me the same leaflet that I had destroyed in the waiting room. 'Go away, read it and we can answer any questions you might have if you want to come back in. It's best to take your time about this, as there is no going back.'

I nodded, sniffing horribly, and shuffled out of the surgery.

I travelled home on the tube and walked home from Highgate station on autopilot. As I turned into my road, I spotted Terry driving off from his house extremely fast, his Audi roaring like an angry cat as it sped off. Then I saw Fiona, standing barefoot in the middle of the road, screeching obscenities at the smoke trail left behind by his exhaust.

'Fuck you, Terry. You'll come grovelling back one day and when you do, I'll never take you back, you bloody bastard!' She collapsed in a heap in the middle of the road.

I ran towards Fiona and put my arms around her, gently drawing her up and leading her back into her house. The front door was wide open and there was shattered crockery and spilt coffee all over the hall floor. I closed the door and steered her around the debris until we reached the safety of the kitchen. She slumped down into one of the chairs.

'What happened?' I asked her, pulling up another chair so that our knees were almost touching.

'He's left me,' Fiona whispered. 'I had been at the doctor's surgery for a check-up and when I got back, Terry had packed a suitcase and was emptying the safe. He's taken everything – cash, jewellery, the lot. I think he hoped to get away before I got back, but the doctor was running early for a change.' She snuffled loudly and wiped her eyes, smearing mascara across her cheek.

'What did Terry say?' This was my fault. I had put too much pressure on him.

'He said some truly awful things - some unbelievable things. It was like he had suddenly turned into a completely different person.' Fiona stared at me wide-eyed.

'Like what?'

'He told me that he had never loved me. He said that I had trapped him into marriage with my first pregnancy and that that was bad enough, but he was not going to be tricked twice.' Fiona was sobbing so hard that I was struggling to piece together what she was saying.

'Oh, Fiona, I'm sure he didn't mean it. He loves you. He adores you. He told me so himself.' I was crying now, rivulets of water gushing down my face. I reached out to hold her hand.

'When did he tell you that?' she asked, staring up at me with her huge doe eyes.

'Oh, well maybe he told Bill who told me. But it's obvious to anyone who sees you two together.'

'He hates me, Amanda. I can see it now. He liked fucking me, but that was about it. As long as I didn't get in his way, it was fine, but he was furious about the baby. He told me to get an abortion, but I refused and now he's gone.' She lay her head on the table and wept.

'I'm sure he'll be back, Fiona. He just needs some time to cool off.' I hoped as much as she did that Terry would return, although somewhere in the back of my mind I felt uneasy.

'I hope you're right, Amanda, but he seems to have turned into someone I don't even recognise. He spoke to me in a way that he never has before. It was terrifying.'

'Look, why don't you come next door with me? Bill should be back soon, and he might know where Terry is. They are about to close this deal together, so Terry can't be too far away.' I rose from the table and picked up my bag. As I did so, the leaflet on abortion fell to the floor.

Fiona bent down and picked it up. 'What's this?'

'Oh, it's nothing, I…'

'Are you pregnant too?' Fiona squealed.

'Yes,' I whispered, looking down at the floor.

'But Amanda, that's wonderful. Why didn't you tell me?'

I hesitated. 'I don't really know.'

'Well, it's good news, isn't it? So why this?' she queried, waving the leaflet at me.

'Because I'm not sure I can go through with it after all the other times – and because I'm not sure I want to be with Bill anymore.'

'But you've got to try, right? This baby might be the one who makes it through. It might be your miracle. You can't just let it go.' She hugged me tightly. 'Have you told Bill yet?'

'No, not yet. I needed to get my head around it first, and to decide what I want to do.'

'I get it, I really do. Bill has not been kind to you, but if you manage to have the baby, that could change. You've always said it's what he wants.'

And it's what I want too, I thought, *just not with Bill.*

'I'm thinking about it, but please don't say anything to him. Please, Fiona.'

'Of course I won't. It wouldn't be my place to interfere in your marriage.'

No, you are right, I thought to myself. *And it was not my place to meddle in yours either, yet I did.*

'Come on. Let's go and see if Bill knows where Terry is,' I suggested brightly, heading for the door.

Fiona followed behind like a little pet dog as we walked down her drive and back up mine. I opened the front door and called out to Bill, which, had he been home, he would have found odd in itself. However, the house only offered up silence. I walked through to the kitchen and that is when I spotted Bill's note.

'Look, Fiona. He's due to meet Terry for dinner in town. That's where we will find them.'

We grabbed our handbags and coats and ran to Fiona's car. She drove into town like a maniac, jumping lights and cutting up other drivers, with me egging her on. Both of us wanted to get to Terry as soon as possible. Fiona parked on a double yellow line outside the restaurant, and we slammed through the swing door, both of us scouring the room for the men. Then we spotted Bill, sitting forlorn and wilting in the back corner. We raced over, knocking a plate out of a waiter's hand in our haste.

'Sorry,' I apologised, as I carried on past him.

Bill glanced up from his beer as he saw us approaching, looking both surprised and downcast at the same time.

'What are you two doing here? I was expecting Terry. We signed our deal this morning and we were supposed to meet to celebrate over an hour ago.'

'I don't think he's coming,' Fiona and I chorused.

Chapter 37

Fiona

Since that day when he sped off in his car, no one had seen from nor heard from Terry. I called anyone I could think of who might know where he was, but he appeared to have completely disappeared. I visited the wine bars he had frequented, the hotels and the restaurants, but no one had seen him. Bill tried to locate John Travis, the solicitor Terry had used to sign the deal between them, but he did not appear to be listed anywhere, even at The Law Society, and was clearly bogus.

Our problems began to multiply. Bill now realised that, with Terry missing, he knew very little about this deal. Terry held all the information. Demands for payment for the new company, as well as his domestic bills came piling in and he had no ability to pay. Bill missed his mortgage payment for the first time in his life. He felt utterly hopeless.

Amanda appeared utterly distracted and spent almost all of her time with me discussing Terry and all manner of permutations relating to his possible return.

'I wish we knew where Terry was,' Amanda fretted. 'He's left us all alone.'

'Us?' I queried.

'Well, yes,' she responded, looking away from me. 'He's left you all alone, pregnant and penniless. And he's done a runner on Bill and I, hasn't he?'

I made no reply, unable to admit to myself that Terry might never reappear, and we might never be able to recover our losses, both financial and emotional.

One morning a few weeks after his disappearance, I rang Amanda's doorbell insistently. Before I had even crossed their threshold, I began screaming hysterically.

'The house. It turns out that we don't even own it,' I cried. 'It was rented apparently, and Terry hasn't paid the rent for months. He hasn't paid the gas, the electric, the water. In fact, he's paid for absolutely nothing. The credit cards are maxed out and I am being chased for payment by everyone. And what is even more criminal is the fact that he put all of it in my name.' She waved a wad of bills in my face. 'What the bloody hell am I supposed to do?' I burst into tears as both Bill and Amanda stood there helpless.

They ushered me into the kitchen.

'I'll put the kettle on,' Amanda offered, filling it up. 'Sit down and we can try to figure out what to do.'

I flumped down, cradling the slight swell of my belly as I did so. Amanda took the chair next to me and stretched her arms over her head. And she did so, a similar shape showed against her own dress. I glanced up at Bill, but he did not appear to notice.

Chapter 38

Amanda

A week or so later, we were grouped around my kitchen table having yet another powwow.

'So, this is what I've done,' Fiona informed us. 'I've spoken to Citizen's Advice, and they are helping me to contact all the banks and other creditors to tell them that I have been a victim of economic abuse, because apparently, it's illegal for Terry to open all these accounts and cards in my name without my knowledge or my permission. We are attempting to ask the banks and everyone else to write off all the debt, but it will take forever.' I sighed. 'In the meantime, I've decided that I am leaving the house and moving to my parents' place in Wales. They live quite close to Cardiff and Mum reckons I could get a job in one of the hair salons there.'

'Will they give you a job if you're pregnant?' Bill asked.

'Bill! Fiona's going through enough without your discouragement,' I barked.

'It's OK, Amanda. He's right. It could well be a problem, but if it is, I'll try to set up as a mobile hairdresser. Mum says she has a few friends she could introduce me to.'

'And what about the baby?' Bill interjected. 'What will you do when it's born?'

'Jesus, Bill!' I huffed. 'Leave her alone.'

'My mum will help me out and they're portable, aren't they, babies?' Fiona laughed half-heartedly. 'So, what are you two going to do?'

I looked at Bill and he spoke. 'Well, as you know, I've been to see the police about Terry several times now and I've reported him for fraud, but I'm not confident that they will do anything about it. Every time I explain the situation to them, the officers look at me like I'm a total mug and I guess I am.'

Neither Fiona nor I disagreed, but we had all been taken for fools, so we could not blame him. Bill looked completely broken, with dark, pendulous bags hanging down under his eyes, carrying the weight of the world in them.

'I've got another job on a new site. It doesn't pay very well, but at least it's some money coming in. But we are having to sell the house, as I can't afford the payments, even with the small amount Amanda brings in as well from the supermarket.'

'But you'll have to stop work at some stage, won't you, Amanda?' Fiona blurted out, before blushing scarlet and clapping her hand over her mouth.

'Why?' Bill demanded.

'I don't know what you're talking about,' I blustered.

Fiona stared at me hard. 'You're going to have to tell him sooner or later.'

'Tell me what?'

'That I'm pregnant, Bill,' I whispered, staring at the floor.

Bill lowered himself back into his chair in slow motion. 'Say that again.'

'I'm pregnant. I hadn't told you because of everything that's been going on, and because I wanted to wait until I had passed twelve weeks to be sure. You know, because of what's happened before.'

I could see Bill calculating in his head. 'So, it's more like fourteen weeks at the moment then?'

I nodded.

'So, we are out of danger then, are we? Or almost.' Bill did not smile. He just looked defeated. 'How bizarre that you are both pregnant at the same time. It's really weird.'

'Yes, it is, but it's exciting too, Bill, isn't it?' Fiona chirruped. 'And I have a feeling that this time things will stick.'

Yes, because it's not Bill's, I thought, so clearly in my head that for a moment I thought I had spoken it aloud

'But we won't be together when we give birth because Fiona will be in Wales, and we will be somewhere else as well. It's a shame,' I muttered, thinking about the half-siblings who would never know each other. It was probably just as well.

I realised in this moment that I could never tell Bill the truth, and I certainly could never tell Fiona. They had both been double-crossed by Terry, as I had been, but I was not going to twist the knife even further into them both by telling them that I was as much of a liar as Terry.

'We can't let Terry get away with this,' I shouted, suddenly jumping up from the table. 'He has ruined us all, and we need to find him and make him suffer before he does it again to someone else. Because – and I've thought about this a lot – I don't think this can be his first swindle.'

'But we've tried to find him and so have the police – although, truthfully, I don't think they've tried hard at all. He might have changed his name or fled abroad or something. We simply don't know where to start.' Bill sighed heavily.

'Well, there is one way,' Fiona mused. 'I've been racking my brains to think of any trail he might have left behind and actually it was my dad who suggested it. He never liked Terry. He didn't meet him until after we were married, but that didn't stop him telling me that Terry was a flash git. 'All mouth and no trousers' was the exact phrase I think he used. Anyway, Dad said to me, what's the one thing that Terry refuses to be parted from?'

'His bloody Audi!' Bill and I shrieked in unison.

'Exactly, that fucking noisy penis of a car. He thinks we will all roll over and cry ourselves to sleep - but if we find that car, we can find him.'

Chapter 39

Fiona

I was done with feeling sorry for myself. Now I was simply furious for having been so naïve and trusting. I had taken Terry at face value far too easily. I mean, why would I not have? He had seemed to me to be the perfect man, glamorous, rich, clever and besotted with me. I guess I should have thought more carefully before marrying him, but Terry had a way of bamboozling you with his overwhelming charisma.

When I finally stopped crying, however, I began to retrace our steps, and I realised that there was a distinct pattern. Every time we had settled into a place, we had to leave again - and it was always in a hurry. So, Terry – if that was even his real name, which I would not be surprised now if it wasn't – was a serial conman, blinding the world with his incessant schmoozing and utter bullshit. I felt like a total idiot, but I owed it to my unborn child to wreak my revenge. I only hoped that Terry's genes did not prove to be dominant.

The car was the key, as my father had suggested, but I soon found out that you cannot locate someone's whereabouts from a registration number via the DVLA, even if you are married to the bugger. I had drawn a complete blank.

Then the phone rang.

'Hi, Fiona, darling, how are you doing?' It was my mother, who had taken to calling me several times a day since everything happened. She meant well, but it was extremely irritating, especially when nothing had changed from one hour to the next.

'I'm fine, Mum. Can I speak to you later? I'm trying to sort a few things out.'

'Your dad wants a word,' she replied. 'Hold on.'

I never understood why my father could not call me himself. It was always Mum who rang for him and made the introductions.

'Hello, Fiona,' my father intoned in his deep, growly voice. 'I think I might be able to help you to find that bastard of a husband of yours.'

'OK,' I replied, still unhappy to hear my father label Terry as such, even though I knew he was right.

'I've got a contact who might be able to do some digging. He's an ex-policeman who I used to work with before I retired from the insurance company. I've outlined our little problem to him, and he says he's happy to look into it.'

'But won't that be expensive, Dad?' I was too painfully aware that I had no money, and I did not want my parents to be out of pocket, especially when they were about to take in me and the baby.

'It won't cost anything, sweetie. Don't worry about it. He owes me several favours and he's more than happy to help. In fact, I think he's rather excited about the challenge. Can I just check the registration number with you?'

I supplied the number of the Audi and listened while Dad scribbled it down at the other end of the phone.

'How's it going with the banks and everything?' he asked.

'Slowly,' I replied, 'but I have made all the relevant calls and sent the letters out, so now I'll just have to wait for them to reply. Hopefully, it won't take too long.' I wound the telephone cord round and round my hand until it almost stopped my circulation.

'Well done, love. Now, you take care of yourself, and I'll call if I get any good news.'

'Thanks, Dad,' I whispered, suddenly feeling phenomenally weary. I replaced the receiver on its cradle and went upstairs to have a lie down.

Chapter 40

Amanda

So, Bill now knew that I was pregnant, and we were having a baby, or potentially having a baby. I had lost all the others before they reached twelve weeks, so maybe this time it would be different, given the genes.

Bill was clearly excited, but equally, this was the worst possible time to have a baby. We had no money. In fact, we were mired so deeply in debt that it would take the rest of our lives to recover, if we ever did at all. It was going to be a terrible struggle. But maybe, just maybe, this was meant to be. It was fated if you like. Perhaps we had to suffer like this in order to be happy again, and this child would bring us together as the product of the two of us as individuals, combining the best of both of us. We had certainly spoken to each other more civilly and more often since Terry absconded than we had in a long time. And fundamentally, Bill was a good person.

Fiona rang hard on the bell. I sometimes thought that she may as well move in given how often she came over here since Terry left her. When I opened the front door, she was beaming, which was unusual.

'Hi, Amanda. I've got good news. Is Bill in?'

'Yes, he's upstairs.'

'Call him down. It's important,' she insisted, bustling into the kitchen, and putting the kettle on.

I huffed, but went upstairs anyway and found Bill shuffling papers in the spare room, looking worn out and defeated.

'Fiona's here. She says it can't wait,' I told him.

'I'll be right down,' he replied to the ceiling.

When I returned to the kitchen, Fiona had made a pot of tea and was busy pouring it into three mugs. Bill appeared at the door and mooched over to a chair. I sat down next to him, and Fiona remained standing, nursing her tea.

'Well?' I said, 'what's the big news that can't wait?'

Fiona took a sip of tea. 'Ouch, that's hot. I've burnt my tongue.'

'Fiona,' Amanda moaned. 'Get on with it.'

'I know where Terry is,' Fiona exclaimed, joining us at the table.

'Where? How?' Bill and I asked in unison.

'You remember that mate of my father's that I told you about. Well, he traced the car to Bristol. Don't ask me how he did it because I really don't know, but anyway, he says Terry is staying at a hotel in the city centre. I've got all the details written down.'

Bill and I were both silent for a moment.

'So, what do you think we should do?' Bill questioned. 'I guess we could call the police and let them deal with it.'

I shook my head. 'No, I don't think that's the way forward here at all. Terry will find a way to get away from the police by denying everything. Or bribing them even. He's far too slippery.'

'So, what do you suggest?' Bill responded.

It was Fiona who replied. 'I think that the three of us should go to Bristol and confront him together. He's wronged all of us. If we go together, he can't deny any of it and we will have him cornered.'

'And what do you suggest we do when we accost him, Fiona?' Bill quipped. 'Make a citizen's arrest?'

'No, but we can demand our money back in return for not shopping him to the police. Terry is nothing if not pragmatic. He won't want to get nicked.'

'I'm not sure about all of this,' I mumbled. 'It could get ugly.'

'It's already ugly, Amanda. How much worse can it get?' Fiona questioned.

I looked down at my feet and I thought I was about to burst into tears. Hormones, I was guessing.

'Right. I suggest we go tomorrow before he buggers off again. Bill, you can drive. We leave at eight.'

And with that, Fiona drained her tea, got up and left.

Chapter 41

Fiona

The three of us arrived in Bristol late morning on the following day in Bill's car. Amanda sat upfront and I was in the back, which made me feel a little car sick, so I was glad when we finally arrived and I could breathe in some fresh air. We had booked two rooms in a bed and breakfast in Clifton, which turned out to be where all the students lived. It was a beautiful, leafy part of town. The B&B itself, however, was not so attractive. It was more than somewhat run down, with elderly paint peeling from the front door and wallpaper edges inside hanging from the corners, limp and tired. The bedrooms themselves were extremely basic, with beds barely lined with paper-thin covers. The towels in the communal bathroom were threadbare and holed. But what else could we expect, given that we were effectively penniless.

Terry, by contrast, was residing in the top luxury hotel in the centre of Bristol, with its highly polished marbled lobby that you could skate on and liveried staff to cater for your every whim. Dad's friend had confirmed that he had taken the penthouse suite there, presumably and rather gallingly paid for with Bill's money. Once we had checked into the B&B and had been provided with a key to let ourselves back in after the ten o'clock curfew imposed by the landlady, we headed out towards the hotel, leaving the car there and travelling on foot. There was a bar opposite the hotel, where we managed to nab a table by the window and the three of us sat there nursing two lemonades for two pregnant ladies and a beer for Bill. We barely spoke to one another, partly from exhaustion, but mostly because we were keen to keep our eyes peeled for any sign of Terry, as it would be a tragedy to come all this way and miss him.

'We are a cracked surveillance team,' I quipped. The others did not laugh.

The time turned just past midnight and the bar was closing in half an hour.

'I think we should call it a night,' I suggested to the others, stretching my arms over my head and letting out a strenuous yawn. 'I'm not sure he's going to show up tonight. He might already be in the hotel tucked up in bed, although knowing Terry like I do, that sounds unlikely.'

Amanda made no reply, merely fiddling with the straw in her glass. She had been extremely quiet ever since I suggested that we come to find Terry. I assumed that she was feeling tired due to the pregnancy, and maybe also that she did not feel as vitriolic towards Terry as Bill and I did, given that he had not crossed her directly.

Bill peered into the bottom of his empty pint as if it was a crystal ball that would provide the answer as to whether we stayed or went home. 'We may never see him, Fiona. He may not even be here at all. We've only got your dad's friend's word for it, and he might well be wrong.'

'Well, Dad said that this guy knew what he was doing, and I wouldn't have suggested we come all this way if I didn't think he had found him. Don't be so negative all the time, Bill.' I pouted. I found Bill quite difficult at times, and thought that it was unfair that I was already being blamed for dragging everyone to Bristol and failing to find Terry when I was only trying to do my best.

'Listen,' Amanda said, suddenly turning her head. 'Can you hear that?'

We all perked up our ears and, at that moment, Terry's car raced into view, skidding to a sudden halt outside the entrance to the hotel. The driver's door was opened immediately by the doorman and suddenly there he was, Terry, resplendent in a mauve silk shirt open to the waist and a pair of extremely tight trousers. Terry skipped around to the passenger door and pulled the handle. A statuesque blonde, taller than Terry in her sky-scraping heels, was manoeuvred out of the car, Terry wrapping his arm tightly around her waist and leading her through into the foyer. They were laughing together at some shared joke, or probably some inappropriate sexual innuendo knowing Terry. As they entered the reception, he stopped and kissed her ostentatiously in the centre of the lobby, before grabbing her left buttock to steer her towards the bar.

I thought I was about to throw up. I had considered how I might feel when I saw Terry again, but I certainly had not contemplated that he might be with another woman. He really had lost no time in moving on.

'What an utter git.'

Amanda nodded and gripped the Formica tabletop.

'We should go over there straight away,' Bill declared, standing up from the table.

'I, well, what, now?' Amanda asked alarmed.

'Yes, now, Mand. We came here to confront the bastard. You two can stay here if you like, but I'm going in.'

I had never seen Bill like this before. He seemed incensed, but in a powerful way. I had a sudden vision of him and Terry butting heads like a pair of antelope in some wildlife documentary. Amanda, on the other hand, was whiter than the walls.

'Are you OK?' I whispered, rubbing her arm.

She nodded, but made no reply.

'Right, I'm going over there before he disappears up to his room with that floozy,' Bill announced, before throwing a few quid onto the table and striding across the road to the hotel.

I glanced at Amanda and held out my hand. 'You coming?'

She nodded and together we waddled after Bill to the hotel, traipsing through the lobby and into the bar. Terry and his lady friend were mauling each other in a velvet booth in the corner, and as a result of his distraction, he failed to spot us until we were right in front of him.

'Hello, Terry,' Bill announced, clearing his throat.

Terry turned his head and jumped slightly.

'Ah well if it's not the three musketeers. Bill, hello. What brings you here? And ladies, how lovely to see you. You're both thriving, I see.' Terry turned to the girl. 'Listen, Princess.'

Princess.

'I just need to have a little chat with my friends here. You order yourself some more champagne, and I'll be back before you know it.'

The girl pouted.

'Seriously, I won't be long,' Terry reassured her. He slipped out of the booth. 'Let's chat in my room,' he suggested, clearly eager to avoid a scene in the bar.

'Not a problem for us,' Bill replied.

Terry strode across the lobby to the lift, taking out his controlled anger on the button, which he jabbed incessantly until it arrived. Once we were all inside, he smashed the button to the top floor.

'What the fuck are you all doing here?' he hissed, even though we were completely alone in the lift.

'I would have thought that was bloody obvious, Terry,' I screeched in reply, somewhat louder than I had intended, my voice emerging high-pitched and strangulated. 'You can't just fuck off and leave me pregnant and in debt with no warning, nothing. I mean, what the fuck, Terry?'

Terry smiled and I wanted to hit him hard in the balls, but at that moment, the doors opened, and an elderly couple got in.

'Good evening,' they greeted us. 'Have you all had an enjoyable evening?'

We nodded in unison, and then there followed an uncomfortable silence until they exited a few floors up. After they left, we continued up without speaking until we reached the penthouse floor. Terry led the way out of the lift and opened up the door to his room. There was a vast atrium with a bizarre stainless-steel sculpture that consisted of spikes of various lengths and extended across most of the floor. To the left was a narrow, ornamental spiral staircase with those gaps that I hated because they always made me feel dizzy. Terry sprinted up the staircase, making it judder rather alarmingly as we followed in his wake. At the top was the suite, which was spectacular, with a panoramic view over the harbour through floor-to-glass doors which led from the living room onto the enormous terrace. There were a couple of other doors off the main room, which presumably led to some playboy-type bedroom and bathroom. It appeared bigger than our entire house.

'Drink?' Terry offered, moving over to the dresser below the television without making eye contact.

'This isn't a social call, Terry,' Bill replied.

'I didn't think it was, Bill. I'm only trying to be hospitable, which is decent of me given that you've all turned up unannounced. Look, let's just calm down, shall we and see if we can't work things out, OK?' Terry suggested, gesturing for us to sit down on the capacious sofa. We all stayed standing except for Amanda, who slumped down, disappearing into the deep cushions. Terry opened the concealed minibar and removed three miniatures of whisky, which he proceeded to pour into a glass and down in one gulp.

'Well, Terry, seriously what the fuck? If you think you can just walk out on me, leaving me in such deep shit, then you're crazier than I think you are. Not only have you left me and your unborn child to fend for ourselves, but you've left me up to my neck in debt for everything and never even told me about any of it. You're a total liar. How could you do that to me? I thought you loved me,' I cried, my lower lip wobbling dangerously. I had promised myself that I would not get emotional, but I could feel a tsunami rising, which was about to engulf me.

Terry made no reply, merely staring straight past me onto the terrace.

'Have you nothing at all to say to me?'

He turned to face me. 'OK, Fiona, this is why I left you. You tricked me into having a baby. For all I know, you've actually done it twice - once so that I'd marry you and now again, for reasons I can't quite fathom, but probably because you're a spoiled, little cow who just wants everything on her own terms. So, if you want to talk about dishonesty, I think you should examine your own conscience before you start criticising me. And as for the debt, if you hadn't gone out every day and shopped like you were fucking Ivana Trump, we wouldn't be in this bloody mess. Quite frankly, you've only got yourself to blame.'

'But Terry, you put it everything in my name. All the bills, the rent – and I thought we owned the house – the credit cards, everything. You know that that's illegal without my consent. And it was you who told me to go out and buy stuff. You positively encouraged me.'

'Only to get you off my back, Princess. I mean, you were a decent shag and all that, but otherwise, you're not the greatest intellect, are you? You're just a provincial hairdresser who I plucked from obscurity and gave a decent life to for a few years. You should appreciate the time we had together and move on.' He ambled back to the minibar and hauled out a bottle of wine. He unscrewed the cap and started drinking directly from the bottle.

I sank to my knees on the floor, fatally wounded by his sadistic cruelty.

'Terry,' Bill began, 'you are a reprehensible human being.'

'Oh, listen to the clever man with his big words,' Terry mocked.

'Fuck you, Terry. If you really think you can rob me of everything I own and just disappear in a puff of smoke, I can tell you categorically that that's not going to happen. I want my money back.' Bill was puce and pumped up. I realised what a strong guy he was physically. It was just well-hidden by his flab.

'Now, Bill, mate, listen, I never robbed you. The deal just did not come off, that's all. I always told you it was a risk. The investment fell through, and it's going to take me a while to sort things out. I'll try to get some of the money back for you. I'll get as much as I can for you, obviously, but I just can't promise. My solicitor is working on it.'

'You must think that I'm a bloody idiot. That solicitor guy doesn't even exist. He was a plant,' Bill yelled. 'And as for the deal falling through, you left the minute I'd signed the papers, so it can't have been a very robust deal. In fact, it never existed at all, did it, Terry?'

Terry laughed. 'You've been watching far too many detective stories, Bill.'

Bill let out a huge roar and marched over to Terry, grabbing him by his silk shirt, which tore easily with a satisfying rip.

'Don't talk to me like I'm stupid, Terry,' Bill spat in his face.

'But you are fucking stupid, Bill. Not only did you risk everything you had on what was always a highly speculative investment, but I was also able to seduce your wife, and impregnate her right under your nose. And what's more, this time it seems to have stuck. I reckon it was the first time she'd ever been rogered good and proper. And what's more, I can tell you that she really enjoyed it. I know that because she kept hounding me afterwards to give her more. She begged me to leave Fiona and shack up with her. Not that that was ever going to happen. I mean, look at her,' Terry cackled.

Bill loosened his hold on Terry and both he and I turned our stares to Amanda.

'Is this true, Mandy?' Bill whispered.

Amanda nodded, tears cascading down her face.

'How could you?' I choked. 'I thought we were friends.'

'So, the baby isn't mine?' Bill asked.

Amanda shook her head.

Bill emitted an animal howl, raw and raucous.

'See, I rest my case. You're all fuckwits, all three of you.' Terry smiled. 'So, I don't care. Go to the police and tell them everything, but I will also tell them absolutely everything, warts and all, and see how it all turns out. They wouldn't trust anything any of us said, given that they'll assume it's some menage a trois gone wrong. I wish you all the very best of luck.' He turned, lighting up a cigarette. He stood with his back to us, smoke curling into the air.

I stayed on my knees, fossilised by Terry. Bill remained where he was, stunned. For a few moments, there was complete silence and then, without warning, Amanda jumped off the sofa and ran towards Terry. She moved so quickly that he did not hear her. She shoved him in the back and Terry swayed backwards, steadying himself on the banister of the staircase. For a moment, I thought he might topple over, but he recovered himself and grabbed Amanda, shoving her hard onto the floor.

'Get the fuck away from me, you crazy bitch,' Terry yelled.

Amanda screamed as she landed.

'Are you alright, Amanda?' I called from the lounge.

'I think my arm might be broken.' She winced and cradled her elbow, which did appear to be jutting out at an odd angle.

I began to get up from the floor to tend to Amanda, but before I could do so, Bill rushed Terry, charging at him as if possessed. He hit Terry hard in the middle of his chest and Terry staggered backwards, before recovering to swing his fist at Bill. He landed a hard punch onto Bill's nose, which began to bleed profusely down his shirt. Bill did not even hesitate before punching Terry in return in the centre of his sternum.

Amanda cowered where she had fallen, just next to where the two men were fighting. Bill pounded Terry and Terry swiped back at him, grabbing Bill in a headlock. Bill elbowed Terry in the stomach, so that he loosened his grip momentarily, before pushing Bill against the edge of the banister of the spiral staircase. Terry grabbed Bill's shoulders to steady himself. Suddenly, there a sharp crack like a lightning bolt, and the flimsy banister gave way. Locked in their pugilistic embrace, Terry and Bill stopped and glanced at each other for a brief moment, their eyes wonderous like lovers, before they both fell together down onto the sharp spikes of the sculpture below. There were no cries of pain, just dull thuds as they landed on the skewers.

I thought that I pierced the air with a shriek, yet no sound emerged from my mouth. Slowly, I edged towards the top of the edge of the staircase and peered down, and then turned back at Amanda and screamed.

Part Three

2012

Jack and Clare

Chapter 42

Jack

I knew that she was the girl for me from the very first moment we met. I know people make such idiotic statements all the time, and believe me, before I met Clare, I would have agreed that they were stupid. But she was something else.

Our meeting was totally random. One afternoon, there was a ring on the door of the flat I shared with two other guys from university. We lived on the Lower Bristol Road in the Twerton area of Bath in a rather shabby terraced house; but frankly shabby suited us well. We were students, so a less than pristine house was perfect given that we were never going to look after it. Bob and I were reasonably tidy, in that we occasionally emptied the bin and used the toilet brush, but Freddie was far more of a troglodyte and general hygiene tended to be low-to-non-existent on his list of priorities. Despite this, we rubbed along very well together. We had first met when we were placed on the same floor in our first-year accommodation. It was extremely lucky that we gelled immediately, when so many other people had corridor mates who were diametrically opposite to themselves, and who, as a result, found it far harder to settle into university life. Bob, Freddie, and I immediately discovered a communal love of football, darts, drinking and unattainable women. From then on, we were inseparable, choosing to share together in our second year in university accommodation and then renting a house in our third year off-campus.

None of us had been very successful with women, and it was definitely not for lack of trying. Bob always fell for the most beautiful girl in the room, which usually meant that she either already had a boyfriend, or if not, men swarmed around her like flies on an open beer bottle. Such girls never picked Bob out of the crowd. He was one of the most genuine blokes you could ever wish to meet, and I think for women, that was his downfall. He was just far too nice. With his brown curly hair, freckled face and shortage of height, they all wanted to be his best friend which, as you can imagine, was extremely frustrating for him.

Freddie, conversely, was six-foot-six and pipe-cleaner thin. When he sat, he folded himself into chairs in order for them to accommodate his length. He sported a scrubby blond beard, and his hair was straggly as though it had never been introduced to a brush. When at home in our flat he wore nothing except his underpants, because despite his leanness and the fact that the house was usually freezing cold, he was always overheating. His body lacked any form of muscle tone whatsoever, yet he wandered around flexing and admiring himself in the bathroom mirror, or in fact in any shiny surface available, be it a window or a cupboard door. Freddie had to lean down to speak to anyone so that they could hear him and so that he could be heard - hence he had a permanent stoop like an old man in a young person's body. He said that his perfect woman was a taller, bigger version of Beyoncé. Funnily enough, he had not located her yet.

I had had my dalliances during my time in Bath. It sounds boastful to say it, but women did tend to find me attractive. I was just a little over six foot with thick, wavy blondish hair and a muscular physique despite never entering the gym. My mother told me that I looked just like my father, whom I never knew, because he left my mother when she was pregnant. I had never even seen a photo of him because she was so angry that she could never bear to look at him ever again, so she destroyed all their pictures and albums. It seemed a terrible shame to me, as I would like to have known what he looked like, even if he was a bit of a shit to my mother. I myself had never met anyone who kept my attention for very long. I tried not to upset girls I went out with when I finished with them, but my problem was that I did get bored rather easily. Bob and Freddie reckoned that I had a phobia of commitment. I just thought that I had not met the right woman yet.

So anyway, I was in the flat one afternoon on my own, desperately trying to write an economics essay - which was late as usual and for which I had neither attended the lectures nor read the required material - when the doorbell rang. Quite often, I ignored the bell because I simply could not be bothered to move to answer it, but on this occasion I was desperately in need of a distraction. I sauntered downstairs to the front door we shared with another flat and flung it open, expecting it to be a delivery. Couriers to our flat were frequent, either from one of our mothers who sent food and clothing parcels on a regular basis as some form of parental fourth emergency service, or more often than not, take outs because we could never be bothered to cook and when we did, the results were generally inedible. However, this time it was neither. It was a girl.

'Hello.' She smiled, squinting at a small piece of paper in her hand. 'Is Ruby in?'

'Ruby? No, I'm afraid she's not.'

'Do you know when she might be back?' the girl asked, looking slightly disappointed.

'No, I'm afraid I don't.'

'Do you think you could give her a message?'

'No, I don't believe I can.'

'Oh, right. Well, thanks for your help – not,' she huffed, turning to go.

'Wait,' I called to her, 'the actual reason I can't give her a message is that no one called Ruby actually lives here.'

'Oh, right. I see.' She unfurled the piece of paper in her hand and re-read it. 'That's odd. I thought this was her address.'

'Let me see.' I took the paper from her. 'Well, this *is* our address. Maybe there is a digit missing or something. It is a very long road.' I handed it back again.

'Maybe you're right. Never mind.' She flashed a gap-toothed smile. She was not my usual type at all, but there was something in that smile that stopped me.

'Look, it's a shame for you to come all this way for nothing and I need a break from not writing my urgent essay, so would you like to come up for a cup of tea?' I asked her.

The girl hesitated.

'Oh, come on. I'm totally harmless. The worst thing that will happen to you is that you will have to drink your tea black because our milk will be off.'

'Alright then, thank you. I'd love a drink.' She followed me inside the front door and closed it behind her. 'I'm Clare, by the way.'

'And I'm Jack.'

Chapter 43

Clare

Ruby had offered to lend me a book that I needed for my coursework. I did not know her all that well, but she was in the same seminar group as me. I had been moaning to another friend that I could not find a copy of this critical book in the library, as everyone else had beaten me to it, and now I was stymied, as I could not afford to buy one. Some of the textbooks were so expensive that you needed to take out a mortgage to afford one. Ruby overheard and very kindly said she had a copy of her own that she was not using, so I could borrow it. That's how I found myself on the Lower Bristol Road at the wrong address.

To be fair, my handwriting was atrocious, and I could not read it myself most of the time, which meant that other people had no hope. I was sure this was the right flat, but then a boy answered the door and informed me that Ruby did not live there. I was annoyed about the book, obviously, but this guy was easily the most handsome person I had ever seen, so it was not exactly a wasted trip. He had thick, blond hair and the most amazing physique. I had seen him around campus quite a few times, but I doubt that he had ever noticed me.

But despite this, when I was right in front of him on the doorstep, he invited me in for a cup of tea and, even more remarkably, I agreed. I was normally quite shy and nervous around men. I suppose some of that might have stemmed from growing up without a father, and also from being raised by a mother who seemed to take an extremely dim view of the male sex in general. *What you must remember Clare is that all men are obsessed with one thing. They cheat and they lie to get it. And afterwards they bear no responsibility for any resulting emotional chaos they create.*

'Was Dad like that?' I asked her once, staring over at a faded framed photograph of my parents outside the registry office where they got married.

'Your father?' she paused and glanced at the same photo. 'No, not really. He was different – difficult, but in other ways.'

'So why do you generalise about all men then if Dad wasn't like that?'

'I've got too much to do, Clare, and no time to be talking to you about this,' she replied, bustling about the kitchen, and running the tap in the sink.

'But.'

'Look, Clare, just be careful, alright?' she barked, banging the crockery in the sink so hard that I was surprised it did not crack.

Anyway, Jack invited me in. Now, if I said that his flat was untidy, I would be understating its condition by some distance. At the entrance to the flat there must have been two dozen pairs of shoes, piled randomly as if they were waiting to go to a jumble sale.

'Sorry about all the shoes,' Jack commented, as we stepped over them. 'We tend to leave them there for convenience when we go out.'

'Doesn't it take you more time to locate which are ones your own?'

'It can do, but if we are in a real hurry, we just wear each other's.'

'So, you all wear the same sized shoes, do you?'

'No, not even close,' Jack laughed.

As I entered the kitchen I reeled backwards. It reeked of rotten food, yet Jack did not appear to notice anything. The odour appeared to emanate from the various black bin bags lurking around the actual bin, so I stood as far away from them as possible.

'Tea or coffee?' Jack began to rummage in the sink. It was piled high with dirty pans and plates. 'I think we need to do some washing up,' he quipped, hauling up a couple of mugs from the depths of the pile and rinsing them fleetingly under the tap.

'Coffee, please,' I responded, thinking that coffee had a stronger smell than tea, which might be helpful under the circumstances.

'Did someone say coffee?' a disembodied voice called out.

'Did you want a cup then, Freddie?' Jack shouted in reply.

'If you're making, yes please.'

At that moment, the tallest, thinnest man I had ever seen, wearing nothing but a pair of tatty, grey boxer shorts, entered the kitchen. 'Oh, I'm sorry Jack, I didn't realise you had company,' he commented, walking straight over to me. He took my hand and kissed it. 'Enchante, madame. I'm Freddie, and you must be?'

'Clare,' I stuttered.

'Clare. Such beautiful name for such gorgeous girl. Tell me, Clare, do you have a boyfriend currently?'

'Freddie, leave her alone,' Jack told him. 'Clare was just looking for a friend of hers and had the wrong address. I'm only offering her a drink.'

'And was this friend a boy?' Freddie enquired, bending down towards me so that I could get a better look at his straggly beard.

'Freddie, go away,' Jack laughed, handing him a mug of coffee.

'I can tell when I'm not wanted!' Freddie smiled, taking the coffee and turning to head out of the kitchen, revealing a large ladder running down the back of his sagging boxer shorts.

'Ignore him, he's completely harmless,' Jack said, handing me a mug.

'He seems very.'

'Eccentric, weird, tall, thin.'

'Yes, all of those things,' I giggled.

'So, Clare, tell me, what did you want with this imaginary Ruby girl anyway?'

'She was going to lend me a book for my coursework.'

'Anything interesting?'

'Not especially, unless you are fascinated by the historical factors that have necessitated crime in the twenty-first century.'

'That sounds a lot more interesting than Economics. I'm guessing you study Law or Criminology.'

'The latter, yes. It's quite an interesting course actually, but like everything else, it has its tedious parts. Don't you like Economics?'

'I do quite enjoy it, but the Maths bit gets me down at times. It can be very complicated. I'm far more interested in the theory.'

'I get that. I'm hopeless at Maths, but I don't really need to use it except for stats occasionally.'

'So where do you live?' Jack asked, sitting down at the kitchen table. I removed a wet T-towel and sat on the chair opposite him.

'Here or at home?'

'Both.'

'Here I'm still on campus and home is London. You?' I sipped my coffee.

'Wales, just outside Cardiff.'

'You don't sound very Welsh.'

'Well, my Mum's English and so are my grandparents, so maybe that's why. Some people say they can hear a slight lilt from the valleys, you know.'

'Maybe just a little.' I smiled at him, and he grinned back. I blushed and stared into my mug.

'So, Clare, in answer to Freddie's earlier question, are you going out with anyone?'

I shook my head, my cheeks burning.

'So, how about a drink out later?'

I knew I should say that I was busy that night and maybe suggest another day, just so that I did not appear to be overly keen, but this was too unbelievable, and I could not help myself.

'Yes, that would be lovely,' I murmured.

And it was.

Chapter 44

Jack

Clare and I met up that evening in a student bar on Second Bridge in the centre of Bath. It was immensely crowded and loud with incessant, nondescript music droning on in the background. We spent an hour yelling at each other over the din, before deciding to retreat to the local pizzeria for something to eat and some hope of conversation at a lower decibel. I thought she was extremely cute. I liked her cheeky smile and there was less glamour to her than many of the girls I hooked up with, who tended to be all spidery eyelashes and full lips. Clare was natural both in looks and in personality and it made such a refreshing change. I did not feel I had to impress her, yet I found myself willing her to like me. We chatted with ease.

'So, what do you want to do when you leave Bath?' Clare enquired, biting down on a floppy piece of pizza, the end of which appeared to elude her mouth for a moment.

'I'm not sure, to be honest. I think I'll worry about that once I've managed to get my degree. The application processes are so involved that I think they will be a full-time job in themselves.' I glugged down the end of my beer. 'I might just apply for a load of different graduate schemes once I leave here and see if I get anywhere, just to give myself more of a clue about what I really want to do. What about you?'

'Same really. Joining the police is a natural fit with my degree, but it doesn't really appeal to me. I don't think I'm tough enough. Or I might think about becoming a paralegal, as I really enjoy the law elements of the course. Like you, I need to concentrate on my finals first, but I can't leave it too long to get a job, as I'll need to earn money straight away, even if I just do temp work. I can't ask Mum to help me out anymore. She's done more than enough.'

'What about your dad? Are they still together?' I stared into my empty glass. 'Sorry, maybe I shouldn't ask. It's a really personal question.'

'That's OK.' Clare smiled, a small dimple appearing in the middle of her left cheek as she did so. 'I never knew my dad because he died in an accident before I was born.'

'Oh, Christ, Clare, I'm so sorry. What kind of accident?'

'It was totally freak apparently. He fell from a great height on a construction site where he was working. I don't know much more about it than that because my Mum doesn't like to discuss it, and I don't like to press her. It was clearly extremely traumatic for her.' She fiddled with a silver ring on her index finger.

'That's dreadful, Clare. Did your mother receive any form of compensation or anything?'

'I don't know, but I don't think so. If she did, it can't have amounted to much, as Mum has always had to work at least two jobs just to keep us both going.'

'What does she do?'

'She worked in all sorts of places – shops, restaurants, supermarkets. She thought about being a taxi driver for a while, but she can't drive, so that was a bit of handicap!' She sipped her drink. 'What about your mum and dad?'

'Well, like you, I grew up without a dad, but he's not dead, or at least, I don't think he is. I've genuinely no idea. Apparently, he just upped and left my mother when she was pregnant with me and has never been heard of since.'

'Have you ever tried to trace him? Sorry, it's the criminologist in me coming out.'

'I've asked Mum for details as I have thought about it, but she won't tell me anything about him. I don't even have his surname, as I carry her name, and she won't tell me what his was. She says he's almost certainly either in jail or dead and she says that she doesn't care which.' I paused. 'Would you like another drink?'

Clare nodded and I waved to the waiter to order another round.

'That must be hard for you – not knowing anything about him,' Clare sympathised.

'Yes, I guess so, but he obviously hurt my mum terribly and I need to respect her desire not to talk about him. But sometimes I see her looking at me and I know I must remind her of him, even if she never admits it. And I wonder if me looking like him pains her.' I felt choked suddenly and coughed to cover it up.

'I'm sure she loves you very much,' Clare soothed. 'It's weird though, isn't it?'

'What is?'

'How we've both grown up without fathers. It's not that common.'

'I guess not,' I mused. 'But I've never known anything else.'

'Has your mum never wanted to remarry?'

I rolled my eyes. 'She's never even wanted to go out with another man, never mind remarry. My father clearly put her off men for life!'

'How odd,' Clare muttered. 'That's exactly what my mum says.'

Chapter 45

Clare

Jack and I quickly became inseparable. I found it so easy to be in his company, as if we had known each other our entire lives. Yet, whenever I was with him, I felt like pinching myself to check that I was not in the middle of a wonderful dream, as I found it difficult to believe that someone as handsome, athletic, and popular as him would have anything to do with me. When we were out together, I felt more confident, even if other girls did give me the onceover - as if to ask how the hell I had managed to hook a guy like him. When we were alone together, he was funny, kind, and considerate. I decided that I must have done something extraordinary in a previous life – and Jack was my reward.

We did not sleep together straight away. Jack put me under no pressure, and I was nervous of spoiling things. I was worried that, when he discovered how disappointing my body was and my inexperience when it came to what to do with what, he would finish with me. He must have bedded so many girls, I reasoned. But after a while, when we had kissed and cuddled, but had not ventured further for several congenial dates, I began to panic that he did not fancy me at all and that he just wanted to be friends.

'Maybe he bats for the other side,' Katy quipped.

"I really don't think so, Katy!'

'No, neither do I actually. Well, I think in that case, you need to make a proper effort to seduce him.' Katy had been my best friend at Bath ever since we had met in halls in the first week of our first year and now we shared a flat together. She was stunning, statuesque with fabulous strawberry-blonde hair that fell in natural waves to the base of her back. Men fell over themselves trying to date her, so she could afford to be picky, and I doubt whether she had ever had to work at seduction.

'That's easy for you to say,' I moaned over a hot chocolate in our local coffee shop. 'You have men fighting over you. I've only ever been out with a couple of losers and sex was perfunctory at best. I have no idea how to seduce anyone.'

'Don't be ridiculous, Clare. And have some self-respect. You are gorgeous and don't you ever forget it,' Katy insisted, flicking her hair. 'Now, what you need to do is invite him over for dinner at our place. I'll make myself scarce for the evening. You can cook a pasta or something. Keep it simple, but avoid sauces like vongole or arrabiata, or anything too spicy, which might lead to burping or worse later on. Buy a gooey chocolate cake from Tesco's. At worst, you can eat it for dessert, and at best, he can lick it off you.' She cackled.

'Funny,' I replied, stony-faced.

'Buy a couple of bottles of wine to make sure you've got plenty to drink,' she counselled.

'Are you suggesting that I have to get him drunk in order to get him interested?'

'Not at all, but it will loosen things up – especially you! Look, Jack's a decent guy and maybe you're simply giving off the wrong vibe. Let's face it, you're super under-confident and you've told me a thousand times about your fear of him seeing you naked because you think he will flee in utter disgust, or some such idiocy. Maybe, just maybe, that's putting him off. Maybe, just maybe, if you took off your over-sized sweat top which you think hides your bum but actually makes it look bigger and put on a nice shirt or, God forbid, a dress, maybe, just maybe, he might get your come-hither message.' She smiled and drained her cocoa.

'Tell it like it is, why don't you,' I mumbled into my mug.

'Look, Clare, it might sound harsh, but you know I'm right. You're willing him to make love to you while warding him off at the same time. The poor chap is probably mightily confused.'

'Hmm, maybe.'.

'Another alternative – if it's more palatable to you – is we invite Jack and his two flatmates over and we find another girl to invite as well to even things up and then we can support you from the side lines.'

'Have you met his flatmates?' I asked Katy, frowning.

'No, but I'm sure they're fine if Jack likes them.' She continued with dogged determination to outline her plan. 'Then, when dinner is finished, I'll drag everyone else out, and you and Jack can stay behind to, you know. But I still insist on the removal of your sweat top prior to their arrival if this idea is to have any chance of working.'

'Alright, I agree,' I laughed.

'Good,' Katy replied, 'because if you don't shag Jack soon, I'll be forced to do it for you!'

Jack arrived three nights later with Bob and Freddie in tow. Katy and I invited Hannah, another friend of ours from Belfast who was always up for a meal and a laugh. Hannah was the first to arrive, a bottle of cheap plonk stuffed into her bag. She banged it onto the kitchen worktop and began to unscrew the lid before she had even taken her coat off. 'Right, Ladies, let's have a glass before the fellas get here,' she instructed, removing three tumblers from my carefully laid kitchen table.

'Hannah, can you use some other glasses?' I whined. 'I've just finished setting the table.'

'I didn't realise it was such a posh affair, Clare. And can I tell you that I've never met a bloke who slept with me because of my perfect table arrangements. You might be barking up the wrong tree there.'

Katy snorted.

'Christ, can you both stop it? The boys are coming for dinner - which was Katy's idea, by the way, not mine - and under no circumstances can they think I have any kind of ulterior motive. OK?'

'OK,' Katy replied, 'but you are wearing a layer less than usual, so you are already screaming "take me, take me!" Katy guffawed.

'Highly amusing, Katy,' I smirked.

The doorbell rang. 'I'll get it,' said Hannah. 'I want first dibs out of the other two.'

'Good luck with that,' I commented as she headed out of the kitchen.

Hannah returned scowling with the three boys following behind her in height order, with Freddie at the front and poor Bob, dwarfed by the other two trailing at the rear. It was one of the few occasions when I had seen Freddie wearing more than his underwear, which was a great relief. Instead, he wore a pair of dirty, ripped jeans and a torn T-shirt, which hung off his gaunt frame as if he were a sagging washing line. Bob, conversely, was wore a smart, well-ironed shirt and chinos. I could not tell you what Jack wore, but he looked irresistible as always.

'Hi, ladies,' Freddie gushed, stooping down to offer me a bottle of red. 'You're all looking delectable tonight if I might say so.'

I ignored him. 'Freddie, Bob, this is my flatmate Katy and our friend, Hannah,' I said, introducing everyone. 'Jack, you know the girls already, don't you?'

'I do indeed. Hi,' Jack responded, giving them both a peck on the cheek before kissing me and giving me a lingering hug.

Freddie followed suit, kissing all of us and hugging us for an inappropriate length of time. 'Ah, ladies, it's so good to be outside of our male-dominated existence,' he crooned. 'I haven't been invited to a dinner party before in Bath. I've sat through loads of stuffy ones at home, mind you, but never one with three such attractive women.'

Jack handed him a glass of wine with a side order of an extra hard stare.

Everyone grabbed a chair around the kitchen table while I emptied a few packets of crisps onto a plate and plonked them in the centre. I sat down on the empty chair next to Jack, who smiled at me. Then everyone started talking at once and the evening disappeared in a blur of chatter, pasta, wine, and chocolate cake.

'My compliments to the chefs,' Bob called, raising his glass.

'Here, here,' shouted everyone.

'Coffee anyone?' I asked, woozily standing to thread my way towards the kettle.

'Guys, why don't we head into town and hit a club?' Hannah suggested, grabbing Freddie's arm.

Freddie almost exploded in his excitement. 'A club? I'm well on for that, ladies,' he shrieked, leaping up from the table and almost braining himself on the low ceiling.

'Me too,' announced Katy, grabbing Bob by the hand, who looked as though he might faint from the shock of being touched.

'You up for it, Clare?' Jack asked, turning to me.

Katy and Hannah stood behind him, shaking their heads at me with vigour.

'I'm not sure I'm feeling like clubbing tonight, Jack. Do you fancy staying here and having a quiet coffee with me?' I paused. 'Although, if you want to go out with the others, that's fine with me too. I just.'

The girls rolled their eyes at me.

'You do look a little tired, Clare. Why don't you stay with her for a bit, Jack, and check she's OK?' Katy suggested.

'Fine by me,' Jack replied.

'Excellent,' Katy responded. 'Right, chaps, let's go.' She turned back to me. 'Clare, sit on the sofa with Jack and relax, and for Christ sakes, leave the bloody washing up!'

Chapter 46

Jack

Clare nestled into my chest as we lay in her narrow, single bed.

'Are you OK?' I asked her, kissing the top of her head.

She nodded, her nose brushing my chest hair.

'You're very quiet, Clare.'

She rolled her head and looked up at me. 'Was I alright?' she whispered.

I answered her by kissing her for a very long time. 'Clare, you were great. No, scrub that, you were perfect, are perfect, in fact. Look, I've been out with many girls, but I can honestly say that I have never felt the way I feel about you with any of them. Making love to you, just being with you, is so different that I really don't know how to explain it. It's as if I've found my soulmate.'

Clare stared back at me, tears flooding her eyes. 'I feel exactly the same way, Jack. I mean, I've not had many boyfriends, so I can't make the same comparisons as you can, but I think you are the one for me. Maybe we are star-crossed lovers, like in *Romeo and Juliet.'*

'Doesn't star-crossed mean that they were doomed though?'

'Oh, well, maybe not then. My Shakespeare is even worse than my Maths. Anyway, you know what I mean.' She snuggled into my chest again and I stroked her hair.

'What are your plans for the Christmas holidays?'

'I usually just spend them at home with Mum, and if I can get any temp work, I tend to do that to earn a bit of cash for next term. You?'

'Much the same. But it's very quiet in our little Welsh village. Not much goes on. I suspect London is more fun.'

'Well, why don't you come home with me for a couple of days? You could meet my Mum and I can show you the sights,' Clare suggested. 'Unless, that is, you'd rather not, or you think it's too soon, or.'

'I'd be delighted. In fact, I've hired a car to get back this time, as it's such a huge faff lugging all my gear across most of the UK's rail network. I could drive you home.'

'Only if you let me pay towards the petrol.'

'All contributions gratefully received,' I laughed. 'And then, if you wanted to, you could come back to Wales with me for a few days before Christmas, if you'd like to, and if your mum wouldn't mind.'

'She probably will mind a bit because she really looks forward to me being back at home, but I'm sure she'll understand once she meets you. I bet she'll wonder what a gorgeous guy like you is doing with boring old me.'

'Clare, this is what I'm doing with you,' I said, rolling her over and kissing her neck. 'But that's probably not what you should tell your mother!'

We began to make love again. I took my time, savouring every inch of her body. Clare moaned with pleasure. Suddenly, I stopped moving.

'Jack, what's wrong?'

'Listen. Can you hear something outside your door?'

We were both silent for a moment.

'I hear it,' Clare sighed.

There were loud whisperings.

'Give me a minute, would you?' Clare sidled out of bed and pulled on her dressing gown which lay on the floor by the end of bed. She tiptoed to the door and opened it a crack. 'What the fuck, guys? We're not deaf, you know.'

'So, how did it go?' Katy cackled like a hyena. 'Did you, you know?'

'Go away,' Clare hissed.

'Oh, I think he's still in there. Is Jack with you?' It was a male voice. Bob?

'Sorry to disturb you,' Katy shouted whilst shushing herself with her own finger as she wobbled around on the landing.

'Goodnight,' Clare replied, shutting the door.

'Was that Bob I heard?' I asked her as she returned to bed, discarding her robe once she was beneath the duvet.

'Yes, with Katy. Sorry about that. She's super nosey.'

'Did you and Katy set me up this evening, so that you could have your wicked way with me?' I stared at her without smiling.

'No, of course not,' she protested, red blotches springing up on her cheeks and neck. 'It's just that normally I leave my door slightly open and anyway, Katy's clearly pissed and.'

I burst out laughing and kissed her. 'If it was a set-up, then all I can tell you is that I'm bloody delighted. I've wanted to sleep with you since the very first time I saw you, but I didn't want to spoil things.'

'And I wasn't sure you were interested, so.'

'So, you little minx, you faked being tired just so that you could seduce me. I'm shocked,' I said with a smirk.

Clare laughed. 'Yes, that's about right.'

'Well, I am so appalled that the only thing I can possibly do now is to make love to you all over again.'

'What a terrible punishment,' Clare responded. 'I am prepared to accept my penance.' And this time, she began kissing me.

Chapter 47

Clare

I was both excited and extremely nervous about taking Jack to London to meet my mother, particularly given her overly suspicious nature and propensity to assume that all men were the devil. I called her the week before term ended to ask her if it was alright if I brought a friend back to stay for a couple of days.

'Of course, you can, Clare. She'll have to share a bed with you, obviously, but as long as she doesn't mind that, I'd be delighted to meet your friend.'

'Actually, Mum, she is a he.'

There was a pause. 'Right, well in that case, *he* can sleep on the sofa. And is this unnamed he a friend, or a boyfriend?'

'A boyfriend,' I stuttered. 'And his name is Jack.'

'Well, you've kept that rather quiet, haven't you, young lady?'

'Not particularly. We haven't been going out that long.'

'Well, I hope you know what you're doing. What's he like, this Jack fellow anyway?' my mother demanded.

'He's a really lovely guy, Mum. I'm sure you'll like him. He's very kind and funny, and super good-looking.'

'If you say so,' she huffed. 'Right, well don't expect me to get too busy for him. I'm working shifts and I haven't got time to roll out the red carpet.'

'That's fine, Mum. Just let's keep everything simple.' I omitted to tell her that we planned to go onto Wales for a few days afterwards, not wishing to antagonise her any further. I reasoned that once she met Jack, she would be as charmed by him as I was, and then she would settle down. I could not have been more wrong.

The meeting was a total disaster. We arrived at Mum's flat in Kentish Town having had a dreadful journey fighting through torrential rain all the way along the M4. Our phone batteries were dead, which was our fault, as we had partied until late the night before and forgotten to charge them, and the rental car had no charger. I knew my mum would be fretting about where we were and why we had not called with a progress report and, sure enough, when I did get my phone up and running again, she had left tens of messages, each of which was slightly more panicked than the last.

However, none of that excused the way she behaved when she met Jack. She took one look at him and reeled back in horror, as if I had brought the Antichrist into her home to accompany her down to hell. She ran off, shutting herself in her bedroom. I wondered for a moment if she had been drinking, but I knew she never touched alcohol. She had an unusual distrust of men – of this I was well aware – but to take it to this extreme at first meeting Jack was absurd. And then, as if her behaviour was not dreadful enough, she told me to get rid of him, and more than that, that I could never even see him again. It was as though I had come home and stepped straight into the middle of some Victorian melodrama on ITV. I found her behaviour bizarre and indefensible.

I shouted at her, telling her that if Jack had to leave, then so did I. I did not think she believed that I would go through with my threat, not me, her only daughter. The two of us were inseparable. But now that Jack and I were attached, my mother's fierce rejection of him cut me to the core. I was furious with her for being so instantly judgemental before she had even taken the time to get to know him. It was unforgivable.

I stormed out of her bedroom and returned to Jack, who mouthed 'what the fuck?' silently while shrugging his shoulders.

'Grab your coat and the bags, Jack. We're leaving,' I instructed.

'But we only just got here, Clare. What the hell is going on?'

'I have absolutely no bloody idea, but for some unfathomable reason my darling mother has taken an instant dislike to you and told me to get rid of you. As I have absolutely no intention of doing that, I suggest we leave immediately and drive to your place.'

'You want me to drive all the way back to Wales now, in this weather, which is further than we have just driven?' Jack stared at me, his eyes weary with fatigue.

'Yes,' I muttered. 'Or we can find a really cheap place to stay en route if we have to, but whatever happens, we are clearly not welcome here.' I felt my chest tighten as I held back my tears of fury.

Jack moved towards me, and I buried my head into his chest. I began to sob hard.

'It's alright, Clare. We'll go if we must, and then tomorrow you can call your mum and hopefully we can straighten everything out. Maybe she's feeling unwell, or just being overly protective. It's always been only you and her, so maybe she feels overwhelmed by me coming into the picture. It'll be alright in the end, I promise you.'

I lifted my head up and he wiped the tears off my face with his hand and kissed me. I waited for a moment, both of us standing stock-still, hoping that my mother would emerge from her bedroom and apologise. But there was no sound. 'Come on, Jack, let's go,' I whispered. We picked up our bags and headed back out into the filthy night.

Chapter 48

Jack

In the end, we drove right through, stopping only for petrol and to charge our phones, arriving home in Wales in the early hours. I texted my mother from the services on the M4 to let her know that there had been a change of plan, and that I was on my way home with a friend. Clare's phone began to beep incessantly the moment she had it on charge, with every text coming from her mother asking the same two things: "Where are you?" and "Are you with Jack?" Clare deleted each one without replying.

'It's as though she thinks that, if she asks the same questions often enough, I'll change my mind and give her the answer she's looking for.' Clare banged her phone down onto the dirty, plastic table in the services. 'It's pathetic.'

I received a text back from my mother, asking me if everything was alright, and saying that she was looking forward to seeing me. She would hide the key in the usual place, a strategically placed stone covering a small hole in the ground beside the back door.

Clare and I travelled through Cardiff and out the other side, the densely populated urban sprawl melting into sparse housing dotted here and there in a random pattern. The track up to our farmhouse was rutted and dusty. Clare and I bounced around inside the vehicle, while I hoped that the suspension on the hire car would hold out without costing me any money in repairs. When we reached the house, there was a solitary light on over the front door illuminating the darkness. I stopped the car and turned off the ignition.

'It's so quiet here,' Clare remarked.

'Yes, well, there's no other house for about five miles and the only neighbours are sheep, although they can be pretty noisy when they want to be. Come on, let's go in. I'm shattered.'

We unfolded ourselves from the car, moving like septuagenarians after such a lengthy time sitting down. The night air was arctic, and we both shivered involuntarily as it slammed into our faces. I grabbed the torch that we always kept by the front door and used it to navigate our way around to the back door without stumbling over logs and other various pieces of debris that always lay strewn around the outside of the house. Clare followed in my wake. I moved the stone, located the key and opened the back door. Inside, the last embers of the fires were still glowing behind the grate.

'Do we need to bring the bags in?' Clare asked.

'No, let's do that in the morning. No one will steal them round here. Come on, let's go up to bed.'

We tiptoed upstairs to my room. It looked the same as it always did, with my Cardiff City duvet cover neatly pressed and my old teddy bear sitting on the pillows patiently waiting for me. 'This is Walter,' I whispered. 'Hi, Walter, my old mate, I'm afraid you'll have to sleep on the side table tonight.' Walter looked a little miffed as I moved him, falling onto his side as I placed him on the bedside table.

'The bathroom is just across the landing. You go first,' I offered.

By the time she returned, I had drifted off on top of the duvet. Clare nudged me gently. We undressed quickly and were asleep holding each other within seconds.

When I awoke the following morning, I was still spooning Clare. The harsh winter sunshine streamed through the curtains and the dust particles danced in its beams. I kissed the back of her neck. 'Are you awake?'

'Hmm,' Clare stirred. 'Not really. Any idea what time it is?'

I rolled away from her to find my phone, which was lying on the bedside table next to a still-disgruntled Walter. 'Christ, it's almost eleven. I'd better go down and say hi to Mum. You stay here. There's no rush.'

I peeled myself away from Clare, pulling on my trousers and sweat top from the previous evening.

'Could you bring my bag up with you when you come back?' Clare asked.

'Which one? There are a few,' I laughed.

'The big suitcase, please. My clothes and wash bag are in it.'

'Will do,' I replied, opening the bedroom door. 'I'll bring you up a coffee as well when I've said my hellos.'

I closed the door behind me, heading down the stairs and into the kitchen. Mum was at the sink with her back to me peeling potatoes. She turned as I entered, her face one wide smile. She was still attractive, even though she was now in her early fifties. She kept her hair a permanent peroxide blonde, although it was shorter than it had been when I was a child. But she was as slim as ever in her jeans and red, checked shirt.

'Jack, sweetheart, how are you?' She dried her hands quickly on a piece of kitchen roll and scooted over to give me a tight hug. 'I didn't want to wake you. You must be knackered after that terrible drive. Did you sleep OK?'

'I slept like the dead,' I replied. 'It was a very long day. A really weird day, actually.'

'Why? What happened?' she asked, pouring me a coffee from the filter machine which ran constantly, and placing four slices bread in the toaster. 'Do you want a fry-up?'

'No, toast will be fine. I'll eat more when Clare comes down.'

'OK,' Mum answered, setting the butter and a knife onto the table, and then popping the toast onto a plate. She set it in front of me and then sat down opposite. 'So, tell me, what's going on?'

'Clare is just upstairs, and I said I'd take her bag up to her, so that she can get dressed, so I'll have to give you the potted version,' I whispered.

'Alright, shoot.'

'So, listen to this, right. We rock up to Clare's mum's place after the worst journey in the world last night, as I think I told you in my text. Anyway, we go inside the flat, and Clare's mum takes one look at me and acts like she's seen the devil himself. Then she orders Clare to break up with me.'

'You're kidding? What's up with her? Is she mental or something?' My mother sipped her coffee, her eyes bright with indignation on my behalf.

'I have absolutely no idea. All I know is that she gave Clare that ultimatum, Clare chose to up and leave with me, and that was it. Clare says she has never seen her mother act that way before. It was so bloody odd.' I chewed on my toast.

'Mouth,' said my mother.

'Sorry,' I replied. 'I'm suddenly starving hungry.'

'Do you think she was pissed? Clare's mum, I mean.'

'No, I don't think so. Clare says her mum hasn't had a drop of alcohol since the day she buried Clare's dad. She got very drunk that day, or so she tells Clare, and made a fool of herself at the funeral. She hasn't touched a drop since.'

My mother stared at me, and her mug tilted slightly, spilling coffee onto her jeans.

'Mum?' She was staring at the stain on her jeans, seemingly lost in another world.

'Sorry, love. I was just thinking about something else. Clare's mum – what's her name?'

'Why?'

'No reason, I just wondered.' She dabbed at the coffee stain with her hand.

'Amanda,' I replied.

Mum's mug crashed onto the kitchen tiles, shattering into myriad pieces.

'Mum, are you alright?' I asked, jumping up from my chair and beginning to pick up the shards of pottery off the floor.

'Yes, sorry love, I just lost my grip, that's all.' She rose, ashen-faced, and moved over to the door in the corner of the kitchen, behind which we kept the cleaning stuff. She fetched the dustpan and brush and began to sweep up the smaller pieces.

'Amanda. Right. And they live where?' Mum returned to the table and sat down. Her hands were shaking.

'In London, Kentish Town. Not that it's relevant, is it?'

Mum ignored my question. 'What does Amanda look like?'

'I don't know, Mum. I didn't see her for long enough to describe her all that well,' I barked, suddenly feeling extremely tired, as well as becoming increasingly irritated by my mother's strange line of questioning.

At that moment, Clare tiptoed through the kitchen door wearing her clothes from the previous evening. 'Hello,' she murmured, walking over to the kitchen table, and holding out her hand to my mother in greeting.

My mother simply stared back at her, her mouth hanging open like a codfish.

'Mum?'

'Ah, Clare, hello, welcome,' Mum replied, shaking herself out of her reverie. 'It's lovely to meet you. Jack has told me so much about you,' she spoke, while addressing the stain on her lap.

'All good, I hope,' Clare replied.

Mum smiled. 'Breakfast?' she suggested, rising from the table, and moving towards the stove.

'That would be lovely, thank you,' Clare replied, 'but please don't go to any trouble. I can have cereal, or I can make some toast for myself.'

'Nonsense,' Mum blustered. 'Let me do you both a fry-up. It won't take me more than a few minutes. I'll go and get the eggs from the pantry.'

My mother scurried out of the kitchen.

'You forgot my bag and I didn't think I could hide upstairs for much longer without appearing to be rude,' Clare admonished me.

'Sorry. I was filling Mum in on last night.' I paused, polishing off my crusts, which I always left until last. 'I think there must be a full moon or something at the moment, because my mother is acting very oddly as well. She wanted to know your mum's name, and then dropped her mug onto the floor. I thought she would have some helpful advice to give me, but she just started asking irrelevant stuff like what your mother was called and where she lived. I just don't get it.'

'She's probably just trying to show interest, Jack, and I'm sure she is very excited to see you. Don't read too much into it. At least she hasn't taken one look at me and told me to piss off!' Clare laughed.

'Not yet!'

Chapter 49

Fiona

'Christ, I can't believe this is actually happening.'

I was strolling into the village with my father. Progress was slow. These days he walked with the aid of a stick as he suffered from crippling arthritis in both his knees. He was on the waiting list for replacements, but despite my continual badgering, no date had been forthcoming from the NHS. I, in contrast, was full of nervous energy and desperate to stride on ahead instead of shuffling along.

'I mean, of all the universities in the whole country, these two end up at the same place. And not only that, but they also then somehow meet each other and fall in love. There must be a one-in-a-billion chance of that happening.'

My father listened as I ranted, partly because he liked to mull issues over before pronouncing judgement and partly because his hearing was quite poor.

'I've spent the past twenty-two years trying to move on from Terry and his infidelities, and then this girl comes along and totally poleaxes me. It's hard enough looking at Jack every day, who even though I love him more than anyone in the world, resembles his father as if he has been cloned, but now to meet his lover who looks just like Amanda – who was one of Terry's many mistresses, as it turned out. It's like being trapped inside a horrifying nightmare.'

Dad nodded, but I had no idea how much of this he was following. He patted my arm. 'The much bigger issue, of course,' he shouted, assuming he was speaking at an acceptable volume, 'is that you know that Terry might be her father and that means the two of them might be siblings.'

I stopped dead in the middle of the lane, the bitter wind lacerating my cheeks. He had been taking it in. 'I know that, Dad. It's the first thing that crossed my mind when Jack told me the story of meeting Amanda.' I felt the unstoppable pain of tears strangling my throat. 'They must be separated, but how the hell do I do that without telling them the truth? It would devastate both of them. Neither of them knows anything about what actually happened – the lies, the affairs, the way their father, or fathers, actually died, who their father even is. I lost Terry and I've learnt to live with that, because I taught myself to hate him, but I cannot, I will not, risk losing Jack. It would kill me.'

Dad stopped and took me in his arms, wobbling slightly with the effort. 'Yet you cannot let their relationship go any further either, Fiona. It's morally and ethically unconscionable. If you think about it, their possible shared genetic make-up might be why they are so attracted to each other. It might be alright in the end for them to love each other, but only as brother and sister.'

'But Dad, they are sleeping together. It's incest, isn't it, even though it's entirely innocent on their part. How will they live with themselves once they find out? It's unthinkable.'

'In my opinion, there is only one solution to this,' Dad pronounced, stopping to rest on a stone bench along the side of the path. I sat down beside him, exhausted.

'Which is what?'

'You need to contact Amanda and agree on a way forward together.'

'But I haven't spoken to her since Terry's funeral – and that was a day that neither of us will ever forget.'

'This is no longer only about you and Amanda. It's about your children. You each have a responsibility to sort this out with as little damage as possible to both your relationships with your children.'

I nodded, hot tears streaming down my icy cheeks.

We walked the rest of the way into the village in silence, each of us lost in our own thoughts. I left Dad nursing a coffee in the local cafe to make sure that he stayed warm and buzzed around buying the food and some other items that I needed. We caught the bus home. It ran infrequently but to time, and we trundled back home in relative warmth. I felt exhausted, weighted down by the emotional strain. I had thought that I had managed to survive the trauma of my past and to create a steady, if unexciting, existence for Jack and myself. But the tentacles of Terry's treachery could clearly still reach out to me from beyond the grave, threatening to drag me back down to him.

Chapter 50

Amanda

I had behaved very badly indeed. I knew that I had, but that boy had brought Terry back into my home. Terry, the man I had alternately loathed and desired for the best part of the last twenty-two years. Terry, who was responsible both for my loveless seduction and my husband's financial ruin and ultimate death. Terry, who I was sure was the father of my beloved child, Clare. Terry, the man I had worked so hard to forget, yet who was completely unforgettable. Terry who continued to ruin me.

My darling Clare looked so utterly lost and confused when I told her that she had to break up with Jack. But how could I expect her to behave in any other way, when I must have appeared to be a total madwoman, offering no explanation of why I was making such demands? Quite clearly, she and Jack could never be, and yet they already were. How could such a situation ever be explained to either of them?

I had not heard from Clare since the night she fled with Jack, despite my leaving her a constant barrage of voice and text messages. I had no idea where she had gone, but I assumed she was with him. But if she had gone to his home, what had happened there? Did Fiona suspect anything? Did she think that Clare bore any resemblance to me or to Terry? Everyone had always told me that Clare looked just like me, but I could see Terry in her so clearly. She had his twinkling, mischievous eyes and his sharp wit. There was nothing about her that remotely reminded me of Bill.

Over the years, I have spent too many lonely nights in bed reimagining my singular experience with Terry, and also wondering what it might have been like if he had left Fiona for me. And then I think about Fiona, and I realise what a total fool I was. If he was cheating on a stunning woman like her with a dumpy bag like me, he clearly lacked any moral compass and was solely led by the continuous ache inside his own trousers. Yet I had foolishly continued to dream.

I was haunted by Bill as well. Poor old Bill, who had never taken a risk in his entire life and who never thought to think outside the box, was equally charmed and bamboozled by Terry. I had come to realise, since Bill's terrible death, that he was not a bad man. It was simply that he never stood a chance. Yes, he was controlling and unkind to me at times, but I think deep down, I believe he loved me as much as he was capable of loving anyone. I disappointed him because I was not his mother. I disappointed him because I had failed to become a mother. We were obviously unhappy together, yet in a funny way, I missed him; and above all, I felt terribly guilty. Bill was so pleased when he believed that he was finally going to be a father, even if he did not quite know how to show it. Then, when Terry exposed the awful truth, it killed the two of them. Terry arguably deserved his fate, but Bill, well, he was merely an unfortunate bystander, swept up in the traitorous carnival that was Terry. Bill led a rather sad life from beginning to premature end.

The home phone rang, and I leapt up from the sofa and raced into the kitchen to answer it, hoping beyond hope that Clare had decided to make contact.

'Hello, Clare?' I gasped.

'Hello, Amanda, it's Fiona.'

My breathing stopped for a second. 'Fiona?'

'Yes. Look, Amanda, I know it's been many, many years since we have spoken, and I was very reluctant to make this particular phone call, for obvious reasons, but we have a dangerous situation on our hands, and we need to find a way to sort it out.'

'I know,' I nodded into the phone, 'but I have absolutely no idea what to do.' My heart was pounding so fast that I was forced to lower myself down onto the kitchen floor. I sat there, panting like an old dog.

'Me neither.' Fiona gulped, as if she was attempting to hold back her tears. 'But what I do know is that if we don't try to do something, we will lose both our children – and I for one am not prepared to let that happen.'

'Me neither,' I agreed.

'I've been discussing all the possible options with my dad, and we think the best thing to do would be for you to come here to Wales so that you and I can talk things through in person. Then we can sit the kids down and attempt to remedy the situation in the most palatable way we can think of with without destroying everything.'

'I've been over and over every scenario in my head already, believe me, but whatever we tell them, it's going to involve some extremely unpleasant truths, or versions of the truth – and I'm not sure they'll cope with it.' I was crying now, sending deep sobs down the phone to Fiona.

'I've done a great deal of thinking as well,' Fiona whispered, 'and I think we've all lied more than enough, don't you? If we don't tell the children the whole truth, warts and all, they'll never forgive us, or indeed understand why you and I are so concerned for them. We are going to have to face up to our sins and let them make their own decisions.'

'But you didn't do anything wrong, Fiona – quite the opposite, in fact,' I cried.

'I am well aware of that, Amanda. But I did make one fatal mistake,' she blurted out.

'And what was that?'

'I trusted all of you. And I've never been able to trust anyone since.'

Chapter 51

Clare

I had been staying at Jack's place for three days, continuing to ignore my mother's desperate attempts to get hold of me. She kept texting to tell me that I had to trust her, but she never explained why. My mother and I had always talked about everything, and I had never had any secrets from her. I had assumed that this worked both ways, but clearly not. She appeared to have metamorphosed overnight into someone I did not even recognise. Yet I was scared. I did not want to lose my mum. She was the only constant in my life, given that I had never known my father, and I had no other family. I did not want to be orphaned completely.

Life at the farmhouse was quiet. We had returned the rental car to Cardiff a few days after our return and I had enjoyed Jack's tour of the city, including his excitement at showing me the stadium of his beloved Cardiff City. I felt that it was a tad disappointing in comparison to Arsenal's Emirates stadium near our flat in London, but I was no football expert, so I said nothing. Once back at the house, Jack and I took regular walks into the village of Cadoxton to get shopping for the family and spent hours rambling across the fields.

Fiona was a strange combination of friendly yet remote. She was not rude to me exactly, but she was certainly offhand, never engaging me in conversation for longer than was necessary. Jack's grandparents were kind enough, but distant for other reasons. His grandmother had dementia and tended to ask me the same questions several times a day and his grandfather was somewhat gruff, as well as being hard of hearing, which made conversion difficult.

Jack and I talked incessantly on our walks, mostly trying to fathom what had happened in London and whether or not my mother would ever see sense.

'I think the only way forward is for you to speak to her,' Jack suggested gently, his arm around my shoulder as we ambled along a slippery lane on a damp, foggy day. The low mist swirled around our ankles, swallowing the ground beneath.

'I am waiting for her to apologise. Not once in any of her calls and messages has she said sorry for the way she behaved. Until she is prepared to take that step at least, I can't see any point in talking to her.' I stopped and turned towards Jack, kissing him on the lips. 'I love you, Jack, and I want Mum to love you too. It is impossible for me to understand how she could fail to do so. But if she won't even make the effort to get to know you, how can she?' I frowned.

Jack hugged me and we continued to pace. 'But if you don't try to talk to her, things will only fester and grow worse. If she won't come to you, you need to go to her and at least give it a shot.'

'You're too nice, you know that, don't you?'

'My mum says that you need to take care not to be too nice to people, as in the end, they always disappoint you, even people you have gone out of your way to help in difficult circumstances. I think it's rather cynical attitude personally, but she says that she learnt that particular lesson the hard way and that it's the best advice she can give me. I guess when your husband bogs off and leaves you pregnant and broke, you're inevitably going to become rather bitter.'

'I can see that in your mum. She puts distance between herself and other people to protect herself.'

'Do you think so? I've never noticed that about her,' Jack commented.

'Well, maybe it's just me that has that effect on her,' I said, pouting.

'Now you're being completely paranoid, Clare. She really likes you. I can tell. And above all, she wants me to be happy. She has always told me that my happiness is her ultimate goal in life. And you make me happy, ergo she must love you.' He hugged me tighter and then pulled my beanie hat down over my eyes in jest.

I hoicked it back up, smiling. 'So, do you really think I've made a good impression?' I asked.

'How could you not?' Jack replied, patting my bottom.

We were nearing the farmhouse and Fiona's car, which sat in the drive unless she was visiting one of her clients to do their hair, was missing.

'Mum normally tells me if she's going to be out with a client. She must have forgotten.'

A couple of hours later, Fiona was not home yet, and Jack was worried. 'Granddad, did Mum say where she had gone exactly? She's very late. Do you think I should walk into the village and see if I can find her? She might have had a puncture or something?'

'Your mum's fine, I'm sure,' his granddad reassured him. 'I think she said she was meeting a friend after work or something,' he yelled over the sound of the television, which was turned up to on the highest possible volume.

'What friend?' Jack shouted back.

His grandfather rolled his eyes. 'Your mother is a big girl, Jack. She'll be home soon. Now, why don't you go and make your granny and I a nice pot of tea. And see if there are any of those nice, malted biscuits left. I'm feeling a bit peckish.'

After feeding and watering his grandparents, I managed to distract Jack by taking him upstairs and entertaining him under the duvet for a while. But as soon as we had finished, he was anxious again, peering out of the bedroom window.

'Anyone would think she was your child, not vice versa,' I teased him.

'I know. I just worry about her that's all.' He paused. 'It's weird, isn't it, how you worry about someone when you're with

Deborah Stone

them, whereas when I'm in Bath I never worry about where Mum is. Hang on, I think that's her now.'

Jack pulled on his sweatpants and ran downstairs. I dressed hurriedly and followed him.

'Hi, Mum, are you alright? You're back very late,' Jack called as he ran downstairs.

'I'm fine, Jack. Sorry I wasn't here to make dinner.'

I followed Jack into the kitchen. Fiona looked tired and drawn, her eyes red and swollen and her face drained of any colour. She slumped down into one of the kitchen chairs and ran her hands through her hair. Then she took a deep breath.

'Clare, love, just to let you know, your mum is going to come over tomorrow to see you.'

'My mum?' I replied. 'Why? How?'

'I contacted her and suggested it might be a sensible idea. It's no good for a mother and daughter to be arguing and not talking.' She sniffed and pulled a dirty, sodden handkerchief from her sleeve, blowing her nose into it.

'But how did you manage to contact her?' I asked, glaring at Jack.

'Jack had nothing whatsoever to do with it, Clare,' Fiona countered. 'I tracked your mother down via directory enquiries. Old people like your mum and I still have landlines, you know.'

'Mum, don't you think you should have asked Clare first? I mean, it's rather presumptuous and interfering of you, don't you think?' Jack barked, his face puce with embarrassment.

Fiona stared at her lap. 'I'm sorry if you feel that way, Jack. But as a mother, I could only empathise with how Clare's mother must be feeling, not knowing where her daughter was and having left everything on such bad terms. I'm sorry if you feel I've done the wrong thing.' Fiona made no eye contact with either of us, focussing on a patch of dried mud on the floor

'What did she say when you called her?' I demanded, as shocked as Jack was that Fiona had contacted my mother behind my back, but not wanting to say so, because I did not want to get on the wrong side of Fiona for Jack's sake.

'She was extremely relieved to hear that you were safe and well. She asked if she could come to see you, as you had apparently been avoiding her calls, and I said that it was alright with me. I appreciate that maybe I should have asked you first, but my own motherly instinct suggested to me that you would say no.' She paused and looked up at me. 'Sometimes, things need to be brokered by a third party to make the peace.'

I scowled at Fiona, unsure exactly what she meant by this statement. 'So, when is she coming?' I asked.

'She arrives around noon tomorrow, I believe.' Fiona hesitated. 'I've arranged a taxi to collect her from the station and to bring her straight here.'

Chapter 52

Fiona

Of course, Amanda was already in Cardiff. I had met her off the train that afternoon and taken her to the nearest Premier Inn, where we could talk well away from anyone who might see us. It was inevitably going to be a conversation we were better off having in private. I waited on the freezing platform, peeling my gels from my nails, which I made a rule never to do, as it wrecked them, but this was an exceptional circumstance. By the time the train arrived, my gels only covered the tips, and I was disgusted with the state of them. I pulled on my woollen gloves to hide them away.

The train was packed with people returning to Cardiff for Christmas. Passengers emerged onto the platform overladen with suitcases and bags of gifts. People streamed past me, their luggage banging into my legs, as I strained to recognise Amanda. I had no idea what she might look like these days. I waited at the barrier, stamping my feet to stop them from losing all feeling on the concrete floor. The train was almost empty by now and only a few stragglers remained along the platform. I began to wonder if she had bailed out and decided not to come after all. But then I spotted her.

Amanda looked almost exactly the same as when I first met her all those years earlier, except somewhat fuzzier around the edges. She was heavy, about a size eighteen I would have guessed, encased in an ill-fitting purple puffer coat and wearing threadbare Ugg boots, which had suffered from over-exposure to the rain and snow over the years. She carried a small duffle bag slung across her body, which made her list to one side like a holed ship.

Amanda spotted me and raised her hand almost imperceptibly. I nodded in reply. When she reached the barrier, she stopped. 'Hello, Fiona. You look amazing, just as you always did.'

I was unable to return the compliment, so I simply asked how her journey had been.

'The train was rammed. It was standing room only, so there was no chance of getting to the buffet car. Otherwise, it was fine.'

'Good. So, if it's alright with you, I've booked you a room for tonight and tomorrow at the Premier Inn around the corner from here. I thought we could chat in your room rather than in the lobby, given the sensitivities of the situation.' I began to march out of the station concourse without waiting to see if she was behind me, but I sensed that Amanda was struggling to keep pace. When we reached the hotel, I did all the talking at reception and the only thing Amanda had to do was hand over her card.

'I'm afraid I don't have a credit card,' Amanda mumbled. 'Is cash OK?' she asked the receptionist.

'Yeah, but you'll have to pay upfront. That's £89.80.'

Amanda fumbled for her purse in her handbag and handed over the requisite amount of cash. I waited with irritation while she counted out eighty pence in small coins.

We headed to the lift and went up to the room. 'I'll make some coffee,' I offered.

'Thanks,' Amanda replied. 'I need the toilet.'

She disappeared into the bathroom for what seemed like a prolonged period of time, while I picked the tips off my nails and broke three of them.

Amanda emerged from the bathroom having removed her puffer jacket. Underneath she wore an ill-fitting red sweat top and grey, baggy trousers. Close up, she looked worn out, with deep labial lines around her mouth and dark rings under her eyes. Her hair was grey and hung lifeless to her shoulders. In a previous life, I had helped her do something about her appearance, but she had reverted to type. She slumped onto one of the two narrow, single beds and I handed her a coffee.

'I added some milk and sugar. Is that OK?'

'That's fine, thank you.' Amanda took a sip. 'It's perfect.'

'Well, it's as good as it can be with these horrible milk sachets.'

'So,' Amanda sighed, raising her head and staring at me.

'So,' I replied. I suddenly felt both exhausted and nauseous. I found it difficult to believe that I was here with Amanda after all these years. When Terry and Bill died, I swore I would never see or speak to her again, but yet here we were, drawn back together by our children.

'Look, Amanda, neither of us wants to be here, and neither of us wants to face up to this bizarre situation, but we have to, so let's just get on with it.' I paused, breathing deeply in an attempt to retain my composure. 'I suggest that we sit both of them down tomorrow and tell them what actually happened. Only by revealing everything to them will they come to realise that they can never be together.'

Amanda gasped, her coffee cup rattling on its saucer. She placed it down onto the brown, nylon carpet. 'But if we tell them everything, they will never trust us again, will they? We will effectively be telling them that everything they think they know about themselves is false. It will destroy them.' She began to cry soundlessly, tears travelling down her cheeks.

'But if we don't tell them everything and they defy us and continue to see each other, they might end up with a child and they could be brother and sister. It's unthinkable, never mind illegal. I don't see any other way out of this bloody mess,' I shrieked rather louder than I had intended.

'And are you suggesting we tell them how Terry and Bill died as well? To tell them that their mutual father was a philanderer and a fraudster who left both families totally destitute? How far into the truth are we intending to go?' Amanda rose from the bed and went back into the bathroom, emerging a moment later with the toilet roll. She tore off a few sheets and blew her nose before handing it to me. She moved over to the window, staring out at the grey, wintry skyline. 'Look, Fiona, I can't tell Clare that I've lied for all this time about who her father is and how he died. She thinks Bill died in a construction accident. She believes that Bill is her father. If she finds out that I have lied to her about such fundamental truths for her whole life, that I have constructed a completely false reality, she will never speak to me again. I'll lose her forever.'

Amanda turned back to face me, snot running from her nose.

'Perhaps you should have thought about that before you slept with my husband,' I shot back. 'Perhaps you should have thought about that when I was the only one who looked after you when you nearly died, yet you still went ahead and betrayed me. Lying obviously comes as second nature to you, Amanda. You've lied to me, to Bill and now to your own child. This is your all fault, not mine at all, and I'm not about to let you screw up Jack's life as you did mine.' I stood right in front of her now, so close that I could have opened the window and pushed her through it.

'But you've lied too, haven't you? Clare told me that Jack's father ran off when you were pregnant. He doesn't know that Terry is dead, does he?' Amanda spat back at me.

I raised my hand and slapped her hard across the face. Amanda reeled backwards, her eyes wide with shock, hitting her head on the windowpane.

'No, he does not know that Terry is dead,' I screamed, my chest tight with anguish. 'But it's the only lie I've ever told him, and I think he would forgive me if he knew why. You, on the other hand, are wading so deep in the shit that you'll never be able to step out of it. But frankly, that's not my problem. There is no way that you are going to drag my son down to your level.' I flung myself onto the bed nearest the window, glaring at Amanda.

'I know what I did to you, Fiona, and I know I can never undo it. I've lived with the guilt every single day since. But if you insist on telling the kids everything, you will destroy the only person I care about.'

I raised my head from the bed and tried to focus on Amanda, but my tears were blinding me. I wiped them away with my sleeve. 'Fuck you, Amanda. You have no right to demand anything of me. You couldn't even let me bury Terry in peace, could you?'

Amanda gulped. She moved across the room and sat down on the opposite bed. 'I was overwhelmed at the time, Fiona. I had just buried Bill and I had no idea what I was doing. I'm so ashamed, but I couldn't help myself.'

'Why were you even there? You weren't invited to Terry's funeral. You were not at all welcome. Yet, not only did you come, but as they were about to commit my lying, cheating git of a husband to the eternal flames, you decided to howl and scream out Terry's name. The celebrant had to stop the proceedings and have you taken outside. You weren't his widow. You were only one of the many, many women Terry screwed. You were no one to him. You were utterly meaningless.'

Amanda slipped down from the bed and onto the floor curling into a plump ball, her body convulsing with grief. 'I loved him, Fiona,' she murmured. 'I still love him.'

'Well, you're more of a fucking idiot than I thought you were, because he thought you were a total joke. Terry loved no one except himself. You know, I used to feel sorry for you. I thought that Bill mistreated you and made you miserable, but actually, I suspect that living with you probably made him the way he was. I thought you were in a coma due to some bizarre food poisoning, but Bill told Terry you tried to top yourself. That's why Bill felt that he couldn't visit you, as he felt betrayed by you. And then, to cap it all, you killed the poor man. Yes, Terry defrauded Bill, but he could have recovered from that, but it was you who murdered him. Once he knew that he was not the father of your child, he no longer wanted to live. Think about it for a moment. Bill was so much physically stronger than Terry. He could easily have pushed Terry over the bannister that night and let go in order to save himself. But he didn't do that, did he, Amanda? No, he chose to hold onto to Terry and to fall onto that horrific spiky statue to his terrible death rather than spend the rest of his life raising a bastard child with you. I saw it in his eyes. It was you who killed Bill. No one else.'

I leapt up from the bed and grabbed my coat and bag. Amanda remained quivering in her foetal position.

'I'm telling the children everything at noon tomorrow. I've ordered a taxi to pick you up at 11.15. If you choose not to come, I'm going ahead with it regardless. It's completely up to you.'

Chapter 53

Jack

I slept extremely poorly the night before Clare's mother arrived because Clare insisted on keeping me awake – and not in the way I would have preferred. She wanted to talk.

'I mean, what the fuck, Jack? Where does your mother get off interfering in my life? I'm not her child, for Christ sakes. She hadn't even met me before I arrived here with you. I'm seriously pissed off with her.'

'I know, Clare. I understand, really, I do. I'm not happy with her either,' I soothed, stroking her arm. She lay on her back, staring up at the yellowing, Anaglypta ceiling as though tracing its weird patterns it might provide some solutions for her. 'But, in all fairness, I think Mum was probably only trying to do her best. That's not to say that I don't agree with you completely that she should have talked to you about it first.'

Clare turned her head to face me.

'Did you know about this? Be honest with me, Jack. Was it you who gave her Mum's address?'

I glared back at her, withdrawing my arm. 'I've already told you a thousand times. I heard that your mother was coming at exactly the same time that you did. It's seriously hacking me off that you don't believe me.' I rolled away from her.

'I'm sorry. I just don't understand how your mum could have found her, that's all, and if you didn't tell her, then.'

'Goodnight. I'll see you in the morning,' I grunted, closing my eyes.

But rest eluded both of us and we tossed and turned all night, finally falling into a deep sleep in the early hours of the morning. When I woke up again, it was almost eleven. I shook Clare.

'Clare, your mum will be here in an hour. We'd better move ourselves,' I whispered, kissing her neck, momentarily forgetting that I was supposedly angry with her.

'Oh shit,' she growled, flinging the duvet off herself and padding towards the door, where my robe hung on the hook. I watched her as she covered her naked body which I loved to explore and excite.

'I love you, Clare.'

She left the room without a word, and I heard the bolt shoot on the bathroom door.

We ate toast and jam at the kitchen table in silence. Well, I ate my toast and then I ate Clare's as well, as she claimed to have lost her appetite. The house was eerily quiet. My grandfather had wheeled my grandmother, swaddled in blankets and topped with a woolly hat and gloves, down to the village for a check-up with the GP. Mum had been out early seeing clients who needed their colour touching up before beginning their Christmas festivities. She arrived home around eleven forty-five, but instead of coming into the kitchen she went straight to her room. I assumed she did not want to start another argument with either of us prior to Mrs Whiteread arriving.

Just before midday I heard the sound of tyres crunch on the gravel outside and I scooted into the front room to peer through the net curtains. Clare's mother emerged from a taxi and paid the driver through his window, fiddling with her purse to locate the right change. The taxi reversed off the drive at speed, throwing up a vast cloud of dust. Clare's mum stood there for a moment, cocooned in her enormous purple puffer. Eventually, she took a visible deep breath and walked to the front door, ringing the bell. Before I could answer it, Mum came pelting downstairs.

'Amanda, come in,' she intoned in a flat voice. 'I think the kids are in the kitchen.'

'Hello again,' I called out, leaping out from behind the door of the front room. Both women jumped simultaneously.

'Jesus, Jack, I thought you were in the kitchen,' my mother gasped.

'Sorry,' I smiled. 'Can I take your coat, Mrs Whiteread?' I offered, having promised myself to be scrupulously polite in an attempt to win this strange woman's approval.

'Thank you, Jack,' she replied, addressing my mother rather than me.

'Where's Clare?' my mother demanded.

'She *is* actually in the kitchen,' I replied.

I led the way with the two mothers following slowly behind me. Clare was seated at the table, her head bent towards her coffee mug, the contents of which remained untasted.

'Your mum's here,' I announced.

'I noticed.'

'Hi Clare,' her mother stuttered.

Clare ignored her.

'Right, Amanda. What can I get you? Tea? Coffee?' Mum asked, marching towards the kettle.

'A glass of water will do me fine, thank you,' Mrs Whiteread muttered.

Mum fetched four glasses from the cupboard and filled them up at the sink, one by one, as the rest of us sat at the table, staring into nothingness rather than making eye contact with each other.

'Here you go,' Mum pronounced, placing the glasses onto the table and taking the empty chair. 'So.'

She paused, her face taut. She wiped a bead of sweat nestling on her forehead with her handkerchief, despite the chill of the room. 'Amanda, do you want to kick off, or shall I?'

Amanda said nothing. Clare glanced at me, and I shrugged my shoulders. The atmosphere was so awkward that I felt as if the air itself might shatter.

'OK, right then, I'll go.' Mum took a deep breath. 'Right, well, Clare, Jack, the thing is that your mum and I, well, what it is… we know each other from many years ago. We were in fact neighbours in London before you were born.' She stopped and took a gulp of water.

Amanda fiddled with the hem of her sweat top.

'How weird is that?' I exclaimed. 'How long ago was that?'

'About twenty-two years ago, give or take. Amanda and Bill already lived in the semi-detached house next door when your dad and I moved in.'

'And let me guess,' Clare smirked, addressing her mother for the first time. 'You fell out, or had an argument over the garden fence, or something completely petty like that, and that's why you now think that Jack and I can't see each other. Is that it?'

'Not exactly,' Amanda muttered, her bottom lip wobbling.

'Clare, please let me tell you the whole story before you start jumping to conclusions,' Fiona continued, her face drawn despite the fact that she had clearly applied a heavy face of make-up that day. 'So, as I was saying, we were neighbours for quite a while, but the relationship between us grew complicated.'

'So, you did fall out!' Clare shouted.

'Yes, in the end, we did,' Amanda whispered almost inaudibly.

'Well, whatever happened between the two of you is nothing to do with Clare and I, so I strongly recommend that we all move on, rather than dwelling on the past.' I got up from the table, hoping to end this pointless chat.

'It's not a simple as that, I'm afraid, Jack. Please sit down and hear me out,' Mum pleaded.

I slumped back into my chair, crossing my arms over my chest and rolling my eyes at Clare, who replied in kind.

'As I was saying, we lived next door to each other. We became quite friendly, particularly because Terry, my husband obviously, was trying to persuade Bill to invest in one of his property deals. So, the two men met up quite frequently.'

'Is any of this at all relevant?' I enquired, yawning.

'Yes,' Amanda interjected. 'Please, listen to your mother, Jack. It's really important.' A tear dropped onto the table from the tip of her chin.

'None of this is making any sense,' Clare said. 'Can you please just cut to the chase?'

Mum scowled, two wrinkles appearing between her eyebrows. 'All in good time, Clare. Please bear with me because none of this is easy for any of us.'

Mum began to cry noiselessly, and Clare and I shifted in our seats, suddenly nervous.

'So,' Mum's voice wavered, 'your mum and I, Clare, well, we were also close friends, or so I thought.'

Clare shot a look at her mum, who studied the contents of her handkerchief.

'But then it turned out that your mum had cheated on me and on your dad as well.' Mum glowered at Amanda with a look of pure hatred.

'I didn't mean to do it,' Mrs Whiteread blurted out. 'It just happened. It was only the one time, I promise.' She began to sob, her face ugly with red blotches.

'Didn't mean to do what, Mum?' Clare demanded.

Mrs Whiteread merely howled even louder and blew her nose with force.

'Your mother slept with my husband. She slept with Terry,' Fiona shrieked. 'She betrayed me, even though supposedly I was her only friend in the world.'

'She slept with Jack's dad? Mum, is this true?' Clare demanded, her voice shrill.

'Yes,' Mrs Whiteread muttered, 'I did, but it wasn't my fault. If you'd known Terry, you'd understand. He was so charming, and I was so shocked and so flattered that someone like him would bother to pay me any attention at all, and your father and I, well, you know, we had our own problems, and we were weren't too happy together, and...'

'Don't say anything else, Mum. Just shut the fuck up,' Clare screamed, slamming her hands over her ears to block out any more words.

I felt a cold fear creeping around my body. 'Mum, are you saying what I think you might be saying?' I spoke quietly, a cold terror beginning to creep around my body.

'What I am saying, Jack, is that this woman slept with your father and became pregnant shortly afterwards, around the same time that I did as a matter of fact. So, what I'm trying to tell you is that you and Clare might be related. You're…'

'Brother and sister,' Mrs Whiteread yelled out. 'You two are half-siblings. That's why you can never be together. That's why we need to leave here, Clare, right now, and you must never, ever, see Jack again.' She rose from her chair, stumbling over the leg of the table. 'Get your things, Clare. I'm calling a taxi.' She stood rigid in the doorway of the kitchen, blocking out the light.

Clare opened her mouth to speak, but instead of emitting any words, she vomited violently across the table, spraying all of us with the foul-smelling, fermented contents of her stomach. In turn, Mum retched, reaching the sink only just in time before she threw up as well. I ran upstairs, returning with towels for everyone to wipe themselves down. I found clean glasses in the cupboard and fetched more water. Then I grabbed the kitchen roll and attempted to wipe the table down. Amanda did nothing, merely standing sentinel in the kitchen doorway with her bag.

Mum remained bent over the sink. I moved over to her and put my arm around her shoulders. 'Is that why Dad left, Mum? Because you found out about the affair?'

She turned to face me. 'No, not exactly, Jack. Your father wasn't really the remorseful type.'

'Stop, Fiona. They've heard more than enough for one day,' Amanda yelled, steadying herself on the doorframe.

'No more lies, Amanda. Remember what we agreed?' Mum croaked.

'You may as well tell us everything,' Clare moaned. 'My whole identity is clearly a total fake, so please tell us the rest of it. We need to know.'

I left Mum holding onto the draining board and walked over to Clare, squatting on the floor by her chair.

'Your father did not leave due to the affair, Jack, as I didn't know anything about it at that point. The reason he left was because he embezzled all of Bill's money and all of my money as well, leaving the three of us completely broke. In fact, I was worse than broke, because he saddled me with huge debts. Your beloved father took out all the credit cards, the mortgage, everything, in my name without my knowledge or consent, and that meant I couldn't pay for anything. I didn't even have a job at the time. Bill lost all his life savings and had sold his business as well as re-mortgaging his house. Your father screwed all of us – literally and physically.'

'Christ,' I whispered, reaching out and squeezing Clare's hand.

'That's right, he cheated on all of us,' Mrs Whiteread agreed hurriedly, nodding her head. 'We were all completely taken in by him.'

'What the hell did you do?' Clare asked, sipping carefully on her water, her face alabaster.

'The three of us tracked him down to a hotel in Bristol with the help of a friend of your Grandad's. We travelled there together to demand our money back.'

'And what happened? Was he there?' I questioned, following the story now as if it was a gripping television drama rather than real life, part of my own life.

'He was there alright.' This was Mrs Whiteread speaking now. She had collapsed onto the floor in the doorway and was addressing the kitchen tiles. She had stopped crying and appeared weirdly calm. 'Terry was there with some busty, leggy blonde, who he dumped in the bar when he saw the three of us bearing down on him. He ushered us up to his penthouse suite – nothing but the best for Terry, especially when it wasn't his money that he was spending. We went to demand our money back and to get some sodding justice, but of course, Terry had an ace up his sleeve. He had thought of bloody everything. When Bill demanded that he pay us all back, he informed Bill that my baby wasn't his. He told Bill about our affair – although it had only happened the one time as I said and could hardly be classed as an affair - and that he, Terry was the father. Bill, well, Bill totally lost it, didn't he Fiona?' Mrs Whiteread stared at Mum for confirmation, but Mum remained motionless. 'Bill and Terry fought in the room. It was terrifying, but there was nothing that Fiona and I could do to stop them. They brawled and they hit each other. There was an awful lot of blood and then.' Mrs Whiteread dissolved into a barrage of sobs.

'And then, the bannister gave way and they both lost their balance. They fell locked together to their mutual destruction,' Fiona finished, gripping the edge of the sink.

'So, Dad didn't die on a construction site either? That was also a lie.' Clare murmured.

'And Dad is dead? He didn't just run off?' I confirmed.

Our mothers nodded.

'So, do you see, Clare? Do you understand now why you and Jack cannot stay together? Not as lovers anyway. You can be friends if you want to be, you can be siblings, but nothing else. I'm sorry, Clare. I'm so sorry.' Mrs Whiteread resumed her howling.

I was incandescent. 'Mum, if you've known all of this the whole time that Clare has been staying with us, why the fuck did you never think to tell me? And you've lied about Dad my whole life. When I think about all those times I've considered trying to trace him. Can you imagine if I had actually started to look for him? What the fuck is wrong with both of you?' I screeched. 'Where are Clare and I supposed to go now, as we sure as hell can't stay with either of you two, and we can't be together either – or at least not as we were. We may as well be dead ourselves.'

'Don't say that Jack. Don't ever say that,' Mum cried, rushing over to me.

I pushed her away. 'Get away from me. I can't bear to be in the same space as any of you.'

Clare stared at me, wide-eyed and so pale. Then she vomited once again all down her front.

'Well, I'm afraid that gives Jack and I an even bigger problem to deal with,' Clare groaned, resting her head in her hands, 'because it turns out that I'm pregnant.'

Chapter 54

Clare

I felt so dizzy that I could barely stand, so I leant on Jack as we climbed the stairs to the bathroom. He helped me to undress without looking at my body, as if we had never been intimate, as if I was a totally different person. I wondered if I now revolted him, and the thought made me feel even more nauseous. Jack shoved my stinking, vomit-stained clothing into a plastic bag and disappeared, while I stood naked under the hot shower, shivering with shock.

I had been intending to tell Jack that I was pregnant, but the news of my mother arriving forced me to postpone it. I had only known for a day as it was. My period had failed to appear, and I was always regular, so I bought some tests when Jack was in the newsagent getting a paper for his grandfather. I purchased three tests, just to be sure, and they all showed the same result – bright pink and positive. I felt completely overwhelmed and was unsure how it had happened at all, as we had used condoms most of the time.

I was furious at first, as well as desperately scared, and then I began to fret about telling Jack. I knew I had to tell him, but I had no idea how he would take the news. After all, we loved each other, but how well did we actually know each other? We had only been going out for three months. I assumed that he would be horrified and that his first instinct would be to ask me to get rid of it. I mean, we were twenty-one years old and in our final year at university. We had careers ahead of us and a baby was certainly not in my plans for the next decade, and I was absolutely sure it was not in Jack's immediate future either.

Yet I knew how my mother had suffered miscarriages when she was young. She had told me that she lost several babies and that when she managed to hang on to me - born healthy, with ten fingers and ten toes and everything else in the right place - she believed she had been granted a miracle. So, what if this was my one shot? If I aborted this embryo, or foetus, or whatever the technical term was for the very early stage I was at, would I never manage to have a child again? This issue had never worried me before, but now, aware that this tiny person was growing and multiplying every minute of every hour inside my womb, I felt a bond that I could never have previously imagined.

All of that worry slammed back into the shadows with these latest revelations from our mothers. Now, I was not only banged up, but I had also committed incest and was carrying my half-brother's child. It would have to be ripped out of me now. Neither Jack nor I would have any choice in the matter.

I collapsed weeping onto the shower tray, hugging my knees and willing this baby to leave me of its own accord, simply for it to let go and run away down the drain. I had already ruined its life, as my mother had ruined my own.

Chapter 55

Jack

I left Clare standing in the shower and went downstairs to put her clothes into the washing machine. Somehow, performing this mundane task meant that, for a few moments at least, I could avoid contemplating how much my life had splintered in a matter of moments. When I had woken up that morning, I had been in love with Clare and hopeful that I could both reconcile her with her mother and that her mother would give me a second chance and accept me as Clare's boyfriend. A couple of hours later, however, I was a young man who had committed incest with his half-sister and, as if that was not crime enough, I had impregnated her as well. I was also half-orphaned – although I was now as good as completely alone, given that I could probably never forgive my mother for lying to me since birth – and I would have to abandon my childhood dream of reconciliation with my father.

What would I do now – and what about Clare? I could hardly abandon her at this point. Could I love her as a sister as I had loved her as a partner? What if she always aroused me and I could never be around her in future? And would she ever want to be near me once she had had to abort our baby? Inside my skull, it felt as though someone was bashing me with a sledgehammer, which thudded down on my bones every second, causing me a pain unlike anything I had ever suffered. I lay down on the floor of the utility room, waiting for it to cease.

Somewhere above me I was aware of voices and then car doors slamming, tyres grinding on gravel. Someone was leaving.

Chapter 56

Amanda

The kids had fled from the kitchen, stepping over me as I lay prostrate in the doorway. Fiona and I were marooned together, both lost in our own private grief. After our husbands died, we at least had had some hope to cling onto and a reason to rebuild our lives through our children. Terry had ruined us, but he had also shaped the future, ensuring that some part of him might be redeemed and loved. Yet, he had also turned both Fiona and myself into consummate liars and - as Terry found out to his cost - liars eventually get rumbled. Fiona and I had both now been outed, and the only two people in the world who we cared for would now never forgive us.

I raised my head and stared at Fiona with my swollen, bloodshot eyes. Fiona, sitting at the kitchen table, stared into space, seemingly broken and aged thirty years in that moment as her universe collapsed.

'We could not have done anything to stop this happening, Fiona. It must have been a minute chance that they would meet, never mind fall in love with each other. Clare must have been pregnant before she came to my flat, never mind to your place. It's not our fault.'

Fiona turned to face me. 'Is that all you care about, Amanda – whose fault it is? As long as it's not your fault, it's all alright, is it? Like it wasn't your fault that you slept with Terry and produced Clare as a result? Like it wasn't your fault that you didn't think about using a condom. So, I'm afraid that this, yes all of this, is your fault, Amanda. If you had just kept your legs shut instead of spreading them wide open the moment Terry came on to you, if you hadn't betrayed me, your supposed best friend, if you had aborted his baby, which should have been the first thing you did when you found out, if you hadn't lied to me and hadn't lied to Bill, then none of this would have happened. We would both still have husbands – or at least been free to choose whether or not we still wanted them – and I would still have a child who loves me. So, Amanda, this is one hundred thousand percent your fault, you lying bitch. I have never forgiven you for sleeping with Terry, or for bearing his child and I will never forgive you for ruining Jack's life.'

Fiona paused and then rose from the table.

'I'd like you to leave my house and never get in contact with me or any member of my family again. Is that clear?'

'But I need to take Clare with me. I'll just go upstairs and see if she's ready to go,' I murmured, backing out of the kitchen.

'I don't think Clare will ever come within a hundred miles of you now, Amanda,' Fiona spat, newly minted tears falling from her eyes.

I turned away and called upstairs to Clare. There was no answer, so I went up and banged on the bedroom door. 'Clare,' I whispered. There was still no response, and when I turned the handle, the room was empty. I knocked on the bathroom door, and still she did not respond, but the door was clearly locked from the inside. 'Clare, I know you're in there. Please come out. We can sort everything out and find a way through this, I promise, but you need to come home with me now. I appreciate that this has all been a terrible shock and that right now you're not so fond of me, but we can work it out, I promise. Clare, please, you have to trust me.'

I could hear Clare weeping and I was desperate to console her, as I had so often before. 'Mum, how can I ever trust you again? Go home and don't ever try to contact me again. You're dead to me.'

'Clare, darling, you don't mean that. I know you feel like that now, but it's simply the shock and probably the pregnancy hormones as well. You need to come home so that I can look after you and so that we can decide what to do from here.' I waited outside, my ear pressed to the door.

'*We* are not deciding anything together. From now on, I'm on my own. Go away, go home, go anywhere, I really don't care, but whatever you do, don't try to contact me ever again.' I heard the sound of running water, as Clare had switched on the shower and all the taps.

I yelled Clare's name repeatedly and pummelled on the door, but I was drowned out.

Chapter 57

Fiona

The house was deathly quiet now. Mum and Dad were in bed, and I sat alone in the sitting room bundled up in an old blanket. Everyone had left.

Amanda slunk out of the house that same afternoon. I did not offer to drive her to the station or to call her a cab, and she did not ask me to. Clare was the next to leave early that evening, piling all her bags into an Uber. Before she left, she came to find me in the sitting room, where I had collapsed onto the sofa.

'Mrs Wainwright, I'm going now. I just wanted to thank you for having me and to apologise,' she muttered, her face as white as paper.

'Apologise? What for?' I questioned, lifting myself into a sitting position.

'For my mother, and for the fact that she cheated on you with your husband. It's an unforgivable thing to do and I cannot imagine how you managed once you knew. And I am sorry about getting mixed up with Jack and for getting pregnant.' She paused. 'But I want you to know that I'm not like my mother. I love Jack, or rather I did love Jack, even if I can't anymore. I didn't want to get pregnant – not for a long time, anyway. I had no intentions of tying Jack down – or myself, for that matter.' She paused and heaved her duffel bag back onto her shoulder, as it had slipped down. 'You're a good person, and so is Jack. And I am so sorry that any of this has happened.'

'Where will you go?' I questioned her, concerned for this young girl; worried for her, despite myself.

'I'm not sure, but I'll sort something out.'

Clare turned to go.

'Where's Jack?' I asked her.

'I don't know, but tell him I'll be in touch. I don't want to face him right now. I don't know what to say to him. Can you tell him I'll message him please?'

'Alright. Take care of yourself, Clare.'

She nodded and was gone.

Once I was sure that Clare's taxi had left, I roused myself and went in search of Jack. He was not in the kitchen or the pantry, where I often found him scavenging for biscuits or a piece of leftover cake. I headed upstairs and knocked on his bedroom door. I turned the handle and gasped as I entered the room. All the drawers were open and emptied, apart from some loose, single socks hanging from them and a couple of faded sweat tops. I flung open the wardrobe and that too was decimated, with a few old shirts and trousers falling off their hangers. I reeled around in panic and saw that Jack's laptop and wallet, which were always on his desk, were gone.

'Jack,' I screeched. 'Jack, are you here?'

I raced downstairs and went into my parents' room. They now occupied the dining room. I had converted it into a bedroom when my mother's walking deteriorated such that she could no longer manage the stairs, and as her dementia worsened. It was easier. The radio was blaring. 'Dad,' I screamed over the top of it, 'have you seen Jack?'

'No, I've not seen him all day.'

I reeled around and ran onto the drive and out into the lane, but it was empty and desolate in the winter evening. Jack had disappeared.

Chapter 58

Jack

Clare and I left separately without speaking. The day had been so overpowering that we both needed time to think and to process alone. The blows had kept coming at us - jab, jab, jab - until I felt as if I had been knocked down, if not completely out cold. If I felt that way, it must have been so much worse for Clare.

I packed most of my clothes because I could not envisage returning home any time soon. I slogged into the village carrying a heavy rucksack and dragging my bulky suitcase, which was a struggle, because one of the wheels was wonky and it kept pulling to the left. Once I reached the cafe, I stopped and ordered a full English breakfast. I had only eaten some toast that morning and I was suddenly ravenous. As I waited for the food, I picked up my phone.

Jack: How's things?

Bob: Good. U?

Jack: Not great, tbh. Bust up at home.

Bob: Why?

Jack: Too complicated to explain. Where r u?

Bob: At parents

Jack: Any chance I could crash 1-2 days?

Bob: Sure. When?

Jack: Tonight?

Bob: OK. C u later. Btw, Katy here.

This was not ideal, as I was hoping to talk to Bob alone and Katy was Clare's best friend.

Jack: OK, thx. Txt address pls as forgotten it.

Katy and Bob had been an item since that first night that Clare and I slept together. I wondered now if my instinct to take it slow with Clare had been more than not wanting to spoil something special. Maybe on some deep, subliminal level, I knew that we should not do it. Yet when we did make love, it felt so incredible, unlike nothing I had experienced before. Perhaps that was actually because we shared the same blood. I shuddered just thinking about it.

I polished off my meal and paid, keen not to miss one of the few buses of the day that ran between Cadoxton and Cardiff. I lugged my bags onto the bus and stared out of the window. I had always viewed the world one way until this point - as an only child of a hard-working, single mother who would sacrifice anything for me. Now, I was part of an extended family – something I had always dreamed of – but not a weirdly dysfunctional one like this. Never like this.

Bob lived in Harpenden, a thriving middle-class town in Hertfordshire, surrounded by rolling fields and great pubs. I journeyed into London, crossed the metropolis by tube and set off on the final leg from Kings Cross station, recently reinvigorated with posh shops and a newly renovated swanky hotel. Bob picked me up at Harpenden station, waving at the barrier as I disembarked from the train. I felt sweaty and tired after such a long commute. Katy was not with him. Whenever I did see them together, I smiled at the visual disconnect. Bob was so short and dressed rather preppy, while Katy was willowy and looked as if she had effortlessly strolled off the pages of a leading fashion magazine. When they walked along together, she put her arm around him bending down to kiss the top off his head. They made a highly unlikely, yet happy pairing.

'Hi, mate,' Bob greeted me. 'How was the journey?'

'Too bloody long, but I slept most of the way – apart from on the tube. I'm always terrified I'll miss my stop.' I hoisted my bag into the boot of Bob's old Fiesta. 'You look like you're moving in,' Bob quipped.

'Don't panic. I'll get out of your hair in a couple of days. I just needed some time away from home.'

'Well, I guess you'll want to be back in time for Christmas,' Bob commented.

I made no reply.

He fired up the ignition and we began to crawl slowly along the high street. 'Bloody Christmas shoppers,' Bob moaned, as a woman wheeling a pram laden with shopping bags almost walked straight out in front of the car, causing him to perform an emergency stop.

'Do you fancy going for a drink before we go back to yours? I could murder a pint.'

'Absolutely.' Bob smiled, swinging the car around and heading off in the direction we had just come.

We reached the pub and settled down at the only free table by the door, so that every time someone came in or left again, we were blasted with icy air.

'Before we get home, Jack, you need to know something. Clare is there. She arrived just over an hour ago. She called Katy earlier today in a right old state.'

'Fucking hell. Really? She's the last person I want to see right now.'

'Well, I'm sorry, but Katy didn't feel she could refuse her. The girls have been holed up in my bedroom ever since. Clare looks bloody awful. Have you two had a row or something?'

'Or something, yes,' I replied, staring out of the window as shops gave way to housing. I was not ready to face Clare yet. I needed more time.

'I mean, it's not a problem for me, obviously,' Bob continued, 'but I just thought you should know. Anyway, if you want to talk, I'm here for you whenever, mate.'

'Thanks, I appreciate that,' I replied.

Chapter 59

Clare

Clare: U at home?

Katy: At Bob's x

Clare: Think I can come for a night? X

Katy: I'll ask. What's up? X

Clare: Too long. Can you ask B now? Am on train to London x

Katy: OK, hang on x

Katy: Bob says fine. House massive, so no biggie. Wot time u coming? X

Clare: DK. Where is it? X

Katy: Go Kings X. Train to Harpenden. Will pick u up x

Clare: Thx x

Katy: U ok? X

Clare: No tbh x

Katy: Wanna talk now? X

Clare: No when I c u x

Katy: OK take care x

Bob and Katy had been waiting by the barrier at the station when I got there, waving and seemingly extremely relaxed together. Bob helped me with my bags without commenting on how much stuff I had brought with me, and Katy sat in the back with me on the way home, squeezing my hand so hard that I thought she might break it.

'You don't look too well, Clare,' Katy commented.

'I don't feel all that great, I must admit,' I replied.

'You can have something to eat when we get home if you like,' Bob called from the front seat. 'My parents are away for a few days, but Mum has left enough food to feed at least two armies for a month.'

'Yes, and last night we got a takeout anyway,' Katy laughed.

I attempted a smile in response.

Bob's house was vast, set back from the road along a lengthy drive. The entrance hall alone was more spacious than our entire flat in Kentish Town.

'I hadn't realised that you lived in a mansion, Bob,' I gasped. Bob was so unassuming that I had never guessed that he came from money. There were too many kids at Bath who wandered about pretending they owned the place because their parents were wealthy. It made me like Bob even more than I already did.

Bob led the way up a sweeping, spiral staircase and showed me into a bedroom, where the bed was made up in the whitest cotton sheets, which appeared to radiate their own light. There was a long bank of fitted wardrobes along one wall. 'I just need to show you this one particular door,' Bob pointed out, opening a door in the centre of the length of wardrobes which was identical to the rest. 'There's bathroom through here. I suggest to people that they keep this door slightly ajar to avoid peeing in one of the hanging cabinets if you need to go during the night,' he chuckled.

'Wow, I've never seen anything like that in my life,' I replied, opening and closing the door to reveal and then hide the bathroom. 'It's like a magic trick. What an amazing house.'

Bob blushed. 'Do you want something to eat? You must be starving.'

'I'm OK, thanks. Can I just grab a glass of water?'

'Sure. Why don't you unpack, and I'll go and get it.'

'Thanks, Bob,' I sighed, leaving my bags exactly where they lay and throwing myself onto the bed the moment he left.

Katy knocked and came in. 'So, what's the scoop?' she enquired, at which point I simply burst into tears.

Chapter 60

Jack

Two pints down and I had finished telling Bob the full story. He was a good listener, never interrupting me, even though his mouth hung open in shock for a good part of the narrative.

'So, there we have it. I've impregnated my own sister,' I concluded. 'My round?'

'I'm driving, Jack, but I'll happily get you another pint.' Bob signalled to the barman, who seemed to understand the local code and a fresh pint arrived at the table in under a minute.

'Great service round here.'

Bob looked glum. 'You've definitely got yourself a situation,' he commented.

'I reckon that if I submitted it as a script to *Eastenders,* they would reject it as too far-fetched.'

'I think you're right, Jack. It's truly bizarre.'

'It's certainly is, but it's also unforgivable that Mum never told me any of it. She's lied to me my whole life and now I can't see how we can ever go back to having a trusting relationship.' I finished off my third pint.

'But she clearly did it to protect you, Jack, not to hurt you – I think you know that. I guess you can't tell a small child that their father was a criminal and that he suffered a terrifying death.' Bob peeled the top off a beer mat as he ruminated. 'Maybe, once you've invented an alternative story, it's too hard to change it back as your child gets older. I kind of get that.'

'I think you're post-rationalising. And she should at least have told me about my dad and Clare's mum. If she had, none of this would ever have happened.'

'That simply can't be true though, can it?' Bob retorted. 'Even if you had known about the affair, you would never have known that Clare was that child. You were highly unlikely ever to meet that child. You would not have known if it was male or female. And you could not have gone through your whole life assuming that everyone you met was possibly them. It's insane.'

I scowled into my empty pint glass. "I suppose you're right. But even so, my whole life is a sham.'

'Your life so far has been pretty happy as far as I can tell. You have a loving family, who have worked hard so that you could have a good education and a happy life. You're tall, handsome, and funny. Girls fall at your feet. Everyone has blips in life. This is one of yours.' Having destroyed the beer mat, Bob began to fiddle with his car keys.

'A blip? And it's only one of them! It's incest, Bob!' I shouted, far louder than I had intended. There was a lull in the conversation amongst the other drinkers in the pub. 'It's incest,' I whispered again, as the revellers strained to listen.

'But is it? Clare bears no resemblance to you whatsoever. If she was your half-sister, wouldn't she look like you just a little bit?'

'Not necessarily. It depends on which genes were dominant, doesn't it? And both mothers seem pretty sure we are blood relations. It's a fucking nightmare.' I started to fidget on the uncomfortable wooden settee that Bob and I had grabbed at the back of the pub for privacy. 'We should have been more careful with the condoms, but you know how it is when you're in the moment.'

'I don't think any contraception is guaranteed anyway. You've just been unlucky, that's all,' Bob sighed.

'Fuck, yes,' I agreed. 'Anyway, Clare will have to have an abortion and then what? We both finish our degrees, but ignore each other forever more? Or we learn to get along as brother and sister, having been to bed together countless times? It's a total shitfest.'

'I think you need to talk it all through with Clare. It's the only way you're going to work this out,' Bob suggested, standing and picking up his keys. 'Come on. You need to face her, and it may as well be now.'

Chapter 61

Clare

Having related the whole saga to Katy amidst a torrent of tears, I had fallen asleep on the pillowcase, which was no longer pristine white, but now smeared in black mascara and tinted moisturiser. When I awoke again, Katy was lying beside me on the bed, her laptop open beside her. I groaned at her as I struggled to focus.

'Clare, I've done some digging around and there is an abortion clinic in London which has availability this week. If not, you'll have to wait until after Christmas, which isn't ideal, I guess,' she announced, her fingers scrolling across the screen.

'I don't want to wait,' I croaked, my throat dry from so much crying. 'If I don't get on with it, I think it will be harder for me to make the decision the longer it goes on. But how much is it? I don't have any money at the moment.'

'Don't worry about that for now. Most clinics won't charge, especially in a case like yours. But before we arrange that, let me pose a hypothetical. If you and Jack were unrelated and you had suddenly got pregnant, would you rush to have an abortion?'

I rolled onto my side to face her. 'I'm not sure. On the one hand, definitely, as I'm way too young to have a child. I haven't finished my degree or got a job, and I don't have any dosh. But on the other hand, my mum suffered loads of miscarriages, so I might have considered keeping it, in case I couldn't have kids in future. Oh, I don't know, Katy and it's not relevant anyway.' I sighed and rolled onto my back, closing my eyes.

'DNA,' Katy replied.

'Excuse me?'

'What if your mum is wrong? If there is the slightest doubt about your paternity whatsoever, you and Jack should get a DNA test before making any decisions. That's the only way you'll know for sure.'

'I bet they cost a fortune.'

'It's around £200 for each of you from what I can see,' Katy replied, clicking on a link.

'And where would I get hold of that kind of money?' I asked her. 'I could only just afford the train fare to get here. And Jack's broke too.'

'I'll lend it to you,' Katy replied, letting go of one side of her laptop and reaching out to hold my hand. 'You can pay me back in the future when you're a famous criminologist, pathologist, paralegal or whatever you end up doing. Grandma always gives me a wad of cash for Christmas, and I may as well spend it on something important this year rather than on more clothes that I like to have, but don't really need.'

'Katy, it's incredibly kind of you, but I couldn't accept it, especially if it turns out to be a total waste, which it almost certainly will.'

'But what if it isn't, Clare. Then what?'

'I think you're clutching at straws, Katy.' I sat up and grabbed her laptop off her. 'Let's make an appointment at the abortion clinic to get the thing over and done once and for all.' I began to scroll.

'But surely you're going to talk to Jack first? Don't you at least owe him that?'

'Maybe, but I don't even know where he is.'

Chapter 62

Jack

I was feeling the effects of the past twenty-four hours, magnified by the beers, by the time Bob and I reached his house. I had visited several times before and so was not as overawed as I had been on the first couple of occasions. The contrast with the opulent yet understated elegance of Bob's home with the ramshackle dilapidation of my own was immense, yet Bob appeared to be comfortable in either location.

I dropped my bags in the hallway and followed Bob into the kitchen, where he put a large homemade lasagne in the oven.

'Forty-five minutes, I reckon, but I can keep it warm if you're not ready to eat yet. Clare is in the room you normally stay in if you want to head on up there,' Bob instructed me.

'Where's Katy?' I asked.

'Upstairs with Clare, I imagine. Can you tell her I've opened a bottle of wine and send her down? I'm sure she won't want to be a third wheel, and I know I don't want to be. And here's one for you.' Bob handed me a bottle of red and two glasses.

'Thanks, mate,' I replied. 'Wish me luck.'

Bob gave me a thumbs up with each hand and I turned to head upstairs, my heart thumping me in the ribcage as I climbed.

I knocked on the door and entered. The two girls were sitting up on the bed looking at something on a laptop, which they snapped shut the moment they spotted me. 'Hi,' I greeted them.

Clare jumped when she saw me. 'What the hell are you doing here?'

'I could ask you the same question.'

'Well, Bob's my friend and I had nowhere else to go.'

'And Katy's mine.'

'I think I'd better go downstairs and do something useful, like make a salad or something,' Katy announced, unfurling her long legs from underneath her and fleeing past me. She closed the door behind her.

'How are you doing?' I asked Clare, standing by the bed awkwardly with the bottle and glasses.

'I'm not sure,' she replied. 'You?'

'Same.'

Clare patted the bed, and I sat down next to her, placing the wine on the floor, my love for her overwhelming me. Tears sprang unbidden from my eyes and I hastily wiped them away.

'I'm sorry,' Clare whispered.

'What for? None of this is your fault.'

She shrugged and reached out to hold my hand. 'Well, firstly I'm sorry for getting pregnant. Parental fuckups aside, that is one that I should have avoided.'

'I know, Clare. And it's not just your fault. But it does leave us up shitcreek without a paddle. I don't know what we should do about any of it.' I was crying properly now, not bothered about hiding it. The emotion I felt was so painful and so raw that it physically hurt.

'I keep trying to unpack everything,' Clare sobbed. 'The baby is one issue, but the far bigger problem is us. If we are really related, if I can't love you in the same way as I do now, if we can't see each other anymore, I don't think I can keep going.' She paused and grabbed a box of tissues, blowing her nose loudly. 'I feel as if someone has dropped a lead weight on top of me and I can't move from underneath it. I can't even think straight. I just don't know where to start.'

She collapsed onto the bed and instinctively I reached for her, lying down beside her, holding her with her back against me. 'I know, Clare. It's impossible. I can't bear to think about what we should do, about what we have to do.' Her hair was damp from my tears. 'What did Katy have to say?' I sniffed.

I felt Clare's body heave with the weight of her sobbing. 'She, well she was trying to be optimistic. She was attempting to persuade me, to persuade both of us, to get a DNA test.' She shifted and turned to face me. 'She thinks we need to be completely sure that our mothers are really right about this. I don't believe for a moment that they're not, as why would they tell us such a dreadful story and ruin our relationships with them and with each other forever if it was false, but it's always possible as they haven't exactly been honest so far.' Clare reached over my head for the box of tissues on the side table, and I grabbed a handful as well. We blew our noses. Synchronicity.

'I agree that it's highly unlikely, but then this whole situation is ridiculous. You couldn't make it up. So, maybe Katy's right. Maybe it is worth checking it out. It would help us to be clearer, even if it just confirms the worst. Then we can make the decisions we have to make.' I stroked her hair and kissed her forehead.

'I couldn't bear to be without you, Jack. I need you in my life one way or another.'

'I need you too – I just don't know how to treat you anymore. Right now, more than anything, I want to kiss you and to make love to you, but I know that I can't. I might never be able to do so again. And if I can't love you like that, I don't really know how I can love you in a different way, or if I can even ever stand to see you again. I feel like my heart would shatter into a million shards every time I did.'

Clare wiped her face on the duvet cover, mascara smeared all down her face. 'I feel exactly the same way and that's why we need to be completely certain of the truth. Let's face it, our mums hid all of this from us so far, and even now they've told us what they say is the truth, but we can't know that for sure. We can't rely on anything they tell us anymore. We need to find out for ourselves.'

Chapter 63

Clare

We went ahead with the DNA test during the first week of January. We both stayed with Bob and Katy until the new year and then moved back to Bristol a week prior to term beginning again, each to our own flats. We thought it best to conduct the test away from our mothers and our friends so that we could deal with the consequences of whatever the result turned out to be alone, before having to involve anyone else.

The test was performed at a specialist clinic, and we had to wait four excruciating days before we knew our fate. During this time, Jack and I stayed away from each other. There was little point in being together while we remained in complete limbo. Neither of us were good with small talk. On the day of the result was due, I waited anxiously in front of my laptop waiting for the email. When it finally blinked into life on my screen, it took me an hour before I could actually summon up the courage to read it.

I texted Jack and told him that I was on my way over. I owed it to him to give him the news face-to-face. He opened his front door, pale as a ghost, and led me silently by the hand into his living room. We sat there for what seemed like an eternity until I finally summoned up the courage to speak.

'So, Jack, the DNA test,' I took a huge breath, 'has proved categorically that we are *not* related.' I gulped, fat tears cascaded down my cheeks, as if the dam holding back all my emotion for the past few weeks had suddenly burst and flooded my body.

Jack gasped and then embraced me, holding me so tightly that I struggled to breathe. 'That's amazing, it's so amazing,' he kept repeating. He loosened his grip and looked at me. 'Clare, I love you so much. I cannot put into words what a relief this is. I know that we still have some huge decisions to make, but at least now we are free to make them. And we've done nothing wrong, have we – except perhaps use a faulty condom.' He smiled, wiping away tears from his eyes. 'Don't you think this is the best news you're ever had literally ever?'

'Of course I do. I have gone over every single scenario in my head a billion times ever since that dreadful day at your mum's, and I had convinced myself that we must be siblings and that we would go to jail for the rest of our lives and not only lose each other, but also our liberty. I was sure that we would be ruined forever through no fault of our own.' I sniffed noisily and wiped my nose on my sleeve. 'But now, you're right, we can move on.'

We made love in a frenzy, tearing at each other's clothes and then repeatedly, more leisurely, for the rest of the day until both of us were utterly exhausted. Then we made cheese on toast and chased it down with a beer each. 'I know I'm not supposed to drink, but apparently the odd one doesn't harm the foetus.' I patted my flat belly and smiled. I nestled into Jack's broad chest, and we fell into a deep sleep amidst the toast crumbs and empty beer bottles.

The next morning, we were woken by the harsh wintery sun streaming through Jack's flimsy curtains. I rolled over to find Jack was already awake, looking at me.

'I think what we should do is this,' I stated, wiping sleep from my eyes. 'Before we make any decisions about what we should do about the pregnancy or make any other future plans, we should celebrate this day and designate it Non-Sibling Day for the rest of our lives.'

Jack laughed and stroked my arm.

'So, what I propose,' I continued, 'is that I make you the best dinner you have ever eaten tonight at my flat where we celebrate that we are not, and never have been related to each other. What do you think?'

'Sounds like a plan.'

'Great.' I rolled away from him and began to pull on my clothes.

'Surely you don't have to leave now. Couldn't we begin the celebrations right here in bed?'

'We did enough of that yesterday. Right now, I've got some important shopping and cooking to do. I'll see you at my flat at seven. Don't be late. I've got a big surprise waiting for you.'

Chapter 64

Jack

I drifted in and out of sleep for the rest of the morning after Clare left, my body and brain worn out from the stress of the past few weeks and the relief of yesterday. But as I pottered about in the afternoon, hanging around not quite knowing how to entertain myself until I went over to Clare's flat later on, I felt an increasing weight bearing down on my chest as I began to think about what lay ahead of us. Of course, we could celebrate our lack of mutual DNA and our freedom to be together and that was fantastic in its way. Yet the fact remained that Clare was still pregnant, and neither of us were mature enough to raise a child, nor did either of us have any money. I just could not see how we could go forward with a baby.

I had no idea how Clare felt about this. We had both been so shellshocked by the thought of being brother and sister, of having potentially committed incest, that we had never discussed the actual baby, or foetus, or whatever it was called at this stage of its existence. After tonight, we needed to talk seriously, but I resolved in my own mind that whatever Clare's decision was, I would stand by her. After all, her family had suffered enough as a result of my own father's actions and I was determined not to follow in his footsteps.

I shaved and made an extremely poor attempt at ironing a shirt. When I finished and put it on, it looked worse than it had before I started. I inspected myself in the mirror; I looked quite tired and had a few painful spots appearing on my forehead and chin which would clearly erupt into something nasty over the next day or so. I smiled wanly. At least Clare and I were past the stage where appearances were vital. She was happy to take me as I was, and I her.

I stopped at Tesco's on route to her flat and bought a bottle of Valpolicella. I would have bought a better bottle, but I had very little cash on me and I had stupidly left my wallet behind at the flat. When Clare answered the door, I presented the bottle with a flourish. 'Tada!' I announced, handing the wine over to her as if I had been to Spain to buy it. 'Sorry it's a bit crap, but there wasn't much available in my price range.'

She wrapped her arms around my shoulders and leaned up to give me a kiss on the lips. 'Don't worry about that. I have bought a good bottle more in keeping with our Non-Sibling Day celebration. We can keep this one for another time.'

I followed her into her lounge, where the small dining table was set with posh paper serviettes and several candles flickered away stuck into the tops of old wine bottles. The rest of the room was unlit.

'Well, you have gone to a lot of trouble. This all looks very romantic,' I commented, patting her bottom.

'Are you ready to eat? I don't know about you, but all this cooking has made me ravenous.'

'You know I'm always ready to eat. But what about my surprise? I've been speculating on what it might be all day.'

'You'll find out soon enough,' she replied, turning away rather abruptly. 'Right, well I'll go and get the food. Help yourself to the wine.' She paused. 'None for me, obviously.'

I smiled faintly and poured myself a generous glass, as Clare disappeared through to the small kitchen.

'Here you go,' she announced, placing a large portion of pasta in front of me. 'Puttanesca, your favourite.'

'It smells amazing.' Clare sat down and we both began to eat. 'This wine is very good. It tastes quite sweet.'

'I wish I could have some,' she replied, shovelling more pasta into her mouth, strands of spaghetti hanging inelegantly from the side of her mouth. 'The guy in the local off licence recommended it and said it was decent. Here, let me top you up.'

We finished the pasta. 'Would you like some more? There's bit left in the pan.'

'Sure, if it's going.'

'I'll go and get it. Hang on.' She topped my glass up again and gathered up my plate.

As I sat there waiting for Clare to return, I began to feel rather woozy. I tried to stand up, but I felt too dizzy, falling back into my chair and almost toppling over. I knocked my fork onto the floor.

Clare returned with my plate, half full of more pasta. 'Are you OK?' she asked, placing the food in front of me.

The sight of it made me retch.

'No, I'm feeling a bit odd suddenly, quite sick, in fact,' I slurred. 'Maybe I've drunk too much wine too quickly. I might just lie down on the sofa for a minute.' I knew what I was saying, but when the words left my mouth, they sounded muffled, strangled. I attempted to stand up, but collapsed onto the floor and vomited all over the rug.

Clare stood in front of me as I lay on my side, but made no effort to help me. She was smiling.

'Is he still conscious?' a disconnected voice asked from somewhere behind me.

'Yes, he's still with us,' Clare responded.

'Good. There are a few things I'd like to say to him.'

I heard a switch being flicked and the main overhead light came on directly above my head. The harshness bored into my eyes and my head felt as if it was about to explode with pain. I felt footsteps reverberating across the floor.

'Jack, it's Amanda here, Clare's mother. I'm sorry you're feeling so poorly.'

I could only lie there shaking, looking at two pairs of feet.

'I'm sorry too, Jack,' Clare's voice echoed. 'I did love you once, truly I did, but when I found out who you really were and when I understood how your father had betrayed my mother, I had no choice but to let you go. You see, at first, I blamed my mother for lying to me about how my father died. But when she explained it all to me afterwards, I could see that none of it was really her fault. It was your father who seduced her and who gave her the hope of a new life together. And then he ruined everything by absconding with her money, abandoning her while pregnant when he must have believed it was his, and then killing my own father to boot.'

Amanda pulled out one the of dining room chairs and sat down. She bent over towards me. I could smell her musty breath. 'And in all that time, you and your mother never really suffered, did you? You lived a happy life when Terry died. Your mother was only too glad to be rid of him once she knew how he had cheated on her and stolen from everyone, and anyway, she had you, didn't she, her little Terry replica to carry around with her. And what did I have? Yes, I had my lovely, irreplaceable daughter, and no one will ever take her away from me, most certainly not you. But your father used me, Jack, even though I loved him. He used me for just sex and to get at Bill. I wanted your dad to leave your mother and run away with me, to care for his unborn child, but instead, he told me to get an abortion and then he ran away from us all and killed Bill into the bargain.' She paused and leaned down a little closer to me. 'You have bad luck genes, I'm afraid, Jack, and bad genes need to be destroyed.'

'The baby,' I mumbled. 'What about the baby?'

'Oh, I've dealt with that already,' Clare stated as if she had just ticked something minor off her to-do list. 'In actual fact, I got rid of it the day we got back to Bristol. I couldn't give bear to give birth to bad blood, whether we were related or not. It was Mum who made me see total sense.'

I closed my eyes and vomited again.

'We are going to leave you now to die in peace,' Amanda informed me. 'You've drunk enough antifreeze to finish you off in the next few hours. You might fit a few times, but then soon after that, it will be all over. Goodbye, Jack.' She stood up and turned away. 'Come on, Clare. Stop blubbering. It's no time to get all upset now. It's done, just as we planned. The priority now is to get out of here before it's too late. Get your coat. Our cases are already in the hire car.' She switched off the light.

And they left me, alone, choking on my own vomit, shivering and shaking in the wavering candlelight.

Epilogue

2022

Chapter 65

I was jolted awake by four small hands shaking my shoulder. I opened one eye and looked at the clock. 'Shit,' I screamed, realising that I had overslept by over an hour.

'Mummy said the s word,' laughed Ruby, which caused Ben to titter into his tiny hands.

I leapt out of bed and ran across the hallway to pee. The kids followed me into the bathroom and watched.

'Why don't you stand up to wee like Daddy?' Ben asked with a solemn face. He already had a wrinkle between his eyes when he concentrated, which would one day become a permanent fixture when the worries of adulthood caught up with him.

'Because Mummy doesn't have a willy like you and Daddy,' Ruby informed him smartly.

'Never mind discussing my anatomy. You two need to get dressed for school. We are going to be late. Ruby, help your brother to put his uniform on while I make some toast for us to take on the way.'

Much to my surprise, Ruby obeyed immediately, taking her little brother by the hand, and leading him into his room. Ruby did like to take charge given any opportunity – she took after me in that respect - but I knew I did not have too long before they began to argue. I splashed some water onto my face and ran the toothbrush around my mouth, before grabbing my sweats from the floor where I jettisoned them the night before. I would have to shower when I got back from the school drop-off.

My mobile trilled to the sound of *The Pink Panther* theme tune.

'Hi,' I shouted into the speaker. 'Look, it's not a good time, darling. I've overslept and we're late for school and work.'

'Just letting you know I'm boarding the plane now. I'll be home this evening around seven.'

'OK, have a safe flight. Love you.'

'Love you too.'

I hung up and raced into Ben's room. Ruby was nowhere to be seen. Ben was wearing his Thomas the Tank Engine pants back-to-front. I shrugged and threw him into the rest of his uniform before taking him by the hand and leading him down to the kitchen. Ruby followed a moment later, fortunately fully dressed.

'No time for toast,' I shouted at myself, looking at the clock. 'We'll grab a croissant on the way.'

Ben's small face lit up. 'Croissant. Yummy. Can I have a chocolate one?'

I nodded, grabbing my keys from the hook by the front door. We set off at speed, Ben's tiny legs struggling to keep pace, so that in the end I had to pick him up and carry him most of the way. We made a short pit stop at Starbucks before I finally deposited them at the school gates, still munching their breakfast. Ben's mouth was smeared with pain au chocolat, but there was no time to clean him up. I kissed them both lightly on the tops of their perfect heads and they ran in, Ruby disassociating herself from her younger brother as soon as she saw her own friends.

I raced home and showered, slapping some make-up on my face before hurrying back to the tube. By the time I got to work, I was sweaty and exhausted, and it was only nine-thirty. I worked as a paralegal for a leading firm in the city. It paid well and they allowed me to work a short day until three so that I could manage the children. I finished up anything I had not done during the day at home once the kids had gone to bed. Thank goodness for Grandma, as she was the one who helped me with the food shopping and who collected the kids if I got stuck at work, as well as babysitting regularly for us. With my other half travelling so much of the time, I simply could not have juggled everything without her.

I got through the day relatively painlessly, and anyway, it was Friday, so tonight we would have dinner all together and then, when the kids were tucked up in bed, we would polish off a bottle of Rioja and catch up on each other's news. I hated the long-distance phone calls, where we ended up having the briefest of conversations while one or other of us was half-asleep due to the differing time zones.

Jack did not travel all the time, but his job as an investigative reporter for *The Times* took him all over the world quite regularly. I missed him horribly when he was away, but our reunions were always great – even if sometimes he was tired and a little crochety with the children due to the jet lag.

It was Jack who had suggested that Fiona sell up in Wales and move down to London once his grandparents had passed away. She was still able to work as a hairdresser, although she did not see as many clients these days, preferring to be on hand for her grandchildren should we need her. The children adored her, and she was besotted with them, so the mutual adoration society worked well. And she never overstayed her welcome, recognising that Jack and I saw little enough of each other as it was and needed our time together.

It was a long story about how Jack and I ended up together.

Bob and I had returned to Bath early for the Epiphany term of our third year at the beginning of a particularly miserable and cold January. Jack and Clare had spent all of the holidays constantly discussing the pregnancy and the DNA test, desperately trying to decide what they should do. They also discussed it separately with Bob and me. After a tug-of-war between emotion and pragmatism, eventually they settled on returning to Bath early, getting the test done and going from there. When they had been back in Bath for almost a week, however, and we had heard nothing from either of them, Bob suggested that we head back there a couple of days before term began, just to check on them and to make sure they were alright.

We arrived back late in the evening around ten. We went to my flat first, as Bob was driving his car and he offered to take me and my stuff home. When I opened the door to the flat, it was in total darkness, except for the faint flicker of candlelight coming from the lounge.

'Looks like we might be interrupting something romantic,' I whispered to Bob as he deposited my heavy suitcase onto the lino in the hall.

I knocked on the door of the lounge, but there was no reply.

'Clare?' I called, entering the room.

And that is when I saw Jack, lying there motionless in a pool of vomit. I screamed and Bob rushed in and knelt beside Jack. He put his head on his chest.

'His heart is still beating, just. At least, I think it is. Call an ambulance, quickly.'

I fumbled in my bag for my phone, finding everything except my phone in my sheer panic.

'Here, use mine, there's no time,' Bob shouted, throwing his to me from out of his jacket pocket. 'Come on, mate, you can get through whatever this is. Katy and I are here now, and the ambulance is on its way.' He kept talking calmly to Jack until the paramedics arrived, while I just stood there trembling and useless.

Jack was in hospital for a couple of weeks. We had no idea what had happened, or what he had eaten or drunk, but after running a whole series of tests, the doctor diagnosed that he had ingested antifreeze.

'Antifreeze?' Fiona asked stunned. She had driven down from Wales the moment we called her and had not left Jack's side since, apart from when she was forced to do so by the doctors when they were examining Jack or administering drugs. 'Why the hell would he have drunk antifreeze?'

Bob and I were equally shocked. Jack liked a drink, but he never touched other substances, so this was all utterly bizarre. Could he have drunk it by mistake? Regardless of the why, the doctor administered ethanol as an antidote, but as he had no idea exactly when Jack had ingested the poison, he could not be sure of the lasting effects, which he told us could include significant kidney damage.

'He may have to be on dialysis for the rest of his life,' the doctor warned Fiona. 'We just won't know until we see how he responds to treatment.'

And meanwhile, none of us knew where Clare was. She and Jack were inseparable, yet now she appeared to be missing. No one could reach her by phone, and she was clearly not in the flat or at Jack's flat. Fiona overcame her distaste and tried to call Amanda to see if she knew where Clare might be, but Amanda's phone just rang out without answer.

'Do you think they were both poisoned by someone?' I asked Bob.

'But why is all Clare's stuff gone?' Bob questioned. 'None of this makes any sense.'

'Kidnap maybe?'

'What sort of kidnapper packs up all your stuff and takes it with them?' Bob shook his head. 'This whole thing is utterly bizarre.'

Jack made a slow recovery, and he did have to have dialysis, but only for a couple of months until his kidney function recovered. And as he got better, he was able to explain to us what had actually happened.

'If I ever find either of them, I will tear them into tiny pieces with my own bare hands,' Fiona promised.

The police traced Amanda and Clare, but only so far. Apparently, they had boarded a flight from Bristol to Amsterdam on the evening that they had poisoned Jack and from there they flew on to Thailand, but the trail appeared to end there. But I know that Jack had never stopped looking for them. Whenever he came back from a trip, I asked him if he had managed to get any further information, but he had still not found a credible lead as yet.

The whole affair took its toll on Bob and I. We were shellshocked by the whole dreadful event and both of us needed time alone to process it. Jack took a year out from university to recover while Bob and I eventually went our separate ways at the end of that year. After we graduated, we all offered our farewells and the group splintered. Only Freddie kept in touch with each of us separately, but only for a while, until he fell head over heels with a very short physiotherapist from Scotland and moved up to Glasgow. We exchanged emails at Christmas.

A couple of years later, Bob, Jack and I all ended up in London when we managed to get jobs after graduating. We began to meet up once a month or so in The Crusting Pipe in Covent Garden to share a bottle of wine or to eat pasta in the piazza. Bob and I were back on good terms, but just as friends. He was, he is, one of the kindest people that I knew and was never one to bear grudges about anything. He had still not found a permanent partner, but he remained forever hopeful and cheerful, and in the meantime, he was godfather to both Ruby and Ben.

Jack and I fell into our relationship by stealth, in that odd way that friends do sometimes, when affection melds slowly into love. One moment you are platonic and amicable, supporting your friend through emotional trauma, and the next, you realise that you are in love with them. In truth, I think I had always loved Jack. It was simply that at first, he was taken and then he was off-limits because of our previous relationships. However, one evening seven years ago, Bob had left the two of us behind in Bella Italia on St Martins Lane and Jack and I were polishing off a second bottle of Frascati. Jack said something which made me laugh and I took hold of his hand. Instead of letting go, he held onto it and sidled closer. Before I knew what was happening, we kissed, slow and lingering. It was the most delicious kiss that I had ever enjoyed. There have been many more of those delectable kisses since, although time-limited these days because of the small people careering around the house.

We married within the year and Ruby followed shortly afterwards. Sometimes, when Jack is away and I am feeling a little lonely with too much time to think at night, I wonder what life would have been like if he and Clare had had the baby and stayed together. Would I still be with Bob? I think it would have been unlikely, but who knows. And what would Jack and Clare's relationship have been like?

But right now, here today, I must collect my children from school and make dinner for them. Jack should be back in time for bath time and when that chaos is over and the kids are in bed, we can cuddle up on the sofa with our wine and maybe devour some chocolates that he might have brought home from his trip. We will talk about work, laugh at the silly things the children have said and done while he has been away and count our many blessings, while always being on the lookout for our enemies, both to bring them to justice, but also to ensure they cannot harm any of us in the future.

Napoleon and Dr Verling
on St Helena

Napoleon and Dr Verling on St Helena

J. David Markham

Pen & Sword
MILITARY

First published in Great Britain in 2005 by
Pen & Sword Military
an imprint of
Pen & Sword Books Ltd
47 Church Street
Barnsley
South Yorkshire
S70 2AS

ISBN 1-84415-250-2

A CIP catalogue record for this book is
available from the British Library

Typeset in 11/13pt Plantin by Mac Style Ltd, Scarborough, N. Yorkshire
Printed and bound in England by CPI UK

Pen & Sword Books Ltd incorporates the Imprints of Pen & Sword Aviation,
Pen & Sword Maritime, Pen & Sword Military, Wharncliffe Local History, Pen
& Sword Select, Pen and Sword Military Classics and Leo Cooper.

For a complete list of Pen & Sword titles, please contact
Pen & Sword Books Limited
47 Church Street, Barnsley, South Yorkshire, S70 2AS, England
E-mail: enquiries@pen-and-sword.co.uk
Website: www.pen-and-sword.co.uk

Contents

To Proctor Patterson Jones
His love of life and dedication to Napoleon were
infectious and remain with us to this day.

Illustrations

Acknowledgements

In 1996 I received a scholarship to study at Oxford University that summer. While my classes had little to do with Napoleon, I spent much of my 'free' time poring through material available at the Bodleian Library. There, I found a unique piece of Napoleonic history. Dr James Roche Verling had been a doctor on St Helena when Napoleon was there and had kept a very detailed Journal. In 1915, one A. E. Ross made a transcript of the original Journal. That transcript, apparently one of four in existence, is now in the Curzon collection (MSS C 1). The Journal has been quoted in various books, but has never been published in its entirety. With the outstanding co-operation of the staff at the Bodleian, for which I am most grateful, I was able to type a copy of the transcript, which was subsequently provided me on microfilm as well.

On the weekends, and in several subsequent returns to the UK, I went to London, where I gained access to the Lowe Papers in the British Library. There, again with the kind co-operation of the excellent staff of that extraordinary institution, I was able to pore through literally thousands of letters and copies of letters, seeking out anything to do with Verling or related topics. I made transcripts of all that I found.

Verling's original Journal passed to his heirs and eventually to a nephew, Dr Ellis, who was a surgeon in the Navy. Ellis mistakenly left the Journal on a ship and shortly thereafter died. The Journal was eventually presented to Napoleon III and today is in the National Archives of France. From the staff I was able to obtain a microfilm of the original. I can assure you that the typed transcript in the Bodleian is far easier to read! Indeed, in a few cases I was simply unable to determine what was written and have so indicated in the text.

The primary reason for this book is to publish, for the first time, the complete Journal as well as letters in the Lowe Papers dealing with Dr Verling. This material offers a fascinating and rare insight into the circus of the absurd that was life on St Helena. I hope, and believe, that this book makes a significant contribution to the scholarly study of Napoleon. To my knowledge, this is the last significant primary source document from St Helena to be published. When combined with the letters, most of which are also published here for the first time, this book provides a significant window into Napoleon's exile. Historians of all levels will now have easy access to all of the material from Napoleon's exile on that island.

I have produced the Journal and letters almost exactly as they were written. To make it easier to follow, I have standardized all of the dates for the entries and added the year, and have standardized the spelling of Bonaparte. I have also added subheadings indicating the year. Finally, I have made minor spelling and punctuation corrections. Otherwise, nothing has been changed. Please note also that I have added in brackets English translations of French phrases used in the Journal.

Sir Hudson Lowe and other British officials had their letters copied prior to being sent, and it is often these copies that are found in the Lowe Collection. Of course, James Verling is copying letters into his Journal. It is not therefore surprising to find occasional small discrepancies when the two copies of the same letter are compared.

There are many people who greatly deserve my thanks. The staff at the Bodleian and British Libraries were most helpful. Those at the Bodleian seemed especially pleased that the Journal was finally going to be published. My thanks also to the staff at the National Archives in Paris for their assistance in this project. Of course, Rupert Harding and Pen & Sword Books have my undying gratitude for their willingness to take on this project. Special thanks go to Susan Milligan for her excellent work as editor.

Then, of course, there are (in the famous words from the movie *Casablanca*) 'the usual suspects'. Proctor Patterson Jones was very interested in this project and gave me numerous ideas. When, in the course of his own important research, he found material related to Verling, he promptly sent it to me. International Napoleonic Society President Ben Weider is a friend whose support and encouragement have meant so very much to me. My longtime friend and colleague Don Horward of the Institute on Napoleon and the French Revolution at Florida State University helped open some doors on this project and encouraged me to present my preliminary research at a meeting of the Consortium on Revolutionary Europe.

Most important of them all, of course, is my wife, Barbara Ann Markham. Her encouragement and help have made all the difference.

As always, I am indebted to all of these people and more, and it is to them that much of any success is owed. Any errors are mine alone.

J. David Markham
Olympia, Washington, USA
January 2005

Major People Mentioned in Verling's Journal

Antommarchi, Dr Francesco (1789–1838). A Corsican physician practising in Italy, Antommarchi was chosen by Cardinal Fesch (Napoleon's uncle) and Madame Mère (Napoleon's mother) to be Napoleon's physician on St Helena. They were given this opportunity by Sir Hudson Lowe when Napoleon refused to accept any physician selected by Lowe. Antommarchi first visited Napoleon in September 1819 and stayed until his death in 1821. He conducted the post-mortem exam but refused to sign the official report. Napoleon had little faith in his abilities, a lack of confidence that was probably completely justified. In 1825, Antommarchi published his memoirs of his experience on St Helena in *Derniers moments de Napoléon* (Last Moments of Napoleon), which was soon thereafter translated into English. He also claimed to have made a death mask of Napoleon, though that claim is considered suspect.

Arnott, Dr Archibald (1771–1855). Arnott moved through the ranks, eventually becoming Surgeon to the 20th Foot Regiment. He played an active role in the Peninsular Campaign and travelled with the regiment to St Helena in 1819. In April of 1821 he attended Napoleon and the two of them established a good relationship. Napoleon gave him a gold snuffbox and an endowment of 600 francs. Arnott attended Napoleon until his death and participated in the post-mortem exam. His 1822 book, *An Account of the Last Illness of Napoleon*, upset Sir Hudson Lowe.

Balcombe, William (1779–1829). Balcombe came to St Helena in 1807 as Superintendent of Public Sales for the East India Company. He also served as partner in a firm that was the purveyor to ships that entered the harbour at Jamestown. When Napoleon took up residence at a pavilion on his property known as The Briars, Balcombe's daughter Betsy struck up a friendly relationship with him, a relationship that soon included the entire Balcombe family. As a result, Balcombe was appointed purveyor to Longwood, Napoleon's home several months later, and the Emperor and the

Balcombes continued to socialize after Napoleon moved to his new home. The closeness of this relationship was too much for Sir Hudson Lowe, who rightly suspected Balcombe of helping Napoleon correspond with the outside world. He left the island under a cloud but in time was reconciled with Lowe and was appointed Colonial Treasurer of New South Wales, Australia, where he died in 1829.

Balmain, Alexander Antonovitch (d. 1848). The Russian Commissioner, Balmain arrived on 17 June 1816 and stayed until 3 May 1820. He married a stepdaughter of Sir Hudson Lowe and generally approved Lowe's actions.

Bathurst, Henry, Earl, Colonial Secretary (1762–1834). Lord Bathurst was the British official responsible for the safety and confinement of Napoleon and was in frequent communication with Sir Hudson Lowe.

Baxter, Dr Alexander (1777–1841). A surgeon from 1799, Baxter served in the Mediterranean with the 35th Foot Regiment and then with the Royal Corsican Rangers. He was with Sir Hudson Lowe at the surrender of Capri in October 1808. Baxter's career also took him to the Battle of Albuera in Spain and, in 1814, to America where he was present at several actions. In 1816, Lowe took him to St Helena as Deputy Inspector of Hospitals. He was heavily involved in the politics that surrounded Napoleon's medical care, and saw Napoleon several times, though not as his doctor. Baxter left St Helena in 1819 and subsequently received his medical degree from Edinburgh. His final assignment was in Barbados.

Bertrand, Fanny, Countess. British-born wife of Count Bertrand, she supported Napoleon's surrendering to England to retire there and was outraged when he was sent to St Helena instead. She agreed to go to the island with her husband and her daughter, Hortense, on the understanding that they would stay one year only. Her son Arthur was born there.

Bertrand, General Henri Gatien, Count (1778–1844). Bertrand was one of Napoleon's more able generals and loyal companions, and served with distinction in many campaigns. Napoleon made him Grand Marshal of the Palace in November 1814, and he went to Elba in that capacity. He had the same duties on St Helena and was with Napoleon until his death in 1821. Bertrand eventually became the Commandant of the *École Polytechnique* and active in politics. He was one of those selected to return to St Helena to bring Napoleon's body back to Paris.

Bingham, Brigadier General Sir George Rideout (1776–1833). A veteran of the Peninsular War, Bingham was placed in command of the troops sent with Napoleon to St Helena and stayed there until 1820. He treated Napoleon with respect and maintained a friendly relationship with him, despite Lowe's efforts to make that difficult.

Blakeney, Captain Henry Pierce (1782–1823). A veteran of the Peninsular War, Blakeney served as the Orderly Officer at Longwood from July 1817 to September 1818.

Buonavita, Abbé Antonio. Toward the end of Napoleon's captivity, his uncle, Cardinal Fesch, sent Buonavita to serve Napoleon. Though his credentials included service as a missionary in Mexico, the selection was a disaster. Buonavita was elderly and not particularly useful to the Emperor.

Cipriani. See Franceschi, Cipriani.

Cockburn, Admiral Sir George (1772–1853). A decorated and distinguished admiral, Cockburn's career included service under Nelson and throughout the Empire. In 1812 he was sent to America and provided outstanding service on the Chesapeake, Sassafras and Potomac rivers, as well as the battles of Bladensburg and Baltimore. He was also involved in the burning of Washington. Cockburn escorted Napoleon to St Helena on the *Northumberland* and remained in command until Sir Hudson Lowe's arrival in April 1816. Cockburn eventually served as First Naval Lord. His account of his experience with Napoleon is an important source of information.

Cole, Joseph. A member of Balcombe's firm, Cole also served as the Postmaster of St Helena.

Croad, Lieutenant Frederick. Croad served as an aide to the Orderly Officer, Captain Nicholls. His ability to speak French led to his occasional use as a translator. Croad retired as a Major in 1845.

Crokat, William (1789–1879). A veteran of the Peninsular War (where he was wounded) and of Walcheren, in Holland, Crokat served with the 20th Foot on St Helena. When Captain Lutyens resigned as Orderly Officer in April 1821, Crokat took his place. He saw Napoleon on his deathbed and arranged for the post-mortem examination. It was Crokat who took the news of Napoleon's death back to England. He eventually became a general and narrowly escaped an assassination attempt in Paris, evidently by someone who resented his role in the captivity of Napoleon. Crokat died at the age of ninety in 1879, the last to die of those who saw Napoleon on his deathbed. Unfortunately, he never wrote any memoirs of his experiences on St Helena.

Dodgin, Colonel Henry Duncan. Dodgin arrived in St Helena in 1816 and was later presented to Napoleon along with other officers. His major contribution to history is the series of sketches of Napoleon that he made. After retiring from the army he served as Inspector of Police in Barbados.

Franceschi, Cipriani (d. 1818). Almost universally known only by his first name, Cipriani served as Napoleon's Maître d'Hôtel. A fellow Corsican, Cipriani was Napoleon's 'eyes and ears' throughout the island and probably his closest confidant. He died mysteriously on 26 February 1818.

Gentilini, Angelo. Originally from the island of Elba, Gentilini served as one of Napoleon's footmen. He and his wife, Juliette Collinet, left the island in October of 1820.

Gorrequer, Major Gideon (1781–1841). Gorrequer's military career took him to Sicily and the Ionian Islands, where he became acquainted with Sir Hudson Lowe. When Lowe was appointed Governor of St Helena, he took Gorrequer with him as aide-de-camp and Acting Military Secretary. He was fluent in French and meticulous in his writing. Gorrequer was involved in almost every aspect of Napoleon's captivity, and his notes and letters are the single largest source of written information from that period.

Goulburn, Henry (1784–1856). As under-secretary to the Colonies from 1812 to 1826, Goulburn was involved in much correspondence during the captivity of Napoleon.

Gourgaud, General Gaspard, Baron (1783–1852). An artillery officer who served in several campaigns and also as one of Napoleon's personal staff officers, Gourgaud served as Napoleon's Master of the Horse until he left the island in March 1818, the result of an ongoing feud with Montholon. He took countless hours of dictation from Napoleon and his account of that time is of vast importance. He was present at the exhumation of Napoleon's remains in 1840 and placed Napoleon's hat on the coffin in ceremonies before the King.

Harrison, Captain Charles. Brigade Major and then Captain in the 20th Regiment, Harrison was present at the post-mortem examination. Harrison was one of only four officers to come to St Helena on the ship with Napoleon and stay until his death.

Henry, Dr Walter (1791–1860). Surgeon Henry served in the Peninsular War and then in India. He transferred to St Helena in 1817 and stayed until after Napoleon's death. Present at the post-mortem, his writing on his St Helena experience is a valuable resource.

Hodson, Major Charles Robert George (1779–1858). Hodson served as Town Major, Major in the St Helena Regiment and Judge Advocate. He and Napoleon got along well, with each visiting the other's house. He was present at Napoleon's funeral as well as the 1840 exhumation of Napoleon's remains. He died in Bath in 1858.

Hook, Theodore (1788–1841). Hook visited St Helena in November of 1818. The following year he published an account of Napoleon's treatment that was quite favourable to Lowe, and may have been encouraged by him. Dr O'Meara published a reply and Hook's writing is generally considered to be too biased to be of much value.

Jackson, Lieutenant Colonel Basil (1795–1889). Jackson accompanied Sir Hudson Lowe to St Helena and, as a Lieutenant in the Staff Corps, was in charge of preparing Napoleon's quarters. His fluency in French helped him get along well with Napoleon and his entourage. Jackson was an artist and his watercolours of Napoleon, Longwood and other St Helena scenes are invaluable snapshots of life there, as are his plans of Longwood. He also published a book, *Reminiscences of a Staff Officer*, which is a useful description of his experiences. Jackson left St Helena in July 1819. He died at the age of ninety-four, the last survivor of those connected with Napoleon's captivity.

Las Cases, Marie Joseph Emmanuel Auguste Dieudonné, Count (1766–1842). As a nobleman, Las Cases fled France for England at the onset of the French Revolution. He returned as a result of a general amnesty granted by Napoleon as First Consul and, in 1810, became Napoleon's Chamberlain, having distinguished himself in several earlier assignments. One of Napoleon's most loyal supporters, Las Cases was with Napoleon when he surrendered to the British, acting as his representative during negotiations. Las Cases' real importance, however, stems from his having accompanied Napoleon to St Helena. There, he took an enormous amount of dictation from the exiled Emperor until Sir Hudson Lowe deported him in 1816 for having sent unauthorized correspondence to Napoleon's family. He was held prisoner for some time, but eventually allowed to return to France. In 1823, Las Cases published *Mémorial de Sainte Hélène: Journal of the Private Life and Conversations of The Emperor Napoleon at Saint Helena*. While Las Cases is clearly attempting to help establish the Napoleonic legend, his work has nevertheless become one of the most important sources of direct insight into the mind of Napoleon.

Livingstone, Dr Matthew. Livingstone served as Surgeon and Medical Superintendent for the East India Company. He frequently provided medical services to members of Napoleon's staff, including the Montholons and the Bertrands. He had a disagreement with Dr Verling over the state of Madame

Montholon's health and her need to return to Europe. He attended the post-mortem but did not stay for its completion, leading to some suspicions on Lowe's part. That report's controversy was fed by Livingstone's name being omitted from the first draft but added to the final version. Livingstone remained on St Helena and died there in October 1821.

Lowe, Lieutenant General Sir Hudson (1769–1844). A career military officer, Lowe saw action in numerous campaigns, including Toulon, Corsica, Portugal and Egypt. He held various staff positions, including staff officer to Blücher, but his most famous duty was as Governor of St Helena from April 1816 until he left the island in July 1821. His narrow approach to his dealings with Napoleon has tarnished his image in spite of his long career. He was, however, knighted in 1817 and most would admit that his assignment was a difficult one, for which he was particularly ill suited. After St Helena, Lowe served as Governor of Antigua and staff officer in Ceylon. He was eventually made Lieutenant General before he left the service.

Lutyens, Captain Engelbert (1784–1830). A veteran of the Peninsular War with the 20th Foot Regiment, with whom he went to St Helena, Lutyens was made Orderly Officer at Longwood in February 1820. However, the petty politics of the island soon caught up with him and he was criticized for accepting a book, *Life of Marlborough*, from Napoleon on behalf of the Regiment. He resigned his position in April of 1821, shortly before Napoleon's death. His daily reports are a useful resource.

Lyster, Lieutenant Colonel Thomas (d. 1841). A figure of some controversy on St Helena, Lyster had served with Lowe and went with him to St Helena as Inspector of Coasts and Volunteers. In July 1818, Lyster was made Orderly Officer at Longwood, replacing Captain Blakeney. Napoleon and his staff objected to the appointment on the grounds that he was not in the regular army, and the dispute became so heated that Lyster challenged Grand Marshal Bertrand to a duel. Lowe removed Lyster from the position and reappointed Blakeney. Lyster died in 1841 on the Isle of Man.

Marchand, Louis-Joseph (1798–1876). Napoleon's most faithful valet and executor of his will, Marchand, whose mother had served as nurse to the King of Rome, was with Napoleon throughout his exile and present at the exhumation of Napoleon's body in 1840. Following Napoleon's wishes, Marchand married the daughter of a general and was rewarded for his long service to the Emperor by being made a count in 1869.

Montholon, Charles Jean Tristan, Count (1783–1853). A generally undistinguished career included service as an aide-de-camp to several generals and marshals, including Berthier, and service as an Imperial Chamberlain. While he served as an aide to Napoleon at Waterloo, he and Napoleon were never close. Still, Montholon and his wife Albine accompanied the Emperor to St Helena, where he became one of Napoleon's most trusted associates. He was amply rewarded in the will, and is seen by some as a suspect for a possible poisoning of Napoleon. After Napoleon's death, he wrote his memoirs and eventually became involved with Louis-Napoleon's attempted coup in 1840. After serving some prison time, Montholon closed his career as a deputy in the National Assembly.

Montholon, Madame Albine Hélène (b. 1780). Wife of Count Montholon, Albine left the island in July 1819. Many historians believe that she and Napoleon had an affair and that he was the father of one of her children.

Nicholls, Captain George (1776–1857). A veteran of the Peninsular War with the 66th Foot Regiment, Nicholls came to St Helena in 1818 and was soon thereafter appointed to the post of Orderly Officer at Longwood. He served in that position until February of 1820. His journal is an excellent source of information, especially as regards Napoleon's efforts to remain secluded.

O'Meara, Dr Barry Edward (1782–1836). Surgeon on the *Bellerophon*, the Irish O'Meara was chosen by the British at the last minute to accompany Napoleon as his physician. He recognized the likely difficulties that would be encountered by anyone who had to work so closely with Napoleon while reporting to the British, and especially to Lowe. Controversy over the relationship between O'Meara and Napoleon eventually led to his removal in July of 1818. While serving as Napoleon's doctor, O'Meara kept copious notes on everything Napoleon said. His book on the subject, *A Voice from St. Helena*, is a major source of information for students of Napoleon's exile.

Plampin, Rear Admiral Robert (1762–1834). Plampin's naval career included service in North America, France, the siege of Toulon and India. In July 1817 he was given command of the St Helena and Cape of Good Hope naval stations, a post he held until 1820. He lived at The Briars and was generally very supportive of Sir Hudson Lowe's policies toward Napoleon. Not surprisingly, there was no love lost between Napoleon and Plampin.

Power, Major James (1778–1851). Power was involved in the Peninsular War and Waterloo and served as commander of the Royal Artillery Corps on St Helena for most of the time that Napoleon was there. He managed generally to avoid involvement in the politics of Napoleon's exile.

Reade, Sir Thomas (1785–1849). After Reade's extensive service in the Mediterranean, he was selected by Lowe to join him as Deputy Adjutant

General, and the two arrived together in 1816. Reade was heavily involved in the internal affairs of Napoleon's exile, especially after being appointed Inspector of Police in 1819. It may be that he was even more zealous in his desire to restrict Napoleon than Lowe. He read letters between the principals, including Verling, and often commented on them. He was present at the post-mortem examination and provided Lowe with a useful account of that process.

Solomon, Mrs Lewis. The wife of Lewis Solomon kept a store and lodging house, along with brothers Saul and Joseph. News from Europe and St Helena moved through the house and it was often involved in the sending of clandestine correspondence from Napoleon or his entourage. The company is the only one from the period of Napoleon that exists today.

Stanfell, Captain Francis, RN. Stanfell served in the West Indies, the Channel and North America before being made Captain of the *Phaeton*, the ship that brought Sir Hudson Lowe to St Helena. He was friendly to and supportive of Lowe and his policies and was eventually given command of the *Conqueror*. He was presented to Napoleon in 1817 but the two had no significant relationship.

Stokoe, Dr John (1775–1852). Stokoe's career included action at Copenhagen and Trafalgar before being assigned, in 1817, as Surgeon to the *Conqueror*. Stokoe was introduced to Napoleon by O'Meara and was assigned to attend Napoleon on 17 January 1819 and paid Napoleon several visits until 21 January. The developing close relationship between Stokoe and Napoleon caught Lowe's eye, however, and he was eventually court-martialled and dismissed from the Navy. His memoirs, *With Napoleon at St. Helena: Being the Memoirs of Dr. John Stokoe, Naval Surgeon*, provide an interesting insight into the petty politics of the island.

Vignali, Abbé Ange. Appointed by Cardinal Fesch to be Napoleon's personal man of the cloth, Vignali, who arrived in September 1819, was of very little use to Napoleon. He presided at Napoleon's funeral and left about three weeks later.

Wortham, Lieutenant Hale Young (1794–1882). After seeing service in the Peninsular War, Wortham went to St Helena with Lowe as second-in-command of the Engineers. He supervised the maintenance of Longwood but after a flap over the nature of the work he resigned the position in April 1821.

Wynyard, Colonel Edward Buckley (1780–1865). Wynyard became known to Lowe during service in the Mediterranean and arrived on St Helena in May 1816. He served as Lowe's Military Secretary but played only a minor role in the captivity of Napoleon.

Major Locations Mentioned in Verling's Journal

Alarm House. Located some two miles from Longwood, about halfway between Jamestown and Longwood, Alarm House served as the residence of Colonel and Mrs Wynyard. Though he lived in Jamestown, Sir Thomas Reade stayed there upon occasion. The house came equipped with a gun which could be fired to alert the island of something happening. The gun was fired to announce Napoleon's arrival to the island.

Castle. As the centre of government, the Castle, located in Jamestown, served as Sir Hudson Lowe's office. Verling and others would see Lowe at either the Castle or Plantation House, and Lowe's correspondence could come from either location.

Deadwood Plateau. A short distance from Longwood, Deadwood was the primary location of British soldiers. It was a dreadful location, too hot in the summer and bitter cold in the winter.

Hutt's Gate. A small house several miles from Longwood that served as Bertrand's house until his home was built in the grounds of Longwood.

Longwood House. Napoleon was assigned Longwood by the British and took up residence there soon after his arrival on St Helena. The house was on a plateau with no protection from the fierce winter winds and torrid summer heat, and had no readily available water. In time even the British recognized its inadequacy and built Longwood New House, but Napoleon died before he could move there.

Plantation House. Residence of the Governor and thus of Sir Hudson Lowe, Plantation House was a little over three miles from Longwood. Clearly the best residence on the island, it was situated on some 200 lush acres with a beautiful view of the sea. Plantation House was considered a possible residence for Napoleon but the idea was not looked on favourably by Sir Hudson Lowe.

Prologue: Napoleon, Verling and St Helena

Napoleon Bonaparte has always been a subject of great fascination to historians and generalists alike. Countless books have been written on every aspect of his career, and his image is familiar to people throughout the world. One of the most interesting periods of Napoleon's life came towards the end, when he was in exile on St Helena from 1815 until his death in 1821. His treatment there by the British was humane and cruel, appropriate and unimaginable, generous and miserly. Napoleon was allowed to maintain his own imperial court in miniature, complete with staff and servants brought from France. The British laid the groundwork for an honourable and decent, if decidedly lonely, exile.

Unfortunately, Napoleon's court soon came into conflict with another, namely that of the Governor of the island, Sir Hudson Lowe. The relationship between the two men began on a reasonable and hopeful note, but soon deteriorated into a petty and dangerous feud between two men who were determined not to give an inch in their dispute. While Napoleon initially was given wide latitude in his movements on the island, Lowe soon instituted restrictions that forbade Napoleon to go very far without British accompaniment. This was unacceptable to Napoleon, but it would soon get worse. Lowe began to demand that a member of his staff make a personal sighting of Napoleon each day, to assure him that Napoleon had not escaped. Now, escape from this island was impossible, but Lowe was insistent.

Napoleon was outraged and refused to co-operate. The entire affair became a cat and mouse game, with Napoleon ever more reluctant even to emerge from his home at Longwood. This was detrimental to his health, of course, as he got very little exercise. Napoleon and his staff, and Lowe and his staff, engaged in a long and often absurd battle of wills. Both sides took part in a level of scheming and bickering that was embarrassing in its absurdity.

The Lowe Papers provide a perfect mirror of Lowe's obsession with maintaining a visual contact with Napoleon. This duty generally fell to Captain Nicholls, and there are numerous letters from him and others with such statements as 'I saw Napoleon'; 'I didn't see Napoleon'; 'I think I heard

Napoleon'; 'I fancy he is in his bath.' Notes flew back and forth at a furious pace. Napoleon, anxious not to be seen, would often get his exercise by walking in the billiard room. In one August 1819 episode, it seemed Nicholls might actually break down the door to Napoleon's room, but cooler heads prevailed and Nicholls was able to observe Napoleon in his bath through a window.

Nowhere was the absurdity of this game more obvious than in the relations between Napoleon, Lowe and an assortment of doctors assigned to provide much-needed medical care for Napoleon. Doctors O'Meara, Stokoe and Verling each became the subject of mistrust, suspicion and accusation from both courts. This situation destroyed the medical careers of the first two doctors. Only Verling managed to escape with his reputation and career intact.

James Roche Verling landed right in the middle of the conflict between the courts of Napoleon and Lowe. Fortunately for modern historians, he kept a very detailed journal, which included copies of letters as well as his recitation of events. This journal gives a reflection of all that was going on in St Helena and is an important document for understanding the interaction between the two courts. Incredibly, it is published here in its entirety for the first time.

For their part, Sir Hudson Lowe and his staff communicated with all concerned through letters, which were copied and saved. These letters give fascinating insight into the politics of the island. Those included here are all that relate to James Verling. The Journal and the letters combine to give us a unique picture of life on St Helena.

Part One

End of a Career, Beginning of a Legend

Chapter 1
Napoleon's Last Campaigns

Napoleon Bonaparte was born of modest parentage on the island of Corsica on 15 August 1769. Through hard work and good fortune he had risen to the heights of power, leading armies to victory after victory and becoming, in 1804, Emperor of the French. At its height in 1810–12, his empire and alliances gave him control of virtually all of Europe.

Napoleon brought liberal reforms to much of his empire and he was wildly popular in France. He was less popular in the halls of power in London and in the ancient courts of Europe. In time, these forces wore him down. In Spain, Napoleon misjudged the feelings of the common people and the determination of the British. Over a period of years, the 'Spanish Ulcer' cost Napoleon valuable soldiers and, more important, his aura of invincibility.

In 1812, war with Russia had become inevitable. Napoleon chose to fight on Russian soil rather than wait for them to attack, so he led his *Grande Armée* (Great Army) of 600,000 men into Russia, hoping to force one great, decisive battle. He got his victory at Borodino, but his capture of Moscow would prove useless. In the end, numerous delays led to the disastrous winter withdrawal from Russia. He had lost 90 per cent of his army and any remaining reputation of being unbeatable.

By the beginning of 1813, Napoleon was in Paris raising an army and seeing to it that his Russian misadventure had no domestic repercussions. Tsar Alexander of Russia had moved his armies into the Grand Duchy of Warsaw and encouraged Prussia to switch sides. By March, the Prussians had done exactly that, and declared war on France. A new alliance was in the works and Napoleon was in trouble.

Even so, Napoleon had a number of important cards to play. He was already organizing a new army and his marriage to Marie Louise, a daughter of the Emperor of Austria, gave him an important alliance. Napoleon could not imagine that Emperor Francis would declare war on his own daughter, and on the grandson born of that marriage.

Napoleon moved quickly against the Russian and Prussian threat, soon defeating them at the battles of Lützen and Bautzen. But promised Austrian troops never arrived to support Napoleon. Instead, Francis proposed mediation with Russia and Prussia, led by Austrian Foreign Minister Count Clemens Metternich. The resulting talks were little more than a sham, with Austria, Prussia and Russia essentially wanting Napoleon to give up all of his gains since coming to power. This would never be acceptable to the French people and was certainly not acceptable to Napoleon. In the end, the armistice and negotiations gained Napoleon nothing and in August Austria switched sides and declared war on France. So much for family ties! England, sensing an opportunity to defeat her old foe, opened her coffers in support of the new coalition against Napoleon. Napoleon, no longer feared, was on the defensive.

The armies drawn up against Napoleon were better trained and more modern than those he had faced earlier. His enemies had learned from the master of warfare. Still, Napoleon himself was formidable. The allied armies planned to avoid him when possible and concentrate on defeating his subordinates. This approach worked. Napoleon was generally successful but his subordinates were not. Former allies began to desert Napoleon, and even his marshals were beginning to lose heart and question the advisability of continued fighting. When Napoleon lost the Battle of Leipzig in October 1813, the rout was on. Stunned by the treachery of the Saxons and Marshal Bernadotte and devastated by the premature destruction of a bridge, costing him 20,000 soldiers and the life of Marshal Prince Poniatowski, Napoleon was forced to withdraw into France. His empire gone, deserted even by his sister Caroline and her husband, Marshal Murat, the King of Naples, Napoleon was now fighting for his very survival. He had not done well in the campaign of 1813. In 1814, in the Campaign of France, he would be more like his old self.

After arranging for the defence of Paris (and further peace negotiations), Napoleon struck at the approaching armies with a fury. He quickly defeated a Russian corps and followed that with several other successes. Stunned, the allies suggested an armistice.

In Paris, the treacherous foreign minister Talleyrand was deserting Napoleon's cause in favour of that of the Bourbons, the ruling family of France until the overthrow of Louis XVI by the French Revolution. Groundwork was being laid to replace Napoleon with a Bourbon king. On the battlefield, the allies were approaching Paris. Napoleon decided to race them to Paris. Marshal Marmont was already being pushed in that direction and the rest of the marshals insisted on joining him there. It was a reasonable approach to take, offering the possibility of presenting the allies with a fortified Paris with Marmont's troops in their front and Napoleon at their rear. As Napoleon later told Count Montholon 'they [the Allies] would never have given battle on the left bank of the Seine with Paris in their rear.'[1]

Paris, however, was in no mood to resist and suffer the consequences. The defeat and subsequent defection of Marshal Augereau at Lyons on 23 March did nothing to stiffen their backbone. Countermanding Napoleon's instructions, Napoleon's brother Joseph, who had been placed in charge of the defence of Paris, sent the government, along with Marie Louise and her son, out of the city, leaving the political future of Paris, and France, largely in the hands of Talleyrand, who remained behind. Marie Louise tried to intercede with her father, the Emperor of Austria, but to no avail. Joseph was of little use to Napoleon in Paris and he left at the end of March. When Tsar Alexander arrived in Paris, he stayed at Talleyrand's home. Napoleon's future was bleak.

Talleyrand led the provisional government and prepared the way for the return of the monarchy that so many had died to remove. Tsar Alexander was willing to consider passing the throne to Napoleon's son, but it was not to be.

On 3 April, Marshals Ney, Berthier, Oudinot and Lefebvre told Napoleon that he had to abdicate in favour of his son and leave the area. Napoleon reluctantly agreed and the next day abdicated in favour of his son, with Marie Louise as Regent. Tsar Alexander was prepared to accept this proposal. However, Marshal Marmont, under the influence of Talleyrand, marched his 11,000 soldiers into the Austrian camp, thus ending any hope for Napoleon or his son. Without those soldiers, Napoleon no longer had any bargaining power.

On 11 April 1814, Napoleon abdicated unconditionally, saying, 'there is no sacrifice, not even that of life, which he is not ready to make for the interests of France.'[2] Louis Stanislas Xavier, brother to the deposed and executed Louis XVI, became King Louis XVIII. Napoleon was exiled to the island of Elba, just off the coast of Italy, where he would be given the title of Emperor of Elba. It was to be an honourable exile to a pleasant island where they even spoke Napoleon's native Italian. But the good faith of the allies was brought into question when they refused to allow his wife and son to join him there. Napoleon, awaiting his fate at the chateau of Fontainebleau, was so distraught that he attempted suicide with poison that he always carried with him. The poison had lost much of its potency, though, and the effort failed.

On 20 April, Napoleon said goodbye to the soldiers of his Old Guard, and left for Elba with a personal guard of 1,000 personally selected soldiers.

Elba

Arriving in Elba, he was saddened by the unexpected death of his first wife, Josephine; another tie to the past was gone. However, Napoleon engaged in a serious effort to improve conditions on Elba. He revised the legal and tax system and built new roads and fortifications. His mother joined him, as did his sister, Pauline. Countess Walewska, his Polish mistress, made a final visit, bringing their young son with her. Napoleon held court to many foreign visitors and was generally seen as busy and happy.

All was not as well as it seemed, however. Louis XVIII refused to give Napoleon his pension, leading to financial difficulties. Worse, it was clear that Talleyrand was interested in arranging an entirely different fate for the Emperor of Elba, perhaps prison, perhaps worse. The powers of Europe were meeting at what was called the Congress of Vienna, and there was no telling what they would do. Napoleon began to hear of French dissatisfaction with Louis XVIII and negative moves toward Napoleon by Talleyrand in Vienna. These two factors led Napoleon to decide to leave Elba and attempt to regain control of France.

The One Hundred Days

Napoleon landed in France on 1 March 1815. After a slow start, he began to make his way north. He was determined not to fire a single shot on his way to Paris, fearing that would lead to disaster. He therefore took the mountain road to Grenoble, off the main road. This route, now known as the *Route Napoléon*, was through difficult terrain and Napoleon was not sure what kind of reception he would receive along the way. But things went well, and after winning over troops sent to capture him at Laffrey, Napoleon entered Grenoble to the cheers of its citizens. He later wrote, 'On my march from Cannes to Grenoble I was an adventurer; in Grenoble I once more became a sovereign.'[3]

On his way to Paris Napoleon also picked up the support of Marshal Michel Ney, who had promised Louis XVIII he would bring back Napoleon in an iron cage. Ney had been the King's last hope, and Louis left Paris just hours before Napoleon entered the city.

Napoleon had two problems to solve. First, he had to reorganize the government and gain the political support of all of the various factions. Second, he had to try to get the rest of Europe to let him reign in peace. If he could get even a few of them to agree – his father-in-law Francis of Austria, for example – his gambit might just work. Along the *Route Napoléon* he had repeatedly professed his desire for peace and promised no more war. But would the rest of Europe believe him? It was his only hope.

Napoleon moved quickly to organize the government and gain support of the factions. He convinced Benjamin Constant, the leader of Parisian liberals, to join in writing a new constitution. It was a brilliant political move, though the two-chamber legislative body established by that constitution would prove problematic.

Dealing with the governments of Europe was far more difficult and far less successful. Had the governments been safely in their respective capitals, Napoleon's efforts might have worked. He could divide and conquer, starting with Austria. But they were still all in Vienna, and so was Talleyrand. Louis XVIII had signed a secret treaty with England and Austria, a treaty that Napoleon hoped to use to avoid war with those two countries and perhaps with all of Europe. But Talleyrand, aided by King Murat's absurd military moves against Austria, was able to convince the allies that Napoleon simply could not be trusted. Peace was out of the question, and the allies began to mobilize their forces.

Napoleon moved quickly, planning to attack the English and Prussian armies that were in Belgium. He rapidly organized the government and mobilized the country, and was able to raise an army of 300,000 soldiers. But staffing his leadership proved to be disastrous. His old friend and chief of staff, Louis Alexander Berthier, fell or was pushed to his death from a window in his estate, depriving Napoleon of the one person who could have filled that job adequately. Marshal Soult, Berthier's replacement, was an outstanding general but not up to the job of chief of staff.

Napoleon left Marshal Davout as Minister of War in Paris, appointed Marshal Michel Ney to command the left wing of the army and Marshal Emmanuel Grouchy to command the right wing. All of these appointments were disasters.

Faced with the European powers against him, Napoleon had to take the first action. He could not afford to wait until a combined force of perhaps 600,000 moved in from two directions across the borders of France. The English and Prussians were in Belgium: Napoleon would march to meet them, hoping to keep them apart and to defeat each in their turn. It was his only chance. It was a good choice, and it nearly worked.

On 12 June, Napoleon's army of about 125,000 men marched toward Charleroi, in Belgium. On the morning of the 15th, they routed the Prussian force, who had no idea the French were coming. As in 1805 when he marched to Ülm, Napoleon had managed to maintain a very high level of secrecy.

Wellington was at a ball in Brussels when he was given the astounding news of Napoleon's actions so near to his army. He and the Prussians decided to make their stands a few miles south at Quatre Bras and Ligny, respectively. Wellington had some 96,000 men under his command and Blücher had about 117,000. Napoleon needed speed, secrecy and a perfect execution of his plans. He accomplished only the first two of those requirements. Almost from the beginning there were delays and confusion. Even so, by the evening of 15 June, Napoleon was in a good position. He had seized Charleroi and had kept the two allied armies apart. The normal course of action would be to turn on first one, and then the other, allowing him to have at least some level of numerical superiority.

Instead, on 16 June, Napoleon did what he almost never did. He split his forces into two wings to fight two separate battles: Ney against Wellington at Quatre Bras and Napoleon and Grouchy against Blücher at Ligny.

Both Ney and Napoleon were slow to begin their engagements. Ney should have moved right away to secure the crossroads at Quatre Bras; had he done so, Wellington would have been kept at bay and the road to Brussels would have been clear. Grouchy and Napoleon were also later than expected in beginning their major offensive. The plan had been to crush the Prussians so that Napoleon could then turn on Wellington and the English army.

At Ligny, Blücher was being pushed back, but the failure of General Jean-Baptiste d'Erlon's troops to join Napoleon at the critical time allowed the Prussians to escape. Confusing and contradictory orders from both Napoleon and Ney led to d'Erlon's spending the day marching first toward one battle and then toward the other, never participating in either.

The Battle of Ligny over, the French should have pursued the retreating Prussians. Unfortunately, Napoleon delayed until the next day sending Marshal Grouchy with 33,000 men. Then, Grouchy further delayed his departure and took what some historians believe was a leisurely pace of pursuit. As a result, the Prussians were able to withdraw in good order and move north, which allowed them eventually to support Wellington at Waterloo.

Napoleon and Ney joined forces and followed Wellington toward Brussels in heavy rain. By early evening, the French had arrived at the fields near the small town of Waterloo.

Napoleon expected to win the battle of 18 June 1815. But time was essential, and the heavy rains delayed the start of the battle, which eventually allowed Blücher to arrive just in time.

Napoleon could have won the battle, but a series of errors and misfortunes led to his defeat. A long and wasted effort against the walled farm called Hougoumont, cavalry attacks by Marshal Michel Ney that were unsupported by infantry (and thus doomed to defeat), the timely arrival of Marshal Blücher, and the failure of Grouchy to arrive at all combined to defeat Napoleon in the early evening of the 18th.

Seeing that all was lost, Napoleon left the battlefield and eventually made his way back to Paris, hoping to rally the government and the people to his cause. It wouldn't happen. News of Napoleon's defeat preceded his arrival and it was already clear that he would not be able to maintain power. He tried to abdicate in favour of his son, but his former Minister of Police, Fouché, manipulated things to ensure the return of Louis XVIII. The Assembly voted to support a continuation of the Bonaparte dynasty, but in the end it was Wellington himself who decided that the Bourbons should return once again, notwithstanding their lack of popular support.

At Malmaison, Napoleon both encountered and created delays in his departure. He seemed unable to decide where he wanted to go, and time was running out. America was a strong possibility and transportation was available. Marie Walewska offered to join him in exile, but Napoleon sent her home and they would never see each other again.

Chapter 2

Journey to Immortality

Napoleon applied for safe conduct passes to America and on 29 June said goodbye to his family. He went to the coastal city of Rochefort, where he discovered that the British ship *Bellerophon* now guarded the harbour.

Though it soon became clear that the allies would not grant him safe passage to America, there were still several options available. He could have used available and willing neutral ships or tried to flee on a French frigate, two of which were immediately available. Either of these approaches might well have worked, but Napoleon decided against them. America did not have the appeal to Napoleon that one might have anticipated. He feared that he would become nothing more than a farmer, sinking into obscurity. He wanted to establish his legend and legacy, and this was not the way to do it, far from the centre of European politics. He also had some concern for his safety in America, ever fearful of an assassination attempt.

Instead, Napoleon decided to retire to England. The English had let other deposed monarchs do that, and Napoleon had no reason to expect different treatment. There, he would write his memoirs, receive distinguished guests, and work on developing the image he wanted to have in history. He sent word of his decision to Captain Frederick Lewis Maitland of the *Bellerophon*, who promised to give him an honourable escort to England. Napoleon agreed, writing a letter to the Prince Regent:

> Your Royal Highness, faced with the factions that divide my country and the enmity of the greatest powers in Europe, I have ended my political career; I come like Themistocles to sit by the hearth of the British people. I place myself under the protection of their laws, which I request from Your Royal Highness, as the most powerful, the steadiest, and the most generous of my enemies.[1]

Napoleon boarded the *Bellerophon* on the morning of 15 July 1815. Captain Maitland gave him full honours and treated Napoleon respectfully. In his journal, Maitland wrote:

> to such an extent did he possess the power of pleasing, there are few people who could have sat at the same table with him for nearly a month, as I did, without feeling a sensation of pity, allied perhaps to regret, that a man possessed of so many fascinating qualities, and who had held so high a station in life, should be reduced to the situation in which I saw him.[2]

Maitland's superiors had other plans for Napoleon. They were determined not to allow Napoleon even to meet with the Prince Regent, for fear that Napoleon would charm him into allowing him to retire to England, and they kept him isolated on the ship. The last thing the government wanted was Napoleon living in England, where he might well become involved in any number of intrigues.

There were a number of possible options for dealing with Napoleon. If Blücher had captured him after Waterloo, he would probably have had Napoleon shot on the spot. Prison, execution and even exile in America were possibilities. Foremost in the minds of all was the need to make certain that Napoleon was never again able to become active in European politics. But there was also the need to remember that he was very popular with many people in France and elsewhere, including a significant minority in Great Britain. Obvious mistreatment of Napoleon would have potentially significant risks, especially given the reasonable treatment normally accorded deposed monarchs.

Thus, while several options were considered, the decision was made to exile Napoleon to the remote island of St Helena, off the coast of southern Africa. Napoleon had returned from one island; he would not return from this one. At the same time, he would be given a house and allowed an entourage of staff and servants. His remaining years would be comfortable and fairly pleasant, while keeping him closely guarded and safely away from European politics.

The next decision that needed to be made was what to call Napoleon. This would not appear to be a difficult decision, as all deposed monarchs were called by their former titles. However, using logic best described as tortured, the British decided that Napoleon was no longer Emperor of France or Elba, and no longer First Consul of France. He would be treated as a mere general, a decision that rankled with Napoleon and upset his supporters to this day. They also reverted to the original spelling of his name, Buonaparte, another insult.

Napoleon's entourage included the following people:

General Henri Gatien Bertrand, Grand Marshal of the Palace, his wife
  Fanny, and their three children;
Charles Jean Tristan, Comte de Montholon, his wife Albine, and their
  youngest son;
General Gaspard Gourgaud;
Emmanuel Auguste Dieudonné, Marquis de Las Cases (whose English skills
  were critical);
Barry Edward O'Meara, a British Navy surgeon serving as Napoleon's
  physician;
Louis-Joseph Marchand, valet to Napoleon;
Numerous other valets, servants and other staff members.

Selecting a Doctor

The British, concerned with public opinion, were determined to provide
Napoleon with a doctor with whom he would be comfortable. They also
expected the doctor more or less to serve as their spy and to be their first line
of defence against any complaints about the effects of the climate on
Napoleon's health. Napoleon naturally wanted a doctor he could trust.

Prior to Napoleon's departure for St Helena, both sides sought a solution
that would satisfy all requirements. The British allowed Napoleon to choose
Foureau de Beauregard, a French doctor. Beauregard was willing to go to
America, but had no interest in the remote island of St Helena. He declined
this dubious opportunity. There was no other French doctor immediately
available and the British were anxious to hustle Napoleon and his entourage on
their way. The British suggested Barry Edward O'Meara, surgeon of the
Bellerophon. O'Meara accepted the appointment, but insisted that he remain a
British officer, as Napoleon's ability to pay him was unclear at best. This
insistence on remaining a British officer, subject to British regulations, would
prove to be a problem. He would find himself caught between the conflicting
demands of Napoleon and Sir Hudson Lowe, Napoleon's eventual gaoler.
Looking back on his appointment, O'Meara commented on the difficulty of
the assignment:

> I never sought the situation; it was in some degree assigned me; and
> most assuredly I should have shrunk from the acceptance of it, had
> I contemplated the possibility of being even remotely called on to
> compromise the principles either of an officer or a gentleman.
> Before, however, I had been long scorched upon the rock of St
> Helena, I was taught to appreciate the embarrassments of my
> situation. I saw soon that I must either become accessory to
> vexations for which there was no necessity, or incur suspicions of no
> very comfortable nature.[3]

These words foreshadowed the very similar words of Dr Verling, still years away from his appointment as Napoleon's physician.

On 9 August 1815, Napoleon, O'Meara and the other members of his entourage sailed for St Helena aboard the *Northumberland*, along with a company of the Royal Artillery. The surgeon of this company was a young Irish doctor named James Roche Verling. Born in Queenstown, Ireland on 27 February 1787, Verling had, at the age of twenty-three, graduated as a Doctor of Medicine at Edinburgh University. His service in the Peninsular War earned him some honours, and he was appointed to the fairly high rank of Assistant Surgeon. Verling, who was able to speak both French and Italian, impressed Napoleon and his staff, but there is little record of their conversations. Napoleon was generally friendly with the soldiers on board the ship.

The voyage to St Helena lasted until 15 October. It was a difficult voyage, with boredom causing difficulties between people. Napoleon played cards and held many discussions with Rear Admiral Sir George Cockburn, whose diary gives valuable insights into Napoleon's view of his history.[4]

St Helena is a tiny island of 85 square miles that served as an outpost for the East India Company. It is 1,100 miles from South Africa, 700 from Ascension Island and 4,400 miles from England. Approaching ships would be easily spotted and the British soldiers stationed there would thwart any escape attempt.

One of the first questions was where to house Napoleon. The Prince Regent had instructed that Napoleon be made comfortable. Plantation House was probably the best choice, as it had one of the best locations with regard to climate and was a nice facility. Instead, Napoleon was assigned Longwood House, which was in a state of disrepair and had a very poor location on a wind-swept plateau with no trees. The British made improvements, but the place was still less than adequate. Napoleon's valet, Marchand, wrote of Napoleon's housing situation:

> there are pleasant residences such as Plantation House, Rosemary Hall, and Sandy Bay. The cottages of The Briars, Dewton, and Mason present them with fine hospitality and cool shade to rest from the hot sun. These advantages were nonexistent at Longwood. This land possessed no more than a plateau ... constantly beaten by southeasterly winds ... [T]he climate of Saint Helena is generally unhealthy, particularly in the area occupied by the Emperor.[5]

Napoleon was first given quarters in Jamestown. He didn't like this arrangement, and was anxious to move out of the city. Although he was eventually to be sent to Longwood, the house was not yet ready when Napoleon arrived on the island. He had a very pleasant stay with the William Balcombe family, whose home was known as The Briars. Balcombe was a partner in a firm that served as purveyors to the many ships that put into the harbour at Jamestown. Their home was situated in a garden-like setting, one of the best on the island.

William Balcombe's property included a pavilion, essentially a summerhouse, and Napoleon seized on the opportunity to stay there. The style was simple but elegant: here, Napoleon could relax in comfort and begin to write his memoirs. Balcombe, of course, offered Napoleon the use of his home, but Napoleon insisted that he would be quite content in the pavilion. The local garrison quickly built a dining room and study for Napoleon's use, and he settled in.

These may well have been the happiest times of Napoleon's stay on the island. He and the Balcombes socialized often, and Napoleon even remarked that William's wife, Jane, reminded him of Josephine. Napoleon exercised often and was in generally fine health. But it was the fourteen-year-old Betsy Balcombe that provided Napoleon with his greatest treat. They took to each other instantly. Her informal ways and playful nature delighted the Emperor, and she was the only person allowed to interrupt Napoleon when he was meeting with someone. No doubt missing his son and Josephine's children when they were younger, Napoleon showered attention on his young friend. He was saddened when he had to leave their home for Longwood on 10 December 1815. The Balcombes visited him often after his move and Napoleon and Betsy remained friends, with him even escorting her to a ball. Eventually, Sir Hudson Lowe became displeased with the close relationship between Napoleon and the Balcombes and they were forced to leave the island on 18 March 1818. Many years later, Betsy wrote her memoirs of her times with Napoleon, and they stand as one of the best insights into Napoleon as a person.

Napoleon's early days at Longwood went as well as could be expected. Enjoying good health, he entertained visitors and dictated his memoirs. Relations with Admiral Cockburn (serving as Governor) started fine, but deteriorated as British control of Napoleon's movements tightened. There was no possibility of Napoleon escaping, but the British insisted on escorting him if he went beyond the ever-diminishing boundaries around Longwood. This would depress any prisoner, and certainly one who had once been the most powerful person on earth.

Bad as things were, they would soon get worse. Sir Hudson Lowe was appointed Governor of St Helena and arrived in April 1816. He was well meaning and wanted to establish a good relationship with Napoleon. But he suffered from a lack of imagination and a determination to interpret and follow rules strictly, no matter how absurd that might be in any given situation. Even Lord Bathurst, Lowe's immediate superior in England, implied that Lowe would have discretion in his treatment of Napoleon, writing:

Herewith you will receive the King's Warrant under my Grant and Seal authorizing you to detain keep and treat Napoleon Bonaparte as a Prisoner of War; and you will receive at the same time the Act of Parliament lately passed giving powers to the above effect. You will be pleased to regulate your conduct according to the spirit of the above Instruments.[6]

Of course, if Napoleon was a prisoner of war, and England and France were at peace, he should have been released! This little rule of international law or custom would be ignored when it came to Napoleon. The former Emperor would remain their 'guest', the term used in their internal communications.

Initially, Lowe and Napoleon got along reasonably well. Both were friendly and spoke in Napoleon's native tongue, Italian. Lowe even agreed to build a new home for Napoleon. But he was convinced that Napoleon was going to attempt to escape, and would therefore not reduce any of the restrictions on Napoleon's movements. This led to bitterness on the part of Napoleon and his entourage. Relations deteriorated, and the two men fell into an adversarial relationship that was often petty and certainly demeaning to them both. In a famous incident, Lowe refused to allow Napoleon to receive a book as a gift because it was inscribed to *Emperor* rather than *General* Napoleon.

The restrictions on Napoleon's movements probably had a negative impact on his health. In time, Napoleon took fewer and fewer walks, finally stopping them altogether. This lack of exercise was not good for either his mental or physical health. As he told Betsy Balcombe:

Would you have me render myself liable to be stopped and insulted by the sentries surrounding my house, as Madame Bertrand was some days ago? It would have made a fine caricature in the London print shops, – Napoleon Bonaparte stopped at the gate by a sentinel charging him with fixed bayonet. How the Londoners would have laughed![7]

Chapter 3
Napoleon's Doctors on St Helena

Napoleon had agreed to accept Barry O'Meara as his doctor, and the two men generally got along fine. O'Meara retained his position with the military but was assigned as Napoleon's full-time physician. His close relationship with Napoleon would soon get him into trouble. Napoleon wanted him to see his primary responsibilities as service to his patient, namely Napoleon.

Napoleon, O'Meara and, unfortunately for them, Lowe, began to see O'Meara as serving in the capacity of *l'homme de l'Empereur* (the Emperor's man). This meant he served as Napoleon's personal physician first, and military doctor second. Indeed, O'Meara soon became quite enamoured with Napoleon and quite disillusioned with Sir Hudson Lowe. He came to feel that the British, through Lowe, were trying to encourage an early death for Napoleon. By insisting on sending him to an island noted for its bad climate, situating him in a house on the worst part of the island in terms of climatic conditions, and then restricting his movement so much that Napoleon eventually all but gave up meaningful exercise, the British, in the eyes of O'Meara, were trying to send Napoleon to an early grave.

O'Meara also resented what he considered was Lowe's effort to use him as a spy. While medical ethics of the day might not match those of the twenty-first century, O'Meara nevertheless was uncomfortable with Lowe's persistent questions regarding the situation at Longwood. Of course, Napoleon also tried to use him as a spy and had extracted a promise that O'Meara would not reveal any information to Lowe save any that he might hear regarding a possible escape by Napoleon.

In fact, O'Meara was in a very difficult position and may have tried to have it both ways. He did reveal more information to others than to Lowe, and it eventually became clear that his sympathies were much more with Napoleon than with his gaolers. Various memoirs and later historians have provided differing accounts of the exact nature of O'Meara's activities, and his own memoirs, *A Voice from St. Helena*, makes his antipathy towards Lowe quite clear. Biased though it might have been, it was an instant best-seller in England and quickly went through a number of editions.

In time, Lowe found the situation between Napoleon, O'Meara and himself intolerable. He became convinced that O'Meara was conspiring against him, and, indeed, there is evidence that O'Meara attempted to bribe one or more people to support Napoleon in his ongoing feud with Lowe. Things came to a head and in July 1818, Lowe removed O'Meara from his position with Napoleon. O'Meara left the island and was subsequently dismissed from the Navy. He died in 1836.

With O'Meara gone, Lowe needed to find another doctor for Napoleon. One possible choice was Dr Alexander Baxter, the Deputy Inspector of Hospitals on the island. He had travelled to the island with, and at the request of, Lowe, which as far as Napoleon was concerned eliminated him from consideration. Baxter was familiar with Napoleon's medical condition, having worked with O'Meara writing up medical reports for Lowe. This was necessary because Napoleon refused to allow any physician to issue written reports calling him by any title other than 'Emperor', while Lowe refused to accept any written reports calling Napoleon by any title other than 'General'. So O'Meara verbally gave reports on the condition of 'Emperor Napoleon' to Baxter, who then wrote formal reports on the condition of 'General Bonaparte' for Lowe.

Verling and the Two Courts

Lowe then turned to the best doctor on the island, James Roche Verling. On 25 July 1818, Lowe directed Verling to 'immediately proceed to Longwood, to afford your medical assistance, to General Bonaparte and the foreign persons under detention with him; there to be stationed until I may receive the instructions of His Majesty's Government on the subject.'[1] Verling dutifully moved into a room at Longwood.

Lowe had good reason to appoint Verling. Verling and Napoleon had had friendly interaction on the long voyage to St Helena, so the two men had already established a relationship of some friendship and trust. Surgeon Walter Henry, who was Assistant Surgeon to the 66th Regiment at Deadwood, thought very highly of him, saying, 'Dr Verling is an esteemed friend of mine; and I know that he was well qualified in every respect for the duty on which he was employed; being a clever and well educated man, of gentlemanly and prepossessing manners, and long military experience.'[2] The historian Frank Richardson calls the selection of Verling 'an excellent choice, and one more indication that Lowe really did try to accommodate Napoleon and the French'.[3]

Napoleon's own supporters, anxious that their Emperor should have the best possible medical care, and recalling their own positive impressions of Verling on the trip to St Helena, encouraged him to accept Verling as his doctor. Napoleon's valet, Louis Marchand, relates that:

the grand marshal and Count de Montholon urged the Emperor not to remain any longer without a doctor, and suggested the one who had replaced Dr O'Meara, Dr Verling ... but the Emperor flatly refused. This refusal was not aimed at the doctor, but at the Governor, who with this doctor would have had a man of his own choosing. The Emperor considered Dr Verling a perfectly honest man, he had spoken with him several times on the *Northumberland*, either at the table when he was invited there, or during his strolls on deck.[4]

Napoleon's mameluke, Ali, says essentially the same thing:

It is true that he could command the services of Doctor Verling, of whom I have written, but the Emperor had never admitted him to his private apartments. It was enough that the doctor had been stationed at Longwood by the Governor for the Emperor to refuse to receive him or to see him. Yet Dr Verling was a serious man, who seemed very capable. The care which he had taken of the Grand Marshal's family and some other people at Longwood, among them Marchand, whom he had cured of a very serious illness, had gained him the confidence of all of us, and I have no doubt that if the Emperor had found himself seriously ill he would not have hesitated to call in the doctor, whom he knew perfectly well, having seen him on board the *Northumberland*.[5]

Verling was a good choice for any number of reasons. He was cultured, courteous and a good conversationalist. His friendship with O'Meara gave him some potential entrée to Napoleon's trust, which along with the fact that he was very well qualified made him a good selection. But he came at a bad time, just as Napoleon had been deprived of a doctor whom he trusted. It is also possible that his age worked somewhat against him, as at thirty-two he was quite junior to the other medical officers that were available.[6]

Napoleon was determined not to see anyone who was put in that position by Sir Hudson Lowe. The noted historian of Napoleon's time on St Helena, Frédéric Masson, reflects Napoleon's attitude when he describes Verling as Lowe's 'man',[7] and Dr John Stokoe, a British doctor whose own difficulties with Sir Hudson Lowe we will shortly discuss, called Verling 'one of his [Lowe's] puppets'.[8] Napoleon obviously would not accept anyone who could be seen in these terms. He wanted someone who would serve as *l'homme de l'Empereur*, and would accept no one else. Even Lowe understood this reality, as Verling records that, in a conversation of 19 August 1818, Lowe said that Montholon told him 'that he believed the only reason why Napoleon did not see me, was that Sir H. Lowe had sent me, and not from any personal objection to me.'[9]

Verling also records that Count Bertrand echoed this idea, telling Verling 'that Napoleon's objections to me were not personal, that Napoleon had often said so, but that he had declared when I first came to Longwood, that he would never see me since I had been selected by Sir H. Lowe.'[10]

Lord Bathurst, Lowe's superior in London, himself indicated to Lowe that Napoleon was to have a doctor of his choosing, although the conditions were somewhat unclear:

> you will not fail to acquaint him [Napoleon] at the same time that, should he have reason to be dissatisfied with Dr Baxter's medical attendance, or should prefer that of any other professional man on the island, you are perfectly prepared to acquiesce in his wish on the subject, and to permit the attendance of any medical practitioner selected by him, provided that he conform strictly to the regulations in force.
>
> I have only to add that you cannot better fulfil the wishes of his Majesty's Government than by giving effect to any measure which you may consider calculated to prevent any just ground of dissatisfaction on the part of General Bonaparte on account of any real or supposed inadequacy of medical attendance.[11]

For his part, Sir Hudson Lowe was convinced that Napoleon was determined to shift the blame for Verling's unacceptability to him, and said so on more than one occasion. His letter to Lord Bathurst of 9 November 1818 goes on at some length on the matter. Lowe calls Verling 'unsuspecting in the matter', but it is clear that Verling is already caught in the middle.

The British, fearful of charges by Napoleon's supporters in England and elsewhere of medical maltreatment, wanted Napoleon to have good medical care. As Napoleon would only accept a doctor who was willing to serve in much the same capacity as any doctor to his or her patient, one might question why Sir Hudson Lowe would not work toward more of an accommodation with Napoleon, especially as they were willing to provide Napoleon with a French doctor of his selection, whose loyalties would clearly be to Napoleon rather than to the British. There is no answer to that question, but the underlying tension was the basis for Napoleon's own efforts to replace Dr O'Meara with a British doctor willing to serve as *l'homme de l'Empereur*.

Napoleon made two such efforts. Upon the loss of O'Meara's services, he approached Dr John Stokoe, surgeon of the *Conqueror*, whom O'Meara had introduced to Napoleon. On 16 January 1819 Napoleon fell seriously ill. Bertrand wrote to Dr Stokoe, asking him to see Napoleon:

> The Emperor has just had a sudden and violent attack. You are the only medical man at present in this country in whom he has shown

any confidence. I beg you not to lose a moment in hastening to Longwood. On your arrival ask for me. I hope that you will arrive in the course of the night.[12]

Of course, Verling was in Longwood, but Bertrand, mindful of Napoleon's orders, sent for Stokoe, an action that resulted in a six-hour delay in getting treatment for Napoleon, who was very seriously ill. That Bertrand, and Napoleon (who had declined offers to send for Verling), were willing to risk even death to avoid seeing Verling says a great deal about the strength of feelings on the matter.

Lowe ordered Stokoe to report to Dr Verling, who was to accompany him to see Napoleon. Napoleon would not allow Verling to see him, so Stokoe saw the Emperor on his own. The two got along fine, and Napoleon decided to ask Stokoe to serve him as had O'Meara. He had Bertrand present eight conditions under which Napoleon would accept Stokoe as his personal physician. These allowed Stokoe to make appropriate medical reports as well as reports of any activities that called upon him to exercise his patriotic duty (such as escape plans), but otherwise to serve as Napoleon's doctor without interference from the British. Stokoe 'saw nothing in the articles incompatible with the honour of a British officer and a gentleman,'[13] attended Napoleon and left. Montholon presented the conditions to Lowe, who seemed to agree and forwarded the list of conditions to Admiral Plampin, Stokoe's immediate superior. Meanwhile, Stokoe continued to see Napoleon as needed, a total of five times by September.

Initially, it seemed that Stokoe's superiors would accept the conditions set forth by Napoleon. In time, however, Stokoe paid a heavy price. Verling was consulted by Lowe's aide-de-camp, Gorrequer, and correspondence became heated. Lowe was convinced that Stokoe was engaged in a conspiracy of some sort, and there were allegations of assorted misdeeds. Perhaps worse yet, Stokoe's diagnosis appeared to support Napoleon's belief that the climate of St Helena was ruining his health. If the British public began to believe that, they might demand that Napoleon be allowed to retire to England. The government was determined to see that the climate, and therefore the British, were not held responsible for any of Napoleon's ailments.

Stokoe left the island on leave, but was forced to return immediately and face a court martial. He was convicted and drummed out of the service. He had foreseen these possibilities, and had tried to avoid such entanglements, but all to no avail. It was one of the most shameful episodes of Napoleon's exile and a classic example of Lowe's irrational obsession.

Verling could see the distinct possibility of the same thing happening to him and was very much on his guard. He made every effort to remain on good terms with Lowe and the other military staff associated with Longwood. He gave numerous reports to Major Gorrequer, Lowe's aide-de-camp and Sir Thomas Reade, Lowe's Deputy Adjutant General, regarding Napoleon's activity. These activities cannot have escaped the attention of Napoleon's staff, and certainly must have made Verling even less acceptable to Napoleon.

Still, Napoleon wanted his own doctor and Verling's good relations with the Bertrands and Montholons made him an obvious possibility. On 19 January 1819, Bertrand met with Verling. The historian Forsyth felt this was an effort to remove Verling from Longwood,[14] but it seems more likely that it was the first step in an effort to get Verling to accept conditions like those offered Stokoe. Verling's journal entry on the subject reads:

> He [Bertrand] then produced a letter from Sir H. Lowe, stating that he had received orders from Earl Bathurst to remove O'Meara and to replace him by Mr Baxter, but in case of Napoleon disliking Mr Baxter's attendance, that he should have the choice of any medical man on the Island, but that he had sent one in the meantime, that even a momentary want should not be felt. [Bertrand said] 'Napoleon declined at that time making any choice, invited as he was, and declared he never would see you, whom if you had not been sent here, we should all have pointed out, from our knowledge of you aboard ship. Our influence has been repeatedly used to induce him to see you, and in vain, even when he thought he was going to die. The Governor now recedes from Lord Bathurst's letter, Napoleon has made a choice, obstacles are thrown in the way, he is about to refuse him. The correspondence is becoming more warm (the Governor is a man who never feels a blow until he is knocked down). He perseveres in wishing to force you upon him, and I warn you that motives will soon be attributed to him for this line of conduct in which your name will unavoidably be implicated, and in a manner in which your name ought not to appear. I therefore advise you to retire immediately from the situation.'
>
> I replied to Count Bertrand, that as a military medical man, I was here in obedience to orders and that my conscience would enable me to disperse any false imputations.[15]

Some time later, Madame Bertrand tried to convince Verling to become Napoleon's doctor, which he dutifully reported to Lowe, recorded in his journal entry of 25 February 1819.

Napoleon would not accept Verling so long as Lowe appointed him. However, he might well accept him under conditions that removed at least some of that connection and guaranteed some level of confidentiality between the two men. Montholon met with Verling on 1 April 1819, and made some direct proposals regarding possible service to Napoleon. An obviously nervous Verling described the proposal in a memorandum to Lowe, and expressed his great desire to be 'removed from Longwood'.[16]

Montholon's proposal was straightforward. If Verling would become *l'homme de l'Empereur*, Napoleon would pay him an annual salary of 12,000 francs, and this should protect Verling from the possibility of his acceptance of the position having a detrimental effect on his military career. As was the case with Stokoe, Napoleon would not expect Verling to do anything amounting to treason, but wanted his primary loyalty to be to Napoleon rather than to Lowe. Verling, of course, recalling the problems encountered by Stokoe, wanted nothing to do with this offer.

Montholon's memoirs, which are often quite suspect, do not relate this offer to Verling. They do mention a letter of 1 April 1819 from Montholon to Reade, written at the behest of the Emperor, deploring the loss of Dr Stokoe and suggesting conditions similar to those offered to Verling, under which Napoleon might select a medical officer from the island as his physician.[17]

The next day, Lowe wrote a long letter to Lord Bathurst describing the offer made to Verling, and closed it with these words:

> Dr Verling after informing me of what was said when they [the conditions] were shown to him ... proposed to quit Longwood; but ... I desired Dr Verling would remain at his post ... when if no French Surgeon came, I would immediately appoint another English Medical Officer to relieve him.[18]

Verling was not yet out of the woods, and in September Madame Bertrand made one last pitch to convince Verling to take a position as Napoleon's personal physician, suggesting that Napoleon would prefer an English surgeon rather than one from another country. She also expressed surprise that Verling would not want to be associated with someone as great as Napoleon.[19]

Verling had resisted all efforts to make him *l'homme de l'Empereur*, but Sir Hudson Lowe, who seldom seemed to trust his fellow man, suspected that Verling was getting too close to the residents of Longwood. While Lowe was officially supportive of Verling's reaction to the letter of 1 April 1819, his secretary, Major Gideon Gorrequer, was saying just the opposite. In his encoded diary, he relates this conversation of 4 April:

> Old Mach [Lowe] mentioned to me ... that Magnesia Terzo [Verling] had done things as bad as either 1st or 2nd Naval ones. That he had agreed to the propositions offered by Veritas [Montholon] ... Afterwards Mach said 'I do not consider him fit for such a situation. He is not trustworthy, particularly after all that he had said to him, and all his cautions.' There were several things in him he did not like. 'I assure you Mr Verling is not the person I expected to find. He has been talked over.'[20]

William Forsyth and other apologists for Sir Hudson Lowe claim that all was well between Verling and Lowe. But Verling's journal and other evidence show this was not at all the case. Gorrequer, for example, makes these entries for 6 April 1819 and 8 September 1819 respectively:

> The hostility he began displaying about Great Gun Magnesia [Verling], and his angry remarks at his not having reported to him sufficiently of his palavers with the satellites of Neighbour [Napoleon] ...[21]
>
> Mach [Lowe] said Magnesia Great Gun [Verling] had played a double part. The rancour he showed against him. His jealousy. He said that any other [doctor] should be chosen in his place – and the vingtième [20th] Magnesia [Dr Arnott] in particular.[22]

Lowe, apparently wishing to tarnish Verling's otherwise sterling image, wrote to Lord Bathurst with the 'shocking' news that Verling might have had certain Irish connections. Verling was, of course, Irish. Fortunately for Verling, Bathurst was a supporter of Catholic emancipation and was not interested in such trivial matters.[23] His aide, Henry Goulburn, responded to Lowe, in part:

> Lord Bathurst has also desired me to take this opportunity of replying to one of your private letters in which you communicate certain information respecting Mr Verling's opinion and connections in Ireland which you had derived from him and which you had thought it right to make known to Lord Bathurst. I am to assure you that the whole of Mr Verling's conduct appears to have been so discreet and proper on occasions even of no little difficulty that Lord Bathurst cannot avoid expressing his entire approbation of it, and in case Mr Verling should have been aware of your having communicated to Lord Bathurst the circumstances contained in your private letter . . . Lord Bathurst is desirous that you should assure him that they can make no impression on his Lordship's mind & that whatever may be his connections in Ireland and the religious faith either of himself or them Lord Bathurst cannot permit any circumstance of that nature to invalidate the confidence to which his uniform discretion and propriety of conduct, up to the date of your last communication so justly entitle him.[24]

Despite the efforts of Napoleon's entourage and of Lowe, James Verling never did attend Napoleon. He did see Napoleon at a distance from time to time and was constantly asked for reports by Lowe and his staff. Verling did provide medical services for the Montholons and the Bertrands, but even this placed him in an uncomfortable position, especially with Sir Hudson Lowe.

For example, he and Doctor Livingstone had a major disagreement on an ailment of Count Montholon. Verling's diagnosis was consistent with the French complaint that the climate was unhealthy, while Livingstone, unwilling to lend any support for such an argument, questioned the seriousness of Montholon's illness.[25] Only departure from Longwood or, better yet, St Helena, would return Verling to some degree of normality. Napoleon would not accept the services of any British doctor unless that doctor would agree to conditions that Sir Hudson Lowe was never going to accept. Any effort by Verling to get on the good side of Napoleon and his companions would be very suspicious to Lowe. Verling understood this, writing:

> Upon the tenor of this conversation [with Sir Hudson Lowe], which I have not fully detailed, I have to remark that it has left upon my mind the impression that the situation of Physician to Bonaparte is one which cannot be held by a British subject, without the certainty of sacrificing his peace of mind for the time he holds it, and with more prospects of ultimate injury than benefit.[26]

All of this still left Napoleon without appropriate medical attention. The British were understandably concerned and agreed to allow Napoleon to have a French doctor. Napoleon's mother, Leticia, and his uncle, Cardinal Fesch, selected a Corsican physician named Francesco Antommarchi. He arrived in St Helena on 20 September 1819. He met with Lowe and Verling, naturally expecting a full medical update. But the meeting was a disaster, as he had been unaware that Verling had never actually seen Napoleon. The embarrassment was so great that Verling actually withdrew from the meeting, though the two did have subsequent meetings.[27]

Antommarchi was an incompetent doctor. Napoleon knew it and never had any faith in him. Verling was truly the doctor who might have been, and was certainly superior to Antommarchi. If circumstances had allowed him to serve as Napoleon's doctor, the quality of Napoleon's health care would have been considerably improved. If the cause of Napoleon's death was stomach cancer, then perhaps he would have had greater comfort. If Napoleon died of other causes, including poisoning, then the quality of health care could have made a difference. A removal from the island for health reasons or the recognition of symptoms of poisoning were both more likely with Verling in attendance. Verling was the right person at the right time, but circumstances prevented him from achieving his own potential destiny.

The arrival of Dr Antommarchi was not necessarily good news for Napoleon, but it certainly was for Verling. His long-standing request to be given a leave of absence to return home was granted, but his departure was delayed. While he was waiting to leave, Madame Bertrand made several requests to have Verling attend her. Verling, by now completely intimidated by the politics involved with any medical treatment of anyone at Longwood, had secured prior permission for such visits. Lowe told Verling that he had no objection to his visiting Madame Bertrand to provide medical services or even to pay a social call, and that Verling's name was on the list of people approved to visit Longwood. This was not enough for Verling, who insisted that he would not visit Madame Bertrand without specific orders from Lowe. This dispute over the difference between Lowe's blanket approval and Verling's desire for actual orders went on for several months and did nothing to improve the relations between Verling and Lowe, a fact clearly reflected in Verling's journal and numerous letters between the principals. Lowe even thought it necessary to write a very long explanation of the situation to Lord Bathurst (see letter of 3 November 1819).

Verling was finally able to leave St Helena on 25 April 1820, and never returned. Amazingly, he left in the good graces of Napoleon's entourage and, perhaps most amazing of all, of Sir Hudson Lowe. Verling returned the favour in 1823 when he wrote an affidavit supporting Lowe in a dispute with O'Meara. He continued to have an outstanding military career, highlighted by his 1827 promotion to full surgeon, his 1843 promotion to senior surgeon and his 1850 appointment as Deputy Inspector General of the Ordnance Medical Department. Four years later he retired from the service as Inspector General, and died four years after that, aged seventy-one.

Chapter 4

Epilogue: Death and Immortality

By the time Antommarchi arrived, Napoleon's health had deteriorated. Increasingly isolated and getting almost no exercise, he seemed to have lost much of his optimism and even his will to live. He showed very little interest in the quality of his health care, and had very little use for Dr Antommarchi. By early 1821 the end was clearly near. Napoleon suffered from sharp pains in his side and had severe vomiting attacks. He made out his will and then added several corrections and additions.

Napoleon died on 5 May 1821, shortly before six in the evening. It was an ignominious end. He was not allowed to return to France even in death, and was buried in a pleasant location on the island where he had relaxed in earlier, happier, years. British, or at least Lowe's, pettiness literally followed Napoleon to his grave. Napoleon's staff wanted the gravestone to read 'Emperor Napoleon'. But Lowe would only allow 'Napoleon Buonaparte'. The impasse resulted in Napoleon being buried in an unmarked grave.

To his credit, Lowe provided a dignified and solemn burial ceremony. On 9 May Napoleon was dressed in his favourite uniform of the chasseurs of the Imperial Guard and placed in a multi-layered casket of tin, lead and mahogany. After mass, British grenadiers carried the casket to the hearse. The procession passed by lines of troops, under arms in a sign of respect for a fallen soldier. The garrison soldiers joined the procession, which marched to the sound of funeral music. Guns from the flagship and forts fired salutes. After prayers at the graveside, artillery fired three honour salvos of fifteen rounds each. A large stone was then lowered to cover the tomb, which was placed under constant guard. Marchand recorded 'the scene was overwhelming in its sorrow and grief'.[1]

Napoleon was buried, but the saga was not quite over. In July 1840, King Louis-Philippe's son, joined by Bertrand, Marchand and Las Cases' son, went to St Helena to return Napoleon's body to France. In a moving ceremony, Napoleon was presented to the French people and laid to rest. In 1861, his tomb under the gilded dome of Les Invalides finally ready, Napoleon's body was placed in a resting place befitting his extraordinary career.

Part Two
The Journal of James Roche Verling

Chapter 5
1818

Saturday, 25 July 1818. Ordered by Lieutenant General Sir H. Lowe, to repair to Longwood as Medical attendant to General Bonaparte's establishment. Arrived about half past 6 o'clock. Found Lieutenant Colonel Wynyard, Captain Blakeney and Lieutenant Jackson waiting for Dr O'Meara who was with General Bonaparte; Colonel Wynyard and Dr O'Meara left Longwood about half past 8 o'clock.

Sunday, 26 July 1818. I met Count Bertrand and Madame walking in the grounds, conversed with them for a short time, Madame Bertrand expressed her intention of sending for me in case of illness in her family. I afterwards called on General Montholon who, as well as Madame, expressed pleasure in seeing an old acquaintance (having known me on board the *Northumberland*).

Madame Montholon complained of great liability to catch cold, and to slight rheumatic pains, on the slightest exposure to the open air. This she attributes to her having taken calomel some time back for a pain in her right side. She showed me a prescription of Dr O'Meara's for the Mercurial pill, 5 grains of which she took night and morning for 3 weeks, occasionally interposing the infusion of Senna and Sulphate of Magnesia, when the pains ceased though her gums were not affected.

Monday, 27 July 1818. Went to Jamestown, saw Sir H. Lowe who inquired what had passed at Longwood; told him General Bertrand and Montholon were glad to avail themselves of medical advice for their families, but had intimated to me that General Bonaparte, though suffering much from pain in the side, had resolved to see no medical man sent by Sir H. Lowe, and had ceased to take the mercurial medicine which he had been using for some time back under the direction of Dr O'Meara.

Tuesday, 28 July 1818. Wrote to Mr Webb informing him that a medical officer of the line had taken charge of the detachment of the Royal Artillery.

Wednesday, 29 July 1818. Had a long conversation with General Montholon, in concert with Lieutenant Jackson. He talked on various points of the treatment of Napoleon by Sir H. Lowe and contrasted the conduct of Sir G. Cockburn, in whose time, he asserted, nothing clandestine had been done by the persons detained at Longwood. He did allow that this line of conduct had not been followed since Sir Hudson's arrival and he asserted the impossibility of preventing them from sending letters and corresponding with whom they pleased. To Sir Hudson Lowe's treatment he attributed the total seclusion of Napoleon and his resolution to have no intercourse with the Governor, which (said he) has been so complete that for the last six months he would defy Sir Hudson to take his oath *sur l'Évangile* [on the Gospel] that Napoleon was actually at Longwood.

To my inquiries concerning his health, he said he thought him better, that his countenance indicated it, and that he attributed it to his having left off mercury, from which he had suffered great inconvenience, whatever good it might have done to the disease of the liver.

The weather very bad, raining all day. Thermometer at 4 p.m. 59 in my room.

Had a long conversation with Count Bertrand, who at length launched into violent abuse of the Governor, commencing with the removal of O'Meara and going back to the measures obnoxious to him – took my leave hastily.

Thursday, 30 July 1818. Went to town.

At the request of Marchand, Napoleon's personal attendant, ordered Solomon to send to England for two Glyster Apparatus to be made in silver according to a model in lead sent by Marchand.

Heard that Dr O'Meara had written a letter to Admiral Plampin complaining that his luggage had been robbed and that he had lost a gold watch, chain and seals, an onyx ring and diamond ring, etc. to him of inestimable value, as they were all presents.

Dr O'Meara was summoned by the police to come on shore and swear to his loss, which he refused unless ordered by the Admiral, which was done. Sir G. Bingham as sitting magistrate investigated.

Sunday, 16 August 1818. Wrote to Dr Baxter informing him that I had no opportunity of gaining any satisfactory information concerning Napoleon's health – that, however, I had learnt from General Montholon that Napoleon had been too unwell yesterday (being his birthday) to entertain them all at dinner, as he had proposed, but from Montholon's manner I did not conceive there was anything serious in the illness; his words were *Qu'il se sentait un peu incommodé* [that he felt a little ill], and that he had gone to bed, but had sent to the children that he would have them to dinner and bestow his annual gift of *joujoux* [toys] in a few days, when he feels himself *un peu gai, en bonne humeur* [a little merry, in good temper].

Weather cold and rainy, Thermometer at 10 o'clock a.m. 58, within doors.

Monday, 17 August 1818. Sat for half an hour, from half past 3 to 4 with Madame Bertrand, talked on the health of her children etc. Hortense came in to tell her Mama that she had just come from the Emperor, and to show a necklace of false pearls and two jewels which he had given her as a birthday present.

Thursday, 20 August 1818. Count Montholon came in to the quarters of Captain Blakeney, where I was sitting, conversed on indifferent matters with me, Blakeney having gone out, told me that he could not say whether Napoleon was better or not, *qu'il était toujours souffrant et qu'il ne dormait pas* [that he always suffered and that he didn't sleep]. Told me that Napoleon (contrary to what I had been told) did not speak the Italian fluently nor willingly, that O'Meara spoke that language to him because at first O'Meara could not speak French. Napoleon had quickly acquired the Italian during his campaign in Italy. Offered me again the use of the Library and apologized for not sending me the catalogue, which he said Napoleon had himself. He repeated the names of some authors and I pointed out the tragedies of Corneille. He went out and shortly returned bringing with him 3 volumes of *Répertoire Général du Théatre Français* and Lord Holland's 'Lives of Lope de Vega and De Castro' in two volumes, neatly bound in Russian leather. In the first volume was the following:

> *H. R. Vassal Holland*
> *Napoléonis fortitudini, et ingénio*
> *non fortunae Minusculum mittit*

[H.R. Vassal Holland sends this small work to Napoleon, unfortunate but of great character and spirit]

Went towards evening to see Hortense Bertrand, found Madame Bertrand apparently much distressed, in a short time she began to talk on the dispute between her husband and Colonel Lyster, said she fancied that the British Officers treated her and Count Bertrand with less politeness and less cordiality, on account of this dispute, expressed great anxiety on the mode in which the quarrel might be represented in England, etc.

She told me that Napoleon had been more unwell than usual, last night very restless and out of bed frequently, and that when she called at 3 o'clock in the afternoon he was only supping and could not be seen. Montholon in the morning said nothing of all this, he added that the pain in his side had been more acute than he had experienced for some time and only yielded to the warm bath.

Thursday, 27 August 1818. Visited Madame Montholon who complains of pain in her right side. Conversed with General Montholon on the campaign of 1814, who extolled the view of it in R. Wilson's tract on Russia, which he offered to lend me, and requested me to procure him the *Edinburgh Review* upon it.

Friday, 28 August 1818. Being in town, borrowed and lent to General Montholon the number of the *Edinburgh Review*, containing the critique on Sir R. W.'s Pamphlet. Learn from Madame Bertrand that Napoleon appeared better.

Thursday, 3 September 1818. Napoleon walked out, in the space enclosed by railing under his window; one of the servants who had never seen him before, described him to me as looking old, pale and sallow.

Wednesday, 16 September 1818. Weather very fine. Thermometer 64 at 2 o'clock p.m.

Napoleon has not been seen out since the 3rd. The grounds of Longwood now present a more lively appearance, large working parties being employed in carrying stones to the site pitched on for building a new house. Lieutenant Jackson is employed in building a park wall, by which the new building and workmen may be kept out of Napoleon's sight, and a distinct entrance is given to workmen.

Sir H. Lowe visited Longwood today, mentioned to me that he thought it proper to request General Montholon to propose to Napoleon that I should be introduced to pay respects to him as an individual who had come out in the same ship, independent of my present functions at Longwood. On going away he requested that I should introduce this subject when conversing with Montholon.

Conversed with General Montholon on indifferent subjects, talked of the possibility of the allied troops being withdrawn from France, told him of the British force going to India, reverted to Sir R. Wilson's pamphlet in which I told him Sir H. Lowe had controverted the accuracy of his views and contradicted some of his statements relative to the campaign in Germany, lent him a sketch of the campaign of 1813, published at Weimar, in German and French. He asked if I had heard any particulars relative to General Gourgaud as he was surprised his name had not been mentioned in the *Morning Chronicle* for May, which had been sent to them. I told him that General Gourgaud had been detained for some time aboard ship, but had afterwards been permitted to proceed to London and that I had heard nothing further.

Friday, 18 September 1818. Sir Hudson Lowe finding that I had not had an opportunity of stating my wish to be introduced to Napoleon to General

Montholon, sent to General Montholon to request to speak to him in the Orderly Officer's room, and in presence of Captain Nicholls and myself, explained to General Montholon that it was his wish and request that Captain Nicholls and myself should be introduced to Napoleon. General Montholon made reply in a very low tone of voice, which I could not distinctly understand, but which I afterwards heard from Sir Hudson Lowe, referred to Count Bertrand being the proper channel for such communication. Sir H. Lowe answered aloud, that he had hitherto always found the intervention of Count Bertrand fatal to any effort at conciliation or mutual good understanding, and he had therefore expressly chosen the agency of General Montholon on this occasion. That whatever might be the result, he wished the proposal to be made. The other replied that it was his wish to conciliate, that he believed he had always been found pliant, and that he would state the proposal, but could not answer for the result.

Sunday, 20 September 1818. Sir H. Lowe came here for a few minutes. I was sitting with the Countess Montholon and saw him at the railing, went out and spoke to him. He asked if I had heard any account of Napoleon's health. I answered no, asked a few other indifferent questions, mentioned to him that Count Bertrand had paid a visit whilst I was sitting in Captain Nicholls' room. Captain Nicholls was at Deadwood, told him of this conversation at his return.

Monday, 21 September 1818. Went to town, nothing particular, saw Captain Stanfell who requested me to give his compliments to Madame Bertrand, and say that he intended to pay his respects to her in a few days. On my return to Longwood in the evening, found a packet containing 2 Books and the following note from Sir H. Lowe.

Dear Sir,

I have received the book of which you spoke yesterday. Several are not returned, I enclose a list of them. It is quite sufficient for me to know that they are at Longwood, but I should be sorry any of them were not forthcoming when wanted, as I could not readily obtain other copies of them.

I enclose two publications I have received by the *Lusitania* which I conceive might be interesting at Longwood, and you may therefore show them to Count Montholon. I am not quite certain, they have not already the *Memoirs of Fouché*, but the account of Savary in the *Pamphleteer* they can as yet have only seen extracts of.

Yours very faithfully,
H. Lowe

20 September 1818

List of books sent with foregoing as having been lent to General Bonaparte, and not returned.

1. *Actes, ordonnances, décrets et manifests, tierés du Moniteur,*
   par Goldsmith   6 Volumes
   [Acts, Ordinances, Decrees and Manifestos, Drawn from
   the *Moniteur*]
2. *Bonaparte peint par lui-même*   1
   [Bonaparte, A Self-Portrait]
3. *État de la France sous Napoléon Bonaparte*   1
   [The State of France Under Napoleon Bonaparte]
4. *Alliance des Jacobins français avec le ministère anglais*   1
   [Alliance of French Jacobins with the English Ministry]
5. *Cinq mois de la révolution française*   1
   [Five Months of the French Revolution]
6. *Histoire de la guerre de Russie*, par un médecin de l'Armée   1
   [History of the Russian War, by a Doctor of the Army]
7. *Guerre de Russie et d'Allemagne*   1
   [The Russian and German War]
8. *Guerre d'Espagne et du Portugal*   1
   [War of Spain and Portugal]
9. *L'Ambigu*   2
   [The Ambiguous]

Wednesday, 23 September 1818. Sent to Count Montholon the *Memoirs of Fouché*, and the number of the *Pamphleteer* containing Savary's letters which he returned in 2 or 3 hours, observing that he had only kept them until he had read the letters of Savary, as he was already in possession of Fouché's *Memoirs*.

Friday, 25 September 1818. Returned to Sir H. Lowe the *Pamphleteer* and the *Memoirs of Fouché*. In the evening received from him Madame Staël's posthumous work on the French Revolution, in consequence of my having told him that Madame Montholon had expressed a wish to read it. It was accompanied with the following note:

Dear Sir,
    I send you the work of Madame de Staël on the French Revolution. It will excite the interest of Napoleon more deeply whither as affecting his present situation, or his name in History than perhaps any work that has ever appeared, or is likely to appear regarding him. In giving it to Count Montholon, say it is in consequence of his having spoken of it to you.
                        Yours faithfully,
                        H. Lowe
25th September

I gave the work to Madame Montholon, who was the person who had expressed the wish to see it. Count Montholon was present and they both seemed gratified at having obtained the work, though disappointed in not finding it in the original <u>French</u>.

Sunday, 27 September 1818. Made a visit to Madame Bertrand. She told me that she had dined yesterday with Napoleon, complained much of extreme heat of his rooms to which she attributed a rheumatic cold. Indulged herself in a Philippique against the Duke of Fitz-James and thus passed to the subject of the young Napoleon. She said she had yesterday pointed out the strong likeness of his mother in the bust sent out here, and regretted much the countenance did not resemble the father. I asked after Napoleon's health, which she said was always indifferent, and that she had lately observed that he had become very bald.

Wednesday, 30 September 1818. Madame Montholon sent for me, being indisposed. Sat for half an hour and talked with her and the Count, who were inquisitive about the news of the day, mentioned to them that it was rumoured in Town that a correspondence had been detected, which was carried on clandestinely by O'Meara, and that it was supposed he had been the agent, through the House of Balcombe, of procuring sums of money for Longwood. He combated this idea and remarked that he should not be surprised if Dr O'Meara had compromised himself with the Government by some indiscretion in his letter, as he thought he was fond of endeavouring to appear a confidential man at Longwood, but in his opinion (and he believed he knew whatever had passed) nothing connected with O'Meara could be of any importance to Napoleon. But that he should commit himself on paper would be no matter of surprise to him, since a man of Las Cases' good sense had had the folly to act as we all knew he had done.

Besides (said he) 'to give you my opinion candidly of O'Meara, I looked upon him at first as an agent of the British Government from the time he became Surgeon to Napoleon, during the time Sir G. Cockburn was here, and for a long time after the arrival of Sir H. Lowe, to whom, I was convinced, he was in the habit of detailing what passed at Longwood. What caused them to quarrel, I know not, whither the Governor *exigeait-il un peu trop* [demanded a little too much of him], but it was not very long ago since a very marked change took place in O'Meara's conduct, in his remark on Sir H. Lowe etc. etc. and perhaps he wished Napoleon to look on him as a sort of martyr in his cause and reward him for his devotions. As to Balcombe, you who know the character of the man, will not think it likely that we should have chosen him as a confidential agent. For what purpose was money required, not only for bribing, since the signature of Napoleon might be much more easily applied for that purpose, than the clumsy means of hard cash, and if bribery were applied to people in low life as soldiers or servants, they had furnished them by Government money sufficient for that purpose.'

Saturday, 3 October 1818. I was requested by Madame Bertrand to mention to the Governor that she had received the books, meant for the instruction of her children, but that she understood some letters had been contained in the box and kept back in consequence of not having passed through the regular channel, the Secretary of State's Office.

If there was any attempt at a clandestine correspondence, she begged to assure Sir H. Lowe that she knew nothing of it, and as she expected letters from her Father in Law, on family matters, she hoped if any such had arrived, the Governor would not detain them on account of any informality in the mode of sending them.

Sir H. Lowe begged to assure Madame B. he should not have detained a moment any letter of hers, that none had arrived, and the letters she had heard of as being contained in the box were loose papers not relating at all to her, and apparently of no importance.

Thursday, 8 October 1818. Extraordinary conversation with Madame Bertrand who has been ill for some time and whose illness proceeds in a great measure from mental anxiety, and in fact whose mind is perpetually agitated by female jealousy. She attributed very plainly the influence General Montholon now possesses with Napoleon to the complaisance of his wife, observed that his little Napoleone did not [at] all resemble him, said that Gourgaud had openly declared the little girl was Napoleon's, that Napoleon himself had complained to Madame Bertrand that Gourgaud had said so. For her part had she chosen to be his mistress she might have been so many years back etc. etc.

Friday, 16 October 1818. Sir H. Lowe having had for some days back frequent conversations with General Montholon relative to the necessity of someone seeing Napoleon, and something like a good understanding beginning between them, General Montholon came into Captain Nicholls' quarters where I was, and mentioned that as his children were playing under Napoleon's window, it was probable Captain Nicholls might get a sight of him as he sometimes threw up the sash and spoke to them. This did not occur, but Madame Montholon going there a short time afterwards with the children, Napoleon opened the window and continued standing at it for some time speaking to her. Captain Nicholls saw him with a glass from behind the wall which separates Bertrand's house from the garden. He was dressed in a dirty looking morning gown and had a reddish handkerchief tied round his head. The impression made on Captain Nicholls was very strange. He could only compare him to a ghost, his complexion he likened to tallow and the falling of the lower jaw struck him forcibly. I saw him from the bottom of the garden, but could hardly distinguish his dress, Madame Montholon interposing. I thought from the slight view I had occasionally that he looked very ill. I wrote to Mr Baxter and said so, and mentioned his dress. To which I received the following note.

11 October
My dear Verling,

I am glad that you had a sight of the man or ghost, but could have wished you were a little nearer. The time approaches when I think you will be in daily attendance on him, and it would not be surprising if I was also to be of the party.

I met Nicholls near Francis Plain, whose nervous agitation excited by the Imperial <u>Shadow</u> had hardly subsided.

It is impossible not to admire the trick practised by the Arch Impostor in the selection of a dress for his debut. Such a dress smells strongly of the Faubourg St Antoine, in the time of sans culottism. I like the proceedings of Montholon and it appears to be the wish of all parties to come to an understanding. I trust you entertain no doubt of B. selecting you as his immediate medical attendant; when he has once decided on that matter, my visits to you shall be more frequent as I shall then be quite free from every suspicion of a wish to obtrude my services. Should you have the good fortune soon of seeing him again, pray let me hear from you, and if you have an interview, give me a little of the details, should you not come down yourself.

Yours,
Alex Baxter

Wednesday, 28 October 1818. Was informed by Count Montholon that he thought Napoleon rather worse, that he complained a good deal and was *plus jaune* [more yellow]. Said that the only remaining obstacles to mutual understanding between him and the Governor were the restrictions of the limits as they stood under Sir G. Cockburn and the privilege of sending notes <u>sealed</u> through the orderly officer to any of the persons with whom he and they were in the habit of intercourse.

A list of 50 names had been given by the Governor, and these persons were to have the privilege of visiting Longwood without a pass by leaving their names at the officer's Guard.

Another point in dispute was the mode in which the orderly officer's duty was conducted, when he accompanied any of them to town, General Montholon contending that he should merely accompany them on the ride to and from town leaving the disposal of their time when there to themselves as in Sir G. Cockburn's rules, and not accompany them contrary to their inclinations into every house and shop, not insist on even eating with them, should a person have the politeness to ask them to take refreshment, as the orderly officer had done by the orders of Sir H. Lowe. He finished by paying Sir H. Lowe some compliments on his talents, etc., but added *envers nous il est tout à fait aveugle par le peur* [between us, he is absolutely blinded by fear]. General Montholon said that in short they wished to be treated as Prisoners of War, and that though Sir H. Lowe said he considered them as such, yet by his restrictions and suspicions he treated them as Prisoners of State, *prisonniers d'État*.

Saturday, 31 October 1818. Having mentioned yesterday to Sir H. Lowe that Madame Bertrand had asked me to procure for her *Lady Wortley Montagu's Letters*, and *Harrington and Ormond*, I this day received from him several books and the following note.

My Dear Sir,

I send you some new novels which you may give to Madame Bertrand, getting back from her if she has done with them, *Mandeville*, *Beppio*, *Northanger Abbey* and *Persuasion*, *Dance of Life*, and any other books she may have of ours. We have some new novels when those now sent are done with and returned, for there are several readers of them. I send also a Pamphlet called 'Napoleon His Own Historian', you may give this to Montholon, it is I believe written by Napoleon himself, as I know he recently got home some of this nature to try their effect.

Yours very truly
H. Lowe

31st October 1818

Books sent:

Frankenstein	3 vol
Knight of St John	3 vol
Harrington and Ormond	3 vol
Edgeworth's Dramas	1
Headlong Hale	1
Rome, Florence, and Naples	1

I called on Madame Bertrand after having sent these books; she had already, in consequence of my having told her that the Governor had expressed a wish to get back the books she had, made a packet of them and written a note apologizing to Lady Lowe for having detained them so long. We talked for a long time on indifferent topics, and Napoleon having been introduced, I told her I had found in a drawer of O'Meara's, a lock of hair which appeared to me to be Napoleon's. She said she did not think O'Meara would have been so negligent, that it was most probably a Lady's hair, but as I seemed to be pleased with the idea of possessing a lock of his hair, she would give me one. I accordingly accepted it, and on comparing it with the other it appears exactly the same.

Saturday, 7 November 1818. Not having received from the Governor any written order to occupy my present situation, I addressed to Major Gorrequer the following letter:

Longwood 7 November 1818
Sir,

His Excellency the Governor had the goodness sometime back to say he would address a letter to me, directing me to take charge of the establishment at Longwood and authorizing my removal from the Artillery.

I take the liberty of requesting you will call this circumstance to his recollection as I have not yet been able to send any written Document to the Director General of the Ordnance Medical Department to whom I am extremely anxious to write by the present opportunity.

I have etc. etc.

[To] Major Gorrequer etc. etc.

Sunday, 8 November 1818. Received the following letter.

St Helena, 25 July 1818
Sir,

Dr O'Meara, Surgeon of the Royal Navy, who was in attendance on General Bonaparte, having been removed from that situation in consequence of orders from His Majesty's Government,

I have to request you will immediately proceed to Longwood to afford your medical assistance to General Bonaparte and the foreign persons under detention with him, there to be stationed until I may receive the instructions of His Majesty's Government on the subject.

I am Sir Your most obedient servant
H. Lowe

[To] Dr Verling, R. Artillery

Monday, 10 November 1818. Wrote to Mr Webb and enclosed him a copy of the two preceding letters.

Wednesday, 11 November 1818. About a week back, I met Lieutenant Kent RN who had just returned from the Cape; he told me he had a note from Dr O'Meara to me about some books, and I received a few days afterwards the following:

Ascension, 17 August 1818

Dear Verling,

As I have been informed by Lieutenant Jackson that the two last volumes of Lord Byron's works which I lent to him were afterwards delivered to you for perusal, you will oblige me by giving them at the demand of Lieutenant Cuppage of Ascension Island, to whom I have given the work.

Wishing you happiness, believe me to be

Yours most faithfully,

Barry O'Meara

Conceiving it prudent that no communication, however trivial, with Dr O'Meara should be private, I showed this note in the evening to the Governor at Plantation House, where I happened to dine, also to Sir T. Reade and Mr Baxter and heard no more about it, till having met Mr Kent riding into town this day. I told him I should send the books, to which he replied, it was too late as the Vessel had sailed for Ascension and that he expected to be put under arrest and sent home for having been the bearer of the note.

Sunday, 15 November 1818. Conversed with General Montholon, told him that I had heard from Sir H. Lowe, that a French surgeon and a Priest were expected at St Helena by the next arrival.

He said he had received a sealed communication from Sir H. Lowe to be placed immediately *Sous les yeux de l'Empereur* [under the Emperor's eyes], but that he had himself opened it as he had positive instructions to open any paper before he showed it. That it contained an extract from a dispatch of Lord Bathurst, and he supposed in Lord Bathurst's own words, as they were _soulignés_ [underlined], announcing that the British Government had delegated to Cardinal Fesch the choice both of a Surgeon and a Priest, and that their names and the time when they were likely to arrive would be made known by the next ship, that he had not told me this before, as he conceived it a private transaction, and had not mentioned it even to Bertrand, and was surprised that the Governor had made the communication to me.

I inquired into the state of Napoleon's health, which he said was very bad, that he complained of his side, that his bowels were obstinately costive, that Glysters produced scarcely any effect, and that he would not take any medicine by the mouth, since the departure of O'Meara. That his remedies consisted in the management of his diet, that is, said he, in fasting, and the warm bath, and that he scarcely ever slept. I asked him how he passed the night: in walking up and down his room, in reading or in listening to someone reading. He then commented on the removal of Dr O'Meara, and the mode in which I was sent here, to which he applied the word *maladroite* [clumsy], saying that had Sir H. Lowe sent him the positive order of the

British Government for the removal of Dr O'Meara and said, until the arrival of a French Surgeon, *prenez Monsieur un tel ou un tel, il y a cent à parier contre un qu'il vous aurait choisi* [take Mr such and such, it's a hundred to one that he would have chosen you], since you speak French, since you were in a slight degree known to him, and better by us, and since you belonged to the Artillery, to which *Arme* [branch of the military] he has a decided predilection already shown by his taking O'Meara, that he had confidence in British Medical men, and if once you were admitted *dans son intimité* [into his private circle] he would never have changed you.

He said that the Emperor was convinced that Sir H. Lowe had taken upon his own responsibility the removal of O'Meara, that is that he had acted upon his general instructions and in the case of Las Cases, and without any specific order, that this had been his opinion all along and was now strengthened by this extract from Lord Bathurst's dispatch, which must have been subsequent to any order, had any such been given, and which, though dated in April, particularly says that this surgeon is appointed to relieve O'Meara.

In fact, Sir Hudson Lowe has acted from personal animosity; in this instance he has allowed his anger to get the better of his reason, and has placed himself in an awkward predicament. Suppose Napoleon had died either from the progress of the disease with which he was afflicted when O'Meara was removed, or from any sudden attack of illness, from apoplexy, what would Europe say? What would even his enemies think, and what position has Sir Hudson Lowe placed you in?

Whatever was the cause of the quarrel between Sir H. Lowe and O'Meara, if Dr O'Meara was sold, *vendu*, he was so originally to Sir H. Lowe, this I have told the Governor myself and that I had proofs of it, and the fact is that the Emperor had in his possession, and I believe now has a correspondence between the Governor and O'Meara in one part of which it appears that the Governor had returned Bulletins of O'Meara as not consonant to the reports he (the Governor) had already made, and that O'Meara had new modelled (*refait*) his, this correspondence was given to the Emperor some time afterwards in a fit of passion, for O'Meara did not perceive that he compromised himself, since a man who could act thus was not a person *à qui l'on pouvait se fier* [in whom one could trust]. He said that O'Meara was taken by surprise, that he had no idea his removal would have been so sudden, and that he had at the moment completely lost his wits, *perdu sa tête*. I observed that a long interview of nearly two hours which he had contrived to have with Napoleon and of which he no doubt made good use, was no proof of his want of presence of mind. To my astonishment he positively said that O'Meara had only seen Napoleon for a few minutes, that in this instance too he was extremely *gauche* [awkward], for he had obtained nothing tending to his personal interest.

I asked him where O'Meara was during these two hours, as I knew he was not in his own apartments, to which he replied he was not with the Emperor.

He then alluded to the late negotiations with Sir H. Lowe and repeated a former conversation that it had come to nothing because Sir H. Lowe would not concede the point of their sending sealed notes, even through the orderly officer, and would insist that the orderly officer should accompany them as a Gendarme into every house they went.

He mentioned the difficulty still existing in laying papers before Napoleon addressed to General Bonaparte.

He termed it *un enfantillage* [childishness] not to give him the title of Emperor, and asked why since they would not give the title, they had refused to let him assume the name of Colonel Muiron, as he had wished.

This was the name of a favourite aide-de-camp, killed by his side in one of the battles in his Italian Campaigns. Under this name, every communication would have been rendered easy.

Thursday, 19 November 1818. Was informed by Sir H. Lowe, whom I saw in Town, that General Montholon having yesterday visited the Marquis of Montchenu, had mentioned to him in conversation the two points which had been the obstacles to mutual accommodation, and had stated that he believed the only reason why Napoleon did not see me, was that Sir H. Lowe had sent me, and not from any personal objection to me.

Whilst I was in Town, Napoleon walked a short time in the garden with Count and Countess Bertrand, and afterwards remained some time in conversation with them in the Veranda. He was dressed in a plain green coat and wore his cocked hat.

Friday, 20 November 1818. Madame Bertrand lent me a translation of the *Aeneid* by the Reverend Charles Symonds, handsomely bound and sent to her by the author. Inscription: To the Countess Bertrand, from the Author, in Testimony of the most profound respect and the most unlimited admiration.

She also showed me a Head of Christ done in Crayons and sent to her by Miss Plowden.

Sunday, 29 November 1818. Having returned some novels to Plantation House, which had been lent to Madame Bertrand, and requested in her name that some more might be sent, I received the following note:

Dear Sir

I send you some fresh books which you may give to the Countess Bertrand. You had better perhaps leave the list with her.

Yours truly,

H. Lowe

It may be right to observe that the 1st number of the *Quarterly Review* contains a very severe criticism on the letters from the Cape; there is however *France* by Lady Morgan and the *Edinburgh Review* to console! The *British Review* contains a critique on Lady Morgan's work. The novels are good, particularly *Marriage*, the *Literary Gazette* is the work in which the letters supposed to be from the Countess Bertrand are to appear. It contains a critique on the observations on Lord Bathurst's speech.

I sent the books to Madame Bertrand and called on her in the evening. She was very much out of spirits and merely acknowledged having received them without any comment. I asked her if she had read *France*, to which she replied in the affirmative, and finding that I had not, she lent it to me; she did not express any opinion on it. She complained of her health, and I prescribed some medicine for her; finding her relapsing into the subject of her miserable situation and the conduct of Sir H. Lowe, I took my leave.

I, afterwards, paid a visit to Madame Montholon; in the course of conversation, Lady Morgan's *France* met with very harsh criticism from Madame Montholon.

Books lent to Madame Bertrand

France (by Lady Morgan)	2 vols.
Walpole's *Turkey*	1
Souvenirs de Londres [Memories of London]	1
Quarterly Review, November 1817 … February 1818	2
Edinburgh Review, February 1818	2
British Review, February 1818	2
Marriage	3
Women	3
Literary Gazette	

Friday, 11 December 1818. Arrived from England HM Ship *Linnet*, she had left England on the 7th September. Brought papers containing a correspondence between Sir T. Reade, Major Gorrequer, and Dr O'Meara.

Count Montholon came in the evening to inquire about letters and sat for some time with Lieutenant Jackson and myself. He inquired if any intelligence had been received concerning the Priest and Surgeon, talked of O'Meara, and wished to exonerate him of any blame in the affair of the snuff-box.

Thursday, 17 December 1818. Went between 4 and 5 o'clock to Plantation House, by signal from Sir T. Reade, met Captain Nicholls at the gate. Captain Nicholls was first called in to Sir H. Lowe, and shortly after I went in. The Governor showed me a letter from Count Montholon, particularly directing my attention to the last paragraph in which it is asserted that General Bonaparte's health is much worse, and that he has been confined to his bed for the last eight days. The Governor asked me if I had received any information about his health, to which I replied that Madame Bertrand had this morning informed me that he had been in bed, and worse than usual (for with them he is always ill) last night, and that Count Montholon had told me he was complaining of severe pain in his side today. From neither, had I the slightest hint that he had been so long confined to his bed.

In the evening I dined at Count Montholon's where Mr Livingstone also dined. Towards the conclusion of dinner a packet was delivered to Count Montholon from Plantation House; after reading some letters he spoke to me of Napoleon having made a complaint that Mr Baxter had intruded himself upon him, and upon my expressing great surprise that Mr Baxter's conduct should have been so misinterpreted, he requested me to read a letter, which I did, from Mr Baxter to Sir Hudson Lowe.

Having remarked that I thought it very evident the offence taken at Mr Baxter's conduct was totally groundless, he said, '*cependant* [however] as he may possibly (*peut-être*) have expressed his opinion on the looks of the Emperor and drawn inferences as to the state of his health, I have orders to protest against any report coming from him.'

Chapter 6
1819

Friday, 1 January 1819. On my return to Longwood from Town, where I had been at the Subscription Ball, I found on my table a Breakfast Service of plate, and a servant of Madame Bertrand's came to inform me that he had brought it in the morning with Madame Bertrand's compliments. It consisted of a Teapot, cream ewer, 2 Cason's and half a dozen tea spoons. I felt disappointed at the mode in which these things were sent, as I thought that she might previously have requested my acceptance or have written a note to that effect. I therefore sent them back with my compliments, that I should call on Madame Bertrand directly, which I did, and was informed that she and the whole family were at General Bonaparte's.

In the evening, I dined at Plantation House, and informed Sir H. Lowe of the present and of my having declined it. He replied that many people had accepted presents and deemed it sufficient to inform him. That he felt that I had acted with great delicacy, but that he had no objection to my receiving any present, provided that he was informed of it.

Saturday, 2 January 1819. I called on Madame Bertrand and found her much offended. She would admit, she said, of no explanation which could justify my impoliteness, except I acknowledged that I had received the Governor's specific orders, and when I informed her that I had not, but that I called at her house to explain to her that I did not wish to receive any remuneration, and intended to have hinted at the matter, she broke out into a violent tirade against the Governor, and his unjust persecution, said I espoused his quarrels, etc., told me I should find myself mistaken if I expected he would do anything for me, and 'you know very well,' added she, 'or if you do not, he does, that his power here will soon cease, and that Lord Hill is appointed to succeed him.' This was a novelty to me.

I took my leave after some trifling conversation and she looked out of the Veranda, and said she should expect me to continue my visits as usual.

In the evening, I paid a visit to Madame Montholon, and after some conversation about a book she had lent me, *Memoirs of Madame d'Epinay*, she requested my acceptance of a new year's gift, and offered me a gold watch, chain and seals.

This was done in a very handsome manner, saying that the gift was in itself a trifle, that it was one she used herself to wear, and that she presented it as a *Souvenir* and mark of thanks for my attentions during her illness (she had lately recovered). I felt that I was rather awkwardly situated and stammered out some apology and regret that I could not accept it, and mentioned as one reason that I had already declined Madame Bertrand's present. She seemed much astonished and disappointed, but dropped the conversation and made her little girl bring the presents Napoleon had given her to show them to me.

Sunday, 10 January 1819. Madame Bertrand having requested me to apply to Sir H. Lowe for some more books, I received the following note, and some catalogue of books.

Dear Sir,

Have the goodness to return the enclosed catalogue as soon as Madame Bertrand has marked any books she wants. If Madame Montholon wants any books, I beg you will offer her any she wishes.

Yours truly,
H. Lowe

Friday, 15 January 1819. The *Hardy* gun brig having arrived from the Cape, the Governor sent to Longwood *Morning Heralds* to the 18th September and I received from him the following note.

Dear Sir,

Read the observations of the Editor in the *Herald* of the 21st August sent by this occasion to Captain Nicholls with other papers for Longwood.

You will find the arguments not inapplicable to what you were speaking to me the other day [sic].

Yours truly,
H. Lowe

This refers to conversation in which I told him I had perceived on the part of the Count Montholon and his Lady, no evident wish and effort to induce Napoleon to receive me as his surgeon. On Madame Bertrand's side, I thought I had recovered her good wishes, though Count Bertrand evidently retained resentment since the refusal of the presents.

This brought on a discussion relative to any stipulations Bonaparte might wish to make, in which Sir Hudson Lowe seemed to think that no stipulation, but that of acting with honour as a medical man, should be required, and that none should be acceded to where Bonaparte assumed as a possibility, that Sir H. Lowe could send any man capable of acting as a spy, and wanted his stipulations to guard against it.

I replied I should of course enter into no secret engagements.

Saturday, 16 January 1819. I was awoke in the night, or rather about 3 o'clock of the morning of the 17th by Captain Nicholls who showed me a letter from Count Bertrand to Mr Stokoe, stating that he was the person in whom the Emperor chose to place confidence and requesting his immediate attendance at Longwood, as Napoleon was taken suddenly very ill and he, Count Bertrand, was very much alarmed.

This letter was directly sent to Plantation House and a note by Count Montholon's desire was soon after sent to the Admiral. About quarter before 7 o'clock Mr Stokoe arrived and about 12 o'clock I received the following note.

Plantation House, Sunday, 17 January 1819
Dear Sir,

After inquiring from Count Montholon, which you may do in the Governor's name, how General Bonaparte's health is after his attack of last night and whether it has passed over, the Governor would wish to see you any time in the course of the day, unless your medical attendance or opinion on medical matters has been or is likely to be required.

Yours etc. G. Gorrequer

To this I replied:

Dear Sir,

I have yet received no communication from Mr Stokoe, who arrived here quarter before 7 o'clock and told me he was going to Count Bertrand's, and supposed I would be in readiness. I told him I should remain in my own apartments.

I postpone, therefore, the inquiry from Count Montholon and shall have the honour to communicate either personally or by letter with his Excellency in the course of the day.

etc. etc. Verling

I afterwards received the following note:

Dear Verling,

If you should be obliged to go to Plantation House in the course of the day, will you call on me here and I will ride over with you, if anything has been done let me know by the bearer.

Yours faithfully,

T. Reade

Alarm House 17 January

I afterwards received from Mr Baxter the following note, he simply knew that Mr Stokoe had been sent for.

My Dear Verling,

How Stokoe will act, I am at a loss to know, but if Napoleon is really so ill as it is said he is, I have not the least doubt of your being called upon to see him, which is a point gained for you.

I do not entertain a very serious idea of the urgency of the illness from the circuitous mode of seeking relief.

Will see how things turn out. Let me know in the course of the day what happens.

Faithfully Yours,

A. Baxter

Monday, 18 January 1819. In the evening, I rode over to Plantation House in company with Sir T. Reade and Captain Nicholls. Sir T. Reade was much astonished when I told him that Mr Stokoe had been admitted to see Napoleon, and had called on me to say that he had seen him and it had been proposed to him to act as his surgeon upon certain conditions to which he had acceded. Count Bertrand had sent through Captain Nicholls the proposed conditions to the Governor, and Mr Stokoe had gone to the Admiral to submit them for his approbation, with the intention of proceeding afterwards to Plantation House. Mr Stokoe had formerly refused to see Napoleon in consultation with O'Meara unless a third person was called in, and had told me, he supposed and wished me to be the person.

On my arrival at Plantation House, I had a long conversation with the Governor, which terminated by my saying that I supposed and wished that he would remove me from Longwood, since the calling upon Mr Stokoe was an unequivocal reflection on me. He replied that it was by no means settled that Mr Stokoe should be allowed to accept the situation, that at all events many points remained to be discussed and he wished me to remain at Longwood until further communications had passed.

About 8 o'clock in the evening Madame Bertrand sent for me, and I found her and her husband together. Count Bertrand addressed me and said that he regretted he had not seen me in the morning when I was at his house, as he wished to assure me that the calling upon Stokoe to see the Emperor proceeded, not from a want of good will on his part towards me, but from Napoleon himself. That he had been called between 12 and 1 o'clock and found Napoleon extremely ill, when he proposed to call me, which was positively refused. He then mentioned Mr Stokoe whom he also refused to see, though he spoke favourably of him, and that Count Bertrand, himself alarmed at the increasing illness of Napoleon, had himself written to Mr Stokoe without Napoleon's consent, and had afterwards experienced great difficulty in getting Mr Stokoe admitted to him.

He assured me more than once, that Napoleon's objections to me were not personal, that Napoleon had often said so, but that he had declared when I first came to Longwood, that he would never see me since I had been selected by Sir H. Lowe, and though my conduct during my residence at Longwood had not given rise to any personal objection, yet the repugnance to receive me as the choice of Sir H. Lowe, was as strong as ever, and indeed, added he, 'the sudden manner in which you were sent here the evening of Dr O'Meara's removal was the most unlikely to insure your reception.' I interrupted Count Bertrand by saying I was sent thus suddenly that Longwood might not be a moment without a medical attendant; that I was not much disappointed for the failure of the recommendation he had bestowed on me, when I reflected on the extreme delicacy of the situation and how difficult it must be for a British subject to discharge the function.

About 9 o'clock, shortly after I had quitted Count Bertrand's House, he came to my apartments and told me he had been to see Napoleon. That he found him in a state of great weakness, and requested me to give an opinion whether I thought it probable Napoleon might be attacked in a manner similar to what he experienced last night.

I observed that the question was a strange one, as I knew nothing of the progress or nature of Napoleon's disease and whether the attack (*crise*) of last night was the result of previous disease or produced by some sudden exciting cause. He then described vaguely the state in which he found him: <u>You must be aware</u>, he said, that the main disease, '*le fond de la maladie*' [the root of the illness], is a chronic affection of the liver. I found him in a state of great agitation and febrile heat, complaining of great uneasiness in his side and shoulder, of restlessness and anxiety, but above all, of a severe pain in the head and giddiness (*vertigo*), which for a short time amounted to a state of insensibility, <u>*perte de connaissance*</u>. I told him, it was often difficult to form a correct opinion even from minute examination of the patient and therefore, impossible for me to express one on his description. Count Bertrand then said, that Mr Stokoe had declared that in case of the return of the vertigo etc. bleeding would be indispensable. I observed that I was upon the spot by the order of the Governor, that I considered it my duty to afford medical aid under any circumstances, and if called upon, should act to the best of my judgment and endeavour to relieve any illness General Bonaparte might be suffering from.

These conversations I minuted down and sent them and the following note to Plantation House.

Longwood, 18 January
My dear Sir,

I have thought it my duty to detail for his Excellency's information two conversations I held with Count Bertrand last night, as the first states the ground on which Count Bertrand chooses to rest Napoleon's refusal to see me, and the 2nd explains in some measure the nature of the disease he is said to have been attacked with.

I remain Yours faithfully
J. Verling

[To] Major Gorrequer etc. etc.

In the evening, I went to Plantation House, where I had been asked to dine, and found there, the Governor, Admiral Plampin, Sir T. Reade and Major Gorrequer. The Governor showed me a Bulletin which had been made by Mr Stokoe after his first visit, nearly corresponding as to account of the disease with what Count Bertrand told me, and giving as his opinion that no immediate danger was to be dreaded from the hepatic disease but if neglected; that in this climate it must immediately shorten his life, and stating that medical attendance on the spot was absolutely necessary to avert the danger threatened by recurrence of the vertigo, syncope etc.

In consequence of the latter part of this, the Governor requested I would immediately return to Longwood, and make known to Count Montholon that I was upon the spot.

I arrived at Longwood about 8 o'clock and called and spent an hour with Madame Montholon. I understood from her that Napoleon was better.

Tuesday, 19 January 1819. Madame Bertrand early this morning sent for some ether saying she had been indisposed in the night, and would be glad to see me, when at leisure.

I went to her, she told me she had an attack of spasm, but was now quite well, and I asked her why she did not send for me at the time she was ill! and she said she was unwilling to give me the trouble of getting up in the night, as she had observed, since Mr Stokoe had been called to the Emperor, that I had treated her with neglect, and that her husband had told her he plainly perceived by my manner to him that I attributed to his bad offices, Napoleon's refusal to see me. She said I was led into this error by the Montholons, especially Madame Montholon, who hated her, and would not hesitate to say or do anything however false, however atrocious, to injure her.

I told her she had told me, and Count Bertrand had repeated, that he had often urged Napoleon to see me. That I had thanked them both for their good offices, that I had often been away before, 24 hours from her house, and therefore did not think she ought to regard my present absence of that time as neglect, which it certainly was not meant for.

She then told me that she requested I would continue my attendance on herself and family as usual, that the Physician attendant on the Emperor and hers were distinct considerations, and that even when I left Longwood, if any serious malady occurred she would call upon me.

In the course of talk, she let out that she had paid a visit to Madame Montholon last evening, and had told her of her intentions of requesting me to continue my attendance.

About 10 o'clock I was surprised to receive a visit from Count Bertrand, who said, you have seen Madame this morning, and notwithstanding her attack last night (very doubtful if she had one), her health was visibly improved since she had taken the medicine I last prescribed for her. He then professed to feel sentiments of good will towards me, and expatiated upon the praise I was entitled to from everybody <u>at the present moment</u>.

He then produced a letter from Sir H. Lowe, stating that he had received orders from Earl Bathurst to remove O'Meara and to replace him by Mr Baxter, but in case of Napoleon disliking Mr Baxter's attendance, that he should have the choice of any medical man on the Island, but that he had sent one in the meantime, that even a momentary want should not be felt – Napoleon declined at that time making any choice, invited as he was, and declared he never would see you, whom if you had not been sent here, we should all have pointed out, from our knowledge of you aboard ship. Our influence has been repeatedly used to induce him to see you, and in vain, even when he thought he was going to die. The Governor now recedes from Lord Bathurst's letter, Napoleon has made a choice, obstacles are thrown in the way, he is about to refuse him. The correspondence is becoming more warm (the Governor is a man who never feels a blow until he is knocked down). He perseveres in wishing to force you upon him, and I warn you that motives will soon be attributed to him for this line of conduct in which your name will unavoidably be implicated, and in a manner in which your name ought not to appear. I therefore advise you to retire immediately from the situation.

I replied to Count Bertrand, that as a military medical man, I was here in obedience to orders and that my conscience would enable me to disperse any false imputations.

Wednesday, 20 January 1819. I received the following note:

Plantation House, 20 January 1819
Dear Sir,

Will you have the goodness to acquaint me for the Governor's information, whether Mr Stokoe called upon you personally yesterday afternoon previous to his visiting General Bonaparte or calling upon any person of his family, and what he may have said on the subject of giving his attendance to General Bonaparte in conjunction with you, whether as from himself or as speaking of any instructions he might have received.

The Governor will be obliged also for any further information you may be enabled to give him respecting Mr Stokoe's visit or General Bonaparte's malady.

Believe me,
Yours Very Truly
G. Gorrequer

[To] Dr Verling

Answer
Longwood, 20 January 1819
My Dear Sir,

In reply to your note, I beg to state for the Governor's information that Mr Stokoe called on me yesterday previous to his visiting General Bonaparte, and I believe previous to his calling upon any of his Family.

Mr Stokoe showed me the Admiral's pass, and I informed Captain Nicholls, who came into my apartment and read to Mr Stokoe in my presence the paragraph of your letter where it is stated that the Governor is desirous Mr Stokoe's professional visits to General Bonaparte should be made in conjunction with me, following as near as possible the instructions on this head. Mr Stokoe inquired what these instructions were. Mr Stokoe observed to me as he left the room, that he was going to Count Bertrand to whom he would make known the Governor's wish relating to my accompanying him during his visits to General Bonaparte, and that for his part my presence would be very satisfactory.

I afterwards met Mr Stokoe in Captain Nicholls' quarters and heard him observe that the state of General Bonaparte would render his stay at Longwood all night necessary.

My professional attendance being required by Madame Bertrand, I went to her house last night about 9 o'clock, where I met Mr Stokoe and remained some time in his company.

No conversation relative to General Bonaparte's health took place, nor have I obtained any further information on the nature of his malady.

I am, Dear Sir,
Yours very truly
J. Verling

[To] Major Gorrequer

About 3 o'clock, I copied the conversation held with Count Bertrand yesterday, and enclosed it to Major Gorrequer, with the following note:

My dear Sir:

Being unwilling from the Memorandum shown me yesterday by Captain Nicholls to quit Longwood for a moment, I forgo the anxious desire I feel to communicate personally with the Governor, and I commit to writing an extraordinary conversation held by me with Count Bertrand.

I have not wished to urge upon the Governor my personal feelings, upon the extreme delicacy of my position, since Napoleon has proved his intention to adhere to his declaration that 'he never would see me' by selecting another, but I think it my duty to make him acquainted with this conversation and shall feel obliged by your communicating to me his opinion of my answer to Count Bertrand.

Believe me
Yours very truly
J. Verling

[To] Major Gorrequer

Longwood, 21 January 1819
My Dear Sir,

You have no doubt been informed of everything going on here, and as information can only be obtained from Mr Stokoe, I am in darkness as to the exact state of Napoleon's health.

Mr Stokoe has just made up some pills and asked if I had Mercurial ointment at hand, Quassia, Infusion of Columbia, Cathay Ext, and seems preparing for a regular treatment of the liver affection. I have not asked him a single question on the subject, the quantity of blood drawn has been but small as I learnt from Count Bertrand, who put the bleeding to the account of the liver complaint. Madame attributes it to a second attack of Vertigo and from the tenor of Montholon's conversation, I am induced to think there is very little immediate danger. I should have called upon you before this had I not received orders to be always on the spot. I am unwilling to make a formal detail of these slight points, as I suppose Mr Stokoe reports regularly. I have received a letter from Sir T. Reade yesterday ordering me to remain here, if you can give me any insight into the probable termination of this affair you will much oblige me.

I am, Dear Sir,
Yours very Sincerely
J. Verling

[To] A. Baxter Esq.

Plantation House, 21 January

My Dear Verling,

I did not hear that Napoleon had been bled and had taken any medicine till I received your note. I have seen two bulletins by Stokoe which attempt to establish the hepatic affection and the determination of blood to the head. I am still sceptical as to the real disease and what you have heard from Montholon confirms me in it.

As to the termination of the affair, it is altogether beyond even conjecture. I hear nothing about the matter although I have been here for the last five days.

Let me know if any medicine is taken, or any more vivisection going on; there is no chance of your quitting the place as far as I can ascertain.

The Governor is much pleased with the manner in which you have acted throughout the whole business. Do write to me tomorrow if any Dragoon comes here from Longwood.

Very faithfully yours
A. Baxter

22 January

My Dear Sir,

I have nothing to communicate as I have been out all day.

Napoleon has been seen walking in his Flower garden. Bertrand has been urgent to send again for Stokoe and I believe the Montholons are on my side. The Dragoon waits.

Yours very truly,
J. Verling

[To] A. Baxter, Esq.

Friday, 22 January 1819. I received a note from Major Gorrequer requesting me to meet the Governor at half past 2 o'clock at the Alarm House.

I had a long conversation with Sir H. Lowe; he informed me that the Admiral had got from Mr Stokoe, that he had told at Longwood, a conversation which Mr O'Meara had held at Ascension in presence of Mr Hall, surgeon of the *Favourite*, Viz. that had he, Mr O'Meara, followed the directions of Sir H. Lowe, Napoleon would have been dead before this time, and that he supposed he was not long for this world. The Governor seemed to think that the conversation of Count Bertrand with me, warning me that my name would be implicated in accusations to be made against Sir H. Lowe was *à suite* [a result] of this conversation of O'Meara.

In the evening, I told Montholon of the conversation Count Bertrand had held in my room and that I had thought it my duty to detail it to the Governor, adding that I had him informed of Stokoe's relating O'Meara's words and that there appeared to be a connection between the two. He said, he did not think so, that he was ignorant whether Stokoe had related the words of O'Meara at Longwood, but that they had known them before Mr Stokoe came to Longwood, and since the arrival of the *Favourite*.

23 January
My Dear Sir,

If you should speak to any person at Longwood on the subject which the Governor mentioned to you yesterday, endeavour to learn in what precise terms Mr Stokoe repeated the information he had obtained from Mr Hall respecting Mr O'Meara's conversation at Ascension, whether as affecting the past, present, or future.

Believe me
Yours very truly,
G. Gorrequer

[To] Dr Verling

Longwood, 23 January
My Dear Sir

I beg to inform you that I have spoken to Count Montholon on the subject mentioned to me by the Governor and stated the idea, that Count Bertrand's conversation with me was in consequence of Dr O'Meara's, but Count Montholon said that he was not aware that Mr Stokoe had detailed or mentioned at Longwood the conversation held by Dr O'Meara at Ascension.

I am not likely to derive any information on this subject from Count Bertrand with whom I have not lately conversed.

I am, Dear Sir,
Yours etc.
J. Verling

[To] Major Gorrequer

Plantation House, 24 January
Dear Sir,

It is quite certain Mr Stokoe did repeat at Longwood during his first day's visit there, the conversation held at Ascension, for it has been confessed by him to the Admiral.

Count Montholon may not have been admitted to the secret and therefore perhaps it may be of importance he should understand it was not to get the information from him that you spoke of it, because Mr Stokoe's avowal renders this unnecessary, but merely to know how far his manner of relating it might bear upon what Count Bertrand said to you.

It appears to have been altogether Count Bertrand's own act and thoughts in mentioning it in the way he did to you.

Believe me,
Very faithfully Yours
G. Gorrequer

Dear Sir

I send you the books for Madame Bertrand.

It will be remarkable if B. himself should not have known of what Count Bertrand said to you and that it should have been an attempt on the part of the latter alone to prevail on you to quit, to render his other work more easy.

The only argument against this suggestion is, the modifying certain expressions regarding you, but what you may have heard on this head from the Bertrands themselves is very poor authority.

Yours very faithfully

H. Lowe

24 January 1819

Monday, 25 January 1819. I wrote in reply yesterday to both of these notes, and a signal was made for me to proceed to town today. Sir H. Lowe asked me if I had any further information and I told him that I had repeated to Count Montholon the words of O'Meara and that he said he did not know what Stokoe had said, but that long before Stokoe came to Longwood, they knew that words of similar import though not so strong had been used by O'Meara.

Sir Hudson showed me a paper containing Mr Hall's statement of O'Meara's conversation and the inference he drew from it, and mentioning that Lieutenant Cuppage had said in his presence that O'Meara had expressed similar sentiments to him.

He showed me a letter from Mr Stokoe to the Admiral declining the responsibility of attending on Napoleon, unless placed in Dr O'Meara's situation, and putting to the attack of the head the danger to be dreaded.

I told the Governor that the liver complaint seemed to threaten no immediate danger, but as I had only Mr Stokoe's bulletins to govern me, that considering Napoleon's age, conformation and confined manner of living, apoplexy was the thing to be dreaded, that immediate assistance was of the utmost importance, and as Count Bertrand had declared he could only call me, in case Napoleon was totally insensible, that the favourable moment for affording medical assistance might be passed. He then said that he had a great mind to send Mr Stokoe to Longwood, place him in Jackson's Cottage and prohibit all intercourse with the people at Longwood, except directly with Napoleon in case of sudden emergency.

He proposed this to Sir T. Reade, who was silent, and then went over to the Admiral, and I saw him no more. Sir T. Reade when I was leaving Town, told me the idea of sending Stokoe to Longwood was given up.

Spent the evening with Madame Bertrand, who was very anxious to know what was passing in Town, told her I knew nothing, asked her if she had not seen the papers, Sir T. Reade having told me he believed the papers to the 24th Oct. had been <u>sent</u> to Longwood, none had arrived.

Tuesday, 26 January 1819. Sir H. Lowe came to Longwood and was again anxious to know if I had learnt from Montholon, the precise words used by Stokoe in communicating O'Meara's conversation at Ascension. I told him Count Montholon had said that he did not know Stokoe had related this conversation until I told him, but that they know of O'Meara's having made use of words of similar import though perhaps not so strong, some time before Mr Stokoe came to Longwood.

The Governor asked if I had any objection to inform him of this circumstance in writing, and I said no. He then turned the conversation on the Commissioners and said I must be careful in any of the slightest communication between the persons at Longwood and them, as however trifling in appearance to me, it led to an intercourse he had been long endeavouring to prevent. He asked me if I had not taken a message from Madame Montholon some time ago to Count Balmain, and I informed him that she had requested me to learn from him what she owed him for some shoes, Orange Flower Water etc., which he had brought her from Rio Janeiro, but that I believed she meant to have settled the account through me. He then said that Count Balmain had put down to a wish to settle this account several visits he had lately made to the vicinity of Longwood.

Longwood, 27 January 1819
My dear Sir,
   In reference to your note of the 24th, I beg to inform you that Count Montholon disclaimed to me ever having heard Mr Stokoe relate at Longwood the conversation of Mr O'Meara at Ascension.

   When I related to him what Mr O'Meara had said, he replied that they knew at Longwood before Mr Stokoe came there, that words similar in meaning, though perhaps not so strong had been used by Dr O'Meara at Ascension.

I am, Dear Sir, Yours faithfully
J. V.

[To] Major Gorrequer etc., etc.

Plantation House, 27 January 1819
My dear Sir,
   If you have a copy of the note you wrote me on the 17th, respecting the arrival of Mr Stokoe at Longwood, I shall be obliged to you to let me have a copy, as the one you wrote to me has been by some accident mislaid.

Yours very truly
G. Gorrequer

Have you heard anything about G. B.'s health?

P.S. The Governor would wish to have a memorandum or a report from you, as to the medicines which Mr Stokoe received from your Dispensary at Longwood or compounded there detailing all you know about the medicines given by Mr Stokoe to N. B. whether taken from you or sent from the Town, mention the day he received the medicine from you, and whether they were sent or taken to General B. by Mr Stokoe.

27 January
My Dear Sir,

I have not a copy of my note of the 17th but I perceive by my Memorandum that it was nearly as follows:

'I have yet received no communication from Mr Stokoe, who came here about quarter before 7 o'clock and told me he was going to Count Bertrand's and supposed I would be in readiness. I answered I should remain in my own apartments in case I should be wanted.

'I postpone therefore the inquiry from Count Montholon and shall have the honour to communicate either personally or by letter with his Excellency in the course of the day.'

By the latter part you will perceive that I was at that moment in expectation of some communication from Mr Stokoe which did not take place and having made the inquiries pointed out by your note from Captain Nicholls, I went over to Plantation House in the evening.

I have made inquiries from both Families on the state of Napoleon B's health, and have been answered similarly by both, that he is much weakened by the bleeding and very low in spirits (*abattu*) [worn down].

I herewith send a memorandum of medicines given by me to Mr Stokoe.
I am etc., etc.
J. V.
[To] Major Gorrequer etc., etc.

On the 21st Mr Stokoe asked me if he could have access to my Surgery, to which I replied certainly. We went there together. He asked if I had any blue pill; I gave him the mass, out of which he weighed 3 Drams and divided it himself into pills, I should think about 3 doz.; he also took a small box of strong Mercurial ointment, and asked if I had Cathartic Extract of Calomel and some other medicines.

Mr Stokoe in the course of conversation observed that he supposed he could get any medicines he wanted made up in Town, to which I replied, certainly.

I do not know whether Mr Stokoe took the medicines he got from me into General Bonaparte himself or whether he sent them; nor do I know whether any medicines for General B. were sent to Longwood from Town by Mr Stokoe.

Longwood House, 27 January

Plantation House, 28 January 1819

Dear Sir,

Since writing to you yesterday, the note which was missing has been found; it corresponds with what you repeated in your answer. Neither the Governor nor myself, amidst the events which occurred on that day, precisely recollect what you said as the result of the inquiry you made of Count Montholon respecting General B.'s health.

What was the answer he gave?

Can you inform him whether Count Montholon was with General B. before he saw Mr Stokoe on the morning of the 17th, or if Count Montholon only saw General B. after Mr Stokoe had left him. Also, if Count Montholon and Count Bertrand were together that morning.

On the 18th Count Montholon did not see General Bonaparte, til 11 o'clock of the forenoon. It was at 10 o'clock of the morning of the 17th General B. was taken ill and had a bath. Query, at what time of the forenoon of the same day did Count Montholon go to him? His answer to the inquiry the Governor wished you to make respecting General B.'s health will probably enable you to reply to this point, which at all events he is desirous for particular reasons to be informed of.

Believe me, Dear Sir,

Faithfully Yours

G. Gorrequer

I received this letter in Town from the Governor, it having been sent after me from Longwood. I told him that Montholon's answer to my inquiry after General B.'s health was the only point on which I could give an answer, that he had said the attack was past, and that he was better, but very weak.

He said, his reason for wishing to know whether Montholon was with Bonaparte or Bertrand that morning was, that he thought he was not, and if so, as the proposals given Mr Stokoe for his assent were written in Montholon's hand writing, it would be evident that they were premeditated and prepared the night before.

He wished me therefore to endeavour to ascertain this point.

The Governor informed me that Mr Stokoe had applied to go home, on the plea of ill health, and that I might repeat this at Longwood.

Plantation House, 29 January

Dear Sir,

The Governor supposes it to be known at Longwood by this time that Mr Stokoe is going to England. If it should not have already been spoken of by you, at the House of Count Bertrand or Montholon it may as well be made known at both.

It should however be mentioned at the same time, as is the case, that it is at Mr Stokoe's own particular desire that he is sent home.

I am etc. etc. G. Gorrequer

[To] Dr Verling

Longwood, 29 January 1819

Dear Sir,

I have mentioned to Count and Madame Montholon the circumstances attending Mr Stokoe's departure.

I beg you will inform the Governor that I have not obtained any information on the various Query's contained in your note of yesterday.

I am etc. etc.

J. V.

[To] Major Gorrequer

Friday, 29 January 1819. The Governor came to Longwood and I told him that I had heard from Montholon, that General B. was as usual complaining, and from Madame Bertrand who had been in with him that he had a severe cold in his head.

Before he (the Governor) left Longwood, Madame B. sent to ask me if I would ride with her, and I agreed.

When we arrived at the Guard House, she told me her husband was on the road waiting for us, and asked if the sentries would allow them to pass the limits accompanied by me. I said, I thought so, but I would ride back and ask the Governor, to which she objected, saying she was afraid to be left alone on horseback. We rode on and were shortly joined by Major Emmett, and about the Chinese Barrack we overtook Count Bertrand. When Emmett rode on, we passed by Sir T. Reade's who was standing at his door, and we then met Captain Stanfell and another Captain of the Navy. We rode below Mr Brook's and over Francis Plain, saw the Governor at the new Road behind Sir G. Bingham's, and met Sir T. Reade, Captain Stanfell and another Captain at the turn near Mr De Fountain's, at Hutt's Gate met Mr Jackson. Madame Bertrand dismounted to go down the hill to Major Harrison's, and a Sergeant of the 66th having brought a stool to enable her to mount, she desired Count Bertrand to give him some money, which he did. About half way between Hutt's Gate and Longwood, her horse became quite lame of the hind legs and she and I walked the rest of the way.

She complained repeatedly during the ride of a pain in her right side. Napoleon was out in the Flower Garden about half past 6 o'clock.

Saturday, 30 January 1819. Called on Madame Bertrand; found her very angry at the number of persons she had met, especially Mr Jackson; she would have it that these were observing us, and she found fault with me for appearing low spirited the latter part of the ride, attributing it to fear of compromising myself with the Governor. I laughed at the idea of Jackson etc., watching us, and told her that I at first had imagined she only was to have rode out, and that as I had told her we could pass beyond the limits, I did not like to retract when we met Count Bertrand, though I was not certain that I was quite right in going without the limits with him.

I called afterwards on Sir T. Reade, who told me that Bertrand was well aware he might be getting me into a scrape, by his conduct, as a very long correspondence had taken place on the very subject of their riding beyond limits, in which it was clearly explained that the Governor was to be informed of the circumstances, and an officer specially appointed for the purpose.

He told me the Governor found no fault with what I had done, and had no objection to my accompanying Madame B. wherever she wished.

Monday, 1 February 1819. I saw the Governor in Town, who conversed a good deal on the subject of an officer riding out with the French. Mentioned to me that Sir G. Cockburn was the person who had put a stop to Dr O'Meara's accompanying them, and said that he had no objection to my going with Madame Bertrand, but that in case of her going into any house, I should feel myself awkwardly situated if any private communication took place.

Requested me to tell Captain Nicholls that in case Count Bertrand went out, he was not to accompany him, but apply for Mr Croad.

It appears to me evident that the less communication I have with the Bertrands the better, as they are very strongly, and I believe very justly, suspected by the Governor.

Tuesday, 2 February 1819. Visited Madame Bertrand, who consulted me about her liver etc.

Wednesday, 3 February 1819. Count Bertrand called on me to inquire how I was, as he heard my horse had fallen with me; talked on various matters, at last he introduced Ireland, its population, religion, etc. and asked me if I was not an Irishman and from what part, if I had brothers and sisters, if I heard from them often. I told him that I had a brother living in the south of Ireland, near Cork, and sisters.

He asked me if he was in the service. I told him no, and turned the conversation by saying that I heard but very seldom from my family and scarcely ever wrote to them.

Captain Nicholls came into my room, to ask if I had any commands for Plantation House, and told me he was going there to point out to the Governor the impropriety as he conceived, of having a Mess at Longwood, and said that he had already talked to him on the subject, and that he would have done so sooner, had it not have been out of delicacy to me, in depriving me of the society of my friends; but that he found the duty at Longwood could not be carried on with comfort to his feelings so long as so many people were admitted.

I begged of him not to consult my feelings in anything connected with his duty, that if the Governor chose to decide according to his wishes, and that Mr Jackson and Mr Wortham were to leave Longwood I should regret it very much, but put up with it, as one of the many disagreeable things I had experienced since I came to the place.

I met Count Montholon, and told him that I had received a visit from Count Bertrand; he asked me if Bertrand had made any proposition to me, and I answered no.

Thursday, 4 February 1819. Captain Nicholls told me he had mentioned the circumstances about the messing to the Governor and in the presence of Colonel Wynyard and Major Gorrequer, and he expected a new arrangement to take place.

Saturday, 6 February 1819. Mr and Mrs Baynes and a Miss Llewellyn came to Longwood to see the new House, etc. I was at Count Bertrand's when Captain Nicholls came in and said that Mrs Baynes having known some relations of Madame Bertrand's, was anxious to pay her respects. Madame Bertrand desired him to say she would be happy to receive them. I took my leave.

In the evening Captain Nicholls informed me that he had been surprised by a visit from Count Bertrand, who told him that he was much hurt at his having accompanied and remained at his house during the visit of Mr and Mrs Baynes, and that it appeared to him as if he had been there in the light of a spy. I congratulate myself that I had not remained, as I see on the part of Count Bertrand, since I refused the present, an evident animosity against me.

Madame Bertrand, having been tormented and tormenting me with a thousand chimerical complaints arising from a tendency to hysteria and from the want of any force of character to support the monotony of her situation, had latterly taken it into her head that the womb must be affected with some organic disease, as she was ten months without conceiving. This had been the topic of conversation for the last 3 weeks between her husband, herself, and me, and I at last proposed to call an *accoucheur* [obstetrician] who should ascertain by manual examination the position of the womb, as there was no symptom to indicate disease. Mr Livingstone came and the matter of menstruation, of her particular mode of having them, of the quantity of blood she had lost in her *fausse couche* [miscarriage], and the minute details were entered into before, and were occasionally commented on, by the *Grand Maréchal du Palais* [Grand Marshal of the Palace]. As Livingstone maintained that all the circumstances were referable to debility, and to be removed by tonics and the cold baths, I explained to him, that nothing would satisfy her mind but examination *per Vaginam* [through the vagina], and he agreed; they went together in the next room. I remained unmovable on my chair, and I believe the Count would have been a spectator of the operation. After a due time, they returned and Madame informed her husband that Mr Livingstone could find no impediment to procreation on her side.

Sunday, 7 February 1819. Capt. Nicholls read me a note detailing to the Governor what Count Bertrand had said relative to his visit in company with Mr and Mrs Baynes.

22 February 1819
Dear Sir,

As the message you carried from Madame Montholon has given rise to a very unpleasant correspondence with Count Balmain <u>originating in him</u>, <u>I shall be</u> much obliged by your acquainting me with the words, as nearly as you can recollect, in which you conveyed her message to him.

I remain, Dear Sir,
Yours very truly
H. Lowe

Longwood, 23 February 1819
Sir,

In reply to the note I had the honour to receive from you last night, I beg to inform you that I cannot recollect the precise words I made use of to Count Balmain, but the purport of the message was, that Madame Montholon requested he would let her know by me, the amount of the sum she owed him for the commissions he had had the goodness to execute for her at Rio Janeiro in order that she might send him the money.

Madame Montholon has since requested me to speak to Count Balmain on the same subject, as I have informed Sir T. Reade, but not having met Count Balmain, I did not think it necessary to call upon him for that purpose.

I am
J. V.

[To] Sir H. Lowe

Dear Sir,

Your explanation is quite satisfactory.

You will hardly however suppose to what your message has led and what may follow. It would have been quite the same thing had any other person been the bearer.

Yours truly,

H. Lowe

23 February

Thursday, 25 February 1819. I dined this day at Plantation House, and Sir H. Lowe informed me that Count Balmain had made a pretext of my message to write him and state that he did not wish to settle a money transaction with a Lady through a third person, and as he had also received visits both from Count Montholon and Bertrand, he was anxious to return them, and stated his wish to proceed to Longwood. This the Governor had refused, and a long and angry correspondence was the result.

I informed Sir H. Lowe that Madame Bertrand had expressed to me her anxiety that I should become the Physician to the <u>Emperor</u>, and had even asked me if I would accept the propositions offered to Stokoe, and on my declining entering upon the subject, had said that if I did not choose to discuss these points with her, I ought to cultivate the good will of her husband, whose character I did not properly appreciate. I affected to laugh, and told her I had no hopes from what had passed, that the Emperor would never see me, and that I looked upon myself as a mere *locum tenens* [place holder], till the arrival of a French Surgeon. To this she replied, that I had been misled, as the Emperor had never made a formal demand for a French Surgeon, but that her husband, in the discussions about the removal of O'Meara, had suggested to the Governor the propriety of not removing him until replaced from Europe, and if the situation should not be accepted by an Englishman that *un medicin quelconque* [an ordinary doctor] would do, but that Napoleon would prefer a French or Italian one. The Governor replied that he would forward a copy of the letter to England. She mentioned also that this letter was dictated by Napoleon, and that the application for a Priest arose from the circumstances of Cipriani's death, upon which event, Count Bertrand had written to Cardinal Fesch requesting that he might be replaced by another *Maître d'Hôtel* [Master of the House], and that if the English Government had no objection, Napoleon would be gratified by the arrival of a Priest. Cipriani had been buried by the Protestant Clergyman, though he died a Catholic. The Governor had forwarded these letters to England and had had a reply from his Government merely stating that there was no objection on their part.

I mentioned to Sir H. Lowe this conversation, and he was decidedly adverse to any advance or attempt to conciliate Count Bertrand. I told him also that she had requested me to tell Count Balmain, that she was anxious to see him and fix the day for the long projected ride to Diana's Peak, that I had declined it, but that she had again repeated her request.

Upon this attempt to convey through me a message which she could not convey through the orderly officer, Sir Hudson made some severe remarks, and said he need not warn me that any communications were delicate, but those with the Commissioners, particularly so, etc. etc.

Upon the tenor of this conversation, which I have not fully detailed, I have to remark that it has left upon my mind the impression that the situation of Physician to Bonaparte is one which cannot be held by a British subject, without the certainty of sacrificing his peace of mind for the time he holds it, and with more prospects of ultimate injury than benefit.

All the pains I had taken to obtain the good will and good word of the people about Napoleon, the only mode I know of obtaining his, and of which the Governor was aware, seem now to throw a shade of suspicion upon my conduct and the mere idea of an approach to Count Bertrand seems to have cancelled anything that might have appeared praiseworthy.

Sunday, 14 March 1819. Arrived from England HM Brig *Redwing.*

Monday, 15 March 1819. I went to Town, and saw there Sir H. Lowe who told me he had received no intelligence of the coming of a French Surgeon. I told him that General Bonaparte had walked out yesterday evening, and that I had heard that he had caught cold, and had a slight bowel complaint. He told me Count Bertrand had received some private letters, the contents of which he was not at liberty to divulge, but I could see that he thought the arrival of the French Surgeon remote.

In the evening, Madame Bertrand rallied me about the arrival of my successor, asked me if Sir Hudson had given me any information, and ended by saying I should have to remain where I was.

Tuesday, 16 March 1819. I called to see young Arthur Bertrand who has been for some days very ill with an inflammatory sore throat, found Count and Madame Bertrand at breakfast and the *Morning Chronicle* for December on her bed. They seemed particularly pleased with these papers, and laughed at the idea of the plot said to have been discovered, and explained to the Government by the dispatches in the *Mosquito.* As to O'Meara, they said, they were confident his conduct would be generally approved of, and that Napoleon had taken care that the loss of his half pay of 6 or 7 Francs a day should give him no uneasiness.

Copy of a letter addressed to Captain Nicholls, on the subject of Mr Stokoe's attendance at Longwood:

St Helena, 18 January 1819
Sir,

In reference to the verbal communication which Count Bertrand made to you, I am directed by the Governor to acquaint you, that having conferred with Rear Admiral Plampin in respect to the continuance of Mr Stokoe's medical attendance at Longwood, the Admiral has acquainted him, that he cannot dispense with Mr Stokoe's services in the Squadron, so far as to admit of his being entirely removed from it, nor could he release Mr Stokoe from the obedience due to him as Naval Commander in Chief, without the sanction of the Lord Commissioners of the Admiralty.

The Governor himself will have no objection to Mr Stokoe affording his medical assistance to Napoleon Bonaparte, whenever so required, but he is desirous in such case that Mr Stokoe's professional visits should be made in conjunction with the Physician who is in attendance at Longwood, following as near as possible the instructions on this head.

The unsigned to me is returned herewith, to be delivered back to Count Bertrand, as well on account of the Imperial Title being used in the heading of it, and its having no signature, as also, because the first part of this letter renders any deliberation on the proposal it contains unnecessary.

I have the honour to be, Sir, Your most obedient
Humble servant
G. Gorrequer

[To] Captain Nicholls. etc. etc. etc. Assistant Military Secretary

Plantation House, 19 January 1819
Memorandum for Captain Nicholls
On Mr Stokoe's arrival at Longwood, Captain Nicholls will see the pass he brings, and inform himself as particularly as he can of the footing on which the Admiral may have granted him permission to visit General Bonaparte.

If he observes any deviation from the words of the pass or those of my instruction Mr Stokoe may have shown, or made known to him, he will notice it to Mr Stokoe.

Captain Nicholls will communicate to Dr Verling, the letter he received yesterday from Major Gorrequer and apprise him that the Governor desires he may be ready at all times to accompany Mr Stokoe in any professional visit he may be required to make to General Bonaparte.

The same rule is to apply to any conference which may be sought for with Mr Stokoe by any persons of General Bonaparte's family, on the subject of his (General Bonaparte's) malady.

Captain Nicholls after seeing the pass which Mr Stokoe may have brought with him, will immediately wait on Count Montholon or Count Bertrand

and make known Mr Stokoe's arrival for the information of General Bonaparte, and that Dr Verling is also at hand to accompany him.

H. Lowe

Thursday, 3 June 1819
Minute of a conversation with Count Montholon, 3 June 1819
Count Montholon informed me that Napoleon had been unwell for several days, that he again urged him to call me in as his Physician, that it now rested with me to become so, since Napoleon was willing to drop all stipulations as to pecuniary matters, supposing he could at any time remunerate me, and this he would always hold in view, as it was not his practice to leave unrewarded the slightest service rendered to him, that the hint (as he now termed it) formerly thrown out relative to the exaggeration of his maladies came from himself and not from Napoleon, and that Napoleon only required that I should conduct myself *loyalement, un homme d'honneur* [loyally, a man of honour] towards him and that I should pledge myself never to make any written report of his state of health without giving him a copy and also that I should not repeat any circumstances I may hear at Longwood, unless I conceived they were of a nature which rendered it my duty as a British subject to divulge them.

My reply was that I could not enter into any pledge or promise secretly, that if such were necessary they must be made known clearly by me to the Governor. General Montholon observed that nothing was required of me but what was a tacit agreement between every patient and his Physician, to which I replied that I could not admit the necessity of a formal and secret engagement with General Bonaparte, when every other person would be satisfied with the implied one. He assured me that such particular agreements did sometimes occur in the common intercourse of life and requested me to consider them attentively, since should any sudden illness induce them to demand my assistance upon these conditions and I should hold it, any refusal would have a very extraordinary appearance. I replied that medical aid might be afforded in case of emergency without reference to discussion, since my admission to him in a moment of necessity did not bind him to keep me as his habitual medical attendant.

Friday, 4 June 1819. I communicated to Sir T. Reade the purport of the conversation and as the sentiments conveyed by my answer were drawn from the avowed opinions of Sir H. Lowe, I thought it better to place the conversation officially before him, and therefore on June 10th copied it and took it to Town observing to him, that as I had some time back requested in writing to be relieved from my situation at Longwood and frequently since verbally, I now told him that, as he had not complied, and said that he did not comply with my wishes from a consideration of the public service, I had refrained from openly declaring at Longwood my resolution not to accept the situation of surgeon, fearful that this declaration might lead to embarrassment to Sir Hudson by inducing them to call upon another person; but I now wished to know if he had any objection to my putting a stop to all future conversations and propositions, by at once declaring to Count Montholon that I did not desire to be the personal surgeon to Napoleon.

He replied that the false position in which O'Meara had been placed, had led them to wish to continue someone in as his successor, but he had no objection to my making known to them that I only wished to consider myself as a British officer on duty at Longwood, and that I had no desire to form one of Napoleon Bonaparte's suite.

On my return to Longwood, I had a conversation with Montholon and Madame, who were very urgent to me, and to whom I clearly said that though I came to Longwood extremely anxious and ambitious to be in personal communication with Napoleon, yet after 10 months residence there, and being better able to judge of the delicacy and difficulty of the position, I was clearly of opinion that I should decline it.

Montholon left us, and Madame entered into a long argument to prove the facility with which I might fill it, and the various motives which ought to weigh with me and induce me not to leave Longwood without seeing *l'Empereur*.

Monday, 14 June 1819

My Dear Sir,
    The Governor wishes to see you down, tomorrow morning at the Castle; be good enough to come down to breakfast at 9 o'clock, not later.
Yours faithfully,
G. Gorrequer

Tuesday, 15 June 1819. After breakfast, Sir Hudson Lowe told me he had sent for me to know if I had not had a conversation at one time with Count Bertrand upon the propositions made to me by Count Montholon, to which I replied that I never had, but that he once addressed me and urged the impropriety of refusing to give a statement for Napoleon of Madame Montholon's illness, and that I replied abruptly that as this matter concerned Count Montholon, and was already arranged with him, I could not discuss with Count Bertrand; where our conversation ended, but that having mentioned what passed to Count Montholon, he said that he thought Count Bertrand was commissioned to speak to me by Napoleon on the proposition, and that he had merely commenced upon this subject, awkwardly enough since my reply was very natural; and that several times afterwards, Montholon had asked me if Bertrand had spoken to me.

He then asked me if I had heard anything about the protocol, to which I told him, not a syllable; he said this was very odd, as he had also sent other papers of which he had heard nothing.

The conversation turned upon other matters, and ended by his lending me a book which he said I might let Madame Bertrand see; this was *The Follies of the Day*, a translation from the French; he opened it at a chapter termed: 'My Hallucinations' in which he observed Count Bertrand would find many things he might apply to himself.

June 25 1819
My Dear Sir Thomas,

Count Montholon was taken ill the night of the play and continues to complain very much. I have given him some medicines, but am anxious to have the opinion of another medical man on his case, and I will thank you to inform the Governor and let me know whom I shall propose to Count Montholon to call in.

> I remain Yours very truly
> J. Verling

[To] Lieutenant Colonel Sir T. Reade CN, Jamestown

Jamestown, June 26 1819
Dear Sir,

The Governor seeing no reason to interfere in respect to the consultation you desire to have respecting Count Montholon's health, deems it unnecessary to say anything further than that he can have no objection to Dr Livingstone, who has been in the usual habit of attending at Longwood, being called in also on this occasion if you deem it advisable.

> Believe me to be Yours truly,
> T. Reade

Longwood, 27 June 1819
My Dear Livingstone,

I was called to Madame Bertrand this morning, and found her much alarmed having lost some blood from the uterus during the night. A bloody discharge still continues and pain in the loins. She is now nearly in her 5th month. I send you a horse on account which I shall explain when you arrive.

> Believe me Yours very truly
> J. Verling

Saturday, 26 June 1819. A store ship from England having arrived yesterday, *Morning Chronicles* to the 30th March were sent here. Count Montholon brought one into my room and showed me an article from home, saying a physician, a surgeon and a Priest had left that City on the 27th February for Ostend and were to be sent by the British Government to St Helena.

He also showed me a letter from Sir T. Reade stating that the Governor had no objection to permit Madame Montholon to go directly to England, contrary to his instructions, in consequence of the delicate state of health she was represented to be in, and offering her a passage in the *Lady Campbell*, Captain Marquis, about to sail for England. And in reference to the allusion made by Count Montholon in his letter about his being likely soon to follow her! The Governor informs him, that in such case, he must send him to the Cape, in compliance with his instructions, unless (which he had no reason to expect) contrary orders should in the meantime arrive from England.

Count Montholon informed me that he had accepted the offer and that Madame wished to see me about medicines etc. for the voyage.

Mr Livingstone came up and saw Madame Bertrand; her countenance was good; he seemed to think that by rest, cold applications and astringents, a *fausse couche* [miscarriage] might be avoided. He afterwards came to my room, where in conversation he told me that he was at Sir T. Reade's house when my note reached him, which he gave to Sir T. to read, who asked him to explain the meaning or allusion at the latter end of it, which he could not do, as he could not understand it himself, but said he supposed it related to something obscure in Madame Bertrand's case, as I had told him when last I saw him that she entertained doubts whether she was pregnant or not.

I explained that I availed in calling him in consultation to Count Montholon's case and then read to him my note to Sir T. Reade in which the nomination of a Physician to be consulted was left to the Governor, and his reply, where Mr Livingstone's name was mentioned.

I then told him, that I had purposely omitted his name in my application, having frequently been informed by himself that he was not desirous of being called in at Longwood. But that however ambiguous Count Montholon's conduct might appear, as having been taken ill at the present moment when it might appear a feint to get away with his wife, yet I had watched the symptoms with attention, and treated them as I would have done in an ordinary case, and that he certainly got rather worse than better, whether this arose from anxiety and restlessness from the departure of his wife and alone, or from the circumstances aggravating a pre-existing hepatic affection. I told him however, that I had advised Count M. to leave off medicines, as he intended to go to Town the following day, and to go to see his wife embark the day after.

Whilst we were speaking, Count Montholon came in to the room. We asked him several questions, and told him that when Madame was gone we should again see him and commence a regular treatment for the removal of his disease. He told us he had been attacked the night before with a palpitation of the heart and that his nights were very restless. When he went away, Livingstone said that to look in his face was sufficient to convince him his illness was real, but we agreed to see him together again in a few days.

Captain Marquis having come to Longwood to arrange about the accommodations and expenses of passage, Count Montholon requested me to interpret; I accordingly went in with Captain Marquis and Captain Nicholls, where it was settled that Captain Marquis was to give up his own cabin, a very large one on the upper deck, for Madame and her children, and a large cabin below for her servants, for which they agreed to pay £350. Besides which finding on inquiry that his stock of poultry was small, Count Montholon offered to send 12 dozen head.

Monday, 28 June 1819. Madame Bertrand spent a good night, but is by no means well this morning. Wrote to Livingstone.

Thursday, 1 July 1819. Madame Montholon and her children went to Town in Lady Lowe's carriage. They stopped at the Castle, where they took an early dinner in company of the Commissioners etc. In the evening, I accompanied her and her husband aboard the *Lady Campbell*, where the accommodation appeared to be tolerably good. Lieutenant Jackson and Mr Croad came on board with us.

Friday, 2 July 1819. About 3 p.m. the *Lady Campbell* sailed.

Saw Napoleon walking in the lower walk of the garden, with Count Montholon. He was dressed as on board the *Northumberland*, cocked hat, plain green coat and star, light coloured breeches, stockings and shoes.

Saturday, 3 July 1819. Count Montholon looking ill and complaining of pain in the side. Gave him at night: Pulv. Ant' gr. ii Calomel gr. v in pil. Sulphat Magnesia.

Saturday, 4 July 1819. Arrived the Company store ships *Bridgewater* and *Marchioness of Ely*; no letters or dispatches. The rumour brought by the *Laertes's* store ship that Mr Stokoe was returning to St Helena in the *Abundance*, King's store ship, is strengthened by these.

Thursday, 8 July 1819. Spent the day in Town with Lieutenant Jackson who sailed in the evening for England in the *Drana* China ship; Passengers: Mr Robaits, member of the Council at China, Mr Hodson of this Island. Dined at the Alarm House with Major Emmett; arrived at Longwood before 9 o'clock.

Called on Madame Bertrand, found her doing well. She told me that Napoleon had paid her a visit about 5 o'clock in the evening. Showed me a very handsome snuff-box, which he had given her, surrounded by 32 very large diamonds; the miniature in the lid was painted after his return from Elba. The likeness did not appear to me very striking, except in the cadaverous hue of the complexion, and an expression of sadness in the eyes; it represented him too young. Madame Montholon showed me a box precisely similar before they went away.

Sunday, 11 July 1819. Called on Madame Bertrand who had lent me the *Morning Post* for April; she asked me if I had read the debate concerning General Gourgaud. I told her I had. She said she thought it extraordinary that Sir G. Cockburn should repeat to the House a private conversation, that her husband had however made the observation attributed to him, to Gourgaud who came to tender him thanks at the Elysée Bourbon. She added too, that Marshal Soult had often told Napoleon that he could not bear to see Gourgaud *dans l'antichambre* [in the antechamber].

The epithet bestowed by Gourgaud on her husband, as related by Sir G. Cockburn, seemed to have annoyed her, and she was very willing to allow that Sir George had painted him correctly.

Monday, 12 July 1819. In a conversation with Count Montholon today about General Gourgaud having been introduced, he corroborated the anecdote about Bertrand, and mentioned that during the exile of Napoleon at Elba, Gourgaud had been taken great notice of, by the Duke of Berri in consequence of Gourgaud's mother having been the Duke's *nourrice* [nurse] or rather because, and that notwithstanding that he had been employed so immediately about Napoleon's person, yet he was confirmed in the rank of Colonel, and appointed to the command of the Artillery near Paris; that the Bourbons wishing to ascertain correctly what was passing at Elba had picked upon Gourgaud as a proper person to be employed in such an affair, that it was proposed to Gourgaud who accepted, and he was in appearance to have been disgraced, then joined as a discontented person to his old master, but that this scheme was prevented from being carried into execution by Marshal Soult, Minister at War, who was adverse to such a line of conduct altogether, but who could only obviate it, by declaring that Gourgaud was a man of no stability of character and that with whatever intentions he might leave Paris, he would most probably reveal to Napoleon at their first interview the entire plan. It was dropped. Gourgaud made his gunners cry '*Vive l'Empereur*' [Long Live the Emperor] and joined Napoleon on his arrival, when he applied to be appointed *Officier d'Ordonnance* [Orderly Officer]. Soult then related this anecdote, but after some delay the appointment was given to him; he did not owe the appointment to him, but that he should not have had it, did it depend upon him, *Car il n'aimait pas les Girouettes* [Because he didn't like weathervanes]. He added that Bertrand afterwards was unwilling that Gourgaud should have been one of those selected to come to St Helena, but that Gourgaud prevailed by clamour and every species of importunity with Napoleon.

Saturday, 31 July 1819. Count Montholon having been for nearly a month complaining of a pain in his side and other symptoms indicating an affection of the liver, and having given him for some time back with the concurrence of Dr Livingstone the blue pill and occasionally Calomel, without much benefit, I rode into Town today, and finding that Dr Livingstone was occupied in attendance on Lady Lowe for symptoms threatening a bad liver, I took the opportunity of proposing to the Governor that Dr Arnott of the 26th should be called in. He said that he did not wish to introduce to Longwood any stranger unnecessarily and that he thought Dr Livingstone might be called again and that the presence of Dr Arnott was unnecessary unless I should think the danger imminent.

Monday, 2 August 1819. I went to Town, I saw Sir T. Reade to whom I mentioned that hitherto Dr Livingstone had been called upon by me, as a sort of private practitioner and in a friendly intercourse; but that I could no longer look upon his coming to Longwood, but as a public duty, and that therefore I begged Sir T. Reade, that if Dr Livingstone was a person appointed by the Governor to consult with me on the state of Count Montholon's health, that it should be explained to him. To this Sir Thomas agreed.

Tuesday, 3 August 1819. 9 o'clock. Sent a horse and a note to Town, requesting Dr Livingstone to come up, mentioning that Count Montholon had spent a bad night and complained much of pain in his side, though the mercury had begun to affect the mouth.
    About 5 o'clock I received the following letter.

My Dear Verling,
    I am sorry to say I have been up all night with Mrs Lewis Solomon, who was delivered of a son about 2 a.m. I am much fatigued, and I am again sent for to another case, Mrs O'Connor. Therefore it is entirely out of my power to be with you today.
    A blister applied to Count Montholon's side may be of advantage.
                                        I am truly yours
                                        M. Livingstone

The Governor was here in the course of the day, and going through the garden, came close upon Napoleon. He remarked to me that he thought that Napoleon walked firmly, and requested me to explain to Madame Bertrand or Count Montholon that Captain Nicholls had brought him through the garden to show him a wall and paling that Napoleon had requested to have made and that the meeting was totally unpremeditated.

Wednesday, 4 August 1819. Count Montholon appears better.

Saturday, 7 August 1819. Went to see General Montholon, found him much alarmed at having spit up some blood during the night.

He told me often before that he had been near dying in France, from a pulmonic affection. I made light of it to him, told him to leave off his pills, gave him a pectoral mixture. He complained of cough and slight strangury. Wrote to Dr Livingstone, and requested him to come up here. General Montholon complained that the repeated visits of the Orderly Officer about seeing Napoleon, and persisting in sending newspapers only through him, had disturbed and annoyed him a good deal.

A coal ship arrived yesterday from the River; no news of consequence, no intelligence of the *Abundance* and of the Italian Physician. *The Times* Newspapers to the 21st May have been sent to Longwood. Captain Nicholls went last night to deliver them to Montholon who said he was too ill to admit him, and the papers were not given till this morning.

About 2 o'clock Dr Livingstone came here.

We found Count Montholon in the following state. A good deal of heat of the skin, pulse 80 and full and soft; short dry cough, pain in the chest, on face inspection no pain in the region of the liver; mouth sore from the mercury. Bowels confined.

The Governor having been informed by Captain Nicholls that he could not see or obtain information about the presence of Napoleon Bonaparte at Longwood, sent a sealed packet, inscribed, notes from the Governor and enclosures for the information of Napoleon Bonaparte, and signed the right hand corner: H. Lowe.

Captain Nicholls (being informed that in case General Bonaparte declining receiving it, it was wholly unimportant to which of Napoleon's followers it was given, providing he understood to give it to Napoleon) went to Montholon who declined seeing him or receiving any packet.

He then called at Bertrand's house and was told he was at Longwood House, and the blinds being apart saw Napoleon, in his dressing gown, walking up and down with Bertrand. This was about half past 6 o'clock. He wrote and communicated these circumstances keeping the sealed paper.

Sunday, 8 August 1819. Count Montholon has spent a sleepless night.

Capt. Nicholls received a note directing him to deliver the sealed packet, and that it was unimportant to whom providing the person undertook to deliver it. He went to Montholon, whose servant said he had orders not to admit any person; he then sent for Marchand, *Valet de Chambre* to Napoleon, who offered to take the paper to the *Grand Maréchal*, but on being told that Bertrand had already refused it, also declined taking it.

He saw Napoleon this evening sitting alone with a lamp before him on his dressing room table.

Montholon's bowels being well cleaned by the salts, he feels much better. His mouth is very sore. Lotio astringéns.

Monday, 9 August 1819. Sent my returns to Mr Webb by the *Redpole*, and also wrote to Jackson. Received a message from the postmaster that they were too late for the mail, and one from Sir T. Reade that they should be sent.

Montholon continues better. Napoleon has not been seen this day. Madame Bertrand told me that she had expected to hear from him, but that the extreme bad weather had prevented him, rain and wind now every day and all day long.

Thermometer 59 in the morning and seldom exceeds 60 during the course of the day.

Tuesday, 10 August 1819. Montholon's mouth sore still; spent a bad night, cough gone, bowels costive and complains of colic pains.

Capt Mist. Sal. Cath. ad Anum solvendum.

Wednesday, 11 August 1819. Montholon spent, he says, a sleepless night, though he took an anodyne containing Tinct [ ]ii: complains of having suffered during the night from Colic pains, frequent desire to make water, skin moist, pulse 76. Tongue furred, less anxiety in the countenance, cough gone, no difficulty in respiration, pain in the region of the liver on pressure, had four stools from a single glass of Saline Cathartic mixture taken yesterday morning.

> Rx. Mist. mucilaginis
> Spt. Aether nitre[ ]
> fluid. ad lib.

Told me in conversation, that he did not think he could possibly hold out any longer at Longwood; that the ennui was too much and the separation from his wife and children led him perpetually to mournful ideas which destroyed his health; here he seemed much dejected and shed tears. I encouraged him as much as I could and turned the conversation. He said that Bertrand had visited him late last night, and apologized by saying that he had been detained *par l'Empereur qui lisait l'Évangile* [by the Emperor who was reading the Gospel].

Went to Ladder Hill, and came back though Town. Saw the Governor, who asked after Montholon's health; told him he was better but extremely dejected and weak. He said it was no wonder that he should be low spirited, considering that the loss of his wife's society and the position in which he stood, having compromised himself more than once; he did not explain and the conversation terminated abruptly.

On my return to Longwood, I found there Colonel Wynyard and Brigade Major Harrison. On conversing with them I found that Captain Nicholls had been to wait upon Count Bertrand and tendered again to him the paper, marked notes from the Governor for the information of Napoleon Bonaparte, and upon his refusal to take it, told him that he requested he would inform General Bonaparte, that an officer of the Governor's Personal Staff was come to Longwood, to wait upon and deliver to him the said paper; and he also declined delivering this message. They sent for Marchand, Napoleon's Valet, and desired him to deliver the message; he said he would give them an answer in twenty minutes; they waited 35 minutes and no answer nor Marchand returned. Colonel Wynyard and Major Harrison then proceeded to the front door of the billiard room which they found locked and after waiting some time, Gentilini, an Italian servant of Napoleon's, came to them and informed them that Marchand had the key and that he was not to be found. They then returned, and Colonel Wynyard sent Captain Nicholls to the door of the dining room with the paper, but here also admittance was denied.

They went away about 6 o'clock of the evening, and I called upon Madame Bertrand, who had been walking up and down the garden walk as long as these Gentlemen remained, observing what passed; she seemed much agitated and asked me whether I thought they would return tonight, and what they proposed doing, whether they would force open the doors as they knew this should not be done, *sans verser du sang* [without shedding some blood]. I told her to tranquillize herself, that I thought it very improbable they would return tonight, but that I really was totally ignorant of the Governor's intentions.

About 9 o'clock Madame Bertrand sent for me. I found her and her husband together, drank tea with them in the bedroom, and on my wishing them good night, Bertrand came into the Salon with me and began talking of what had passed in the morning. I told him I could not converse upon the subject, and that in fact it was entirely out of my province; he detained me however for some time, asked me what steps they meant to follow next. I told him I was totally ignorant of their intentions. He then said, why do they not communicate in the usual way, through Count Montholon, or since he is sick through me? I made no answer to anything he said, but wished him a good night.

Thursday, 12 August 1819. This morning Captain Nicholls informed me he had received during the night a letter directed to Bertrand and orders to deliver to him both it and the packet. He went to Bertrand who received both, but observed it was useless to give it to Napoleon, for he would throw it into the fire.

Montholon is considerably better, but complains much from Lumbago.

Went to Town and dined at the Castle; slept at Major Power's.

Friday, 13 August 1819. Between 7 and 8 o'clock Major Power's servant brought me a signal made from Deadwood: Dr Verling is wanted immediately at Longwood, and whilst dressing I received the following note. (Immediate on the back):

My Dear Sir

The Governor begs you will please proceed to Longwood so as to arrive there before 10 o'clock to be in the way of anything extraordinary that should occur in the course of the execution of an instruction with which Capt Nicholls is charged.

Very truly Yours
G. Gorrequer

7:15 a.m Friday Morning

I arrived at Longwood before 10 o'clock and Brigade Major Harrison soon after me. Captain Nicholls sent for Marchand, who after some delay came into his room where I was with Major Harrison. On Captain Nicholls addressing him in English, Marchand appealed to me to explain, and I told him after Captain Nicholls, that he had sent for him to deliver a message to Napoleon, that he requested him to go to General Bonaparte and inform him that the Governor had sent him positive orders to wait upon and see General Bonaparte and that Captain Nicholls was now going to the front or billiard room door, where he should wait till Marchand brought him an answer. To this Marchand replied, that the Emperor had passed a very bad night and was at the moment in his bath. He was then asked, if he had been desired by Napoleon to state these circumstances; he said no. He was then desired to deliver the message, that Captain Nicholls was waiting at the billiard room to be admitted to see Napoleon: but this he positively declined, saying that he did not conceive it his duty, but that it ought to pass through the Grand Marshal. Captain Nicholls then proceeded to the billiard room door and knocked, waited for some time, and upon no person coming attempted to go in, but found the door locked.

He then sat down to write for the Governor's information what had passed, and Major Harrison went away. Whilst he was waiting, Count Bertrand came to his room and asked what was the precise object he had in view; he replied: to see Napoleon. Bertrand told him if he passed by the window of the bathroom he would see him. Captain Nicholls accordingly followed Bertrand and passed the window, but he did not see him; he passed again, in a few minutes afterwards, and saw Napoleon sitting in his bath and his *Valet de Chambre* Marchand standing by him. This was about 20 minutes after 11 o'clock.

Nicholls observed to me that he was a very ghostly figure.

I went to see Montholon and found him complaining much of his Lumbago, and that he had passed a very restless night. He was however free from Fever and appeared to me to be doing very well. He complained that he had again been tormented by the Captain's visits last night.

Having more than once thought that no good could arise to me from any interference however indirect in the unpleasant communications occasionally going on at Longwood, I had expressed to the Governor my unwillingness to act as interpreter, and he fully agreed with me, and said he should take care there should be no necessity for it in the future. Major Harrison too agreeing with me in the view of the subject I had taken, and having told me that he had now applied to have an officer who spoke French sent with him today to Longwood, I wrote as follows to Gorrequer.

Longwood, 13 August
My Dear Sir,

I had formerly occasion to converse with the Governor upon the subject of my acting as interpreter when communications were to be made by Captain Nicholls to the persons at Longwood, and he then fully coincided with the ideas I expressed to him.

I have not allowed this to influence me today, having been unwilling to cause any delay. I request however you will have the goodness to mention the circumstance to the Governor and let me know his wishes upon this head.

Very truly Yours,
J. Verling

[To] Major Gorrequer, etc. etc.

Saturday, 14 August 1819. At breakfast, Nicholls gave me his instructions to read, by which I find, if an opportunity is not daily afforded him of seeing Napoleon before 10 o'clock, he is to send a message to him that he is ordered to see him, and to wait at the hall door for admission. Accordingly at 10 o'clock he sent for Marchand, gave him the message and proceeded to the hall door, where he knocked, waited for some time, endeavoured to open the door, found it fastened and came away.

Fearful that Marchand might not have clearly understood him, he brought him to my room, and I repeated to him the message, and that the Captain had been waiting at the door for an answer.

He replied that he believed that the Emperor was in bed, and until he did ring, it was impossible for him, Marchand, to disturb him.

General Montholon continues to improve; complains much of his loins and soreness of his mouth, bowels costive.

> Capt Solut. Cath [ ]
> Ln^th Saponis
> Emp. Lyttae ad F[   ]

About 1 o'clock I received the following note dated 13 August, Jamestown:

My Dear Sir,

In reply to your note of this day, I beg leave to say the Governor does not see any impropriety in the assistance rendered the Orderly Officer in the interpretation of the message you allude to, there not appearing any other person at the time on the spot to do it for him, and when messages are the result of any alleged indisposition on the part of the persons on whom you are in attendance, he conceives there cannot be a more proper channel for the delivery of them, as you are naturally the most competent judge whether the situation of the person is really such as to render him unable to receive a message without injury to his health, in which case, viewing the very serious points which generally form the subject of the Governor's communications, it is of the highest importance that no false pretext be suffered to prevail.

If therefore as in the case of the messages which the Orderly Officer has been directed to deliver to Count Montholon, the Count's state of health has been such as to render him unable to receive them or the letter I sent to the Orderly Officer for him, it ought to be the first question of the Officer to you, whether indisposition really prevails to such an extent as to render it inexpedient that the letter or message be delivered to him, and the Governor will always be happy in such a case to leave it to your own discretion to judge of the proper moment of delivering it, either on the part of the Orderly Officer himself, accompanied by you, by yourself, or by one of the sick person's attendants.

With reference to the only occasion where you spoke to the Governor upon the subject of your acting as interpreter, it was one where the Orderly Officer had employed you as the medium of communication to a servant of Count Bertrand who had infringed the regulations, and as a matter of policy he should have preferred that any other person had been applied to, on the occasion. But the Governor at the same time did not mean to bar you in the exercise of your own discretion where there is an absolute necessity for a message being delivered, and there is no other person at hand to assist, particularly in cases where it would be impossible to ascribe your act to any desire or design of undue interference in matters that did not regard you.

Believe me Very truly yours

G. Gorrequer

Sir T. Reade having come here in the course of the day I mentioned to him that I did not comprehend the drift of Major Gorrequer's note or rather letter, since mine made no allusion to Count Montholon or the message to be delivered to him, or to the sick persons upon whom I might be in attendance, but referred simply to a conversation in which I had expressed to the Governor my unwillingness to be employed as the medium of communication when any discussion of an unpleasant nature should be going on at Longwood, and in which he agreed that I was not the proper channel. That I had thus been employed again in a matter totally unconnected with my professional duty, that I had lent myself to this sooner than cause delay, but that I recalled on the present occasion the former conversation, hoping that both conjoined might prevent my being so employed again. I told him also that the same idea had occurred to Major Harrison, who, when my assistance was found necessary, observed that he had anticipated the difficulty and pointed it out at the Castle, and even named Mr Croad as a proper person to be employed.

Sir T. Reade said that the Governor would be obliged for any assistance I might give the Orderly Officer, to which I observed that I had on trivial and household events been in the daily habit of assisting him, and that here, in a matter so serious as to require the presence of a Staff Officer, besides the Orderly, I had done so sooner than allow any obstacle to remain, but that I then became in case of any doubt or dispute, responsible to both parties for the inaccuracy which may be charged on either.

Sir T. Reade asked me where I got the paper upon which I had written to Major Gorrequer, observant that it had upon it the head of Napoleon. I took some note of paper which was lying by me on the sofa, and holding it up to the light, saw upon it a very good likeness of Napoleon, with the inscription *Empereur des Français Roi d'Italie* [Emperor of the French, King of Italy], and I recollected that seeing a large quantity of note and letter paper upon Count Montholon's outer table and wanting some, I had told him I should rob him of a few sheets, and he requested me to take what I wanted. I had taken a packet of each, letter and note paper; on looking at the letter paper, it had no impression on it. Sir Thomas took the only remaining sheet of the note paper and asked me to procure him two or three more.

He told Nicholls that the Governor wished him to go to Town early in the morning and to remain to dinner, and observed to me, that as tomorrow would be his birthday it would be better to leave him quiet. The whole of the shutters of Napoleon's apartments, upon the appearance of Sir T. Reade at Longwood, were immediately fastened.

Sunday, 15 August 1819. Before Nicholls went to Town, he again showed me a note from Gorrequer about a letter to be delivered to Montholon, in which it was said that he might ask me to explain to Montholon, that it was from Gorrequer and that the Governor could not imagine why he would not receive it, and request to know if Nicholls should bring it to him or send it by his servant.

I delivered this message, and Montholon replied that as this letter must be upon business, must require an answer, and must lead to involve him in business to which he felt totally unequal, he must positively decline it, that he had when it was first offered been under the impression that it was the packet to the address of Napoleon, but he should equally have declined receiving it had he known it was a letter from Major Gorrequer. He complained a good deal of cough and difficulty of breathing and appears much debilitated.

Monday, 16 August 1819. Count Montholon appears better: cough slight.
Mist. pro tuss.
A letter from Bertrand has been sent to the Governor.

Tuesday, 17 August 1819. Montholon still continues better.
A letter received by Captain Nicholls, in the handwriting of Sir T. Reade, addressed to Count Bertrand, and a packet sealed to the address of Napoleon Bonaparte.

Captain Nicholls called on Bertrand and delivered the message that he requested Count Bertrand would let Napoleon know that the Orderly Officer wished to see him in the execution of his duty. Count Bertrand replied that Napoleon was sick, and Nicholls having asked if he was to conceive this as a reply from Napoleon, Count Bertrand said that he was authorized by Napoleon to say he was sick.

Captain Nicholls having received some orders about having two rooms of the suite of Count Montholon fitted up for the reception of the Italians expected, sent to inform Montholon, who desired to speak to him, and went with him into the bath room, being unwilling to give it up.

Count and Countess Bertrand paid General Montholon a very long visit. In the evening about 6 o'clock he sent for me, and I found him complaining much; his skin was hot and dry, pulse 83, and full but easily compressible, dry cough, and pain under the scapulae upon breathing, anxious countenance.

> Rx. Ag. [   ] Acet. [ ]ii
> Ag Pur [ ]i
> Capt [ ] cls.

He attributed his illness to cold taken in the bath room and to the fatigue of a long conversation with the Bertrands.

Wednesday, 18 August 1819. Found Montholon free from fever, skin moist. Still complains of pain under the scapulae upon drawing a full breath, and is very uneasy having been in a very precarious state for a long time in France from an affection of the Lungs, and from which Corvisart told him he had escaped miraculously, warning him to beware of catching of venereal disease, for that his constitution would not bear the exhorbtion of mercury; I laughed off this idea, as it was plain that he was very low spirited and ascribed to the mercury, his present cough etc.

I however thought it prudent to propose to him to call another medical man, and he said he put himself entirely at my directions. I accordingly wrote to Dr Livingstone, about half past nine o'clock.

Longwood, 18 August 1819
My Dear Livingstone,

The Governor having desired me to call upon you in case I should require the assistance of another medical man, I send a horse for you.

Count Montholon was, from the last day you saw him doing very well; the spitting of blood did not reappear and the pain of side ceased. Yesterday morning he caught cold by going into a room with a current of air, and last night he had a good deal of fever, and difficulty of respiration with pain under the scapulae. From the previous Haemoptysis, and having had formerly a severe affection of the lungs, I am uneasy about him and anxious to see you. He is much quieter now, but still complains of being incapable of drawing a full inspiration without pain, and notwithstanding the debility, I am much inclined to take away some blood.

Yours very truly
Verling

A little after 10 o'clock Captain Nicholls went to Count Bertrand and requested him to deliver to Napoleon the message as yesterday. In reply Count Bertrand observed that he did not sufficiently understand the English language to enter into an explanation with Captain Nicholls, but that he tendered him his answer in writing, presenting at the same time a paper. Nicholls declined taking it, saying Count Bertrand surely understood the message; he again presented the paper which Nicholls refused and came away. Captain Nicholls then sent for Marchand who was not at hand, and after waiting some time he sent for Ali, who refused delivering any message and referred him to Bertrand. He then went and knocked at the billiard room and could not see any person to admit him.

About 2 o'clock Livingstone came here, and we saw Montholon. He was much easier, skin moist, pulse moderate. Livingstone seemed to think that the pain under the scapulae etc. proceeded principally from Rheumatism, and the pain in the back from affection of the kidneys; he advised emollients and [illegible word], and 5 Grs. of the Pulv. Ant. at night. I saw him again at night when he appeared to have a feverish exacerbation, gave him the Pulv. Ant.

About five o'clock the Governor came here accompanied by Sir T. Reade, Major Gorrequer and Harrison; after various messages etc., he sent for me, and having asked me if I had seen the Orderly Officer's instructions to which I replied 'Yes' he told me that he had received a very impertinent letter from Bertrand stating that Napoleon was ill, and demanding that Mr Stokoe his physician should be sent to him, if he had arrived, or if he had not, as soon as he should arrive, or if he was not to return to the Island, that permission should be given to such person as Napoleon should select to sign the conditions proposed to Mr Stokoe.

To this the Governor had sent a copy of his answer to these conditions, article for article, given at the time to Count Montholon, a copy of Lord Bathurst's letter in which permission is given to Napoleon Bonaparte, to chose any medical man, providing he agrees to adhere to the regulations in force.

Having obtained no reply to this, he said he wished me to go to someone of the suite of Napoleon, and deliver the following message, which he first repeated verbally, and which at my request Major Gorrequer committed to writing:

> I am directed by the Governor to say, that having understood through different channels, that Napoleon Bonaparte states himself to be indisposed, I am come to request you will be pleased to make known to him, that I am ready at all times to afford to him my medical assistance and beg to be informed if he is disposed to avail himself of it.

Longwood, 19 August 1819
Sir,

In compliance with the orders of his Excellency the Governor, I waited yesterday evening upon the Count Montholon, and informed him, that the Governor having understood through different channels that Napoleon Bonaparte stated himself to be indisposed, I had come to request he would be pleased to make known to him that I was ready at all times to afford to him my medical assistance, and that I beg to be informed if he was disposed to avail himself of it. The Count Montholon being confined to his room by sickness, requested me to address myself to Count Bertrand.

I accordingly repaired to the house of Count Bertrand, and made him the same tender of my services; he replied that Napoleon Bonaparte would not see any Physician who did not previously sign the conditions agreed to by Mr Stokoe, and was proceeding to explain the nature of these conditions, when I told him that I could not enter in any discussion upon the subject. He said, that as I had undertaken to deliver a message, he conceived that I should also be the bearer of an answer, to which I replied that as I had requested Count Bertrand to make the message known to General Bonaparte, I supposed the answer was to come from him.

I saw Count Bertrand again last night about half past five o'clock, when he told me that he had informed General Bonaparte of the message and that he was directed to reply that General Bonaparte was willing to choose a Physician, whenever the Governor would authorize whoever might be selected to sign the conditions agreed to by Mr Stokoe, and that he would not see any person who declined signing these conditions.

I am etc. etc.

Verling

[To] Major Gorrequer etc.

Longwood, 19 August

My Dear Sir,

I have been informed that the malady under which General Bonaparte is said to labour at present, is a constipation of the bowels, and I am led to think that his occasional 'crises', as they are termed here, have arisen from the same cause. Hitherto, this state of health has been treated by the warm bath and frequent Glysters, and by abstinence; but it is said that latterly he has found the bath produces much debility and is afraid to push it to the length he used to do, and that at present Glysters have failed to procure any effect. No mention was made of his having tried medicine, though I have formerly been told that he had taken Cheltenham salts and Castor oil.

Believe me

Very truly Yours

Verling

[To] Major Gorrequer etc. etc.

I was playing a game of chess with Captain Nicholls, about 5 o'clock when Count de Montholon sent for me, to request I would call and see him before I went to bed.

About half past nine I went and found him in bed, with several papers before him. He said that Napoleon had sent for him, but that as it was impossible for him to go they had carried on a long discussion by notes, the result of which, he was now about to communicate to me.

He told me it was my own fault if I did not become his Physician. Napoleon, he said, had wished him to propose to me the conditions accepted by Mr Stokoe, but that he had explained to him that such a proposition would be useless. And he said, I have drawn up in the most unexceptionable form the following paper to which if you are willing to affix your name, you will be called to him tonight, and observe your signature is entirely safe, since the acceptance is conditional and provides that your Government shall give its permission. He then read the paper, which contained pretty nearly the same stipulations as those marked out in his letter of the 1st of April to the Governor. If I was willing to sign this paper which he said was only signing *que j'étais un honnête homme* [that I was an honest man] I should be called up in the night, as if to a sudden illness of Napoleon.

The paper should be presented to me as a necessary preliminary before I had the admission to him. I would see that there was nothing derogatory to me as a man of honour, and as far as my Government was concerned, it was quite conditional and left to them to confirm or to annul it; my acceptance had been given through a laudable desire, not to allow a piece of formality to prevent me from giving medical assistance in a case which was represented as extremely urgent.

I allowed him to go on. He said that Napoleon would that very night give me 3,000 Louis, and in case in the morning discussions or disputes might arise, which should prevent me remaining at Longwood, I had this sum in my possession. But as from the nature of the conditions, there was every probability I should remain, he agreed to pay me for a period to be fixed on, 500 a year, and to secure this income to me for my life time.

I told Count Montholon, this was a mere repetition of an old offer, to which I had before given an explicit refusal, that I could not for a moment think of signing any paper however conditional, or taking into consideration the contents unless previously shown to the Governor and coming to my knowledge through him, and I asked him to put himself for a moment in my place, and leave the 3,000 Louis out of the question, whether he would sign such a paper. He answered certainly he would, as it would be finishing *ma carrière à Longwood* [my career at Longwood] in a very flattering manner, that I should be reciprocally useful to Napoleon and the Governor terminating the present state of *Crise* [crisis] and when the Italian, or if it were possible that Stokoe was coming back, when he should arrive, that I would have in my power to leave Longwood carrying with me the most flattering marks of regard from the Emperor.

I told him that I had clearly explained to him, that my position at Longwood was that of a Military Medical Officer sent by my superiors, and that any attempt to alter it, or any intrigue to be placed near the person of Napoleon, was totally incompatible with my duty and even inclination.

Friday, 20 August 1819. After reflecting during the night upon the conversation it seemed to me unnecessary to communicate it to the Governor. I was however hesitating when Dr Arnott arrived at Longwood and brought me the following letter.

Jamestown, 20 August 1819
Dear Sir,

Count Bertrand having addressed a letter to the Governor stating Napoleon Bonaparte to have fallen down sick last night, he has directed Dr Arnott as the principal Medical Officer in the island to repair to Longwood to give his advice.

This is however not meant to interfere in any shape with the continuation of your attendance, Dr Arnott's visit being one of duty as well as attention, according to the rule laid down to the Governor in his instructions.

Believe me, Dear Sir
Yours Truly
T. Reade

[To] Dr Verling etc.

Dr Arnott told me he had directions to the same effect and to act in conjunction with me. I accordingly went to Montholon and communicated to him, that Dr Arnott was here and for what purpose; he referred me to Count Bertrand, and we went together to his house. Dr Arnott not speaking French fluently requested me to explain to Count Bertrand, and I told him, that in consequence of his report of the illness of General Bonaparte last night the Governor had sent Dr Arnott as *chef des officiers de santé* [head of the health officers] to offer his medical assistance.

Bertrand talked a good deal about his illness, and said he would communicate the offer of Dr Arnott, though he knew its futility, since Napoleon would not accept any person but upon conditions taken by Mr Stokoe, and that in moments of sudden illness, both himself and Count Montholon had urged him to take me. Here he took an opportunity of paying me a compliment.

Count Bertrand then went to Montholon's with his wife, and then to Napoleon. And upon his return we saw him again. He asked Dr Arnott if he possessed his independence of the Governor, to which Dr Arnott replied, in his medical capacity he was perfectly independent and unbiased, and that he was ready to give to the best of his ability assistance to General Bonaparte. Count Bertrand asked him, if he was not a Military man, to which he answered certainly, but Military control had nothing to do with professional medical duty. Count Bertrand asked if he was willing in case of being admitted to Napoleon to give his opinion of the nature of his disease, to point out the proper remedies, and the course of treatment he conceived most likely to restore him, if he would state his opinion in writing and sign it. Dr Arnott said that he would make his statement to the Governor. Upon this Count Bertrand observed that to Napoleon everything proceeded from or connected with the Governor was suspicious, that he knew not among us, to what extent military power went etc. etc. and that therefore he had thought it necessary that the situation of a medical man placed near him should be defined. He then read to Dr Arnott the conditions accepted by Mr Stokoe, article by article, commenting upon them as he went along, pointing out such as related and depended upon the Governor, and such as depended upon the honour of the individual Physician selected, and concluded by saying that the answer to Dr Arnott's offer of his services was that Napoleon would accept them, or those of any Medical Officer who should by the Governor's consent pledge himself to these conditions.

Dr Arnott having left Longwood, I called upon Montholon, and in the course of conversation told him what had passed at Bertrand's. He seemed much astonished and said that Bertrand had certainly exceeded his authority from Napoleon. He asked if Dr Arnott spoke French and I told him that Bertrand had explained himself in English, and he attributed to this circumstance what must be a mistake, since Napoleon had only authorized him to say, that if the Governor authorized these conditions, he would then choose a medical man. On leaving Montholon, I was going to visit Madame Bertrand, and met Bertrand going to Montholon. Shortly after he came where I was sitting with his wife, and told me he was quite astonished at what I had told Montholon, that he had never meant to say Napoleon would accept Dr Arnott or any medical man, since this would be at once conceding to the Governor the power of choosing for him, and he asked me to rectify the mistake, and point out as indeed he had already done to me, and in writing to the Governor that the answer was, that Napoleon would himself choose, when these conditions were conceded to him. I declined interfering any further and he said it did not much signify, he would wait and see how the Governor would act.

Saturday, 21 August 1819. The *Abundance* store ship having arrived, I went to Town. Sir T. Reade informed me that Mr Stokoe had come in her, and in conversation with the Governor he pointed out to me a curious coincidence between the last report of Mr Stokoe when at Longwood, but where constipation is pointed out as one of the principal points to be guarded against as inducing an affection of the head. The information lately given to me of his being constipated, the report of Count Bertrand of his having fallen down, a written application made on the 17th and dated as if by mistake on the 19th. That if Mr Stokoe had arrived he should be sent to Longwood, and if not, that he should be sent as soon as he did arrive, and a verbal application made by Count Bertrand to say, through Captain

Nicholls, that Mr Stokoe should be sent immediately to Longwood. I observed that I had heard nothing of his having fallen down, either from Madame Bertrand or from Montholon. Sir T. Reade then informed me that Mr Stokoe was to be tried by a Court Martial and that an instruction had been sent to Nicholls to communicate to Count Bertrand that the trial would prevent for the present his going to Longwood.

Sir H. Lowe read to me an extract from a private letter of Mr Goulburn where he mentions that Lord Bathurst approved of my conduct in the circumstances of no small difficulty, alluding to my conversation (I believe) with Count Bertrand, shortly after my arrival at Longwood. He also adverts to a conversation I had communicated, where Count Bertrand had made inquiries relative to my family and connections in Ireland and when I had myself thought proper to inform Sir H. Lowe that my friends were Irish Catholics. His Lordship says that the religious persuasion either of myself or my friends could not all influence his opinion.

Sunday, 22 August 1819. Montholon continues to get better. This evening fever and night sweats have not left him.

Castle, 22 August
My Dear Sir,
    The Governor sends a letter for Count Montholon from the Countess. He understands from the Commander of the vessel who has brought it, that the Countess was better before she left Ascension.
                    Yours Very Truly,
                    G. Gorrequer
[To] Dr Verling

Count Montholon sent for me to read to him the first part of the letter which was from Captain Marquis, commanding the ship, noting that Madame was still ill in bed of sea sickness and very low spirited, that Tristan was also ill and the two girls were well. Madame however had herself written, told me she desired to be remembered to me. He seemed low spirited, and I read to him Gorrequer's note and told him that the sea sickness would soon pass away.

Monday, 23 August 1819. I went to Town. Sir T. Reade informed me that he supposed Mr Stokoe would be tried in the course of the week upon ten charges, drawn up by the Admiralty, in a very clear manner against him. I understood afterwards that they had been drawn up by the Attorney General, and that they were accompanied by some remarks from him elucidating the law of evidence.

Montholon's evening exacerbation and profuse sweats continue.

Bertrand this morning in answer to Captain Nicholls' desire to see Napoleon in the execution of his duty as Orderly Officer, put a slip of paper into his hand, in which he says he repeats the demand that Mr Stokoe be sent to Longwood, as his presence becomes more and more requisite.

A large packet sent to Bertrand in the evening.

25 August 1819
Dear Sir,

The Governor wishes to see you at the Castle to morrow, immediately after breakfast.

Yours Faithfully,
G. Gorrequer

Thursday, 26 August 1819. I went to the Castle; the Governor told me, that one of the charges to be brought against Mr Stokoe, was for having repeated at Longwood, the slander propagated at Ascension by Dr O'Meara against Sir H. Lowe, and that it would be necessary to produce to the Court my conversation of the 17th and 19th of January 1819 with Count Bertrand. I observed that the latter one seemed to me to bear upon the calumny of Dr O'Meara, and that unless some particular object was in view, the less of my conversations and communications that were made public, the better. This gave rise to some discussion in which he agreed to make some extracts from my first conversation as would prove Count Bertrand's communication on the subject of Napoleon's health and affect Mr Stokoe's assertion that 'he thought it necessary medical assistance should be always on the spot.'

It ended by my observing that the whole conversation had better be shown.

He then asked me to make a postscript to my report of the 15th of August of that part of my private note, where constipation is stated to be the malady of General Bonaparte, in order to trace a connection between this information and the report of the following day from Count Bertrand, where it is stated that Napoleon had fallen down, and to link this with the expected arrival of the *Abundance* and compare it with the caution given by Mr Stokoe when at Longwood against constipation as tending to produce a determination of blood to the head. I told him that the same information had been given to me often before and however it might appear to him, that I did not think there was any connection or concerted plan in the information and that I had meant my note to be a private one; that however he had the note and might do as he pleased. I left him and he again sent for me and asked me, if the word constipation had been used by Count Bertrand when giving me the information on Napoleon's health. I told him I had the information from Count Montholon, and that I did not think the word constipation had been used, as it was rather a medical term and not in familiar use.

Friday, 27 August 1819. Captain Nicholls went to Town and brought me in the evening, the following note.

Castle, 27 August 1819
Dear Sir,

If you can give any information as to the hour at which Mr Stokoe saw General Bonaparte in the first visit he paid him, Viz. 17th January 1819, be good enough to communicate it to me for the Governor.

Very truly yours,
G. Gorrequer

[To] Dr Verling

St Helena, 27 August 1819
Sir,

You are requested to attend a Court Martial to be held on board HM Ship *Conqueror* on Monday the 30th at nine o'clock for the trial of Mr Stokoe, Surgeon, on charges exhibited against him by the Lords Commissioners of the Admiralty, in order to give your evidence thereon.

I am, Sir
Your most obedient Servant
George Nicholls
Deputy Judge Advocate

To: Dr Verling

Saturday, 28 August 1819. Wrote to the Governor, saying that I could not give any information as to the time Mr Stokoe first saw General Bonaparte, as I had remained in my own apartment most of that morning, and telling him that the date of the two conversations I had held with Count Bertrand was the 17th of January in the evening of the day Mr Stokoe first came to Longwood (as he had thought it was the 18th and had induced me to alter it). I also informed him that I had received a letter from the Deputy Judge Advocate requiring my attendance as an evidence on Monday morning at 9 o'clock.

About half past one o'clock, I went to see Count Montholon and found him a good deal annoyed at a letter he had received from Gorrequer, communicating an application from the house of Balcombe for payment of sums due to them, and enclosing an extract of a letter received by Mr Cole from Balcombe, dated Plymouth, in which he says that he is astonished at being informed that General Montholon had said he, Balcombe, owed the French money.

That indeed O'Meara had wished him to become agent to the French, and had offered him a £3,000 bill to meet their drafts, but that he had refused and that the bill had been given to Mr Holmes who had agreed to transact their business. Montholon said that *Balcombe était un fripon* [Balcombe was a rogue], that he Montholon had put into Balcombe's own hands, and saw him put them in his pocket, two bills, one for £1,800 drawn by Bertrand, the other for £1,200 in favour of Balcombe, and that they had received intelligence that the one for £1,800 had been paid, and that therefore Balcombe was a rogue, who wished to pocket the money supposing that Napoleon would hush up the affair, but that he Montholon would not let it rest, and that the payment of the bills by their banker and other circumstance would eventually prove that Balcombe *s'était fourré dans une mauvaise affaire* [had got himself into a bad business].

The accusation against O'Meara, he said, was false as he himself had given the bills to Balcombe.

About 2 o'clock the Governor came here accompanied by Sir T. Reade and Colonel Wynyard; he asked me if I had heard anything of Napoleon. I told him that Madame Bertrand had told me she intended paying him a visit and said she hoped she might find him dressed. This did not look as if he was very ill.

He said that Bertrand had written to him a letter, in which he stated that Napoleon had fallen down; that this letter was found by the Orderly Officer in the morning and that Bertrand had afterwards told the Orderly Officer that he did not wish to disturb him in bed, and had left it on his table, notwithstanding the urgent illness with which Napoleon is said in it to be attacked, and an application made for Mr Stokoe. When Captain Nicholls delivered this morning the usual message to Count Bertrand, that he wished to be admitted to see Napoleon, the Count gave him as an answer a written paper, stating that they had not received the *Morning Chronicles* as they ought and that there were upon the island *Morning Chronicles* to and for May, which were withheld.

The Governor desired Nicholls to write upon a piece of paper and give it to Count Bertrand, that all the *Morning Chronicles* and papers to the address of Napoleon had been sent to Longwood and the later ones, which had come to the Governor's hands, that there were no *Chronicles* for May upon the island, and that the paper though not an answer to Captain Nicholls' question, was not returned because it afforded another instance in Count Bertrand's hand writing of an assertion without proof.

Jamestown, 29 August 1819
My Dear Sir,

Having accidentally found the enclosed note, the Governor has desired me to send it to you, in the hope that it may aid your recollection as to the time Mr Stokoe was admitted to see Napoleon Bonaparte on the morning of 17 January.

As Major Gorrequer wrote his note after breakfast you could not have sent the enclosed one till near eleven, and as you mention that Bertrand and

Napoleon's greatest victory was at Austerlitz in 1805. This engraving is *c*.1840 by E. Rouargue.

Copper engraving, *Départ de Fontainebleau, le 20 Avril, 1814,* by Swebach, *c*.1816, showing one of the most emotional scenes in Napoleonic history, Napoleon's farewell to his Old Guard after his first abdication.

Rentrée de Napoléon le Grand. 1815 engraving of Napoleon returning from Elba as Caesar. No doubt many in France hoped he would manage to do the same thing from St Helena, but it was not to be.

Surrender of Napoleon, Emperor of the French. Engraved by F. Dixon, from a drawing mad[e] under the direction of a gentleman who wa[s] on board the *Bellerophon* at the time. Published by Edward Baines of Leeds, February 1817.

Gold snuffbox dat[ed] 20 March 1815, the d[ay] Napoleon returned to Paris [for] the 100 days. The image sho[ws] Napoleon, Marie Louise and th[eir] son, the King of Rom[e.] Unfortunately for Napoleon, i[t was] fantasy, as neither his wife nor his s[on] was able to join hi[m]

Napoleon at St Helena, by
C. Currier, *c.*1890.

Denzil Ibbetson's drawing of Napoleon's residence at Longwood, after a watercolour by
Basil Jackson, showing Napoleon, Bertrand and Gourgaud. In Norwood Young,
Napoleon in Exile at St. Helena, 1915.

Dr James Verling, from
a portrait in Arnold
Chaplin, *A St. Helena
Who's Who,* 1919.

Nineteenth-century engraving of Sir
Hudson Lowe, Governor of St Helena
during Napoleon's time on the island.

This engraving shows Sir
Thomas Reade, Deputy Adjutant
General on St Helena and one of
Sir Hudson Lowe's top aides.

Nineteenth-century engraving of General Baron de Gourgaud, Napoleon's Master of the Horse on St Helena.

Nineteenth-century engraving by Martinet of Charles Jean Tristan, Comte de Montholon, one of Napoleon's close associates on St Helena.

Nineteenth-century engraving of Dr Francesco Antommarchi, the doctor finally sent to attend Napoleon on St Helena.

Nineteenth-century engraving of Louis-Joseph Marchand, Napoleon's valet.

Le Comte de Las Cases. Engraved by Müller after a life-painting by Delorme, printed in Paris by Chaillou Potrelle, 1824.

General Count Henri Gatien Bertrand served as Napoleon's Grand Marshal throughout the exiled emperor's time on St Helena.

Ivory sewing device of *c.*1821-40 showing Napoleon's tomb on St Helena.

St Helena: The Shade of Napoleon Visiting His Tomb. A mid-nineteenth-century lithograph published by S. Knights, Lithographers to the King. See if you can find the 'shade of Napoleon' in the trees.

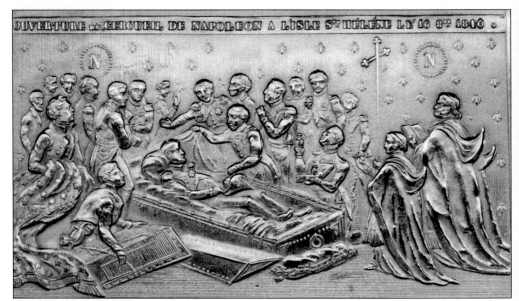

Snuffbox of *c.*1840 showing Napoleon's body being exhumed from his grave on St Helena.

When Napoleon was exiled it was illegal to have his image in one's home. This false-bottom snuffbox was one of the many ways that people got around that restriction.

Wooden snuffbox of 1840 showing Napoleon's body being brought to France from St Helena.

Montholon had been going to and fro between the house of the former and Longwood House very often, it is natural to suppose that Mr Stokoe must during this time have been at Count Bertrand's house, otherwise there could have been no motive for the latter passing backwards and forwards to his own house.

Believe me, Yours Very truly,
T. Reade

Copy of the note alluded to in the preceding:

My Dear Sir Thomas,

Mr Stokoe came into my room about a quarter before 7 o'clock and told me he was going to Count Bertrand's and supposed I would be in readiness.

I said I should be found in my own room if wanted, since then I have heard nothing of him.

Count Montholon and Bertrand have been going to and fro, between Bertrand's house and Napoleon's very often.

I have had a note from Major Gorrequer saying the Governor wishes to see me, unless my attendance on medical service has been or is likely to be required; I am desired to ask after General Bonaparte's health in the Governor's name, which I have delayed doing, expecting to see Mr Stokoe; but as his visit seems undeterminable, I am now going into General Montholon's and if circumstances permit me to leave Longwood, shall call on you on my way to Plantation House.

Yours faithfully
Verling

17 January 1819

This note, which was found accidentally, was marked on the back, in Sir T. Reade's handwriting: 'From Dr Verling, Received at the Alarm House January 17th 1819'.

Longwood, 25 August 1819
My Dear Sir Thomas,

My note to you of the 17th Jan. states explicitly that from a quarter before 7 o'clock until the moment of writing it, 'I had heard nothing of Mr Stokoe.'

I think it was Captain Nicholls who told me Counts Montholon and Bertrand had passed repeatedly between the house of the latter and Longwood house.

Believe me Yours Very Truly,
Verling

[To] Lieutenant Colonel Sir T. Reade

Monday, 30 August 1819. As I was going on board the *Conqueror* to the Judge Advocate's summons, I met the Governor and told him that Count Montholon had sent for me last night, and requested me to state to the Governor that his health had suffered much from the obligation occasioned by forcing letters upon him and messages tending to implicate him in business when he was unable to leave his room. At this moment he had a considerable degree of fever upon him, and pointed it out to me, saying that it was absolutely useless to give him medicine, and that he conceived it my duty to intervene in his favour.

I told Sir H. Lowe that he certainly was worse than I had before seen him, and he seemed considerably annoyed and requested me to call upon him on my return from the Court Martial, as he wished to speak upon this matter.

On my return, I was sent for to the Castle and also Captain Nicholls. We found Colonel Wynyard with the Governor, and he began, by saying to me that he did not see why his character should be attacked for inhumanity to such a person, that I had told him that Count Montholon's illness was much augmented by his forcing letters and messages upon him, and that it had driven him last night to a state almost amounting to delirium, whereas he was not aware that Count Montholon had been so ill, for that I had told him the last day he was at Longwood that Count Montholon was tolerably well and sitting upon his sofa. All this was said in a very angry tone of voice. I told him that he had mistaken what I had said, attributing to me what had come from Count Montholon, and that his being worse last night was the only part which was mine. That since he had been at Longwood Count Montholon was so much worse, as to induce me to call upon Dr Livingstone, who had advised the calling in of Dr Arnott, and that, though I had told him that Count Montholon was on his sofa, yet I had at the same time told him that he was upon his sofa every day and that it was only in the evening he was so very ill, being then attacked with fever. He said that he was left in ignorance that Dr Livingstone had been sent for; I told him, I had taken care to acquaint the chief of his staff.

He then said that I had not followed his instructions of the 13th August, and he then read to me Major Gorrequer's letter of that date.

I replied to him, that I had informed Captain Nicholls early yesterday evening upon his inquiry that Count Montholon was ill in bed and unable to transact the business, that I had been saying so for the last three weeks, and that I did not conceive it proper to come forward every moment obtruding my opinion, and that as far as related to his instructions, I had got the letter in answer to a very short note of mine, upon a different subject, that I should read it over carefully and have the honour to reply to it. He observed that, in my capacity as a British Officer that he thought that I might assist and forward the views of the Governor. I told him that I conceived it my duty to deviate as little as possible from my medical capacity and that in this instance especially I saw nothing further to be required of me than a declaration of the actual state of Count Montholon's health.

He made many remarks upon Montholon's conduct and repeatedly mentioned his insidious proposals to me, to which I replied that as long as Count Montholon stood in the relation of a patient to me, I should perform towards him what I felt to be my duty.

This conversation terminated by his saying that I need not (as he had first required) make any written report on Count Montholon's health, that he was now informed of his illness and should refrain from sending letters or messages upon business until I should report that he was fit to receive them.

Tuesday, 31 August 1819. Remained at Longwood, having requested Dr Arnott to come and see Montholon; did not come.

Wednesday, 1 September 1819. Went to the Court Martial; heard Stokoe make his defence; he asked me two or three questions of no importance. Thought he managed his defence indifferently.

Thursday, 2 September 1819. Mr Stokoe was found guilty upon nine of the ten charges and upon part of the other, and sentenced to be dismissed from His Majesty's Service; but in consequence of 25 years spent in the Navy, the Court recommended him for half pay. I went to the Castle, and in conversation asked the Governor to let me have a copy of the charges made against Stokoe; he said that the Admiral was very delicate about naval affairs and had already refused to give copies, but he did not see where the objection lay. Major Gorrequer said that he had made a rough sketch of the charges, which he could give me, and the Governor desired me not to show it or let anybody know that I had it. He said in talking over the subject at Longwood I should be careful, and explain that the recommendation for half pay was solely grounded upon his length of service. He went through most of the charges, and saw no objection to their being made known at Longwood.

Copy of Gorrequer's notes

1st Charge. Having communicated with General Bonaparte and his attendants on the 17th January 1819, upon subjects not connected with medical advice, contrary to the Naval standing orders at St Helena.

2nd Charge. Having taken notice and given an answer to communications received both in writing and verbally from some of the French prisoners at Longwood, previous to making them known to the Naval Commander in Chief, contrary to the said standing orders.

3rd Charge. Having signed a paper purporting to be a bulletin of General Bonaparte's health and delivered the same to General Bonaparte or his attendants, contrary to the standing orders and his duty as a British Officer.

4th Charge. Having stated facts, in said bulletin, that did not fall under his own observation, confessed by him afterwards to have been dictated or suggested by General Bonaparte or his attendants, not consistent with his character and duty as a British Officer.

5th Charge. Having in said bulletin inserted as follows: 'The more alarming symptom is that which was experienced in the night of the 16th, a recurrence which may prove fatal particularly if medical assistance is not at hand' to create a belief that General Bonaparte was in imminent or considerable danger and that the case was so little urgent, that he had been four hours at Longwood before he was admitted to see him and that Doctor Verling was at hand.

6th Charge. Having communicated to General Bonaparte or his attendants information about books, letters or papers said to have been sent from Europe for them and which had been intercepted by the Governor and having conveyed to them information respecting their money concern.

7th Charge. Having contrary to his duty and character as a British Officer, communicated to General Bonaparte or his attendants an infamous and calumnious imputation cast upon Lieutenant General Sir H. Lowe by Barry O'Meara, implying that Lieutenant General Sir H. Lowe had practised with the said B. O'Meara to induce him to put an end to the existence of General Bonaparte.

8th Charge. Having disobeyed his superior Officer's orders in not returning from Longwood on or about the 21st Jan at the hour prescribed.

9th Charge. Having knowingly and willfully designated General Bonaparte in the bulletin, in a manner different from the Act of Parliament and contrary to the practice of His Majesty's Government, the Lieutenant General, Governor of St Helena, and the Rear Admiral, and doing so at the special instance and request of General Bonaparte and his attendants, though he knew the mode of designation was a point in dispute between General Bonaparte and the Governor and British Government, and thus acting in opposition to the wish and practice of his own superior Officers and the respect he owed them under the general printed instructions.

10th Charge. Having in the whole of his conduct evinced a disposition to thwart the intention and regulations of the said Governor and Rear Admiral, to further the views of the French prisoners, in furnishing them with false and colourable pretence of complaint, contrary etc. etc. etc.

Castle, 6 September 1819
Sir,

The Orderly Officer having reported that when he desired to see Napoleon Bonaparte this morning in the execution of his duty, he was told that Napoleon Bonaparte was indisposed, it is the Governor's direction that should a similar answer be given when the Orderly Officer desires again to see him, that you will call upon the person to whom the Orderly Officer may have addressed himself and make known your readiness to attend upon Napoleon Bonaparte, saying you have received the Governor's directions for such purpose.

The Governor desired you will on the receipt of this letter wait upon the individual who delivered the answer this morning to Captain Nicholls and offer your services as above.

I am etc. etc.
T. Reade

[To] Dr Verling

Longwood, 7 September 1819
Sir,

In obedience to orders conveyed in your letter of yesterday, I waited upon Count Bertrand, and offered my services to Napoleon Bonaparte as therein directed.

Count Bertrand replied that Napoleon Bonaparte was ready to make choice of a medical attendant whenever the Governor would sanction the conditions proposed in the month of January last.

The Orderly Officer having informed me that Count Bertrand had this morning reported Napoleon Bonaparte to be ill, I again tendered my services through Count Bertrand, who replied that he would make known to Napoleon Bonaparte the purport of my visit.

I have the honour to be Sir,
Your most obedient and humble servant,
Verling

[To] Lieutenant Colonel Sir T. Reade etc.

Tuesday, 7 September 1819. Colonel Dodgin lent me a pamphlet entitled *Facts illustrative of the treatment of Napoleon Buonaparte at St Helena,* generally and I believe correctly ascribed to Theodore Hook. I copy the following passage as a specimen of his politeness as far as related to me and of his veracity.

> Madame Bertrand who, to do her justice, though long and lanky, and sallow and shapeless, is somewhat interesting, tries her influence over Dr Verling, the medical attendant, on the subject of her husband's affairs with Colonel Lyster. For finding that instead of being noticed by almost all Military men in their neighbourhood, her husband (whose policy does not lead him so cordially to hate red coats as his master) was universally cut by them. She made an attack upon the Doctor to endeavour, by his interference, to effect a reconciliation between the Count and the Colonel. His answer silenced all further requests. 'Madame,' said he, 'I can have nothing to say on the subject; the insult was afforded to Colonel Lyster in writing, in writing the apology must be made; and only in writing can it be conveyed to that Gentleman.'

Madame Bertrand, at the time, told me that the expressions offensive to Colonel Lyster were only written by her husband, at the express dictation of Napoleon, and that the quarrel seemed to be because they were supposed to proceed from Bertrand himself. She went so far as to wish me to communicate this explanation from her to Colonel Lyster, which I positively declined. I afterwards mentioned the circumstances in conversation to Sir H. Lowe, and to Mr Baxter. But I never presumed to tell her that her husband ought to apologize in writing. Mr Hook puts inverted commas before the words as if he had himself heard these identical words from my mouth or copied them from a paper written by me.

8 September 1819
Dear Sir,

I request you will have the goodness to inform the Governor that Count Montholon's health is much improved. He informed me today, that he had an intention of visiting General Bonaparte. He continues to complain of pain in the right side, but the evening accession of fever had been but slight yesterday and the evening before.

Believe me
Yours Truly
Verling

[To] Major Gorrequer. etc. etc.

I sent the note off, and then wrote the present from memory, so that there may be some slight difference of expression.

About 4 o'clock I met Count Montholon coming from Bertrand's and walked with him to his own house; he asked me in and told me that he had had a long conversation with the Emperor and entirely about me. That after many objections, the Emperor had declared the futility in his opinion of making any attempt to come to an understanding with the Governor. That therefore Montholon had urged him to take me without any conditions, and that he had agreed to ask me not to sign any, and merely required that I should pledge my word of honour to two things:

1st. Not to make any written report of his health without his knowledge and giving him a copy.
2nd. Not to repeat any conversation I might hear at Longwood. My word being given, he would send for me tonight and write to the Governor that by the advice of Montholon and Bertrand and harassed by disease, he had sent for me, and proposed seeing me daily as his Physician, according to the regulations proposed in Lord Bathurst's letter.

Montholon added that Napoleon would not require me to make any bulletin of his health, so that the only positive engagement I took with him was not to repeat his conversation. But should such report of health be required by the Governor, it must be made known and shown to him. He added there were engagements which every medical man took tacitly, such as to conceal any little disease or infirmity to which his patient was liable. Upon my looking at Montholon, he said that he had replied to Napoleon that this was a matter of little consequence since he had none, to which he replied, but suppose it possible I should get *la chaude pisse* [the hot piss] you would not have it inserted in a bulletin.

Montholon told me that he had endeavoured to get Napoleon to see me without asking me to give my word to anything however so simple, pointing out to him, that if I was a man of honour, my pledge was unnecessary, and if not, it could be of no use to Napoleon, but that he persisted in having my word on the two points already stated.

I told Count Montholon, that I had already been explicit in explaining to him my sentiments about any, the most apparently trifling engagement, taken secretly. That I positively declined entering into any; that the arrangement, if any was to be made, must come to me through the Governor, and that I was not at all anxious nor did I wish even then to fill the situation.

He said he was sorry for my resolution as he thought I was losing an opportunity which would not be likely to present itself every day, that it had been the last request of his wife to him, when she left the Island, to exert himself to procure me the situation, that at this moment Madame Bertrand was warm in my interest and anxious to retain me at Longwood, that she had drawn her husband into the same opinion and that as far as the interior of

Longwood was concerned, my situation would be very agreeable. That in regard to the reports of the Emperor's health, he required none, and if the Governor did, I had only to tell the truth and support it.

He added that Napoleon did not think he was worse than he had been for some time back, but that he, Montholon, found him altered much during the five months he had not seen him.

I told him my ideas on the subject were fixed, and wished him good evening.

I walked with Madame Bertrand in the evening, who at first seemed to think everything was arranged, and talked about the conversation I should have with the Emperor, etc. etc. At last she inquired particularly what Montholon had said to me, and was much surprised at my refusal to give my word. She parted with me by saying she supposed I reserved a surprise for her and that she expected to hear next morning that I had been called to the Emperor.

She told me that her husband had been directed to write to Stokoe but that this had been afterwards prevented.

Thursday, 9 September 1819. Captain Nicholls came into my room about 8 o'clock and requested me to explain to him the meaning of a letter which he gave to me and which had been sent to him open. The contents were nearly in the following words:

Sir,
I beg you will come to Longwood as soon as possible, the Emperor Napoleon is in great want of your assistance.
I have etc. etc. etc.
Le Count Bertrand
[To] *Mr le Docteur* Stokoe

He sent it back to Count Bertrand by the servant who brought it, observing to me that he could not receive any paper which contained the title of emperor. Not long after Count Bertrand's servant brought to Captain Nicholls a sealed letter addressed to the Governor.

At 10 o'clock, Captain Nicholls went to Count Bertrand to deliver the usual message about seeing Napoleon, and was presented with a written paper for answer which he declined receiving, saying that he did not understand French, but that he would go and bring an Officer who did; he went to Mr Croad, but on their return to Count Bertrand, he had gone out.

Madame Bertrand made a curious observation to me in our conversation yesterday, talking about the manner in which her husband had been treated by British Officers. She said she should not readily forgive the Emperor for involving her husband as he had done, that she surely believed he had done it on purpose, thinking that they were upon too good terms with the English. About one o'clock, I received the following note:

Castle, 9 September 1819
My Dear Sir,

As you mentioned to me in your note of the 7th that Count Bertrand said he would make known to Napoleon Bonaparte your having called upon him to offer your medical attendance, the Governor desires you will again call upon him simply to ask if he has informed Napoleon Bonaparte, and to know if he accepts your services.

As Count Montholon is now recovered, you may make known to him also, what you have done to Count Bertrand.

Yours Very Truly
G. Gorrequer

The Governor wishes to see you in the course of this day, and would be glad of your company to dinner.

I went to Count Bertrand who was not at home, and I met him coming from Longwood as I left his house. I told him that I had called for an answer to the message delivered the day before yesterday; he made answer that I might reply he was not at home when I called, and upon my observing that I was going from Longwood and should be glad he would give me an answer, he observed that he was not at home. I left him, and in about twenty minutes called at his house and sent my name in, and the servant brought word that he was not at home. As I was dressing the servant came to my room, to request I would go to Count Bertrand and when I got there he presented me with a written paper, as the answer to my offer of my medical assistance. I read it and returned it; it ran thus: '*L'Empereur ne prendra qu'un medecin de son choix* [The Emperor will take only a doctor of his choice] and who shall possess the independence necessary to fulfil his duties (*remplir ses fonctions*) according to the letter of the Count Montholon of April last.'

I went to Town and related this to the Governor, with whom I had a long conversation, about the propositions upon which he seemed to wish me to give a divided opinion.

I told him that I had not a moment's hesitation in refusing to take into consideration any stipulation unless it came to me from him, and that I had informed the French at Longwood that I had no desire to enter into any agreement or to become the medical attendant of Napoleon, and that in fact, I was only at Longwood because I was a military man, and obliged to obey orders. That I had also applied to him in writing to be relieved and frequently since personally, and that he must be well aware how anxious I was to get away from Longwood. He said that every man had occasionally duties to perform disagreeable to him, that this at present was my case, and that a sense of public duty obliged him to keep me where I was. Dr Arnott perhaps would not like to go, and any change might give rise to fresh intrigues. He remarked upon the change of reference from Bertrand to Montholon's letter of April, instead of the conditions of Stokoe in January and I told him I was convinced that they were much inclined to drop many of the objectionable points in the proposals, from various hints I had had from Montholon, and that I could not arrive at certain knowledge of their intentions without a long discussion upon these matters, and an apparent wish upon mine to meet their views.

Friday, 10 September 1819. Before I left Town, the Governor sent for me, and showed me a copy of a memorandum he had sent to Longwood stating that Mr Monro supercargo of a Brig arrived from Rio Janeiro had informed him that he had seen English papers to the 21st January, in some of which it was mentioned that the foreigners destined for the service of Napoleon had left England 6 or 7 days before the mail for Rio and that he, Mr Monro, was much surprised that they had not arrived here. He brought me no newspapers.

Sunday, 12 September 1819. I rode out with Madame Bertrand, she told me they were to have dined with Napoleon but that he found himself too unwell to receive them and had sent to say so.

She reproached me on my refusal, as she termed it, justly to become his Surgeon. Told me he had said it was evident he was no longer anything, since people refused to come to him; she acknowledged that he did not like the coming of the foreign Surgeon and would prefer an English one. That he was astonished, if two were coming, that they should have sent people, whose persons and even names were entirely unknown to him. She said that he still had great hopes, some turn of affairs might remove him from St Helena and again reproached me for not wishing to be in daily communication with so great a man.

We returned about 4 o'clock and about half past five Count and Madame Bertrand went into Napoleon's apartments, Montholon having just left him, after spending the whole day and dining with him. Montholon told me, he (Napoleon) was unwell, not having had a stool for eight days, that he had remonstrated with him and he believed had prevailed on him to take Castor Oil, glysters with salt and oil producing no effect. He told me that they had eaten like two sick men and then walked up and down the billiard room. Montholon walked in the Veranda with me, expressed a wish that some one of the Physician or Priest might be a person capable of filling his place. Abused the Emperor's family for having sent Italians, called Cardinal Fesch *un prêtre fanatique* [a fanatic priest] for having sent, out of three persons, two

Priests, wondered if the cook was also a Priest, and wished himself clear of St Helena.

In the evening drank tea with Madame Bertrand.

Monday, 13 September 1819. Napoleon is taking a warm bath.

Tuesday, 14 September 1819. Montholon continues to complain much of his side. He has been taking blue pill, ten grains at night for some time back. Talked with him about Napoleon, who had not, he said, taken the Castor Oil, but whom he hoped would take it tomorrow morning; said he had taken two Glysters with salt without effect; that he, Montholon, had proposed to him to put in some of the purging salt which I had given him, but he refused because he said Montholon had none in his possession, but would have to ask me for it.

Montholon said that whatever was the nature of his attack in January last, he had not been the same man since; he spent most of his time in bed, the slightest bodily exertion fatigued him and *quant à son travail* [as for his work], it was sometimes so unworthy of his former productions that he was sometimes on the point of telling him so, but that he had read *Gil Blas*.

He said that Napoleon *avait un fond de philosophie* [had a stock of philosophy]. Today Montholon talked of his father who had died in '85.

This immediately produced from Napoleon a rapid sketch of his whole career; about that time his utmost ambition was gratified by getting the commission of *Sous Lieutenant* [sub-lieutenant] of Artillery. His mother and his whole family embraced him over and over again. He then ran on in his career, until he said, the greatest Sovereigns in the whole world spoiled him by the basest flattery. He cited the Emperor of Austria, who had written a memoir to prove that he was descended from the Medici; the King of Prussia, who had presented to him the Prince Royal, asking as a great favour that he might be appointed his aide de camp. He dwelt upon his own inordinate arrogance and obstinacy in having refused the Kingdom of Louis XIV at Chatillon, and finished by saying that he was *tort de se fâcher* [wrong to get angry] at any of the daily inconveniences he at present experienced.

Wednesday, 15 September 1819. Dry cold wind. Thermometer 62.

Montholon complains much of his side; he got from me 1 oz. Mag. Sulp. in 2 papers, increased the blue pill to 10 grains night and morning.

Monday, 20 September. The three foreigners destined for Longwood landed at St Helena. I was in the Castle when they came on shore and was introduced to them. The old Priest Buonavita appears upwards of sixty years and is a respectable looking man; the young one, Vignali, a savage, unpolished Corsican; the surgeon, Antommarchi, appears about 30, rather a gentleman-like man, mild and talkative.

The Governor having conversed with Colonel Wynyard, who seemed to think there could be no difficulty in accommodating them, asked me when I could conveniently give up my quarters, and I told him on the following day, and it was so settled.

They arrived at Longwood about 6 o'clock and were introduced to Bertrand; I met them all in the evening at Madame Bertrand's and found them talking about Rome and the Bonaparte family. None of them saw Napoleon this evening.

Tuesday, 21 September 1819. I had packed up and was sending off my baggage when Count Montholon sent for me, and I found Count Bertrand in his room and Mr Antommarchi. Antommarchi and myself talked about Montholon's illness, and both Bertrand and Montholon then addressed me and expressed their surprise at my leaving Longwood so soon, and their wish that I should remain some time longer, and said that if I did not myself formally oppose them, they would write to the Governor upon the subject, and that as I had been so long amongst them they hoped I would sacrifice a short time more. Antommarchi also expressed his wish that I might remain, as it would afford him an opportunity of becoming acquainted with the mode of treatment I had adopted to Count Montholon etc. etc.

I told them I felt flattered by the confidence they placed in me but that I had settled with the Governor to leave Longwood today, and that I should on all occasions be at hand and willing to afford any assistance in my power, and that as it could create great inconvenience in quarters, and that I was within an hour's ride of Longwood, I thought it better not to remain. Bertrand observed that I was wanted on the spot etc. etc. On going out with Antommarchi he met Colonel Wynyard, and Antommarchi detailed to him what had passed and expressed his own wishes upon the subject. Colonel Wynyard sent for me and told me he thought I had better not leave Longwood until he had seen the Governor, and shortly after I received the following note.

My Dear Verling,

The Governor approves of your remaining at Longwood in compliance with their request until the Surgeon is perfectly established in his situation. I mentioned to him your having sent down your baggage, remaining in light service order.

Yours faithfully
E. Wynyard
Plantation House, 21 September 1819

I went into Count Montholon's on receipt of this and told them I had received a note from Colonel Wynyard, by which I learned the Governor had no objection to my remaining a short time at Longwood, and that I should therefore remain for some days.

I went to Town having engaged some friends to dine at the Mess, and next morning I returned by Plantation House, conceiving it better to learn the Governor's sentiments from his own mouth, as his approval did not appear to me what was necessary and his positive wish was what I required.

Wednesday, 22 September 1819. I found upon conversing with the Governor that he did not know in what light to regard their request, and after some time I perceived that he wished me to leave Longwood. I therefore told him I should quit it tomorrow and he agreed saying that I need not acquaint them with my intention tonight, and not until I was upon the point of leaving.

Thursday, 23 September 1819. The Governor and Colonel Wynyard came to Longwood together, and Colonel Wynyard asked me if I could let him have the note or a copy of it that he had written to me on the 21st, saying that as I considered it of a private nature he had kept no copy, but understanding it had been shown to the French people, he thought a copy requisite. I told him the note had gone with my baggage and he might have either the original or a copy as he thought proper. That he was misinformed as to its having been shown, but it was unavoidable that the nature of its contents should be made known to them as upon its authority I had remained at Longwood.

I said I was surprised to know how such an idea as its having been shown had originated. He said that he did not know, but as this was not the case I need take no further notice of it.

I left Longwood about 5 o'clock in the evening and upon my arrival in Town received the following note, which Colonel Wynyard had written before I saw him.

My Dear Sir,

I shall be much obliged to you to furnish me with a copy of the note I wrote to you on Tuesday, as I understand it has been shown to some of the foreign persons at Longwood and considering it of a private nature, I had not kept any copy.

I remain, my Dear Sir,
Yours Truly
E. Wynyard

Knollcombe, 23 September 1819

I made no reply to this, and Colonel Wynyard the next time I met him said it was unnecessary.

Friday, 24 September 1819. I dined today with Sir T. Reade, in the evening he informed us that the Captain of the *Snipe* transport had attempted to land several copies of O'Meara's book, and upon the officer asking what they were had said they were religious books put on board by the Missionaries, that he had however got possession of them. They were upwards of twenty and were addressed to several officers on the Island; it remained to be seen whether they would receive books from such a man. He mentioned several names to which they were addressed and told Major Power who was present that there was one for him. There was none for me.

Saturday, 25 September 1819. The R[oyal] Artillery and 20th Regt. were inspected at Deadwood. After the inspection I told Sir H. Lowe, that I was going to pay a visit to Madame Bertrand, as she had much wished me to go with her to the races, if he had no objection, I should offer her my services. He said he had none, and that he saw no objection to my going to Longwood whenever my medical attendance should be required, and occasionally to inquire after her health or that of the children. I paid Madame Bertrand a visit for about an hour; when I went in Count Montholon was with her, but went away directly. I told her that I should breakfast with her on the race day and go to the course afterwards.

I went to Count Montholon afterwards, but he was not at home. In the evening, dined at Plantation House, both 20th and Royal Artillery having been asked.

Sunday, 26 September 1819. Attacked with cholera, kept in bed all day.

About 12 o'clock at night, was awoke by a Dragoon who brought me a note from Major Gorrequer.

My Dear Sir,

The Governor begs to see you here tomorrow morning between 8 and 9 o'clock.

Yours Very Truly

G. Gorrequer

Plantation House, Sunday, 26 September

I went to Plantation House, and breakfasted there. Sir H. Lowe informed me that he had received a letter from the Countess Bertrand, where she seemed to say that obstacles were thrown in my way of visiting her, and requesting not only that I might be permitted, but that he would direct me to visit her family daily. He wished to know if I had clearly understood what he told me, and I said that I had, and that I had not given Madame Bertrand any reason to think that obstacles were to be thrown in my way. He said that if Madame Bertrand were a free agent, there could be no more objection to visiting her than any other Lady, but that, though not perhaps aware of it, she was often made the instrument of indirect attacks upon him, and that this letter, though written in her hand, was not hers, but written in complicity with Dr O'Meara's book. I asked him, what connection there could be between me and Dr O'Meara's book, and he said none; but besides mine, the subject of visits to her generally was discussed, and that she would not see that the deprivation of society under which she laboured did not arise from him, nor was it his fault, but arose from the conduct of her husband on various occasions, one of which was his conversation with me and attempt to drive me from Longwood.

We did not force any man's judgment upon the business of Colonel Lyster, each person must judge for himself. I told him my intercourse at Count Bertrand's was ridiculous enough, as though very intimate with her, I had little to say to the Count. He told me that he was aware I had a very disagreeable duty at Longwood, and that he hoped that he should have it in his power to evince his sense of it.

Yesterday, Major Power came into my room told me that Sir T. Reade had called him into his house and at the same time Major Hodson, and shown them each a copy of O'Meara's book with their names on the book; that there was no further inscription on the title page and that he had requested his copy might be returned to the printer; that then Sir T. Reade having asked Hodson what was to be done with his, he had also desired his to be returned. Major Power borrowed my desk and wrote a note to the following purport.

Major Power begs to return to Mr Ridgway a copy of O'Meara's book which was addressed to him and which he understands was attempted to be clandestinely introduced into this island.
St Helena, Sept. 26th

Monday, 27 September 1819. Arrived HM Ship *Menai*. I received no letters. Sir T. Reade dined at the mess.

In the morning, I had mentioned to the Governor that I had long been anxious to get home, that my family affairs required it, and I had spoken more than once on the subject to Sir T. Reade, and I believed had mentioned it to Major Gorrequer, that as I had now left Longwood, and from what had passed was not anxious to continue my intercourse with it, I should feel obliged to him to give me leave to go to England. He observed that no relief had come for me, but I told him that I certainly should have been relieved had I not been sent to Longwood; he said however that the number of medical men on the Island would not permit him to allow me to go.

Before I left Plantation House, I took an opportunity to urge the point again and requested him to take it into consideration.

In the evening Sir T. Reade told me that he believed the Governor would not make any strong objection to my going, if I was very anxious. He told me that there were a great many dispatches and probably there would be something about me from Lord Bathurst in reply to a recommendation long ago made by Sir H. Lowe.

He read us some passages from a letter he had received from Captain Rous, one of which says that Prince Borghese and two of Napoleon's Brothers pay O'Meara an annual pension of 5,000 Francs (£200); that he had spoken to Mottley the editor of the Portsmouth paper about several lying paragraphs which had appeared in it, who had promised to be more circumspect; that he had an interview with Lord Bathurst who had shown him every attention, and that the various misrepresentations about St Helena were entirely disregarded by the higher circles, and O'Meara could find no champion hardy enough to assert his cause.

Tuesday, 28 September 1819. Saw Sir T. Reade who informed me that there was nothing from Lord Bathurst relative to me. Received towards evening the following note.

Dear Sir,

The Countess Bertrand having expressed a wish to see you, the Governor wishes you would make it convenient to come round by Plantation House immediately.

Yours faithfully

G. Gorrequer

Tuesday 3:15 p.m. 28 September

I went to Plantation House, where after some conversation with the Governor, in which, though I could get nothing direct, yet it appeared plainly that the anxiety expressed by Madame Bertrand for a continuation of my visits and frequently, for her letter expressed daily, appeared to the Governor very extraordinary. I gave him to understand that I intended going with her to the races on the following day, an engagement formed before I left Longwood, and that any further intercourse with Longwood as it was the result of my duties performed by his orders, I should look up to his directions as to the nature of it, and that I should address to him a letter upon this subject. In this, he replied that I was right in my notions on this head, and that he should deem it necessary to give me written instructions for my guidance, if I was to continue on the Island, but he had no objection to my visits to Madame Bertrand. As long as I continued, he said, I might make known to her that I had applied for leave, and that it had been granted, but to be explicit and make it clearly understood that it was my own free act.

I went to Longwood and found Madame Bertrand in her usually weakly state; she was suffering from tooth ache, and had a gum boil which being touched with the lancet was much relieved. Count Bertrand being with Napoleon, I dined with her. A little before 9 o'clock, I went to Captain Nicholls' room and found there the Officer of the Guard, sat for a little time, got the countersign and went to Jamestown getting thoroughly soaked with rain.

Wednesday, 29 September 1819. I rode this morning to Plantation House; Gorrequer told me a dragoon had been sent with a note to the Alarm House to require my presence. The Governor asked me, if I had clearly explained to Madame Bertrand that my going from the Island was by my own desire. I told him I had. He asked me more than once if she had endeavoured to prevail upon me to remain; I told him that she had simply expressed regret at my departure and observed that she would apply to have Mr Henry permitted to attend herself and family. I mentioned that I was to accompany her to the races, and he said, that if upon the race ground, she talked to me upon the subject of remaining he wished me to detach myself from her and inform him.

I rode with Madame Bertrand to the race ground and walked with her all day, and saw her home in the evening; the Foreign Commissioners and many others paid her attention. Sir H. Lowe walked and chatted with her. Nothing passed between us which I thought requisite to be communicated to Sir H. Lowe. She requested me to come often and see her.

Saturday, 2 October 1819. I called upon Madame Bertrand and found her at breakfast. I took a cup of coffee and Captain Nicholls came in to say that Mrs South and her daughter were come to Longwood and would be happy to pay their respects to her. She requested Captain Nicholls to detain them at the New House for a quarter of an hour, when she would be ready to receive them and I went off. I afterwards met her on the ground and walked about with her and accompanied her back to Longwood. She made me promise to breakfast with her on Monday at 10 o'clock.

She looked miserably ill and dejected, had sore eyes for which I promised to bring some medicine.

Monday, 4 October 1819. I took some Ung. Hyd. nut. dil. and some Sulphate of Zinc and went to Longwood. I found Madame Bertrand looking very ill, complaining of oppression in breathing and pain in her chest; her eyes were better. I ordered for her a Cough Mixture and a burgundy pitch plaster and advised her to keep within doors.

Tuesday, 5 October 1819. I rode up to the races and before going on the ground I called upon Madame Bertrand, whom I found looking ill and still complaining of her chest. I tried to dissuade her from going to the races, but she attributed her illness to ennui and to low spirits, and said that a little amusement would do her good. I walked with her and Count Montholon on the course and accompanied her back to Longwood.

St Helena, 6 October
Sir,

After an absence of nearly five years from my family, I find that it is extremely necessary for the arrangement of my private affairs that I should return home.

I shall therefore be much obliged to you to forward to his Excellency the Governor, my application for twelve months leave of absence.

I have the honour to be, Sir,
Your most obedient etc. Servant
Verling Surgeon
Royal Artillery

[To] Major Power
Com. Royal Artillery

Jamestown, 12 October 1819
Dear Sir,

Having expressed to the Governor my intention of requesting his particular directions relative to visits which have been or may be required of me to Longwood since the arrival of the Foreign Surgeon, he observed that my departure would render this measure, which he approves, unnecessary. As my stay may be protracted somewhat longer than was at first intended, I request you will make known to his Excellency my anxiety to have clear instructions for my guidance in any intercourse which may take place with Longwood should such be deemed necessary.

I am, Dear Sir,
Very truly yours
Verling

To Major Gorrequer etc.

P.S. The Countess Bertrand having sent for me yesterday to see one of her children, I think it probable that I shall soon be called upon again.

Plantation House, 13 October 1819
Dear Sir,

In reply to your letter to Major Gorrequer, the Governor has directed me to say, he has a perfect recollection of his having told you when Madame

Bertrand wrote to him to request that he would authorize and even direct you to give your daily and personal attendance upon her family, that he approved your intention of not continuing such habitual attendance upon any of the persons at Longwood, unless it should be required of you as a matter of duty, but that he had no objection whatever to your occasional visits and thought it right even that you should make them until she had time to become acquainted with the newly arrived medical man, and as you had applied for leave of absence at the time, he did not enter further into consideration of the matter.

He could not have foreseen at the time the protraction of your stay on the Island, but this circumstance does still not appear to him to require any particular instruction to be conveyed to you.

Madame Bertrand has had opportunities since she first wrote of becoming better acquainted with Dr Antommarchi. The Governor is not aware there can be any <u>necessity</u> consequently for the constant attendance of any other medical person; although as a matter of attention and complaisance towards her, he has not the slightest objection to the continuance of your visits, but he sees no motive for ordering them or conveying any more particular instruction to you on the occasion, than what he might incidentally think is necessary to give to any professional person not belonging to the establishment at Longwood, who might be occasionally called in, or who might have obtained his permission for paying visits there.

Yours Truly,
E. Wynyard

To Dr Verling

Jamestown, 13 October 1819
Dear Sir,

Having attended upon the families at Longwood for 14 months in obedience to the Governor's orders, I conceive that the visits made by me subsequent to the arrival of Dr Antommarchi were in consequence and continuation of the same duty and indeed I proceeded in two instances from Plantation House by the Governor's directions.

I can see no reason for placing myself in any relation to the persons at Longwood different from that in which I have hitherto acted and in which his Excellency was pleased to place me.

I beg therefore to declare my intention of confining myself to my Military duties and consequently of not giving any attendance at Longwood, unless particularly directed to do so.

I am, Dear Sir, Very faithfully yours
Verling

To Colonel Wynyard etc.

Saturday, 16 October 1819. 11 o'clock a.m. On the 12th I dined at Plantation House, but no conversation about Longwood took place, nor was my letter mentioned; on the 13th I received Colonel Wynyard's letter and on the 14th mine was sent though dated 13th. Since I have heard nothing of Longwood, in any shape, or from any quarters.

Sunday, 17 October 1819. About 6 o'clock in the evening, I received the following letter.

Plantation House, 16 October 1819
Dear Sir,

Having showed your letter of the 13th to the Governor, he has desired me to convey the following remarks to you.

When he placed you at Longwood, it was for the express purpose of giving your medical attendance to General Bonaparte, then without any medical person near him. His followers were a secondary consideration. General Bonaparte himself declined to receive your visits, and on proposals being made to you which were contrary to your honour and your duty, you applied to be relieved.

The Governor signified to you that a foreign medical attendant had been written for, and was expected, and that you would be relieved on his arrival, every motive conspiring in the meantime to render it necessary that a medical officer should remain on the spot, and it being deemed inexpedient to make any change, until the foreign medical person should arrive.

On his arrival you were relieved, only waiting sufficient time to give such information as he might desire, and on your quitting Longwood, your relations with the persons there, became precisely the same as those of any other individual.

The application of Madame Bertrand to authorize and direct the continuance of your attendance upon her and her children was not wholly unforeseen, and the more so, as before it was made to the Governor, you had yourself acquainted him with her desire for the continuance of your visits, and he had signified his assent to them, until she might have time to become acquainted with her new medical advisor.

Your application for leave of absence rendered it unnecessary to enter into consideration of the more formal demand made for your being directed or ordered to attend her, and the Governor's desires or suggestions (not his directions) for your continuing your attendance upon her so long as you remained here (the protraction of your stay on the island being wholly unforeseen when the Countess's demand was made) he certainly did not conceive could have been regarded in any other light, than as a simple act of attention towards her, or at most, as an accommodation to the service, in the sphere of which you had been acting.

In whatever light viewed, however, the Governor is fully disposed to admit the obligation to you, and up to the period at which your intentions have been last declared to him, it will be considered.

As in your letters you speak of the families and persons at Longwood in general, the Governor has remarked that there has been no application for your attendance by any other person than the Countess Bertrand, nor since your quitting Longwood has his authority or permission been required any further, than for your visits to her, and for enabling Professor Antommarchi to consult you on any point of his duty.

It will rest with you of course, to continue your visits to the Countess or not, as you may think most fit after this explanation but if they are continued, the Governor desires, it may be on the footing mentioned in my reply to your first letter, as he deems it highly advisable to discourage any expectation on her part or that of any of the followers of General Bonaparte, that a British Medical Officer is likely to be appointed as a fixed attendant upon them, in addition to the foreign one who is already established there.

I remain, Dear Sir,
Yours Truly
E. Wynyard

To Dr Verling

Plantation House, 17 October 1819
Sir,

I am directed by His Excellency the Governor to inform you, that having taken into consideration the additional trouble and inconvenience to which you have been exposed by continuing your professional visits to the Countess Bertrand after you had been relieved from your general duties at Longwood, he has ordered that the allowances which you received whilst on actual duty at Longwood, shall be continued up to the date of your last communication of the 13th October.

The Governor has already conveyed to you, his full approbation of your line of conduct in the very delicate situation, where it was attempted to place you in the occasion of Count Bertrand's conversations with you in January 1819, as detailed in your letters of the 18th and 20th of that month and he has had the satisfaction to acquaint you that it met also the entire approval of Earl Bathurst.

His Excellency desires me further to express to you, his fullest approbation of your having rejected the proposals made to you by Count Montholon on the 1st of April 1819, and to assure you of the favourable sense he entertains of your general line of proceeding whilst still obliged to remain at Longwood, until the foreign medical person who was expected should arrive, after the very irksome and painful situation in which these proposals, and the refusal of General Bonaparte to allow your visits, unless you acquiesced in them, had tended to place you.

I have the honour to be, Sir,

Your most obedient humble servant

Edward Wynyard

Lieutenant Colonel and Military Secretary

Jamestown, 18 October 1819

Dear Sir,

   In reply to the last paragraph of your letter dated the 16th I beg to refer you to the previous declaration in mine of the 13th. The idea of attending at Longwood on any footing than by the direct orders of my superiors never occurred to me, and even of this situation I was not desirous, as is known to the Governor from various applications which I made to be removed.

   The written application for my attendance made by the Countess Bertrand, was by me unforeseen and unknown till communicated to me by the Governor and whatever expectations may exist on her part or that of any of the followers of General Bonaparte, that a British medical Officer is likely to be appointed as a fixed medical attendant upon them, I cannot be the person in view, since they are under the impression that I am to leave the Island immediately, my intention of doing so, having been communicated to the Countess Bertrand, by the Governor's desire, and the alteration in the arrangement remaining unknown to her.

I remain, Dear Sir,

Yours Truly

Verling

To Lieutenant Colonel Wynyard

Saturday, 23 October 1819. A Groom from Longwood brought a horse and a message that the Countess Bertrand was unwell and wishes to see me, I went to Sir T. Reade and informed him of this and of my intention not to go, unless by the Governor's orders, and requested to know through what channel this message should be sent to the Countess; he said he supposed by the Groom, to whom I accordingly gave it. I afterwards called at Plantation House, and informed the Governor, who talked a good deal upon breaking off by degrees, and to my great surprise, said he could not see what reasons I had for so abruptly declining my attendance, that he did not wish, however, to enter into any discussion upon the motives which actuated me. I told him, I had not been able to know what were his wishes upon the subject; to which he replied in angry tone, that he had none.

   He ended by saying that he supposed some explanation must be given to the Countess Bertrand, and that he thought it would be proper in me to ride to Longwood and explain the affair to her in such a manner as to prevent her from conceiving that any personal slight was meant to her, and in consequence to avoid if possible any angry discussion for which the persons at Longwood were always anxious upon the slightest pretext. I objected to this at first, saying that I did not see how any verbal communication of mine, could prevent their writing if so inclined, and feeling that I subject myself to misrepresentation or misconstruction should the explanation now be given by me to become the subject of discussion. It occurred to me on the other hand, that as sickness had been the cause of asking for me, my professional duty required me to go, and again, that as I had several times visited, politeness required that I should make another, and acquaint Madame Bertrand, that she might act accordingly in case of future illness in her family.

I therefore proceeded to Longwood and found Madame Bertrand at first much irritated by the message she had received from the Groom. I talked to her about her health which has long been in a bad state, and explained to her, that having been originally placed at Longwood by the Governor's positive orders with a view to giving medical assistance to General Bonaparte, who had never thought proper to receive me, I could not possibly continue to attend at Longwood upon any footing by the Governor's orders, and that the attending upon her family forming a part of the original duties, must be continued by the same orders or entirely discontinued, however flattered I might be, that I had obtained her confidence, and that I had been of any use to her, yet everything considered, I thought she would exonerate me from any blame in following this line of conduct.

She seemed a good deal affected by the position in which she was placed, saying that she hoped I would occasionally visit her as a friend, in whose house I had been politely received for fourteen months, whom I had known for a longer period and who felt grateful for my attentions and a wish for my welfare. She informed me that Mrs Brooke and her son had called upon her, and that she expected other visitors, Captain and Mrs Power she named.

She did not feel herself compelled to ask the Governor to order me.

I took my leave, without giving my explanation of my intentions as to visiting her, and feeling much for the apparently impolite and harsh line of conduct which necessity compelled me to follow.

I went and dined and slept at Major Emmett's, and did not see the Governor till Monday morning in Town.

Monday, 25 October 1819. When I communicated to him what had passed, he observed that he supposed she would apply for me or for somebody else, when I told him that I had recommended to her to call (if she should wish for a British medical man) upon Dr Livingstone, who had attended as *accoucheur* [obstetrician] upon her and who was well known to her, and who was to be looked upon more in the light of a private practitioner than any other Medical man on the Island.

Tuesday, 31 October 1819. I have heard nothing from Longwood since, from any quarter, and I am in hope no discussion will arise.

Monday, 8 November, 1819. Wrote to Lieutenant Jackson and sent the Return to the end of September. Sailed HM Ship *Bacchus* and *Cosway*.

Friday, 26 November 1819. Last night having called upon Dr Livingstone, he informed me that he had, the evening before, been to see Madame Bertrand and her child, by the Governor's directions, and that he found her suffering with a bad cough and looking very ill; that she told him that she had repeatedly sent for me, that I had refused to go and see her, and that she should never call upon me again, he said that he advised her to lose six or eight ounces of blood, and told her that it would also be of service in preventing a *fausse couche* [miscarriage], she being two months gone with child. He found young Arthur attacked with bowel complaint and looking sallow and unhealthy.

Dr Antommarchi had given him two doses of Calomel which have operated briskly and Dr Livingstone recommended a continuation of it, as an alteration in small doses.

I rode to Plantation House, and informed Sir Hudson Lowe, that as Dr Livingstone had been called to see Madame Bertrand, I looked upon him as selected to give advice at Longwood, and that of course, the subject of my attendance would no longer be thought of, that, however, I was now going to Longwood to pay her a visit, not at all to offer any medical attendance, but as a matter of politeness and respect to her. He said, that Dr Livingstone had been sent in consequence of Madame Bertrand having applied for some medical person to see her child, observing, at the same time to Captain Nicholls that I was afraid to go to Longwood, that if he could have taken the liberty of addressing me as he had Dr Livingstone, I might have been the person selected, but as I had so positively demanded direct orders, he had preferred employing people who were more easily at his disposal.

I replied that he could not possibly mean to say, that he ever thought I was unwilling to give my attendance to Madame Bertrand, and that the fact was I never could have his wishes. He said: You have declared you will not attend unless positively ordered, I have it in writing. You would not act upon your own responsibility. I replied that I was still of that opinion, and told him, however, that I was then going to Longwood. He observed that he did not see how Dr Livingstone being called there made any alteration in regard to me, but that my name was at the Barrier Gate as one of the persons permitted to visit her.

I accordingly proceeded to Longwood. I found Madame Bertrand in bed and looking very ill. Her pulse was about 90, and full. She coughed incessantly and expectorated a greenish matter. I found she had not been bled, as Antommarchi differed in opinion from Livingstone; and she was taking some cough mixture, and had been blistered under the left breast and on the inside of each arm.

Notwithstanding the expectoration, the pulse seemed to me to indicate bleeding, but as I did not come as her medical adviser, I told her to send again for Dr Livingstone, and upon her observing that he and Antommarchi could not understand each other, I recommended her to call Dr Arnott.

She expostulated with me upon my not going to see her and attending upon her, and I told her she must not imagine that it arose from any want of proper feeling and due respect towards her, but that having hitherto attended at Longwood by the Governor's orders, I could only continue my attendance by his directions, which he did not choose to give, and that as these were given to Dr Livingstone, and would be also to Dr Arnott if she required it, she would suffer no real inconvenience, that I had hoped to hear a favourable account of her health from her medical attendants. She requested me to look at the child who was very much altered, and I again advised her to send for Dr Livingstone.

On my return to Town, I took an opportunity of seeing Livingstone and found him impressed with the idea of a serious affection of the lungs being likely to take place.

I told him that she was very anxious to see him, that she had not been bled. He said he would go once more and enlarged upon the difficulty of communicating with Antommarchi and seemed very unwilling to have anything to do with Longwood.

Wednesday, 8 December 1819. I met Sir Thomas Reade in the street, and he took me aside and showed me a note by the Governor's directions, from Captain Nicholls to Major Gorrequer, which stated that the Countess Bertrand had requested him to inform the Governor that if Dr Livingstone's state of health prevented him from giving her medical attendance, she should wish me to be sent to Longwood. This note Sir T. Reade said, he was directed to show me, and on asking if there was no message from the Governor to me, he said he was merely directed to show me the note. I observed the Governor having told me, if I attended at Longwood, it must be on my own responsibility, I had already declined so doing, and I meant to decline it still.

Thursday, 9 December 1819. The Governor was in Town most part of the day, and I spent the evening at Count Balmain's in company with Sir T. Reade, but no further mention was made of Longwood.

Friday, 10 December 1819. Having some business in Town, I met Sir T. Reade, standing at his own door; Captain Stanfell RN and myself entered into conversation, and Sir Thomas took out of his pocket a note which he handed to me, it was addressed 'My Dear Reade' and was from Major Gorrequer; it contained comments from the Governor about my conduct saying that he did not see what additional responsibility attached to me, if I had gone by his consent instead of his orders and given the accommodation of my attendance, especially as it was probable it would only be required for a short interval of Dr Livingstone's illness, and since I had visited so lately as a private individual; his note so plainly inferred that he had expressed a wish that I should go, and that I had refused unless positively ordered; then I requested Sir T. Reade to let me take the note to my room and I should write to the Governor in explanation. To this he objected, I asked him, then, if I was to consider the note as communicated to me and act accordingly. He said I might do as I pleased. I requested to look at the note again and he gave it to me.

I pointed out to him, what I conceived a misconception on the Governor's part of what I had said, or at least an assumption that more had been said to me when Nicholls' note was shown, than was the case, and requested he would inform the Governor that I wished to have the note or a copy of it, where I would explain the motives of my conduct, but as a misunderstanding evidently had arisen from the verbal communication I had already had with Sir T. Reade, I begged to decline making any further explanation in the manner.

I afterwards observed to Sir T. Reade that it was peculiarly hard that I should be obliged to enter into anything like a contest with the Governor, that from our relative situations a wish of his in this instance would be equivalent to a command, but that he had kept me totally in the dark as to his wishes; in a word did he wish me to go to Longwood or did he wish me to stay away, and why did he not send another.

Chapter 7

1820

Friday, 28 January 1820. The Countess Bertrand having miscarried on the morning of the 26th, I thought it incumbent on me to call and make inquiry after her state of health. I arrived at Longwood about 12 o'clock and found her in bed, looking pale and debilitated, but her spirits were good, and she was not so much tormented by the cough, as when I last saw her. She told me she was not offended at my refusal to come to Longwood, as she attributed it to the force of circumstances and not to want of inclination. She informed me that Captain Nicholls had shown her a long letter from Major Gorrequer stating that application had been made to me to give my medical assistance, to do which I had positively declined, and in proof, passages were cited by Major Gorrequer from my letters. I told her that she must be well aware, no disrespect was meant to her by my refusal, and entered into no further explanation. Dr Antommarchi was in the room when I arrived; he sat for a short time and asked me to call upon him before I left Longwood, to which I agreed; but reflecting afterwards, that I had only permission to enter Longwood for the express purpose of visiting Madame Bertrand, I did not call upon him.

Count Bertrand came into the room just as I was on the point of leaving. Young Arthur was quite well, poor little Hortense much emaciated from the febrile complaint she has had for the last fortnight. I met Sir Hudson Lowe and Colonel Wynyard on the road leading to Longwood.

Monday, 7 February 1820. I met Captain Nicholls in Town, who told me that Sir T. Reade had asked him about my visit to Madame Bertrand, and he having said that I had merely paid her a visit of civility as one of those names were in the Guard Room. Sir T. Reade asked him if he did not think it odd that I should visit her after refusing to attend her as a medical man. Capt. Nicholls observed to me that he thought I had sufficiently discharged the duties of civility, and that it would be more prudent not to repeat my visit. He told me he expected to sail for England tomorrow, on the *Cornwall*.

Tuesday, 8 February 1819. Captain Lutyens of the 20th is appointed orderly officer at Longwood, through Sir T. Reade's influence; I believe Major Gorrequer had endeavoured to procure the situation for Captain Crokat.

Captain Lutyens and myself talked about Longwood. He informed me that Sir H. Lowe had read to him Lord Bathurst's letters relative to the absolute necessity of General Bonaparte being seen by the Orderly Officer. He asked me many questions as to the nature of the duty. I told him that from what I knew of it, it did not appear to be very difficult to fill the situation.

Wednesday, 9 February 1820. Captain Lutyens breakfasted at Plantation House, in order to proceed to Longwood.

Monday, 6 March 1820. Sir T. Reade showed me a note from Captain Lutyens, in the latter part of which he says that having met Count Montholon and inquired after his health he (Count Montholon) had complained that he was in a very poor state of health and had taken a great quantity of medicine without much benefit; that he did not wish to call Dr Verling in, formally; or do anything to hurt Dr Antommarchi's feelings, but that if I was riding in that direction, and would pay him a visit, he should be very glad to see me. I told Sir T. Reade that I saw no reason for my acting upon a casual conversation, which might never have occurred had Captain Lutyens not made inquiries about his health. He replied that as my name had been mentioned, he thought it but fair to communicate it to me.

Wednesday, 8 March 1820. Sir T. Reade showed me another note from Captain Lutyens, in which he says that Count Montholon had again requested that I might go to Longwood; this was enclosed with a note from Major Gorrequer desiring that it might be shown to me and saying that I had the Governor's <u>consent</u> to call upon Count Montholon.

To this I replied that if the Governor wished me to go, I should of course do so, but that upon the simple wish of Count Montholon, I could not do so, as I must consider my attendance at Longwood as a point of duty.

He asked me if he should write this to the Governor. I said yes.

Saturday, 11 March 1820. The Governor was in Town Thursday but I heard nothing more about Longwood.

About 6 o'clock in the evening, I met Colonel Power, who took me aside and after premising that what he was going to say must be private, informed me that Sir T. Reade had called him into his room, and asked him if I had informed and conversed with him upon the occurrence that had taken place, since I left Longwood. To this Colonel Power answered in the negative. Sir Thomas told him that he supposed he knew that the Governor had recommended me very strongly, that he had therefore done his part; he observed that I had been with him (Sir T. Reade) to know if anything had come from Lord Bathurst, by the *London*, relative to me, and that he had said, no; but the Governor had since written him a note stating that my name had been mentioned in Lord Bathurst's communication and that his Lordship had expressed much surprise at my having asked for leave, and then not taking advantage of it.

Colonel Power asked him if he was at liberty to communicate this conversation to me and he said that it was a private one. I observed that I felt obliged to him for his telling me, that, however, it seemed that though Sir Thomas said it was private yet it was meant to reach my ears, as probably no injunction of secrecy would have been given, had he not asked the question, and that I thought he might very easily mention again to Sir Thomas Reade that he felt unwilling to be depository of any secret relative to me when my welfare might be concerned and be unable to communicate it.

Sir T. Reade asked him if it did not appear odd that I should apply and then decline taking leave; Colonel Power, said it did not to him, that the season of the year, the object of spending my winter in Edinburgh, the expectation of a successor etc. were in his mind sufficient reasons.

Who suggested to Lord Bathurst the idea that there could be anything improper in my remaining in the Island, that there could be any sinister motive? Sir Thomas also mentioned to Colonel Power that as soon as I had made up my mind to remain I had then refused to visit Longwood without a positive order, though the Governor had never put me under any restrictions and had always placed confidence in me.

I never asked for an order, but went in the first instance, unsuspectingly to Longwood, till I perceived and was made to feel by the conduct of Sir T. Reade and the Governor that this line of conduct was looked upon with a very jealous eye. I then told the Governor I regarded my visits as made under his authority and as a point of duty and that I intended to write to him upon the subject; he said that this was the proper light, but as I was going away, I had better continue them and not write.

I repeatedly asked what were his wishes. I was told by Sir T. Reade that it was a mere matter of informing him whether I went or not, and Sir H. Lowe, stamping his foot upon the ground, said he had no wishes upon the subject. It behooved me, therefore when I perceived that I was to expect no guidance from my superiors, not to act at all but upon specific orders, and after all the matter seems simple enough: I was employed as a Military Surgeon; you cease to employ me, my functions cease.

It is evident I have made a powerful enemy. How far perfect good intentions and how far innocence may be a protection time will show; and as I read, over my cup of tea this morning, 'Of those that by precipitate conclusions involve themselves in calamities without guilt, very few, however they may reproach themselves, can be certain that other measures would have been more successful.'

Saturday, 22 April 1820. I rode to Longwood and called to wish Madame Bertrand goodbye; I sat with her an hour and a half. Count Montholon having heard I was there called to see me; he wished me goodbye and said that he hoped to be soon in Europe, observing that it was very strange his wife said nothing to him in her letters about any person coming out to replace him. Count Bertrand was also in the room.

Sunday, 23 April 1820. I rode to leave my card at Plantation House; on my return I met Sir H. Lowe. He stopped me and asked when I sailed, I said in the evening, and that I had just called at Plantation House. He paused for some time and then informed me that he had just been writing to Lord Bathurst such a letter as would be sure to do away with any unfavourable impressions, which might have been made upon his mind, by my remaining upon the Island; to which I could not avoid replying that if such existed, they must have arisen from erroneous views of my conduct.

A long and angry conversation in consequence ensued which terminated however by my saying that since he had thought proper to declare his opinion of the correctness of my conduct, I begged once more to return him my thanks for his former recommendation. He observed in parting, 'Well Sir, I shall send my letter to Lord Bathurst.'

I saw Sir T. Reade in Town, who asked me if I had seen the Governor, and told me he had desired him to mention the letter to me. I asked him if he had seen the letter and he said that he had copied it, and that it was of such a nature as to remove every unfavourable impression. I made no further remark and we parted.

In the conversation with Sir H. Lowe, on my observing that I had not been treated with the confidence I expected, he remarked that I had not sought his confidence but had endeavoured to fill the situation in as independent a manner as possible.

To this I made no answer, and do not conceive it any imputation on my conduct.

Part Three

Letters Relating to James Verling

Chapter 8
1816

Bathurst to Lowe, 13 April 1816, BM MSS 15,729 (19)

London, 13 April 1816
Sir,

Herewith you will receive the King's Warrant under my Grant and Seal authorizing you to detain keep and treat Napoleon Bonaparte as a Prisoner of War; and you will receive at the same time the Act of Parliament lately passed giving powers to the above effect. You will be pleased to regulate your conduct according to the spirit of the above Instruments.

I also enclose for your further information and guidance a Bill for regulating the Intercourse with the Island of St Helena.

I am, Sir
Your most obedient humble Servant
Bathurst

[To] Lt. General Sir Hudson Lowe KCB

Chapter 9

1818

Lowe to Verling, 25 July 1818, BM MSS 20,149 (1)

Plantation House, 25 July 1818
[To] Dr Verling, Royal Artillery
Sir,

Mr O'Meara, Surgeon of the Royal Navy, who was in attendance on General Bonaparte, having been removed from that situation in consequence of orders from His Majesty's Government, I have to request you will immediately proceed to Longwood, to afford your medical assistance to General Bonaparte and the foreign persons under detention with him; there to be stationed until I may receive the instructions of His Majesty's Government on the subject.

I am etc.
H. Lowe

Verling to Gorrequer, 4 November 1818, BM MSS 20,128 (374)

Longwood, November 1818
Sir,

His Excellency the Governor had the goodness some time back to say he would address a letter to me, appointing me to take charge of the establishment at Longwood and authorizing my removal from the Artillery.

I take the liberty of requesting you will call the circumstance to his recollection as I have not yet been able to send any written document to the Director General of the Ordnance Medical Department to whom I am extremely anxious to write by the present opportunity.

J. Verling
Assistant Surgeon, Royal Artillery

[To] Major Gorrequer

Lowe to Bathurst on Verling et al. (handwritten copy), BM MSS 20,124; 249–252

St Helena, 9 November 1818
My Lord,

A few days subsequent to the last conversation I had with Count Montholon I learned he had spoken to Dr Verling; and mentioned that General Bonaparte had no objection whatever, to receiving him as a Medical person, but that there were still two points unsettled with the Governor.

Dr Verling who has avoided entering into discussion with him on such occasions did not particularly question him on the points that caused this difficulty but understood that one of them regarded the objection to carrying on a correspondence by sealed notes upon the Island; the other the relaxation which was sought to be obtained in the attendance of the orderly officer upon Counts Bertrand and Montholon when they proceeded to the Town.

As both these points had been entirely given up in argument by Count Montholon in the last conversations I had with him in such degree that he did not even offer a word in reply to the Extracts I had taken with me of my previous correspondence with Count Bertrand, nor renew the subject of the sealed notes to the Purveyor, it is impossible to view the mention of them in this indirect manner to Dr Verling after having thus given them up, in any other light, than as seeking a pretext for General Bonaparte refusing to consult medical advice or to avail himself of the relaxations which had been permitted on the ground of obstacles which he ascribed to me.

As nothing however has been said on the subject to me, and as it was only in a kind of confidential way Count Montholon expressed himself to Dr Verling, enjoining him at the same time to secrecy, I have taken no notice of what was said, considering the two last conversations I had with Count Montholon, as final in every point of discussion, which he had brought forward.

There is one circumstance however which may appear deserving of notice in this conversation, and which events might possibly at some future period render expedient to bear in mind being, that if General Bonaparte does not think fit to consult the opinion of the physician who is placed near him, it is not from any personal objection to his character, or any want of confidence in his professional skill; and consequently, that the protest he once made against receiving the visits of any other Medical person than Mr O'Meara on the ground of his being the only one on the Island in whom he placed confidence loses all that force, which those who might think or protest under such circumstances as he presented it merited regard, might be disposed to give to it.

The motives which had been before urged against his taking exercise; this, my refusal to permitting a sealed correspondence within the Island, are now brought forward, however indirectly, as the cause of his not consulting medical advice, but the real fact I presume to be that General Bonaparte, finding matters drawing to an understanding in a way he did not approve and embarrassed how to proceed, has sought to extricate himself from the kind of dilemma in which my last conversation with Count Montholon had placed him by making the obstacles appear on my side, instead of his, and was obliged to shift his ground accordingly. Knowing, however, that if Dr Verling mentioned it to me the truth would be made apparent, Count Montholon enjoined him in so particular a manner to secrecy that Dr Verling says he is persuaded if it was thought I knew what had been said he should never see General Bonaparte, whilst he was left at the same time by Count Montholon's conversation decidedly under the impression that no other obstacles existed to his seeing him than those which he was to suppose I knew but not to speak of to me.

Dr Verling, who was unsuspecting in the matter, had, however, spoken of Count Montholon's conversation to a third person before he mentioned it to me, supposing a reality in the obstacles the Count had stated as if they had not been spoken of again to me. Dr Verling, as well as every person to whom he might have mentioned them, would have been under precisely the impression Count Montholon had endeavoured to excite, and the cause of General Bonaparte not receiving the professional visits of Dr Verling thus silently and covertly insinuated to rest with me.

I have the honour, etc.

H. Lowe

Chapter 10
1819

Gorrequer to Verling, 17 January 1819, BM MSS 20,149 (41)

Plantation House, Sunday, 17 January 1819
[To] Dr Verling
Dear Sir,

After inquiring from Count Montholon, which you may do in the Governor's name, how General Bonaparte's health is after his attack of last night, and whether it has passed over; the Governor would wish to see you any time in the course of the day, unless your medical attendance, or opinion on medical matters, has been or is likely to be required.

I am etc.,
G. Gorrequer

Lowe to Nicholls (memo), 19 January 1819, BM MSS 20,149 (42)

Plantation House, 19 January 1819
Memorandum for Captain Nicholls

On Mr Stokoe's arrival at Longwood, Captain Nicholls will see the pass he brings, and inform himself as particularly as he can of the footing on which the Admiral may have granted him permission to visit General Bonaparte.

If he observes any deviation from the words of the pass or those of my instruction Mr Stokoe may have shown, or made known to him, he will notice it to Mr Stokoe.

Captain Nicholls will communicate to Dr Verling, the letter he received yesterday from Major Gorrequer and apprise him that the Governor desires he may be ready at all times to accompany Mr Stokoe in any professional visit he may be required to make to General Bonaparte.

The same rule is to apply to any conference which may be sought for with Mr Stokoe by any persons of General Bonaparte's family, on the subject of his (General Bonaparte's) malady.

Captain Nicholls after seeing the pass which Mr Stokoe may have brought with him, will immediately wait on Count Montholon or Count Bertrand and make known Mr Stokoe's arrival for the information of General Bonaparte, and that Dr Verling is also at hand to accompany him.

H. Lowe

Gorrequer to Verling, 20 January 1819, BM MSS 20,149 (43)

Plantation House, 20 January 1819
[To] Dr Verling
Dear Sir,

Will you have the goodness to acquaint me for the Governor's information, whether Mr Stokoe called upon you personally yesterday afternoon, previous to his visiting General Bonaparte, or calling upon any person of his family; and what he may have said on the subject of giving his attendance to General Bonaparte in conjunction with you – whether as from himself or speaking of my instruction he might have received.

The Governor will be much obliged for any further information you may be able to give, with respect to Mr Stokoe's visit or General Bonaparte's malady.

Yours etc.
G. Gorrequer

P.S. Please to send the answer by the Bearer.

Copy of following for Nicholls, BM MSS 20,214 (101); 20,125 (146)

Minute of conversation with Count Bertrand [by James Verling]
19 January 1819

Count Bertrand called upon me and after professing sentiments of good will towards me for my attentions to his Family, he expatiated upon the praise I was entitled to from everybody at Longwood, <u>at the present moment</u>. He then showed me a letter detailing Lord Bathurst's instructions relative to Mr O'Meara's removal and his replacement by Mr Baxter or by any other medical Man upon the Island Napoleon should choose. He went on, 'Napoleon, invited as he was, declined at that time making any choice, but declared he would never see you, whom if you had not been sent here we should have all pointed out from our knowledge of you on board ship. Our influence has been repeatedly used to induce him to see you, and in vain, even when he thought he was dying.

> 'The Governor now recedes from Lord Bathurst's letter, Napoleon has made a choice, obstacles are thrown in the way, he is about to refuse him. The correspondence is becoming more warm, and I warn you that motives will soon be attributed to him for this line of conduct in which your name will unavoidably be implicated and in a manner in which it ought never to appear, I therefore advise you to retire immediately from the situation.'

I replied to Count Bertrand that I was here as a military Man, in obedience to Orders from my Superiors, and my conscience would enable me to disperse any false imputations.

Reade to Verling, 20 January 1819, BM MSS 20,149 (44); 20,125 (167)

Plantation House, 20 January 1819
[To] Dr Verling
Dear Sir,
    The Governor has seen your letter and its enclosure; he approves in the highest manner of your replies to Count Bertrand, not only in this instance, but on every occasion he has heard of.
    You will on no consideration whatever quit Longwood, unless by an order from him.

I am etc.,
T. Reade

Copy of letter from Verling to Gorrequer, sent to Captain Nicholls. MSS 20,214 (100); 20,125 (145)

Longwood, 20 January 1819
My Dear Sir
    Being unwilling from the Memorandum shown to me by Captain Nicholls to quit Longwood for a moment, I forgo the anxious desire I feel to communicate personally with the Governor and I commit to writing an extraordinary conversation had by me with Count Bertrand.
    I have not wished to urge upon the Governor my personal feelings, upon the extreme delicacy of my position, since Napoleon has proved his intention to adhere to his declaration that 'he never would see me' by selecting another, but I think it my duty to make him acquainted with this

conversation and shall feel obliged by your communicating to me his opinion of my answer to Count Bertrand.

Believe me

Yours very truly

J. Verling

[To] Major Gorrequer

Gorrequer to Verling, 23 January 1819, BM MSS 20,149(47)

Plantation House, 23 January 1819

[To] Dr Verling

Dear Sir,

If you should speak to any person at Longwood on the subject which the Governor mentioned to you yesterday, endeavour to learn, in what precise terms Mr Stokoe repeated the information he had obtained from Mr Hall respecting the conversation held by Mr O'Meara at Ascension; whether as affecting the past, present, or future.

Yours,

G. Gorrequer

Gorrequer to Verling, 24 January 1819, BM MSS 20,149 (47)

Plantation House, 24 January 1819

[To] Dr Verling

Dear Sir,

It is quite certain, Mr Stokoe did repeat at Longwood during his first day's visit there, the conversation held at Ascension, for it has been confirmed by him to the Admiral.

Count Montholon may not have been admitted to the secret, and therefore perhaps it may be of importance he should understand it was not to get the information from him that you spoke of it, but merely to know how far his manner of relating it might bear upon what Count Bertrand said to you.

It appears to have been altogether Count Bertrand's own act and thought, in mentioning it the way he did to you.

Yours,

G. Gorrequer

Lowe to Verling, 24 January 1819, BM MSS 20,149 (47)

Plantation House, 24 January 1819

Dear Sir,

I send you the books for Madame Bertrand. It will be remarkable if B—— himself should not have known, of what Count Bertrand said to you, and that it should have been an attempt on the part of the <u>latter alone</u> to prevail on you to quit – to render his after work, more easily. The only argument against this supposition is – the modifying certain expressions regarding you – but what you may have heard on this from the Bertrands themselves is very poor authority.

Yours,

H. Lowe

Lowe to Bathurst, 5 March 1819, BM MSS 20,125 (368–369)

St Helena, 5 March 1819
Private
My Lord,

Since addressing your Lordship on the 27th, the following considerations have presented themselves to me, in respect to the succession of Mr Baxter, and which are submitted with the utmost deference to your Lordship's superior deliberations.

The medical officer with the King's troops on this island next in rank to Mr Baxter is Dr Verling. He belongs however to the Ordnance, and could not I apprehend, without some supposed interference with regular succession in the lines, be recommended by me for the appointment of staff Surgeon. The same objection could not however lie against the situation of Physician to the Forces, for which his degree as such, and other qualifications, render him fully eligible. To become a Physician to the Forces, it is not necessary to have passed through any subordinate rank, nor does the appointment, when it is proposed, command any claim to future advancement. There is I have understood, a precedent of an assistant Surgeon of the Ordnance having been appointed Physician to the Forces, in the West Indies.

If Dr Verling was fixed upon to remain with General Bonaparte, the honorary rank must be regarded by him as a great mark of favour and attention, and it would present also a just scale of pay, for the duty he would have to perform, not exceeding what your Lordship had in mind for Mr O'Meara.

If a French surgeon arrives and Dr Verling is relieved from his personal attendance at Longwood, he would as Physician to the Forces be a very fit person as the head of the Medical Establishment on the Island, and not supposed any way objectionable to be called in, as a 'consultant' in any case of emergency at Longwood. Under all these circumstances I do not hesitate to submit Dr Verling's name to your Lordship, as a person whose conduct hitherto has given every reason to suppose, he is activated by right principles, and who is in other respects fully competent to the discharge of all the duties required of him. I am the more induced to speak thus favourably of him, as if he has not been long since appointed to the situation of Mr O'Meara, it arises I am persuaded solely from the resistance he has shown to all design on the part of the persons at Longwood, of employing him in other ways than what regards the duties of his profession, and he has thus furnished no real cause to object against his nomination, should General Bonaparte finally resolve on requiring his attendance, it may be perhaps on the whole the most advisable plan, to give him the proof of confidence I have taken the liberty to suggest, in having no tendency to establish him in the situation, any more than if he did not propose it.

If Dr Verling does become established in General Bonaparte's family, the confinement to which this may subject him, will render it difficult for him to grant that attention which may be required to other parts of his duty, supposing him appointed as Physician, and in that situation as head of his department. In such case I might be under the necessity of applying to the Horse Guards, or the Court of Directors, for another medical Officer – but until information is received respecting the French Surgeon (whose arrival however now appears to excite neither desire or expectation at Longwood) I cannot make any definitive proposals on this head.

If no French Surgeon comes, the expense however will not be affected, as Mr Baxter's appointment did not preclude the necessity of paying a salary to Mr O'Meara, and a Staff Surgeon will be less chargeable than a Deputy Inspector. I have transmitted under an open seal, an official letter to Sir H. Torrens, acquainting him of Mr Baxter's application to return to Europe, but have referred him in a private letter to Your Lordship's opinion as to the succession.

Dr Verling expects to be released at the expiration of three years (now drawing to a close) from his duties with the Ordnance here, but whether a French Surgeon arrives or not, I apprehend I may find it necessary to detain him here, until something is fixed in regard to Mr Baxter's succession.

I have the honour to be etc.

H. Lowe

Gorrequer to Verling, 20 or 26 March 1819, BM MSS 20,149 (65)

Plantation House, 1³/₄ p.m., 26 March 1819
[To] Dr Verling
Dear Sir,

The Governor is exceedingly sorry to hear of Count Montholon's indisposition, but as a pretext seems to be drawn from it for not delivering a paper which it is of importance should be instantly communicated, he wishes you to point out to him, the expediency on account of his own responsibility, to send it by some other hand.

Yours,

G. Gorrequer

Gorrequer to Nicholls, 27 March 1819, BM MSS 20,149 (66)

Plantation House, 27 March 1819
[To] Captain Nicholls
Dear Sir,
    You may ask Dr Verling to translate the accompanying message to Count Montholon, but he is to avoid entering into any discussion upon the matter.
I am etc.
G. Gorrequer

Verling to Lowe, BM MSS 20,214 (16–19)

Longwood, 6 April 1819
Sir,
    I have the honour to enclose for your information a Memorandum of a proposal made to me by the Count de Montholon.
    This proposal I thought it my duty to communicate verbally to you as soon as possible after it was made and I there explained my wish to be removed from Longwood, ...
    I hope therefore your Excellency may be pleased to adopt some measures, by which medical assistance may be afforded to the Family at Longwood, and which may enable me to return to my Military duty.
I have the honour to be your most obedient most humble servant
J. Verling

Memorandum of a proposal made to me by the Count de Montholon on the 1st of April 1819.

Having had a reason to visit at Count Montholon's he took an opportunity when we were alone of introducing the subject of Napoleon choosing a Surgeon. He said, I must be aware that he had long endeavoured to fix Napoleon's choice on me, and how flattering it would be to me should I now be chosen notwithstanding that I was the person selected by the Governor, as this must be attributed to the favourable impressions made by my conduct during the 8 months I had been at Longwood.

    He informed me that propositions which the Governor might perhaps accept, had this morning been made, and if accepted Napoleon would instantly choose a Surgeon, but that he could not think of having near him *l'homme du Gouverneur* [the Governor's man]; by this, he meant he said any person whose views of promotion and of self interest might prompt him to act under the Governor's influences.

    If on the contrary, I was willing to become *l'homme de l'Empereur* [the Emperor's man], to attach myself, *comme le sien propre* [as his very own], he Count Montholon was authorized to make a proposal to me, which he advised me to accept, as I should at once obtain a degree of his confidence by avowing the motives of making my fortune, a motive much more intelligible to him than any vague declaration of admiration of the Man.

He said that Napoleon was willing to give me an allowance of 12,000 Francs p. annum, to be paid monthly and he (Count Montholon) had represented to him the danger I might incur *de perdre mon état* [of losing my position], pointing out the examples of Mr O'Meara and Mr Stokoe, he would at once advance a sum to my practice in Bills upon the house of Baring, the interest of which should equal to my present pay from the British Government.

He asked the amount of my pay and I told him nearly 1£ per day on this Island. He told me Napoleon would not require from me any thing which should compromise me with Government or with any tribunal, or even in public opinion – that Mr O'Meara had never been required to do any thing of this nature – I should be able when I saw him to judge of the state of his liver which he himself thought was much diseased; that in my Bulletins my report might lean rather to an augmentation than a diminution of the malady. That I might draw the line rather above than below, as he was still in hopes that *la force des choses* [force of circumstance] might summon him from St Helena.

He, however (Count Montholon), was much more in dread of apoplexy attacking Napoleon, to which they all thought he had a strong tendency, but advised me to be guarded upon this subject as it was one on which he would not converse and from which he wished to avert his thoughts.

To this proposal I replied that I considered it totally incompatible with my duty to enter into a private agreement with Napoleon Bonaparte.

Lowe to Bathurst, 7 April 1819, BM MSS 20,126

St Helena, 7 April 1819
… On the morning of the 2nd April I was waited upon by Dr Verling, who begged to speak to me in private, and made the following extraordinary communication; viz. – That Count Montholon had showed to him the proposals he had forwarded to me and acquainted him, that if I agreed to them he, Dr Verling, was the person whom the 'Emperor' would select. That he would in such case become *l'homme de L'Empereur*. That he would receive a salary of 12,000 Francs per year, and that he would be put <u>in possession at once of Bills on the House of Baring, the interest of which, would be sufficient to always secure to him the salary he then enjoyed</u>.

The Count told him he would not be required to do anything which might compromise him before any Tribunal, and that Mr O'Meara had never done anything which could be brought against him before any Tribunal; – but Dr Verling then remarked, that if he accepted these proposals, <u>he had good reason to believe it would be expected of him he should exaggerate the state of Napoleon Bonaparte's disorder</u>.

This communication appeared to me altogether so extraordinary, that I did not choose it should remain with me alone, and I asked therefore Dr Verling's permission to make what he had said known to Mr Ricketts, who was then in the House, and to whom I related what had passed.

The design of the proposals in Count Montholon's letter, which vary only in form from those Count Bertrand had exhibited to Mr Stokoe, became quite evident and I was confirmed therefore in the propriety of my having so immediately rejected them.

Dr Verling after informing me of what was said when they were shown to him, mentioned Count Montholon was not aware of the communication that had passed being made known to me, and proposed to quit Longwood; but as I was in daily expectation of information respecting the arrival of a French Medical Attendant by the *William Pitt*, Indiaman, which had been reported on her way hither by a Transport with part of the 20th Regiment, and as the arrival of that Regiment might present to me some fresh choice of a medical officer to station at Longwood, I desired Dr Verling would remain at his post until the *Pitt* arrived, when if no French Surgeon came, I would immediately appoint another English Medical Officer to relieve him ...

I have the honour to be etc.

H. Lowe

Henry Goulburn (aide to Bathurst) to Lowe, 8 April 1819, BM MSS 20,126 (82–84)

Downing Street, 8 April 1819
Private
My Dear Sir,

The continued sitting of the Committee on the Affairs of the Bank and the sudden departure of the *Abundance* have prevented Lord Bathurst from acknowledging the receipt of your several dispatches and private letters relative to the conduct of Mr Stokoe. He has therefore directed me to acquaint you that it has upon consultation with the Lords Commissioners of the Admiralty appeared more advisable to send him back to St Helena in order to his being brought to trial for the offences to which he has been guilty and that instructions have been given to Admiral Plampin to that effect.

Lord Bathurst has also desired me to take this opportunity of replying to one of your private letters in which you communicate certain information respecting Mr Verling's opinion and connections in Ireland which you had derived from him and which you had thought it right to make known to Lord Bathurst. I am to assure you that the whole of Mr Verling's conduct appears to have been so discreet and proper on occasions even of no little difficulty that Lord Bathurst cannot avoid expressing his entire approbation of it, and in case Mr Verling should have been aware of your having communicated to Lord Bathurst the circumstances contained in your private letter of the [blank space] Lord Bathurst is desirous that you should assure him that they can make no impression on his Lordship's mind and that whatever may be his connections in Ireland and the religious faith either of himself or them Lord Bathurst cannot permit any circumstance of that nature to invalidate the confidence to which his uniform discretion and propriety of conduct, up to the date of your last communication so justly entitle him. You will I am sure see that the only object of Lord Bathurst in making such a communication is to remove from Mr Verling's mind any impression that he has been considered undeserving of confidence, as such an impression if entertained by him might naturally operate to produce the very consequences which it is on every account so desirable to prevent.

Believe me
My dear Sir, etc. etc.
Henry Goulburn

Reade to Lowe, 11 April 1819, BM MSS 20,126 (97–98)

11 April 1819

I saw Dr Verling yesterday, but he did not mention anything new. He seems rather uneasy about something and appears to be very anxious to get away from Longwood. I suspect his uneasiness proceeds from having given some kind of promise to Count Montholon regarding a Certificate of his wife's illness. He mentioned the circumstance to Baxter who, I believe said, 'were it his case' he would not give any Certificate whatever nor indeed would he give them anything in writing. Livingstone has pointedly refused giving any …

T. Reade

Lowe to Bathurst, 10 Apr 1819, BM MSS 20,126 (142–147)

St Helena, 10 April 1819
Private
My Lord,

… Your Lordship will be much surprised at the proposals made to Dr Verling – I feel it right to make known to your Lordship the following circumstances regarding them. It was on the afternoon of the 1st April, that is, the same day Count Montholon sent his letter containing the seven articles to me, the conversation took place between him and Dr Verling. He showed to Dr Verling the articles he had proposed in his letter to me, and built the conversation that ensued upon them. Dr Verling expected me that afternoon at Longwood, and did not come over immediately to make known what had passed. I delayed not a moment in sending back Count

Montholon's letter with the seven proposed articles, with a letter written on the same day to him by Sir Thomas Reade, but it arrived late in the evening at Longwood, and was not carried to the Count until early in the morning of the 2nd April. Count Montholon again saw Dr Verling, and showed him Sir Thos. Reade's letter, said he supposed I was not acquainted he (Dr Verling) was the person whom, if the proposals had been accepted, 'the Emperor' meant to select. It was upon this occasion Dr Verling lost not an instant further time in coming over to Plantation House, and acquainting me of what had occurred, seeming to think he could no longer remain at Longwood after making known what had passed betwixt Count Montholon and him. I however desired him to continue at this post, on the grounds which will be found detailed in my public letter on the occasion. He told me then when Count Montholon first showed to him the proposals he had sent to me, he did not see any particular motive as affecting himself to object to them, but he had a distinct explanation with Count Montholon on his returning to Longwood when he acquainted him he could enter into the consideration of no proposals that were not previously approved by me. In fact, I may consider it fortunate that I returned Count Montholon's letter with the proposals immediately, for had I even given them a qualified acceptance, or not rejected them *in toto*, as was done by Sir Thomas Reade's letter, I need not point out to your Lordship, what strong temptations were at work to induce a favourable leaning towards them, on the part of any medical person that might have been offered. Dr Verling has said, he never passed so uneasy a night in his life time, as when he found I did not come to Longwood in the afternoon of the 1st April, and that he could not then tell me what Count Montholon had said.

Dr Verling has ascribed the unguarded manner in which General Bonaparte has committed himself through Count Montholon, to his apprehension of being compelled to receive the visits of the Orderly Officer, and to his desire of instantly procuring a medical attendant, who might answer for him and stand between them. Dr Verling had I understand at first some hesitation in inserting in the written memorandum of the conversation with Count Montholon, what is said about the proposal to exaggerate the state of General Bonaparte's indisposition. The way in which he first spoke of it to me, and as I afterwards mentioned it to Mr Ricketts, is precisely as detailed in my public letter; but finding that Dr Verling had mentioned the other circumstances to Sir T. Reade without speaking of that, I desired the latter would suggest to him my wish to be furnished with a written memorandum of the proposition actually made to him, and particularly of what was said on the point which I regarded as of most importance. Dr Verling seemed to consider it more as a matter of observation than of actual proposition on the part of Count Montholon, but Sir T. Reade having explained that if he left that out that he might as well leave out everything, he then acquiesced in the suggestion presented to him, and furnished the details required …

I have the honour to be etc.

H. Lowe

Lowe to Bathurst, 29 April, 1819 BM MSS 20, 126 (205–206)

St Helena, 29 April 1819
Private
… The very superior claims of Dr Arnott of the 20th Regiment, to that of any other medical person on this island, preclude my following up my former suggestions in respect to Dr Verling's advancement to a Medical Staff situation here, though I shall be happy in his receiving any mark of attention, which his conduct during his continuance in the very delicate situation in which he has been placed at Longwood, may appear to render him deserving of …

I have etc.

Lowe

Memorandum of Major Gorrequer, May 1819, BM MSS 20,126 (186–190)

On the 30th April I met Dr Verling at dinner at Admiral Plampin's, who told me Count Montholon had mentioned to him, the day before, that in the course of a conversation with me on the 28th, I had made some observation, which induced him to infer, it was possible an arrangement might take place with Dr Verling respecting the conditions of his admission as the Medical Attendant of Napoleon Bonaparte, without the necessity of its being formally made known to the Governor. Being conscious I had said nothing which could in any degree warrant such inference, I repeated to Dr Verling the observation that had been made to me by Count Montholon, with regard to him, and my reply, begging that he would put the Count right as soon as possible on this point.

The next morning (1 May being the second day of the race meeting) Dr Verling told me at the race ground, he had mentioned to Count Montholon what I requested him to say, who answered, that although he had received such an impression as above stated, he however had not considered any thing of what passed in our conversation as in any way official, or attached any consequence to it: that he had merely mentioned the circumstances to Dr Verling, so as to make it a matter of after conversation between the Doctor and myself.

A few minutes afterwards, Count Montholon came up to me and said, that in consequence of what Dr Verling had stated to him, he begged me to believe he was perfectly well aware, there was nothing official in the conversation we had together the first day of the races, but that he had never conceived I attached any meaning to the observation I made, beyond the words themselves, and that what he had said to me and I to him, was of no more importance than *si nous avions seulement causé sur les courtes des chevaux* [if we had only chatted on the race course].

I replied, I felt surprised at the manner in which he had spoken of it to Dr Verling, when he interrupted me by speaking nearly the same words he had just done, and bowing to me took his leave.

G. Gorrequer, Maj.

Montholon's letter to Lowe, 27 May 1819, asking for his wife to leave, BM MSS 20,126 (307)

La Maladie de la comtesse de Montholon exige son retour en Europe.

Les Medecins Verling et Livingstone s'ont déclaré qu'ils considèrent un changement de climat comme indispensable au rétablissement de sa santé ...

[The illness of the Countess of Montholon demands her return to Europe. Doctors Verling and Livingstone have stated that they consider a change of climate to be essential to restore her health ...]

Nicholls to Gorrequer, 5 August 1819, BM MSS 20,127 (127–128)

Half past 6 o'clock p.m., Longwood, 5 August 1819

I am sorry that I have not been able to obtain any information concerning General Bonaparte this day, he has kept himself so exceptively close, his bed and dressing room windows have been closed all day.

Napoleon appeared out yesterday two or three times, and paid a visit to Madame Bertrand yesterday afternoon at about five o'clock. Everything seems to go on regular among the servants of General Bonaparte, I have therefore caused the signal to be made as usual this evening.

Count Montholon is confined to his bed with a sickness – a blister was applied to his side last night. St Denis, one of General Bonaparte's Valets applied to me this day for a joiner. I request to be informed, where I am to make application for these kind of artisan when they are required at Longwood.

G. Nicholls

P.S. Dr Verling has just told that he heard Count Montholon say this morning that Napoleon was unwell.

G. Nicholls

Reade to Nicholls, 6 August 1819, BM MSS 20,127 (136)

Castle, 6 August 1819
Dear Sir,
    The papers which Dr Verling will give to you are the Governor's. They are literally the only papers that have arrived by the Vessel from England and the Governor therefore begs when you deliver them to Count Montholon for General Bonaparte that you will explain his wish that they should be returned as soon after perusal as possible.
    Acquaint Count Montholon also that a vessel is delayed sailing this afternoon in consequence of your report not having been received.
T. Reade

[To] Captain Nicholls

Gorrequer to Nicholls, 6 August 1819, BM MSS 20,127 (137)

Castle, 6 August 1819
Dear Sir,
    You will be pleased to call on Count Montholon in company with Dr Verling and say to him that however concerned you are to intrude upon him during his indisposition the difficulty you are again placed under from the want of consideration towards the importance of the duties you have to perform renders it absolutely requisite to have recourse to him to explain that you have not been able to see General Bonaparte either yesterday or today and of the indispensable necessity of your making your report before the day closes.
    Count Montholon although indisposed has every means of making your difficulty known to General Bonaparte through the other persons of the household.
G. Gorrequer

[To] Captain Nicholls

Gorrequer to Verling, 13 August 1819, BM MSS 20,127 (196–197)

James Town, 13 August 1819
Dear Sir,
    In reply to your note of this day, I beg to say, the Governor does not see any impropriety in the assistance you rendered the Orderly Officer in the interpretation of the messages you allude to, there not appearing to have been any other person at the time on the spot, to do it for him, and where messages are the result of any alleged indisposition on the part of the persons on whom you are in attendance, he conceives there cannot be a more proper channel for the delivery of them, as you are naturally the most

competent judge, whether the situation of the person is really such as to render him unable to receive a message without injury to his health, in which case, viewing the very serious points which generally form the subject of the Governor's communications, it is of the highest importance that no false pretext be suffered to prevail, if therefore as in the case of the messages which the Orderly Officer has been directed to deliver to Count Montholon, the Count's state of health has been such as to render him unable to receive them or the letter I sent to the Orderly Officer for him, it ought to be the first question of that officer to you, whether indisposition really prevails to such an extent as to render it inexpedient that the letter or message be delivered to him; and the Governor will always be happy in such case, to leave it to your own discretion to judge of the proper moment of delivering it, either on the part of the Orderly Officer himself, accompanied by you – by yourself, or by one of the sick person's own attendants.

With reference to the only occasion where you spoke to the Governor upon the subject of your acting as interpreter, it was one where the Orderly Officer had employed you as the medium of communication to a servant of Count Bertrand, who had infringed the regulations, and as a matter of policy, he should have preferred that any other person had been applied to on the occasion; but the Governor at the same time did not mean to bar you in the exercise of your own discretion, where there is an absolute necessity for a message being delivered, and that there is no other person at hand to assist, particularly in cases where it would be impossible to ascribe your act to any desire or design of undue interference, in matters that did not regard you.

G. Gorrequer

Verling to Gorrequer, 13 August 1819, BM MSS 20,127 (198)

Longwood, 13 August 1819

My Dear Sir,

I had formerly occasion to converse with the Governor upon the subject of my acting as interpreter when communications were to be made by Captain Nicholls to the persons at Longwood and he there coincided fully with the ideas I expressed to him.

I have not allowed this to influence me today having been unwilling to cause any delay. I request however you will have the goodness to mention the circumstance to the Governor and let me know his wishes upon this head.

Verling

[To] Major Gorrequer

Nicholls to Gorrequer, 14 August 1819, BM MSS 20,127 (200)

Longwood, 14 August 1819

Not having had an opportunity of seeing General Bonaparte this morning by three o'clock, in compliance to my instructions, I requested Marchand, the chief Valet, to acquaint General Bonaparte that I wished to be admitted to see him – and then proceeded to the hall door, which I found locked. I remained in the Verandah about ten or twelve minutes, and not receiving any answer to my message I returned to my own quarters. Marchand afterwards explained to me, through the means of Dr Verling, that General Bonaparte was still in bed, and as the General Bell had not rung he should not disturb him.

G. Nicholls

[To] Major Gorrequer

Nicholls to Gorrequer, 17 August 1819, BM MSS 20,127 (222)

Longwood, 17 August 1819

Dear Sir,

I beg you will be pleased to acquaint the Governor that in quitting my sleeping room this morning I perceived upon my sitting room table a loose paper and upon unfolding it, I saw the writing was French and looking to the bottom of the paper, I observed that it was signed Count Bertrand. I instantly folded it up again and without looking at a single letter further, I proceeded with it, to Count Bertrand's quarters – his servant told me that his master was dressing and that I could not see him immediately – I walked into the Count's Parlour and placed the paper on a table, and then returned, but first pointed out to a servant that I had done so.

My servant tells me that when he first came into my dining room this morning, he saw the above mentioned paper upon the table, but he knew not who put it there.

Dr Verling <u>was present</u> this morning when I first perceived the paper in question and is witness that I neither preserved it or kept it in my possession.

G. Nicholls

Verling to Gorrequer, 19 August 1819, BM MSS 20,127 (239)

Longwood, 19 August 1819

My Dear Sir,

I have been informed that the malady under which General Bonaparte is said to labour at present is a constipation of the Bowels and I am led to think that his occasional 'crises', as they are termed here, have arisen from the same causes. Hitherto, this state of body has been treated by the warm bath and frequent Glysters, and by abstinence; but it is said that latterly he has found the bath produces much debility and is afraid to push it to the length he used to do, and that at present Glysters have failed to procure any effect. No mention was made of his having tried any medicine, though I have formerly been told that he had taken Cheltenham salts and Castor oil.

Believe me etc.

J. Verling

[To] Major Gorrequer

Lowe to Napoleon, 19 August 1819, BM MSS 20,127 (246); 20,149 (125)

Note for the information of Napoleon Bonaparte
The Governor has the honour to make known for the information of Napoleon Bonaparte, that it having been stated he is indisposed, the Governor pursuant to the instruction contained in Earl Bathurst's letter of 16th May 1818, has directed the principal Medical Officer on this island, Dr Arnott, to attend immediately to any call that may be made for his services, should Napoleon Bonaparte be pleased to avail himself of them.

H. Lowe

Castle, St Helena, 19 August 1819

Reade to Verling, 20 August 1819, BM MSS 20,127 (248)

Castle James Town, 20 August 1819
Dear Sir,

   Count Bertrand having addressed a letter to the Governor, stating Napoleon Bonaparte to have fallen down sick last night, he has directed Dr Arnott as the Principal Medical Officer on this island, to repair to Longwood, to give his advice. This is however not meant to interfere in any shape with the continuance of your attendance, Dr Arnott's visit being one of duty as well as of attention, according to the rule laid down to the Governor, in his instructions.

T. Reade

[To] Dr Verling

Notes of conversation between Count Bertrand and Dr Arnott, 20th Regiment, at Longwood, 21 August 1819, for Lowe.

I proceeded to Longwood yesterday for the purpose of offering my medical attendance to General Bonaparte. On my arrival there, I waited on Dr Verling, who took me to the house of Count Bertrand, and introduced me to him. I think the conversation which took place between the Count and myself was nearly as follows:

I communicated to him the object of my visit; that I had been ordered there by you, to offer my assistance in a medical capacity, to General Bonaparte in concert with Dr Verling, to which Count Bertrand replied that the Emperor was very ill, and that although he (the Emperor) entertained a very high opinion of the English Faculty, yet he had refused to be visited by any British Surgeon, unless he would accede to certain conditions. The Count also said that he himself and his family having experienced much attention from Dr Verling, had often recommended the Emperor to see him professionally, but that he had uniformly objected to it, because he (Dr Verling) would not accede to the conditions prescribed by the Emperor. I then signified to Count Bertrand that I could wish the object of my visit to be conveyed to General Bonaparte, and that I would wait at Longwood to know the result. He said that he would communicate the message to the Emperor, and that Dr Verling and I might call on him again. In about an hour afterwards, Count Bertrand sent for Dr Verling and myself to his house. In this second interview he told me he had been with the Emperor and that he would see me, provided I was authorized to give my opinion in writing, to sign and leave it with him. I replied, I would not promise to do that, without first communicating with you, that I considered my visit strictly professional, and that as such I would act to the best of my judgment, but on no other terms would I visit General Bonaparte. 'Oh!' then he replied, 'you are acting under the influence of the Governor.' At the same moment the Count took from his side pocket a written paper from which he read several conditions, the purport of which tended to absolve the person who should have the medical charge of General Bonaparte from your control, and every other military authority. He put the question to me, if I were authorized and willing to give my assent to those articles. I then unequivocally told the Count [end]

Gorrequer to Verling, 22 August 1819, BM MSS 20,127 (272); 20,149 (127)

Castle, James Town, 22 August 1819
Dear Sir,
    The Governor sends a letter for Count Montholon from the Countess. He understands from the Commander of the vessel who has brought it that the Countess Montholon was better before she left Ascension.
Gorrequer

[To] Dr Verling

Lowe to Napoleon (see a shorter version earlier), 23 August 1819, BM MSS 20,127 (280–281); 20,149 (129)

Note to Napoleon Bonaparte
The Undersigned Lieutenant General and Governor of the Island of St Helena has the honour to make known to Napoleon Bonaparte that

Dr Arnott, Principal Medical Officer on this Island, and Dr Verling, Surgeon in attendance at Longwood, upon requesting one of the officers in attendance upon Napoleon Bonaparte, to make known to him that they were in waiting to afford him medical assistance if so desired, were informed that Napoleon Bonaparte would not see any medical person, unless such person agreed to and was authorized by the Governor, to sign the same articles as had been proposed to Mr Stokoe's acceptance, and agreed to by him.

The undersigned has in consequence reverted to a copy of the unsigned articles above referred to, and although he considers them in all the main points to have been already answered by a paper sent to Count Montholon on the 10th April last, he has the honour nevertheless to enclose for the information of Napoleon Bonaparte, a further paper stating those modifications upon which alone he should feel himself warranted, without the express directions of his government, to grant his permission for any person under his authority, affixing his signature to articles that were proposed to Mr Stokoe, and according to which modifications, or upon the plain simple and wholly unobjectionable footing expressed in Earl Bathurst's letter of the 16th May 1818, it rests solely with Napoleon Bonaparte to have recourse to the advice of any medical officer on this island, until the person whose selection has been left to a member of his own family, as communicated to Napoleon Bonaparte, by a note from the undersigned dated 4th November last, may arrive here.

H. Lowe

Castle, James Town, 23 August 1819

Verling to Gorrequer, 28 August 1819, BM MSS 20,127 (318–19)

Longwood, 28 August 1819

My Dear Sir,

I am not able to give any information as to the hour Mr Stokoe saw General Bonaparte on the 17th of January 1819 having remained in my own apartment most of that morning.

On referring to my memorandums, I find that the date of the two conversations with Count Bertrand was the 17th January, they having occurred on the evening of the day Mr Stokoe first came to Longwood.

The error of date was in the note accompanying them.

Believe me etc.

J. Verling

P.S. I beg to inform you, that my attendance as an evidence has been required by the Deputy Judge Advocate on Monday morning at 9 o'clock.

Verling to Reade, 25 August 1819, BM MSS 20,127 (322)

Longwood, 25 August 1819
My Dear Sir Thomas,
   My note to you of the 17th January states explicitly that from ¼ before 7 o'clock until the moment of writing it, 'I had heard nothing of Mr Stokoe.'
   I think it was Captain Nicholls who told me Counts Montholon and Bertrand had passed repeatedly between the house of the latter and Longwood House.
J. Verling

[To] Lieut. Colonel Sir Thomas Reade

Reade to Verling, 29 August 1819, BM MSS 20,127 (341); 20,149 (134)

James Town, 29 August 1819
My Dear Sir,
   Having accidentally found the enclosed note, the Governor has desired me to send it to you, in the hope that it may aid your recollection as to the time Mr Stokoe was admitted to see Napoleon Bonaparte on the morning of the 17th January.
   As Major Gorrequer wrote his note after breakfast, you could not have sent the enclosed note until near eleven, and as you mention that Bertrand and Montholon had been going to and fro between the house of the former and Longwood House very often, it is natural to suppose that Mr Stokoe must during this time, have been at Count Bertrand's house, otherwise there could have been no motive for the latter passing backwards and forwards to his own house.
T. Reade

[To] Dr Verling

Portion of a letter from Lowe to Bathurst, 30 August 1819, BM MSS 20,127 (356–358)

St Helena, 30 August 1819
Private
My Lord,
   … Count Montholon made another attempt to tamper with Doctor Verling, giving him to understand a much larger sum would be at his service than what was first proposed, but Doctor Verling informed me he cut the conversation abruptly. He has said, however, that he clearly sees they will stick at no sum to gain their end.
   The last communication I received from Longwood referred in particular to the proposals offered to Mr Stokoe's acceptance, as those alone upon

which General Bonaparte would allow any English Medical Officer to approach him. I sent an answer to them, and offered any medical persons on the modified answer I had given, or if preferred, on the plain and simple footing expressed in Your Lordship's letter of 16th May 1818, but both have been rejected, on these or any other terms, than those of signing the same conditions as Mr Stokoe had signed ...

H. Lowe

Note of unknown origin regarding Verling, August 1819, BM MSS 20,127 (368)

August 1819

Dr Verling mentioned that at both Count Bertrand's and Count Montholon's they used to laugh at the complaints of a want of provisions at Longwood. It was a subject, they said, which ought never to have been brought forward, either in Santini's Pamphlet or O'Meara's book. That they also ridiculed the idea which Bonaparte seemed desirous to impress of an apprehension of assassination or violence to his person.

Captain Power mentioned that Madame Bertrand had said to himself and Madame Power that Mr O'Meara was a mischief making man – 'a troublesome man', and that had it not been for him things would have gone on much better between Longwood and the Governor.

Reade to Verling, 6 September 1819, BM MSS 20,128 (43); 20,149 (142)

Castle, James Town, 6 September 1819
To Dr Verling
Sir,

The Orderly Officer having reported that when he desired to see Napoleon Bonaparte this morning in the execution of his duty he was told that Napoleon Bonaparte was indisposed, it is the Governor's direction that should a similar answer be given when the Orderly Officer desires again to see him, that you will call upon the person to whom the Orderly Officer may have addressed himself and make known your readiness to attend on Napoleon Bonaparte, saying you have received the Governor's directions for such purposes. The Governor desires you will on the receipt of this letter, wait upon the individual who delivered the answer this morning to Captain Nicholls, and offer your services as above.

I have the honour etc.
T. Reade

[Note also 20,128 (44) copy of letter from Gorrequer to Nicholls telling him to tell Verling 'immediately' if he (Nicholls) is told Napoleon is sick.]

Verling to Gorrequer, 8 September 1819, BM MSS 20,128 (76)

Longwood, 8 September 1819
Dear Sir,
    I request you will have the goodness to inform the Governor that Count Montholon's health is much improved.
    He informed me today that he had an intention of visiting General Bonaparte. He continues to complain of pain in the right side, but the evening accession of fever has been but slight, yesterday and the evening before.

Believe me, etc.
J. Verling

[To] Major Gorrequer

Gorrequer to Verling, 9 September 1819, BM MSS 20,128 (82); 20,149 (144)

Castle, James Town, 9 September 1819
Dear Sir,
    As you mentioned to me in your note of the 7th that Count Bertrand said he would make known to Napoleon Bonaparte your having called upon him to offer your medical attendance, the Governor desires you would again call upon him, simply to ask him if he has informed Napoleon Bonaparte of it, and to know if he accepts your services.
    As Count Montholon is now recovered, you may make known to him also what you have done to Count Bertrand.

G. Gorrequer

[To] Dr Verling

Lowe to Countess Bertrand, 30 September 1819, BM MSS 20,128 (246)

Sir Hudson Lowe presents his respectful compliments to the Countess Bertrand, and in reply to her note of the 28th has the honour to acquaint her, that Dr Verling will possess every facility so long as he remains on this Island, to continue his attendance upon and visits to her and her family.
    Sir H. Lowe begs leave further to acquaint her, that the names of the persons of whom she enclosed a list will be left at the Longwood Gate, as having permission to visit her without applying to him for a pass. He was obliged on this occasion to make a reference to Admiral Plampin which will account for the short delay of this reply.
Plantation House, 30 September 1819

Lowe to Bathurst, 1 October 1819, BM MSS 20,128 (253)

St Helena, 1 October 1819
My Lord,
I do myself the honour to inform Your Lordship, that on Professor Antommarchi relieving Dr Verling at Longwood, the latter whose ordinary term of service on a Foreign Station as a Medical Officer of the Royal Artillery had some time since expired, although no person had yet been sent out to replace him, applied to me for leave of absence to proceed to England.

Under all circumstances, considering the highly delicate nature of the situation in which Dr Verling had been placed, and the attention due to him on such account, I did not think proper to withhold my assent to his request.

A few days after it had been made to me, I received a letter from the Countess Bertrand, applying to me to authorize or direct him to continue his Medical attendance upon her and her family.

This led to a correspondence between the Countess and myself, copies of the whole of which are annexed.

On receiving her second letter, I requested Dr Verling would call upon her, and explain the circumstances of his application to me for leave. She expressed much concern at hearing that he was about to quit the Island, and said, in that case she should apply for the attendance of Dr Henry Assistant Surgeon of the 66th Regiment.

Your Lordship will observe a request upon another subject, to have been made to me by the Countess Bertrand, to which I immediately signified my acquiescence, and which produced a very gracious acknowledgment as will be seen at the conclusion, from her.

Sir H. Lowe

Letter requesting 12 months leave

St Helena, 6 October 1819
Sir,
After an absence of nearly 5 years from my family, I find that it is extremely necessary for the arrangement of my private affairs that I should return home.

I shall therefore be much obliged to you to forward to his Excellency the Governor my application for twelve months leave of absence.

I have the honour to be Sir,
Your most obedient and humble servant,
J. Verling
Adj. Surgeon, Royal Artillery

To: Major Power

Gorrequer to Major Power, 4 October 1819, BM MSS 20,128 (271)

Plantation House, 4 October 1819
Sir,

In reply to your letter to me of yesterday's date, enclosing an application from Dr Verling for twelve months leave of absence, for the purpose of returning to England for the arrangement of his private affairs, I am directed to convey to you His Excellency the Governor's assent to Dr Verling's Request.

G. Gorrequer

[To] Major Power
Comm. Royal Artillery

Verling to Gorrequer, 12 October 1819, BM MSS 20,128 (297)

James Town, 12 October 1819
Dear Sir

Having expressed to the Governor my intention of requesting his particular directions relative to visits which have been or may be required of me to Longwood since the arrival of the Foreign Surgeon, he observed, that my departure would under this measure (which he approved of) be unnecessary.

As my stay may be protracted somewhat longer than was at first intended, I request you will make known to His Excellency my anxiety to have clear Instructions for my guidance in intercourse which may take place with Longwood should such intercourse be deemed necessary.

J. Verling

[To] Major Gorrequer

PS The Countess Bertrand having sent for me yesterday to see one of her children, I think it probable I shall soon be called upon again.

Wynyard to Verling, 13 October 1819, BM MSS 20,128 (298); 20,149 (157)

Plantation House, 13 October 1819
Dear Sir,

In reply to your letter to Major Gorrequer, the Governor has directed me to say, he has a perfect recollection of his having told you when Madame Bertrand wrote to him to request that he would <u>authorize</u> and even <u>direct</u> you to give your <u>daily</u> personal attendance upon her and her family, that he approved your intention of not continuing such fixed habitual attendance upon any of the Persons at Longwood, unless it should be required of you as a matter of duty; but that he had no objection whatever to your <u>occasional</u> visits, and thought it right even that you should make them, until she had time to become acquainted with the newly arrived Medical Person, and as you had applied for leave of absence at the time, he did not enter further into consideration of the matter. He could not have foreseen at that time the protraction of your stay on the island, but this circumstance does still not appear to him to require any particular Instructions to be conveyed to you.

Madame Bertrand has had opportunities since she first wrote of becoming better acquainted with Dr Antommarchi. The Governor is not aware there can be any necessity consequently, for the constant attendance of any other Medical person, although as a matter of attention and complaisance towards her, he has not the slightest objection to the continuance of your visits – but he sees no motive for ordering them or conveying any more particular instruction to you on the occasion, than what he might incidentally think is necessary to give to any Professional Person, not belonging to the establishment at Longwood, who might be occasionally called in or who might have obtained his permission for paying visits there.

E. Wynyard

Verling to Wynyard, 13 October 1819, BM MSS 20,128 (299)

James Town, 13 October 1819
Dear Sir,

Having attended upon the Families at Longwood for 14 Months in obedience to the Governor's orders, I conceived that the visits made by me subsequent to the arrival of Dr Antommarchi were in consequence and continuation of the same duty, and indeed I proceeded in two instances from Plantation House to Longwood by the Governor's directions.

I can see no reason for placing myself in any relation to the persons at Longwood, different from that in which I have hitherto acted and in which his Excellency was pleased to place me.

I beg therefore to declare my intention of confining myself to my military duties and consequently of not giving any attendance at Longwood unless particularly directed so to do.

I am etc.
J. Verling

[To] Lieut. Colonel Wynyard

Wynyard to Verling, 16 October 1819, BM MSS 20,128 (306–307); 20,149 (158)

St Helena, 16 October 1819
Dear Sir,

Having showed your letter of the 13th to the Governor, he has desired me to convey the following remarks to you.

When he placed you at Longwood, it was for the express purpose of giving your Medical Attendance to General Bonaparte, then without any Medical person near him. His followers were a secondary consideration. General Bonaparte himself declined to receive your visits, and on proposals being made to you which were contrary to your honour and your duty, you applied to be relieved. The Governor signified to you, that a Foreign Medical Attendant had been written for and was expected, and that you would be relieved on his arrival, every motive conspiring in the meantime to render it necessary that a Medical Officer should remain on the spot, and it being deemed inexpedient to make any change, unless the Foreign Medical Person should arrive.

On his arrival you were relieved, only waiting sufficient time to give such information as he might desire, and on your quitting Longwood your relations with the persons there became precisely the same as those of any other Individual.

The application of Madame Bertrand to <u>authorize</u> and <u>direct</u> the continuance of your attendance upon her and her children was not wholly unforeseen, and the more so, as before it was made to the Governor, you had yourself acquainted him with her desire for the continuance of your visits, and he had signified his assent to them, until she might have time to become acquainted with her new medical Advisor.

Your application for leave of absence rendered it unnecessary to enter into consideration of the more formal demand made for your being directed or ordered to attend her, and the Governor's desires or suggestions – not his directions – for your continuing your attendance upon her so long as you remained here (the protraction of your stay on the island being wholly unforeseen when the Countess's demand was made) he certainly did not conceive could have been regarded in any other light, than as a simple act of attention towards her, or at most, as an accommodation to the service,* in the sphere of which you had been acting. In whatever light viewed, however, the Governor is fully disposed to admit the obligation to you, and up to the period at which your intentions have been last declared to him, it will be considered.

As in your letters you speak of the Families and persons at Longwood in general, the Governor has remarked, that there has been no application for your attendance by any other Person than the Countess Bertrand, nor since your quitting Longwood has his authority or permission been required any

---

* The following remark was inserted in the margin of the copy of this letter sent to Earl Bathurst: By 'accommodation to the service' it was afterwards explained to Dr Verling, was his pursuing that line of conduct which was calculated to prevent discussion with and complaint on the part of General Bonaparte.

further, than for your visits to her, and for enabling Professor Antommarchi to consult you on any point of his duty.

It will rest with you of course, to continue your visits to the Countess or not, as you may think most fit after this explanation, but if they are continued, the Governor desires it may be on the footing mentioned in my reply to your first letter, as he deems it highly advisable to discourage any expectation on her part or that of any of the followers of General Bonaparte, that a British Medical Officer is likely to be appointed as a fixed attendant upon them, in addition to the Foreign one who is already established there.

E. Wynyard

Verling to Wynyard, 18 October 1819, BM MSS 20,128 (308)

James Town, 18 October 1819
Dear Sir,

In reply to the last paragraph of your letter dated the 16th I beg to refer you to the previous declaration in mine of the 13th.

The idea of attending at Longwood on any footing than by the direct orders of my superiors never occurred to me, and even of the situation I was not desirous as is known to the Governor from various applications which I made to be removed.

The written application for my attendance made by the Countess Bertrand, was by me unforeseen and unknown till communicated to me, by the Governor, and whatever expectations may exist on her part or that of any of the followers of General Bonaparte, that a British medical Officer is likely to be appointed as a fixed medical attendant upon them, I cannot be the person in view, since they are under the impression that I am to leave the Island immediately, my intention of doing so, having been communicated to the Countess Bertrand, by the Governor's desire, and the alteration in the arrangement remaining unknown to her.

I remain
J. Verling

Wynyard to Verling, 17 October 1819, BM MSS 20,128 (312); 20,149 (159)

St Helena, 17 October 1819
Sir,

I am directed by His Excellency the Governor to inform you, that having taken into consideration the additional trouble and inconvenience to which you have been exposed by continuing your professional visits to the Countess Bertrand after you had been relieved from your general duties at Longwood, he has ordered that the allowances which you received whilst on actual duty at Longwood, shall be continued up to the date of your last communication of the 13th October.

The Governor has already conveyed to you his full approbation of your line of conduct, in the very delicate situation where it was attempted to place you in the occasion of Count Bertrand's conversations with you in January 1819, as detailed in your letters of the 18th and 20th of that month and he has had the satisfaction to acquaint you that it met also the entire approval of Earl Bathurst.

His Excellency desires me further to express to you, his fullest approbation of your having rejected the proposals made to you by Count Montholon on the 1st April 1819, and to assure you of the favourable sense he entertains of the general line of your proceeding, whilst still obliged to remain at Longwood, until the Foreign Medical person who was expected should arrive, after the very irksome and painful situation in which these proposals, and the refusal of General Bonaparte to allow your visits, unless you acquiesced in them, had tended to place you.

E. Wynyard

Lowe to R. H. L—, Secretary to the Board of Ordnance, 17 October 1819, BM MSS 20,128 (313)

St Helena, 17 October 1819
Sir,

I do myself the honour to inform you, that Dr Verling of the Royal Artillery, having been relieved in his attendance on General Bonaparte at Longwood by the arrival on this Island of Professor Antommarchi, has resumed his duties with the Ordnance department.

I at the same time beg leave to state to you, that during the time Dr Verling was employed in the above duty, he received no other compensation than an allowance for Table Expenses, and in consequence to submit, that he may be considered as entitled to the full amount of his regular pay whilst employed near General Bonaparte, in the same manner as if he had remained with the detachment of the Royal Artillery.

H. Lowe

[To] R. H. L—
Secretary to the Board of Ordnance

Lowe to Bathurst, 3 November 1819, BM MSS 20,128 (356–361)

St Helena, 3 November 1819
My Lord,

In a letter which I had the honour to address to Your Lordship on the 1st October 1819, I mentioned, that an application had been made to me for leave of absence by Dr Verling, and under the circumstances of Countess Bertrand's demand to me for his being directed to continue his attendance upon her and her family, which might only be the prelude to a further demand for a British Medical Person being attached to the Establishment at Longwood, in addition to the Foreign one, I was not averse to an acquiescence with Dr Verling's application, as it enabled me to reply to the Countess Bertrand's letter, in a satisfactory way, without entering into any particular discussion with her on the occasion. Circumstances however have since arisen, which induce me to take a retrospect of what at first occurred.

Upon the arrival of Professor Antommarchi, Dr Verling became of course immediately relieved from the obligation of that duty with which he had been so long charged at Longwood, and from which it had been so much his own desire to be relieved.

Although not called upon to see General Bonaparte, he had been in attendance upon the family of Counts Bertrand and Montholon, and a request was made by Professor Antommarchi, that Dr Verling might remain a few days at Longwood to give him information upon such points as might be desired. To this, I most readily assented. Dr Verling continued at Longwood three days, and then went to his quarters in the Town.

Dr Verling on quitting Longwood applied to me for leave to proceed to England, and at the same time made known his desire of breaking off all relations with the Persons at Longwood, except when ordered to visit them by me, and if his attendance should be demanded, desiring to have written instructions for his guidance.

The application to me for leave was not wholly unexpected. I told Dr Verling that the unpleasant situation in which he had been so long placed at Longwood, was such as entitled him to every consideration, that I should miss his professional services on the Island, but that I would think of what might be done, and give him my answer accordingly.

A few days after, a Race Meeting was to take place, where Dr Verling acquainted me that the Countess Bertrand had made a request to him to continue to call upon her and her children, and had also requested him to accompany her to the Races. I told him, I had not the slightest objection of his acceding to her wishes in both respects, and even thought it an act of proper attention in him to occasionally call upon her and her children, to inquire after their health.

The next day I was surprised at receiving an application from Countess Bertrand, for Dr Verling being authorized and directed to call upon her. I sent for Dr Verling to show him the Countess's letter, and told him, that I thought the best course of proceeding was for him to call upon her, and acquaint her of the application he had made to me for leave of absence, and that he might inform her, I had granted it to him. That in the meantime, he might continue his visits to her.

I sent my reply to the Countess's letter accordingly; copies of both accompany.

I received a second letter from the Countess Bertrand of which copy also accompanies, together with that of the reply I sent, and of a further note I received from the Countess.

Dr Verling's application for leave of absence, which had been made before any of this correspondence took place, was a verbal one; but in every other respect, formally made and acceded to.

On the 4th October I received a written application addressed to me through his Commanding Officer, Major Power of the Royal Artillery, which was replied to officially on the same day, and as the *Eurydice* Frigate was on the point of departure for England, I was under the impression that Dr Verling intended to apply for a passage in her, or that he would profit of what I considered a real favour to him, in the leave granted, by the next opportunity that might offer; two or three days afterwards, however, he mentioned to Sir Thomas Reade his desire of remaining on the Island until the month of March or April next, grounded on pecuniary motives, and fear of giving offence to the Director General of the Ordnance Medical department, and on the first day afterwards, that I met him, he made known to me his intention to the same effect, desiring at the same time, that the leave of absence which had been granted, might still remain valid.

I had felt a reluctance to part with the services of any Medical Man from the island, when Dr Verling made his first application to me, and could therefore see no motive for objecting to his determination of remaining on it. I told him therefore, he was at liberty to act as he pleased, and that as he had decided on remaining, it would afford time for him to write to the Director General in order that his successor might be arriving here about the time he went away, and I conceived even a reason for protracting his departure, which he himself had not expressed to me: that of his making the voyage home during the summer season.

Dr Verling spoke at the same time about writing to me for instructions on the subject of the continuance of his visits at Longwood, but I told him that viewing the occasional way in which his visits would be made, I did not consider it necessary for him to write me on the occasion, and Sir Thomas Reade to whom he had spoken before on the same matter, had delivered the same opinion to him.

It was not therefore without some regret, and even some surprise, after hearing of his intention to remain on the Island until the month of March or April next, that I received a letter addressed to my Military Secretary, soliciting written instructions for his guidance in visiting at Longwood. Copy of his letter with the reply I ordered to be written to him is annexed.

In my reply, it will be observed, I declined giving the written instructions that Dr Verling required, letting him understand, however, that if incidentally such instruction should appear necessary, it would be afforded to him. Dr Verling wrote again.

I was much struck with that part of his second letter, where he says, 'that he can see no reason to place himself in any relation with the persons at Longwood different to that in which he had hitherto acted'; – with the omission of any precise reference to the Countess Bertrand, who had alone made the demand for his services, and with the mode in which he appeared to consider her demand as being one for attendance upon the persons of Longwood in general.

It was not easy for me to judge what were the views of the persons at Longwood and what were those of Dr Verling.

Whilst General Bonaparte was without any other medical attendant, he would naturally be inclined to consider the British Medical Officer placed near him, in the light of his domestic surgeon, and if any particular restraints were imposed upon the communication of such person, either with him or his followers, he would derive a protest from this to avoid consulting him. Dr Verling therefore during the period of his remaining at Longwood, was left to act almost wholly upon his own discretion.

I never required to be informed of any communications he had there, except upon those points of duty, where he himself was the first to mention them to me; nor, except upon such points of duty, did I ever receive any particular information from him. He enjoyed a habitual free intercourse with all the persons of the establishment, and if a distance prevails between him and Count Bertrand or Count Montholon, it arose from causes over which I exercised no control.

I pursued this line of conduct for the reason above explained, to avoid furnishing a pretext to General Bonaparte for not asking his advice, reserving however the power of giving him my instructions, and of laying them down very precisely in writing whenever a decision might be taken by General Bonaparte himself to receive his visits, and to frame those instructions with the more or less latitude according as I perceived a design to establish Dr Verling as his personal domestic surgeon, or as only to perform the duties provisionally, until a foreign medical attendant might arrive.

In drawing out such instructions, I had only to adopt the principle laid down in Your Lordship's letter of the 10th May 1818, availing myself of the right to enforce an observance of all such parts of the regulations in force on the Island, as I might conceive applicable or required.

In the meantime, the latitude enjoyed by Dr Verling and the persons at Longwood themselves, left no cause of objection, or dissatisfaction, either on his part or theirs.

If he had not become *l'homme de l'Empereur* [the Emperor's man] no pretext was left to him or them, to consider him as *l'homme du gouverneur* [the Governor's man].

On the arrival of a Foreign Medical Person on the Island, matters became changed. General Bonaparte had then obtained the man of his selection – there was no longer any motive for leaving an English Medical person in habitual unrestrained communication with him and his followers.

If the advice of any British medical officer was given, it could only be upon the principle expressed in the last article but one, of the instructions to Sir George Cockburn.

If no foreign medical attendant had arrived, and that Dr Verling himself had been established as the domestic surgeon of General Bonaparte, his reports alone would be in strict form, have been considered in no more binding light, than those of Mr O'Meara, if other medical advice was at the same time refused to be taken.

I saw reasons therefore, why if required to continue his medical assistance at Longwood, his relations with the persons there should not remain precisely the same as they were when he was the sole medical attendant, and when, in order to induce General Bonaparte to consult his advice, whilst awaiting the arrival of a foreign medical person, so little restraint had been imposed upon him.

If in addition to a foreign medical attendant, General Bonaparte could obtain the assistance of a British medical officer whose relations were to be the same as those in which Dr Verling had stood whilst he continued there alone, a double point would have been gained, of two confidential persons who were to be alike reserved in all their communications to the Governor, whether as regarding their professional duty or their private relations with the persons at Longwood.

In replying to Dr Verling's letter, Your Lordship will observe these points were considered, but as there appeared to have been a gleam of dissatisfaction in his manner, arising probably from my not having officially communicated to him my sentiments upon his general conduct, I directed a letter to be written to him, in addition to the reply I sent to that from himself, pointing to the particular delicacy of the situation in which he had been placed, and expressing my sense of his general line of conduct, whilst he had remained at Longwood; trusting this might have some effect on his future proceedings.

He wrote another short letter of which a copy is also annexed; it did not appear to me to require any reply.

On the 22nd, Dr Verling waited on me, and told me Countess Bertrand had sent a message to him, to request he would call upon her, and that he had answered it verbally, he could not go without an order from me; he mentioned at the same time his wish to break off all relations with the persons at Longwood. I told him there were two ways of doing so. The one, abruptly, the other by degrees – That if he called on Madame Bertrand to give his advice to her and her children, but showed at the same time he wished to confine himself solely to medical business, he would probably soon discover that she would discontinue sending for him; that I did not, nor could not presume to judge of his motives for refusing to visit her in such a way, but, that I was not myself aware of any objection to it.

I at the same time explained to Dr Verling, that had General Bonaparte asked for him to become his domestic physician, I should not have failed to have given him written instructions for his guidance, but that never having been called upon to attend him, it had not become necessary for me to do so. At present, now that General Bonaparte had his own medical attendant, such instructions became wholly unnecessary, but if any British medical officer was now called upon to attend him, the instructions might be of a different nature to those given to a person considered as his own domestic surgeon. If he, Dr Verling, still persisted in his intention of not visiting Madame Bertrand, I thought the best way for him would be to wait upon her and acquaint her of it; that he had a ready mode of explaining his objection, by saying he had been fourteen months at Longwood without General Bonaparte's having condescended to see him, and that he was naturally solicitous on such account of not continuing his visits there, but again repeated, I had myself no objection to his occasional visits to the Countess as before expressed.

I saw Dr Verling two days afterwards, when he told me, he had called upon Madame Bertrand and had acquainted her he could not continue his visits to her, unless upon the same footing he had been on before. She then quoted to him my letter, stating he had every facility for visiting her, but he persisted in his resolution.

I asked him if Madame Bertrand's reply was of a nature to make him conceive that she ascribed his determination of not visiting her to any breach of the assurance I had given to her. He told me, certainly not; she must ascribe the discontinuance of his visits to himself alone. I then expressed my regret to him that he should have put his refusal of not visiting her, upon the ground of his not being allowed to do so upon the same footing he was before; he corrected himself by saying, he had so expressed himself to me, by chance, but she had not so understood him; that she perfectly comprehended the objection prevailed on his part, merely on the ground of his not having a written order from me.

I have heard nothing further since from the Countess Bertrand or from Dr Verling on the subject, and am willing to hope therefore, I shall not be involved in any further discussion with the residents at Longwood upon it.

H. Lowe

Lowe to Bathurst, 4 November 1819, BM MSS 20,128 (364–367)

St Helena, 4 November 1819
Private
My Lord,

The enclosed letter marked separate is on a subject which I should hardly think it necessary to intrude on your Lordship's consideration, except so far as circumstances might hereafter require me to refer to it.

It relates to a correspondence into which I was very unexpectedly, and it appears to me, very unnecessarily drawn by Dr Verling, but which was soon brought to a close.

If Dr Verling was sincere in his desire of breaking off all relations with the persons at Longwood, there was a natural and obvious way of doing so, by simply acquainting Madame Bertrand of it, without involving me in any discussion on the subject; but his perfect readiness to attend upon her, and the persons at Longwood in general, if he <u>obtained an order</u> from me, is hardly reconcilable with the desire of breaking off all relations with them, and rather betrays a secret inclination to have become the medical attendant upon them, on the <u>same footing as he was before</u>, if he could cover the renewal of his visits as a duty forced upon him by me, and not as the act of his own free will. His desire of breaking off all communication with them, is at the same time hardly reconcilable with the protraction of his stay on the island, after I had acceded to his application for leave, nor with the letters he wrote after such resolution was taken, knowing that in refusing to visit Madame Bertrand as an act of attention to her (although I had specified my acquiescence to it) unless by an <u>order</u> from me, he was merely seconding the application she had made for a British medical attendant being attached to the establishment, in addition to the foreign one. His construing my acquiescence to, and recommendation of his occasional visits, so long as he might remain on the Island, his leave being at the same time granted, as an <u>order</u> for the continuance of his attendance as before, and when he had resolved on protracting his stay, requiring instructions from me as if such order had been actually given, appeared to me (as it has done to all who know the circumstance) as very extraordinary. My replies therefore I made pretty full, and the official letter with which I concluded them, in giving him every praise to as full an extent as he could possibly lay claim to for his line of proceeding <u>whilst he was at Longwood</u>, will I should trust, have some effect in pointing out to him the proper line to follow, now that he has quitted it.

In the separate letter, enclosed, I have said that except on points of his professional duty, I had received no information from Dr Verling during his stay at Longwood.

In my official acknowledgment of his services, I have expressed my opinion of his conduct in general, as a professional man placed in a very delicate situation, as he was, at Longwood, but if he had been sworn to secrecy, as to his communications with the persons there, upon all other matters than those of his professional duty, he could not have maintained a greater degree of secrecy in regard to them.

The persons at Longwood seemed to have gained their end, in a certain degree, of making him believe that it would be an act of real dishonour to repeat the most indifferent circumstances he might learn, whilst living amongst them, whilst he never appeared to reflect that if admitted to the opportunity of the most unrestrained communication with them, on points no way relating to his professional duty, without even any inquiry on any part of what passed during his daily intercourse with them, it was a sign of favour and proof of my confidence in him, which in matters, at least by which the public service might in any way be affected, merited some kind of return.

When I sent General Bonaparte the extract of Your Lordship's letter of the 28th September 1818 (the same attached to the protocol of Aix la Chapelle) I omitted that part where Dr Verling's name is mentioned, because I conceived a pretext might be derived from it, to demand his removal from Longwood.

It was from Lieutenant Jackson I received information of the particulars referred to, and though I was aware of motives for not introducing his name, yet I felt disappointed in speaking to Dr Verling who had been present during the conversation, at not receiving that kind of confirmation which might have warranted any reference to him. I had resolved not to speak of this whilst he remained at Longwood, although the information was of a nature which he could in no pretext have been justified in withholding for an instant from me; but though he could not contradict what Lieut. Jackson had repeated to me, and even appeared to recollect all that was essential of it, yet, a certain apprehension of having his name appear seemed to outweigh all other considerations.

Your Lordship will probably have observed in the letters that were addressed to me by Count Bertrand about the time of Mr Stokoe's return here, the attempts made to induce a reconsideration of the proposals that had been offered to him. The omission of any notice of the answers I had given to the modified proposals in Count Montholon's letter of 1 April 1819 and when I had sent General Bonaparte my remarks on the proposals made to Mr Stokoe, as they might apply to any other English medical person, in order that he might not say the objection to the appointment of one lay wholly with me, the recurrence made to the modified proposals offered by Count Montholon.

Had any answer to the proposals offered in the first instance to Mr Stokoe's acceptance been more favourable than the reply to the modified ones, or, even in the latter articles, been as favourable, I am persuaded

Dr Verling would have been selected, even though a foreign medical attendant was hourly expected; but in proportion as his arrival became certain, I felt the less necessity to concede.

Dr Verling was earnest to impress upon me at the same time that Count Bertrand had assured him of his having recommended General Bonaparte to employ him, as his private surgeon, without any stipulation whatever; the arrival of Professor Antommarchi put a stop however to all discussion on the matter. The experience I had had of the arts practised with every British medical person who had been admitted to Longwood, did not lead me to encourage their views on this point. I was decided in my opinion, that a foreigner subject to the same regulations as themselves was the proper person, but as Dr Verling appears to have been not averse to the employment, my objections (which were wholly of a public and general nature) he may perhaps have applied to himself. When he first mentioned to Sir Thomas Reade his intentions of remaining on the Island, he alleged 'poverty' as one cause. He has seen the golden hopes held forth to him on one side wholly vanish, without any substantial benefit immediately resulting to him on the other; had he profited by his leave of absence, it was my intention to have addressed a recommendation to Your Lordship of him, to obtain some step in his profession, or for advantage in any other way that presented; the course he has pursued for himself renders it difficult however what to say or do regarding him. He has had no cause whatever given him for dissatisfaction at any part of my conduct toward him, unless he conceives I have been a hindrance to his becoming the private surgeon of General Bonaparte (which he would probably have become had not a foreign one arrived) but on the contrary, where his line of proceeding tended to create doubts, he always found me disposed to put the most favourable construction. I could repeat instances if circumstances required it.

In a letter which proceeds by this occasion from Count Montholon, your Lordship will perceive, he speaks of Count as well as Countess Bertrand going to Europe this Spring; if Count Bertrand has such intention, he will probably not attempt to be sending home any matters for publication, but as it is impossible to foresee what may appear, it is on such accounts principally I have thought it advisable to send the whole detail of what has occurred, as to the Countess Bertrand and Dr Verling.

Count Montholon's letters will be found also to contain some remarkable observations respecting Mr O'Meara and Mr Holmes. I believe Count Montholon meditates still to outstay the Bertrand family, at least such is the opinion I have formed from his letter. The detail I have given respecting Dr Antommarchi requires no further comment. He has shown a disposition to complain from the outset. He wrote a note to me a few days after his arrival, perverting an act of real attention towards him, by the Orderly Officer, into one of *soverchia impolitezza* [excessive rudeness], but he seemed then not rightly to apprehend the distinction of military rank, for in accounting to me why the Abbé Buonavita had not accompanied him in visiting me, he said it was because he did not like to be attended by *un soldato*. As he had so recently arrived, however, I took no notice of what he said, further than to set him right as to facts, though the terms I considered as really impertinent, applied to an officer, who is remarkable for professing very gentlemanly manners, and whose line of conduct had procured to him in general, a real respect on the part of the other persons of the establishment. Some time however has since passed and the Professor appears the better reconciled to his situation.

H. Lowe

Memorandum of Conversation between Sir Hudson Lowe and Dr Verling, at Plantation House, on 26 November 1819, written by Major Gorrequer. BM MSS 20,128 (416–417)

Dr Verling called this day on the Governor, but addressed him at first in so low a tone of voice, as to be quite inaudible to me; the Governor however told me immediately after the Doctor went away, he was then saying that as he found Mr Livingstone was established as the medical attendant of Madame Bertrand, he (Dr Verling) would now call and pay her a friendly visit.

I heard the Governor in answer, explain to Dr Verling that on his going to Longwood, a few days before, the Orderly Officer (Captain Nicholls) had acquainted him, that Madame Bertrand had that day desired to have Mr Livingstone sent for, as she had a blister on her arm, and her youngest child was ill. She at the same time saying that Dr Verling had refused to attend her without an order from the Governor to that effect, that Mr Livingstone had been sent for accordingly, but answered he could not come till the following day. However, whilst he (the Governor) was still at Longwood, Madame Bertrand had once more sent to request that Mr Livingstone might (notwithstanding this answer) be desired to come to her, sooner than he had stated he would; and he was in consequence again sent for, and required to come immediately.

That he (the Governor) would have at once sent for Dr Verling, had it not been for his objections to attend her, without receiving an order to that effect, and that as Mr Livingstone, or indeed any other medical person on the island, might be easily had recourse to without the formality of an order, he had been sent for. Why should he (the Governor) be put to the necessity of giving such an order? He would not give it. He saw no reason for putting matters upon any other footing than they at present were on, or establishing any new relations; they had a medical attendant of their own choice at Longwood, and therefore no necessity could exist for ordering another to attend.

Mr Livingstone, continued the Governor, was not however established as the medical attendant of Madame Bertrand. He was merely requested to call there, as might be Dr Arnott, Mr Henry, or any other medical person she wished to consult, and who would go there on obtaining his permission, without requiring an order.

Dr Verling here said in a very formal way, 'I hope Sir you don't mean to say I ever refused attending Madame Bertrand.' The Governor replied, he certainly had stated, and that even in writing, he would not go without first obtaining an order from him to that effect, but he would give no such order. He had no wish or desire about it, and left it entirely to him. He saw no necessity for his attending, but he had his permission to visit Madame Bertrand, and he left him to act for himself, and use his own discretion.

Dr Verling said, he would not act upon his own discretion, and repeated he would not give his medical attendance to Madame Bertrand and her family without an order, but as he had experienced every civility and attention during the fifteen months he had been in the habit of visiting there, it was his intention to proceed then to Longwood and call upon her, but certainly not to pay her a professional visit.

The Governor said he was at full liberty to go whenever he thought proper. His name was on the list, left at the guard, of persons who had permission to visit Madame Bertrand.

G. Gorrequer

Major

Gorrequer to Reade, 8 December 1819, BM MSS 20,128 (441); duplicated at 20,149 (165)

Plantation House, 8 December 1819
My Dear Reade,

The Governor desires you will show the enclosed note to Dr Verling, who has already had the Governor's consent to his giving Madame Bertrand his medical advice.

G. Gorrequer

[To] Sir Thomas Reade

Gorrequer to Nicholls, 8 December 1819, BM MSS 20,128 (442)

Plantation House, 8 December 1819
Dear Sir,

Immediately on receiving your note the Governor directed me to have it shown to Dr Verling, making known he had the Governor's consent to visit Madame Bertrand, but he has objected without an order to that effect.

Please to acquaint Madame Bertrand of this, and ask her whether there is any other medical person who she wishes to see, in which case you will send directly to him.

G. Gorrequer

[To] Captain Nicholls

Gorrequer to Reade, 9 December 1819, BM MSS 20,128 (443); 20,149 (166)

Plantation House, 9 December 1819

My Dear Reade,

Having mentioned to the Governor Dr Verling's objections to wait on Madame Bertrand viz. 'that he would not take the responsibility without an order to that effect', he remarked, that he does not see why a professional visit made with his consent, as a mere matter of accommodation during the illness of another medical person entails more responsibility than if made by his order, or why visits made on such a ground and probability for so limited a period, should present objections, after his so lately visiting there as a private individual.

G. Gorrequer

[To] Sir Thomas Reade

Gorrequer to Reade, 16 December 1819, BM MSS 20,128 (457)

Plantation House, 16 December 1819

Private

My Dear Reade,

As the Governor has seen the invitations from Longwood to Drs Arnott, Verling and Livingstone, no reference whatever is necessary to him, before the answers are sent.

Drs Arnott and Livingstone if well enough, he supposes, will go. He can however form no guess with regard to Dr Verling.

G. Gorrequer

[To] Sir Thomas Reade

Lowe to Bathurst, 28 December 1819, BM MSS 20,128 (491–494)

St Helena, 28 December 1819

Separate, No. 270

My Lord,

Being uncertain, in what degree circumstances may hereafter render it necessary for me to refer to the subject of my separate letter to Your Lordship of the 3rd November last, detailing the line of proceeding that had been followed by Dr Verling, subsequent to his quitting Longwood, I am led to intrude upon Your Lordship's time, with the relation of some further occurrences, more or less connected therewith.

On the 24th November I had gone to Longwood, where the Orderly Officer, Captain Nicholls, brought me a message from the Countess Bertrand, who had seen me in the grounds, saying that both herself and her youngest child were at the time very unwell – that Mr Livingstone (the medical person most in the habit of attending ladies on this island) had been sent for, and that he had written to say, he could not come up until the next morning, but that she wished very much to see him if possible that day.

I wrote from the spot to Mr Livingstone, to make known the Countess's desire, and he came up directly to her.

Annexed is copy of the note which had been previously sent, to request his attendance, on the part of Doctor Antommarchi.

On the morning following I was waited upon by Dr Verling, who addressed me in a very abrupt manner nearly as follows – 'Now it is established that Mr Livingstone is the medical officer to attend upon Madame Bertrand, I intend to pay a visit to her, as an act of attention.' I immediately replied, that I did not see how Mr Livingstone was established as a medical attendant upon Madame Bertrand, in any different manner than he was formerly, as he had frequently been before in the habit of visiting there; he, Dr Verling, had refused to go without an order, and I presumed that was the reason why Mr Livingstone had been sent for; that if he supposed Mr Livingstone had been directed by me to proceed there, he was in error, as he had been sent for, before I arrived at Longwood; that if Dr Verling, Dr Arnott, Mr Henry, or any other medical man had been sent for, I should have forwarded the Countess's request in the same manner; that in other respects, he Dr Verling was at perfect liberty to visit Madame Bertrand, whether as a private or as a professional person – his name was at the guard in the list of persons permitted to visit there, but I could not admit the sending for Mr Livingstone, in the way that had been done, made any alteration whatever in his relations, or those of any other person, with Longwood – he had refused to go there without an order, and it was therefore natural for Madame Bertrand, to send for a person who did not stand on that form in regard to her.

Dr Verling replied he would not act on his own discretion in giving her his medical advice without an order; that as he had experienced every civility and attention during the fifteen months he had been in the habit of visiting there, it was his intention now to proceed to Longwood, to call upon her, but certainly not as a professional visit.

I said he was at full liberty to go whenever he thought proper.

A few days afterwards Mr Livingstone was taken very seriously ill. The Countess Bertrand also continued in a bad state of health. The Orderly Officer was requested by her, to send for Dr Verling – Copy of the Orderly

Officer's note accompanies; – it was sent immediately to Sir Thomas Reade, who was directed to show it to Dr Verling – annexed is copy of the note written to Sir Thomas Reade, and of his reply.

Dr Verling's refusal drew forth a remark from me which was communicated to him by another note sent to Sir Thomas Reade.

Thought this line of proceeding singularly unaccommodating, and calculated in particular to make it appear to the persons at Longwood that if he did not attend upon them, the fault lay with me, and did not derive from any real objection on his part; if he merely desired to break off all communication with the persons at Longwood, he would have abstained from visiting there as a private person – if he saw no objection to maintain an intercourse with them as a private person, there could be no excuse for his declining to give his medical advice on so unforeseen an occasion, and for so limited a period, as that for which it was required; viz. during the indisposition of the only medical man whom Madame Bertrand had been before in the habit of consulting.

I should not have been disposed to blame Dr Verling for declining a further attendance at Longwood, making known to me and Madame Bertrand his precise motive for doing so; but after declining to visit there as a medical man, he erred it seemed to me in renewing his intercourse as a private person – it being naturally his visit in this capacity, which encouraged Madame Bertrand, in the application for his medical aid. His motive for refusing which could not thus be ascribed to objections against the continuance of any personal relations with the persons at Longwood, notwithstanding the strong motives which had been given to him, for not visiting either at the house of Count Bertrand or of Count Montholon; but to his desire only of obtaining the sanction of my order to continue his visits.

On the 16th December, three open notes were delivered to the Orderly Officer from Dr Antommarchi, for Dr Arnott, Dr Verling and Mr Livingstone – Enclosed is copy of one of them. They contained an invitation to dinner. Dr Antommarchi had verbally also invited Mr Henry, Assistant Surgeon of the 66th Regiment.

I caused the notes to be sent to their addresses immediately, intimating I had seen them and that consequently no reference to me was necessary, before answering them.

Dr Arnott pleaded a prior engagement and declined the invitation. Mr Livingstone was unwell and could not go. Dr Verling and Mr Henry also sent excuses. I interfered not in any shape with either of these gentlemen.

By the letter which was addressed to Dr Antommarchi, dated 4 October, a great facility was afforded to him of communicating with the medical gentlemen on the island, in matters relating to his own profession. From this moment he appeared to cultivate their acquaintance with great assiduity – and although I saw no objections to the ordinary relations of society between him and them, yet, the attempts to form a particular society with them alone, evidenced a disposition already to wander from the principle upon which I had granted each facility for communication with them.

I have the honour to be,
H. Lowe

(1819?) Unsigned discussion (see Forsyth, *History*, III, 162–85) BM MSS 20,127 (30)

Largely contained in a letter to or from Reade (20,207 (163); fragment, unsigned, but evidently in Reade's handwriting). A copy of this letter or fragment can be found in 20,127 (121).

Mr Livingstone head surgeon of the East India Company's Services having been shown the News Paper containing the debate in the House of Commons, where it had been said, the medical men of St Helena had given a certificate to the Countess de Montholon stating the necessity of her going to the Waters of Cheltenham, was greatly surprised at it, and remarked immediately as follows:

That he never signed any certificate regarding Madame Montholon's health, except the one in which 'Mineral Waters' were recommended, although Dr Verling had asked him previously to sign one, wherein the Cheltenham Waters were named. He also says that for some time previous to Dr Verling leaving this Island, they were not upon very good terms, owing to a difference of opinion respecting Count Montholon's health. That Dr Verling stated to him, that Count Montholon was affected with a spitting of blood, a pain on the right side, supposed to be the liver complaint, and also an intermittent fever. That upon all the occasions of his, Dr Livingstone's, visits to Count Montholon, he never could perceive any of the slightest symptoms of the above complaints. That particularly on this last visit, where Dr Verling stated that the Count had a violent fever upon him, he was very much surprised to find a large fire in the Count's room, hot enough to increase the heat to 90 degrees. He instantly mentioned this to Dr Verling, stating his surprise that he, as a pupil of Dr Gregory's of Edinburgh, would have permitted such a thing, and at the same time told him that he believed it had been designedly done, and that he was convinced nothing was the matter with Count Montholon. That he was sure there was something improper intended in all this. Dr Verling and Mr Livingstone had some very unpleasant words upon this occasion, and the visit ended by Dr Livingstone saying that he did not wish to have any more to say upon Count Montholon's complaints either to Dr Verling or the Count himself. Dr Verling wished Mr Livingstone to have given a certificate respecting Count Montholon's health, but took no notice of it, after their quarrel.

Chapter 11
1821

Lowe to Verling, 5 November 1821, BM MSS 20,133 (300)

9 Berkeley Square, 5 November 1821
Sir,

In reply to your letter of the 8th October which did not reach me until the 25th and also to that since received dated the 31st October, I beg leave to refer you to the letter I directed to be addressed to you dated the 17th October 1819 as containing my sentiments of your conduct whilst you continued at Longwood, copy of which I forwarded to Lord Bathurst. I subsequently addressed his Lordship on the occasion of your departure from St Helena for the purpose of removing any unfavourable impressions that might have existed in his Lordship's mind in consequence of your having protracted your stay at St Helena so long after leave of absence had been granted to you.

His Lordship is not at present in town and I cannot consequently refer to him in person, but I received acknowledgments of my letters and of course infer his Lordship's acquiescence in, and satisfaction at, what I had the honour to communicate to him on both the above occasions.

I have the honour to be etc.

H. Lowe

Select Bibliography of Saint Helena

Abbott, John S. C. *Napoleon at St. Helena; or, Interesting Anecdotes and Remarkable Conversations of the Emperor during the Five and a Half Years of his Captivity*. Collected from the memorials of Las Cases, O'Meara, Montholon, Antommarchi, and others. New York: Harper & Brothers, 1855.

Abell, Lucia Elizabeth (Balcombe). *Recollections of the Emperor Napoleon, During the First Three Years of His Captivity on the Island of St. Helena: During the Time of His Residence at Her Father's House, 'The Briars'*. London: John Murray, 1845.

Aldanov, Mark Aleksandrovich. *Saint Helena, Little Island*. First English edition. Translated from the Russian by A. E. Chamot. New York: Alfred A. Knopf, 1924.

Antommarchi, Francesco. *The Last Days of the Emperor Napoleon*. 2v. London: 1825.

Aubry, Octave. *St. Helena*. Translated by Arthur Livingston. Philadelphia: J. B. Lippincott Company, 1936.

Balmain, Aleksandr Antonovich, Graf. *Napoleon in Captivity: The Reports of Count Balmain, Russian Commissioner on the Island of St. Helena, 1816–1820*. Translated and edited with introduction and notes by Julian Park. New York: Century, 1927.

Bertrand, Henri Gatien, Comte. *Napoleon at St. Helena: Memoirs of General Bertrand, Grand Marshal of the Palace, January to May 1821*. Deciphered and Annotated by Paul Fleuriot de Langle. Translated by Frances Hume. Garden City: Doubleday, 1952.

Blackburn, Julia. *The Emperor's Last Island: A Journey to St. Helena*. New York: Pantheon Books, 1991.

Brookes, Dame Mabel. *St. Helena Story*. New York: Dodd, Meade and Company, 1961.

Chaplin, Arnold. *Thomas Shortt (Principal Medical Officer in St. Helena). With Biographies of Some Other Medical Men Associated with the Case of Napoleon from 1815–1821*. London: 1914.

———. *A St. Helena Who's Who; or, A Directory of the Island During the Captivity of Napoleon*. 2nd edition, revised and enlarged. New York and London: 1919.

Cockburn, Rear Admiral Sir George. *Buonaparte's Voyage to St Helena; Comprising the Diary of Rear Admiral Sir George Cockburn, During His Passage from England to St Helena, in 1815. From the Original Manuscript, in the Handwriting of his Private Secretary*. Boston: Lilly, Wait, Colman, and Holden, 1833.

Forsyth, William. *History of the Captivity of Napoleon at St. Helena; From the Letters and Journals of the Late Lieut.-Gen. Sir Hudson Lowe, and Official Documents Not Before Made Public*. 3v. London: John Murray, 1853.

Frémeaux, Paul. *The Drama of Saint Helena*. Translated from the French by Alfred Rieu. New York: D. Appleton and Company, 1910.

Gonnard, Philippe. *The Exile of St. Helena: The Last Phase in Fact and Fiction*. Philadelphia: J. B. Lippincott Company, 1909.

Gorrequer, Major Gideon. *St. Helena During Napoleon's Exile: Gorrequer's Diary. With Introduction, Biographies, Notes and Explanations, and Index of Pseudonyms by James Kemble*. London: Heinemann, 1969.

Gourgaud, General Gaspard, Baron. *The St. Helena Journal of General Baron Gourgaud 1815–1818: Being a Diary Written at St. Helena During a Part of Napoleon's Captivity*. Translated by Sydney Gillard; edited with notes by Norman Edwards; preface by Hilaire Belloc. London: John Lane, 1932.

———. *Talks of Napoleon at St. Helena with General Baron Gourgaud, together with the Journal Kept by Gourgaud on their Journey from Waterloo to St. Helena*. Translated and with notes by Elizabeth Wormeley Latimer. Chicago: A. C. McClurg, 1903.

Henry, Walter. *Surgeon Henry's Trifles: Events of a Military Life*. Edited with an Introduction and Notes by Pat Hayward. London: Chatto and Windus, 1970.

Humphreys, A. L. *Napoleon: Extracts from* The Times *and* Morning Chronicle *1815–21 relating to Napoleon's Life at St. Helena*. London: privately printed by A. L. Humphreys, 1901. [Limited to 50 copies]

Jackson, Basil. *Notes and Reminiscences of a Staff Officer, Chiefly Relating to the Waterloo Campaign and to St Helena Matters During the Captivity of Napoleon*. New York: E. P. Dutton & Co., 1903.

Kauffmann, Jean-Paul. *The Black Room at Longwood: Napoleon's Exile on Saint Helena*. Translated from the French by Patricia Clancy. New York: Four Walls Eight Windows, 1997.

Knowles, Sir Lees, Bart. (ed.). *A Gift of Napoleon, Being a Sequel to Letters of Captain Engelbert Lutyens, Orderly Officer at Longwood, Saint Helena, Feb. 1820 to Nov. 1823*. With Illustrations. London: John Lane, 1921.

Korngold, Ralph. *The Last Years of Napoleon: His Captivity on St. Helena*. New York: Harcourt, Brace and Co., 1959.

Lachouque, Henry. *The Last Days of Napoleon's Empire: From Waterloo to St. Helena.* Translated by Lovett F. Edwards. 1st American edition. New York: Orion Press, 1967.

Las Cases, Marie Joseph Emmanuel Auguste Dieudonné, Comte de. *Mémorial de Sainte Hélène. Memoirs of Emmanuel Augustus Dieudonné, Count de Las Cases, Communicated by Himself. Comprising a Letter from Count de Las Cases at St. Helena to Lucien Bonaparte, Giving a Faithful Account of the Voyage of Napoleon to St. Helena, His Residence, Manner of Living, and Treatment on that Island. Also A Letter Addressed by Count de Las Cases to Lord Bathurst.* London: Henry Colburn, 1818.

——. *Journal of the Private Life and Conversations of The Emperor Napoleon at Saint Helena.* 4v. Boston: Wells and Lilly, 1823.

Lutyens, Captain Engelbert. *Letters of Captain Engelbert Lutyens, Orderly Officer at Longwood, Saint Helena: Feb. 1820 to Nov. 1823.* Edited by Sir Lees Knowles. London and New York: John Lane, 1915.

Malcolm, Clementina Elphinstone. *A Diary of St. Helena: The Journal of Lady Malcolm (1816, 1817), Containing the Conversations of Napoleon with Sir Pulteney Malcolm.* Edited by Sir Arthur Wilson. New York: Harper, [1929].

Marchand, Louis-Joseph. *In Napoleon's Shadow: Being the First English Language Edition of the Complete Memoirs of Louis-Joseph Marchand, Valet and Friend of The Emperor, 1811–1821.* Produced by Proctor Jones. Original notes of Jean Bourguignon and Henry Lachouque. Preface by Jean Tulard. San Francisco: Proctor Jones Publishing Company, 1998.

Martineau, Gilbert. *Napoleon's St. Helena.* Chicago: Rand McNally, 1968.

Masson, Frédéric. *Napoleon at St. Helena 1815–1821.* Translated by Louis B. Frewer. 1st edition. Oxford: Pen In Hand, 1949.

Mills, Lt. Nelson, and Cpt. Thomas Ussher. *Napoleon Banished: The Journeys to Elba and to St. Helena in the Letters and Journals of Two British Naval Officers.* London: The Rodale Press, 1955.

Montholon, Charles Jean Tristan, Marquis de. *Memoirs of the History of France During the Reign of Napoleon, Dictated by the Emperor at Saint Helena to the Generals Who Shared His Captivity; and Published from the Original Manuscripts Corrected by Himself.* 3v. London: Henry Colburn and Co. and Martin Bossange and Co., 1823.

——. *History of the Captivity of Napoleon at St. Helena.* 4v. London: 1846.

Napoleon's Appeal to the British Nation, on His Treatment at Saint Helena. The Official Memoir, Dictated by him, and delivered to Sir Hudson Lowe. London: William Hone, 1817.

O'Meara, Barry E. *Historical Memoirs of Napoleon, Book IX: 1815.* Translated by B. E. O'Meara. Philadelphia: Abraham Small, 1820.

——. *An Exposition of Some of the Transactions, That Have Taken Place at St. Helena, Since the Appointment of Sir Hudson Lowe As Governor of that Island; In Answer to an Anonymous Pamphlet, Entitled 'Facts Illustrative of* the Treatment of Napoleon Bonaparte', &c. Corroborated by Various Official Documents, Correspondence, &c.. 2nd edition. London: James Ridgway, 1819.

———. *Napoleon in Exile; or, A Voice from St. Helena. The Opinions and Reflections of Napoleon on the Most Important Events of his Life and Government, in his own words.* Philadelphia: James Crissy, 1822.

Pillans, T. Dundas. *The Real Martyr of St. Helena.* New York: McBride, Nast & Company, 1913.

Quarterly Review. An Answer to O'Meara's Napoleon in Exile; or, A Voice from St. Helena. From the *Quarterly Review* for February, 1823. New York: T. & J. Swords, 1823.

Saint Denis, Louis Etienne. *Napoleon from the Tuileries to St. Helena: Personal Recollections of the Emperor's Second Mameluke and Valet, Louis Etienne St. Denis, known as Ali.* Translation and notes by Frank Potter. Introduction by G. Michaut. New York and London: Harper, 1922.

Shorter, Clement King. *Napoleon and His Fellow Travellers; Being a Reprint of Certain Narratives of the Voyages of the Dethroned Emperor on the Bellerophon and the Northumberland to Exile in St. Helena; the Romantic Stories Told by George Home, Captain Ross, Lord Lyttelton, and William Warden.* London: Cassell and Company, 1908.

———. *Napoleon In His Own Defence: Being a Reprint of Certain Letters Written by Napoleon from St. Helena to Lady Clavering, and a reply by Theodore Hook, with which are Incorporated Notes and An Essay on Napoleon As a Man of Letters.* London: Cassell and Co., 1910.

Stokoe, Dr John. *With Napoleon at St. Helena: Being the Memoirs of Dr. John Stokoe, Naval Surgeon.* Translated from the French of Paul Frémeaux by Edith S. Stokoe. London: John Lane, 1902.

Tarbell, Ida Minerva. 'Napoleon Bonaparte, Sixth Paper: The Last Campaigns; Waterloo; St. Helena', *McClure's Magazine*, IV, No. 5, April 1895.

Thornton, Michael John. *Napoleon After Waterloo: England and the St. Helena Decision.* Stanford: Stanford University Press, 1968.

Tussaud, John Theodore. *The Chosen Four.* London: Jonathan Cape, 1928.

Warden, William. *Letters Written on Board His Majesty's Ship The Northumberland, and at Saint Helena; In Which the Conduct and Conversations of Napoleon Buonaparte, and His Suite, During the Voyage, and the First Months of His Residence in That Island, Are Faithfully Described and Related.* London: Published for the Author by R. Ackermann, 1817.

Watson, George Leo De St. M. *A Polish Exile with Napoleon: Embodying the letters of Captain Piontkowski to General Sir Robert Wilson and Many Documents from the Lowe Papers, the Colonial Office Records, the Wilson Manuscripts, the Capel Lofft Correspondence, and the French and Genevese Archives Hitherto Unpublished.* Boston: Little, Brown and Co., 1912.

Weider, Ben, and Sten Forshufvud. *Assassination at St. Helena Revisited.* Forewords by David Chandler and David Hamilton-Williams. New York: John Wiley & Sons, 1995.

Welland, Rachel. *Napoleon At Bay: A Letter of 1816.* London: Buttercross Books, 1992.

Young, Norwood. *Napoleon in Exile at St. Helena (1815–1821).* 2v. Philadelphia: 1915.

Younghusband, S. A. C. (Mrs Frank). 'Letters from St. Helena', *Blackwood's Magazine*, No. 1582, August 1947, 144–53.

Notes

Chapter 1

1. Charles Jean Tristan, Marquis de Montholon, *Memoirs of the History of France During the Reign of Napoleon, Dictated by the Emperor at Saint Helena to the Generals Who Shared His Captivity; and Published from the Original Manuscripts Corrected by Himself.* 3v. (London, 1823), II, 265.
2. Napoleon I, Emperor of the French, *Correspondance de Napoléon Ier; Publiée par ordre de l'empereur Napoléon III.* 32v. (Paris: Imprimerie Impériale, 1858–69), 11 April 1814, No. 21558, XXVII, 421.
3. Baron General Gaspard Gourgaud, *Talks of Napoleon at St. Helena with General Baron Gourgaud, together with the Journal Kept by Gourgaud on their Journey from Waterloo to St. Helena.* Translated and with notes by Elizabeth Wormeley Latimer. (Chicago, 1903), 175.

Chapter 2

1. Louis-Joseph Marchand, *In Napoleon's Shadow: Being the First English Language Edition of the Complete Memoirs of Louis-Joseph Marchand, Valet and Friend of The Emperor, 1811–1821.* Produced by Proctor Jones. (San Francisco, 1998), 285.
2. Captain Frederick Lewis Maitland, *Narrative of the Surrender of Buonaparte and of His Residence on Board H.M.S. Bellerophon; with a Detail of the Principal Events that Occurred in that Ship, Between the 24th of May and the 8th of August, 1815.* (London, 1826), v–vi.
3. *Napoleon in Exile; or, A Voice From St. Helena. The Opinions and Reflections of Napoleon on the Most Important Events in His Life and Government, in his own words.* 2nd edition. 2v. (Philadelphia, 1822), I, vii.
4. Rear Admiral Sir George Cockburn, *Buonaparte's Voyage to St Helena; Comprising the Diary of Rear Admiral Sir George Cockburn, During His Passage from England to St Helena, in 1815. From the Original Manuscript, in the Handwriting of his Private Secretary.* (Boston, 1833).
5. Marchand, 346–7.

6. Letter to Lowe from Bathurst, 13 April 1816, Lowe Papers MS 15,729 (19).

7. Lucia Elizabeth Abell (Balcombe), *Recollections of the Emperor Napoleon, During the First Three Years of His Captivity on the Island of St. Helena: During the Time of His Residence at Her Father's House, 'The Briars'*. 2nd edition. (London, 1845), 188.

Chapter 3

1. Letter to Verling from Lowe, 25 July 1818, BM MSS 20,149 (1).

2. *Surgeon Henry's Trifles: Events of a Military Life*. Edited with an Introduction and Notes by Pat Hayward. (London, 1970), 166–7. Henry was a surgeon in the Peninsular Campaign and served on St Helena from 1817 till 1821.

3. Major General Frank Richardson, MD, *Napoleon's Death: An Inquest*. Foreword by James A. Ross. (London, 1974), 132–3.

4. Marchand, 532.

5. Louis Etienne St Denis, *Napoleon from the Tuileries to St. Helena: Personal Recollections of the Emperor's Second Mameluke and Valet Louis Etienne St. Denis, known as Ali*. (New York and London, 1922), 216–17. Ali was wrong about the last point, as is discussed herein.

6. Arnold Chaplin, *Thomas Shortt (Principal Medical Officer in St. Helena). With Biographies of Some Other Medical Men Associated with the Case of Napoleon from 1815–1821*. (London, 1914), 43–4.

7. *Napoleon at St. Helena 1815–1821*. Translated by Louis B. Frewer. (Oxford, 1949), 239.

8. *With Napoleon at St. Helena: Being the Memoirs of Dr. John Stokoe, Naval Surgeon*. Translated from the French of Paul Frémeaux by Edith S. Stokoe. (London, 1902), 82.

9. Verling, Journal, 19 August 1818.

10. Ibid., 18 January 1819.

11. Letter from Lord Bathurst to Lowe, 16 May 1818, in William Forsyth, *History of the Captivity of Napoleon at St. Helena: From the Letters and Journals of the Late Lieut.-Gen. Sir Hudson Lowe, and Official Documents Not Before Made Public*. 3v. (London, 1853), III, 399–400 (No. 131).

12. Stokoe, 84.

13. Ibid., 91.

14. Forsyth, III, 109.

15. 19 January 1819.

16. Dr Verling to H. Lowe, 6 April 1819, BM MSS 20,214 (117–119).

17. Charles Jean Tristan, Marquis de Montholon, *History of the Captivity of Napoleon at St. Helena*. 4v. (London, 1846), III, 76–9.

18. Sir Hudson Lowe to Lord Bathurst, 7 April 1819, BM MSS 20,126.

19. Verling, Journal, 12 September 1819.
20. *St. Helena During Napoleon's Exile: Gorrequer's Diary*. With Introduction, Biographies, Notes and Explanations, and Index of Pseudonyms by James Kemble. (London, 1969), 124–5. Gorrequer's diary was written using code names for the people on St Helena, and Kemble was able to 'break the code' and present a fascinating account of life during the exile.
21. Ibid., 126.
22. Ibid., 140–1.
23. Norwood Young, *Napoleon in Exile at St. Helena (1815–1821)*. 2v. (Philadelphia, 1915), II, 155.
24. Henry Goulburn to Lowe, 8 April 1819, BM MSS 20,126 (82–84).
25. Chaplin, *Shortt*, 54–5.
26. Verling, Journal, 25 February 1819.
27. Francesco Antommarchi, *The Last Days of the Emperor Napoleon*. 2v. (London, 1825), II, 58.

Chapter 4

1. Marchand, 709.

Index